Hooks & Eyes

Part 1
of

The Ambition & Destiny Series

By
VL McBeath

Hooks & Eyes
By VL McBeath

Editing services provided by Katharine D'Souza Editorial Services and Wendy Janes at WendyProof.

Cover design by Michelle Abrahall (www.michelleabrahall.com)

ISBN: 978-0-9955708-1-8 (Kindle Edition)
978-0-9955708-2-5 (Paperback)

Main category - FICTION / Historical
Other category - FICTION / Sagas

First Edition

Explanatory Notes
Meal times

In the United Kingdom, as in many parts of the world, meal times are referred to by a variety of names. Based on traditional working class practices in northern England in the 19th Century, the following terms have been used in this book:

Breakfast: The meal eaten upon rising each morning.

Dinner: The meal eaten around midday. This may be a hot or cold meal depending on the day of the week and a person's occupation.

Tea: Not to be confused with the high tea of the aristocracy or the beverage of the same name, tea was the meal eaten at the end of the working day, typically around five or six o'clock. This could either be a hot or cold meal.

Money

In 1839, the currency in the United Kingdom was Pounds, Shillings and Pence.

- There were twenty shillings to each pound and twelve pence to a shilling.

- A crown and half crown were five shillings and two shillings and sixpence, respectively.

- A guinea was one pound, one shilling (i.e. twenty-one shillings).

For ease of reference, it can be assumed that £1 at the time of the story is equivalent to approximately £100 in 2017

(Ref: http://www.bankofengland.co.uk/ InflationCalculator)

For further information on Victorian England visit: http://bit.ly/victorian-era

Please note: This book is written in UK English

To Tez
The truth is in here ... Somewhere

Condemned by Fate

A Short Story Prequel to The *Ambition & Destiny* Series

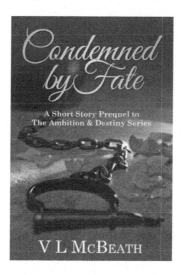

Set in 1839, seven years before the start of *Hooks & Eyes*
Download your FREE copy by visiting
http://valmcbeath.com/condemned-by-fate/

The family trees shown on the next three pages
represent the families at the start of the story.

The Jackson Family Tree

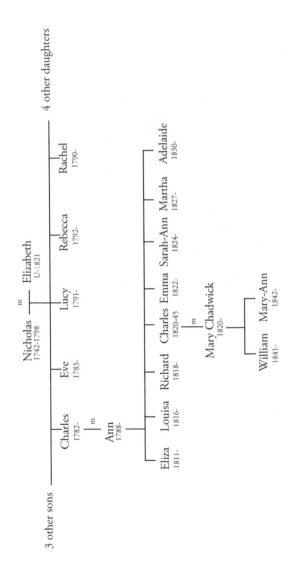

3 other sons

4 other daughters

Nicholas
1742-1798

m

Elizabeth
U-1821

Charles
1782-

m

Ann
1788-

Eve
1783-

Lucy
1791-

Rebecca
1792-

Rachel
1790-

Eliza
1811-

Louisa
1816-

Richard
1818-

Charles
1820-45

Emma
1822-

Sarah-Ann
1824-

Martha
1827-

Adelaide
1830-

Mary Chadwick
1820-

m

William
1841-

Mary-Ann
1842-

NB. All characters are fictitious
U = Unknown
m = Married

The Chadwick Family Tree

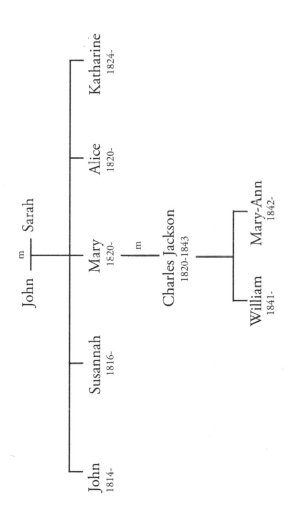

The Wetherby Family Tree

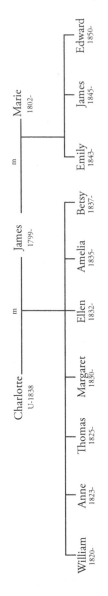

NB. All characters are fictitious
U = Unknown
m = Married

Charlotte U-1838 — m — James 1799-

James 1799- — m — Marie 1802-

William 1820-
Anne 1823-
Thomas 1825-
Margaret 1830-
Ellen 1832-
Amelia 1835-
Betsy 1837-

Emily 1843-
James 1845-
Edward 1850-

Chapter 1

Aldridge, Staffordshire. Near Birmingham, England. September 1846

M ARY STOOD AT THE FRONT door, surveying the fields that stretched out before her. Her eyes darted from one to the next, but after the activity of the harvest all was quiet. With the exception of a couple of labourers, the only people she saw were gathered under the shade of an oak tree not ten yards away. They were waiting for her. She took a deep breath and pulled the door shut behind her, gripping the handle for longer than necessary. Her heart banged against her ribs, but as much as she wanted to stay, she couldn't. Not now. With a burst of determination she threw back her shoulders and, with her head held high, walked down the garden path.

As she reached the gate, she turned to look at the house she had called home for the last four years. The whitewashed stone walls were topped with a grey slate roof through which a tall chimney emerged. Four small windows pierced the front wall and at this time of day the light from the sun reflected from them, causing her to squint. A second similar cottage, occupied by her brother-in-law Richard, stood beside it. With a glance at the house next door she pulled the gate closed and kept walking.

"I'm ready," she said as she joined her mother- and father-in-law, who stood with two of their daughters, and Mary's own two children. "We need to go, I don't want to miss the carriage."

"Are you sure you don't want me to come with you?" her father-in-law said. "I don't like you travelling on your own."

"I'm sure. I'll have to get used to doing things on my own." The sadness in her voice was unmistakable.

"Our Lucy'll look out for you," he continued. "She knows you're travelling today and she has a room ready. Here, take this."

Mary glanced down at the folded paper her father-in-law handed her, a puzzled look on her face.

"Money for your rent," he said. "Lucy won't take much, but as she's my sister I like to help her out."

Mary looked at the two young children who stood with their grandmother. Why was she taking them with her? Even with the help of her husband's family she would struggle to look after herself, let alone William and Mary-Ann too. Her late husband, Charles, hadn't left her much money and she couldn't hope to get a job while the children were so small. Her mother-in-law had offered to keep them until she settled in, but Mary couldn't leave them, not when she was about to lose everything else she cared for. Her father-in-law must have seen her despair and looked down at his grandson.

"You look after your mother, William, you hear me?" he said.

"Yes, sir." William was five years old, but with the events of recent years he had grown up quickly and he pulled himself up to his full height as if to prove it. He went to his mother and squeezed her hand.

"Some money for the waggon as well." Her father-in-law handed her a second package.

"Thank you." Mary blinked to hold back the tears filling her eyes. "I don't know what to say, you've been so good to me."

"Nothing more than we'd do for anyone else in the family," her mother-in-law said. "You won't be on your own in Birmingham and you'll be better off down there. Besides we'll be gone from here in a couple of weeks."

She was right. Mary's brother-in-law Richard had recently married and chosen to take on a larger farm further south. His parents were moving with him to a smaller place of their own and, although she wished she could go with them, she knew she had to go back to Birmingham.

"I'll still miss you all," she said. "This hasn't been an easy decision."

Her sister-in-law, Martha, gave her a weak smile. "I'll be moving to Aunt Rachel's house soon enough. It isn't far from Aunt Lucy's. Sarah-Ann's not far away either, and I know she's looking forward to you being back in Birmingham."

"I know. I felt so guilty leaving her in Birmingham after she'd gone to so much trouble to persuade Eliza to let her stay with her and Mr Rashford."

"Stop worrying." Her mother-in-law took her hand. "Eliza's enjoyed having her sister with her, and I'm sure Aunt Lucy will look after you until you find a new husband."

"If I ever do." Mary looked again to her brother-in-law's cottage. "It's not something I want to think about."

Her father-in-law put his arm around her. "You can come back any time if things don't work out, I hope you know that. Now, I have to go. Those potatoes need storing."

He smiled and placed his hand on William's head before he looked down at his granddaughter gripping the skirt of her mother's dress. A moment later he turned and headed back to the barn.

Mary bent down to pick up her bag but straightened again, leaving it on the ground, when she saw her sister-in-law, Mrs Richard, walking towards her. She was the last person she wanted to see; she hadn't even told her when she was leaving.

"Are you ready to go?" Mrs Richard asked.

"I didn't realise you were home," Mary said. "The house looked empty."

"I'd gone to the barn to see Richard. He's bagging the vegetables and likes me being with him when he's working."

More like you want to keep an eye on him, Mary thought. "Did he come back to the house with you?" She stole a glance over Martha's shoulder.

"Don't be silly; he's far too busy."

So he couldn't even come and wish me well. Mary forced herself to smile. "Never mind. Tell him he's always welcome to call if he's in Birmingham."

As she turned to hug her mother-in-law, Mary saw the smile on Mrs Richard's face fade.

"Thank you for everything," she said. "I'll write as soon as I can. Goodbye, Louisa." She embraced her sister-in-law.

"If only you and Charles were coming with me, like last time."

"You can't think like that." Louisa wiped her own tears. "Neither of us can."

She turned to Martha, and after squeezing her hand, she picked up the linen sack that contained all her belongings, and reached for the hand of her four-year-old daughter. Following his mother's lead, William held onto his sister's other hand and the three of them set off down the track leading to the road and the carriage that would take them to their new lives.

Chapter 2

Birmingham, Warwickshire. England.

MARY SHIFTED HER POSITION ON the back of the waggon and looked at the horses. They had travelled for most of the afternoon but, despite the fact the driver had stopped in Perry Barr to give the animals water, their slow pace made her worry they may not reach Birmingham before nightfall. The base of her spine was bruised from the pounding it received every time they hit a rut in the road, and she couldn't take much more.

William had somehow managed to sleep for most of the journey but as the noise grew louder, he opened his eyes and sat up.

"Are we nearly there?" he said, breaking into a yawn.

"Nearly. Can you see the chimneys up ahead? That's where we're going."

"They're getting bigger." Mary-Ann said from her perch on top of several bags of potatoes.

"All the smoke makes everything look grey," William said. "Where are the trees? And what's that smell? It's horrible."

"It must be brewing day. You can smell the hops they use for making ale. You'll get used to it," Mary said.

"I don't want to get used to it; I don't like it here. Can't we go back to live with Grandfather? He said we could."

"Not yet. Once we're at Aunt Lucy's house everything will look better."

Towards four o'clock, the waggon pulled up outside Birmingham Town Hall. It was an imposing building in the centre of town, styled like a Roman temple with large pillars standing over ornate arches and topped with a gently sloping roof. The pale stonework gleamed in the late afternoon sun, making it look magnificent against the grime of the adjacent buildings.

The town square was full of people and animals; Mary doubted she had seen so many people together in one place. There were children running in every direction, some were playing while others were being chased for being up to no good. There were street sellers selling everything from food to matches, and bootlaces to rat poison while crowds of people stood around them. Outside one of the inns there were several men fighting. The noise was deafening and the children clung to her.

As the carriage drew to a halt, Mary hesitated. She thought she knew where she needed to go but suddenly everything was unfamiliar. She prised the children's hands from hers and eased herself from the back of the waggon before she helped them down and looked about her.

"I need to go towards Snow Hill, which way is it?" she asked the driver.

"Up Colmore Row," he replied, pointing in the direction of the fighting. "Five minutes down there and you'll get to a crossroads, turn left and you're there." Mary didn't remember it like this, but she thanked him and took hold of Mary-Ann's hand. Once again, with William on his sister's other side, they set off.

As they approached the men who'd been fighting, Mary stopped and looked around. She didn't want to get too close to them. She was only a little over five feet tall and even at this distance the men looked twice her size. As she turned to cross over the road she heard her name being called.

"Mrs Charles Jackson?" the voice said again. Mary turned and looked at a tall, intimidating woman standing before her. She had piercing black eyes and her skin was heavily lined with visible moles around the hairline. She wore a thick brown cloak and matching bonnet that looked too warm for the time of year.

"Yes, that's me," Mary said.

"Miss Lucy Jackson," the stranger said. "Or Aunt Lucy if you prefer. I promised Chas I'd look out for you. You weren't hard to spot, looking like you don't belong round here."

Mary didn't recognise her. It had been several months since they had last met and even then the encounter was brief. She sensed the heat building in her face, but Aunt Lucy either failed to notice the reddening, or chose to ignore it, and unexpectedly lavished a broad smile on her.

"Yes, of course." Mary allowed herself a brief smile. "I'm rather confused. I lived here a few years back, but it looks so different."

"It does that," Aunt Lucy said. "The place is getting so busy there'll be no space left soon, but never mind that for now. Tell me, what news is there from Aldridge? How's my brother coping with the planned move?" With that, Aunt Lucy took her arm and steered them towards their new home.

Aunt Lucy's house was beyond Snow Hill, and as they left the town centre the roads became narrower and the houses more densely packed. Children played in the street, and between every fifth or sixth house narrow alleyways offered a glimpse of life in the courts behind them. Within minutes they turned into Weaman Street and found themselves outside a three-storey brick building.

"Here we are then," Aunt Lucy said. "We're round the back, down the entry here." With that she disappeared down the dark passage, but as Mary went to follow her, there was a tug on her hand.

"What's the matter?" Mary turned around to see William pulling Mary-Ann back towards the road.

"I don't like it here," William said.

"You haven't seen the house yet. We just have to go to the end of the entry and we'll be in the court."

"That lady's scary."

"Don't be silly. She's Grandfather's sister, she's going to look after us. I hope you're not going to embarrass me by crying." Mary took his hand and pulled him down the entry.

"I want to go home," William said.

"This is home, now stop that whining."

The court was surrounded on three sides by houses, while the fourth consisted of the washhouse, the privies and a small workshop. Children filled the space as men sat in chairs or leaned against the walls. A few women were busy with laundry or rushing to the tap to collect water.

"Back of number two we are." Aunt Lucy said as she waited for them by a door. It opened into the corner of a small room, and Mary followed her inside and looked around. The grey stone flags on the floor appeared no different to those outside, but in the centre of the room, surrounded by a selection of chairs, stood a large wooden table. In the corner between the fireplace and the window sat a wooden rocking chair draped with a shawl, while a second similar chair stood on the opposite side of the chimney breast. A Bible lay on a simple console table adjacent to the door.

"This is the living room." Aunt Lucy extended her arm into the room. "I'm not here much during the day, I'm often out with Rebecca … my sister. You remember her, don't you?"

Mary vaguely remembered Aunt Rebecca from Charles's funeral, and the memory sent a shiver down her spine. Aunt Lucy continued without waiting for a response. "When I'm at home I spend most of my time by the fire; I don't like to be cold. I get the bread in the morning and usually a bit of meat and cheese as well. On Sundays I get a joint. If you need anything else you'll have seen the sellers in town. Your room's on the top floor. There's a bed and chair up there and a bowl for washing. The water pump's on the other side of the yard between the privies and the washhouse."

"I don't know how to thank you," Mary said, but Aunt Lucy continued.

"Other house rules you need to know. The door will be locked at nine o'clock at night and opened at six in the morning. I don't mind a bit of company of an evening, but I don't want to see any men here. I only let rooms to women and children; it keeps it simple and means we can choose for ourselves how we live. As much as they have their merits, men always want to take charge, but they won't tell me what to do and certainly not in my own house."

Mary smiled at Aunt Lucy's attitude. She'd lived with her father-in-law and his Quaker beliefs for long enough to know how independent their women could be. As much as she loved her mother-in-law, it would make a pleasant change to live with someone who wasn't so preoccupied with finding her a new husband.

She turned to make her way up the stairs, when she remembered the money her father-in-law had given her. She put down her bag and took the envelope from her pocket.

"Your brother sent this for you." Mary handed the packet to Aunt Lucy.

"What's this then?"

"Some money for the rent."

"What's he sent this for? I told him I'd take care of you until you could find some work. Ann's got a lot to answer for. Wait until the next time I see him; I'm managing better than he is. I certainly have more houses than he has. Wait until I tell Rebecca, she'll be furious."

Mary wasn't sure what her mother-in-law had done to upset Aunt Lucy; she had always liked her. Nevertheless, she decided it was better not to ask and turned again to go up the stairs.

The stairs were steep and narrow and she struggled to help Mary-Ann while she carried her bag. Once at the top, she entered the room and saw that Aunt Lucy had described it perfectly. It contained a large bed, standing opposite the door, with a table, chair and washbasin down the left-hand wall. Adjacent to these, a small window overlooked the court, but at this time of day little light came in. The walls and floor were bare and the only colour came from the heavy blue curtains. The fire looked as if it hadn't been used recently, but Mary smiled briefly when she felt the warmth in the chimney breast from the fire downstairs.

Placing her bag on the bed, she peered around for some candles. She found some in a cupboard wedged in the recess between the fire and the window, and after lighting one she sat on the bed. The quilt curled around her legs and she ran her hands over it before William and Mary-Ann joined her. She looked at the two of them and put her arms around their shoulders. William was the image of his father with his thick dark hair and deep brown eyes; Mary-Ann was a picture of her younger self with her slender frame and light brown hair.

"Why did we have to leave Grandfather's house?" William asked.

"Grandfather couldn't look after the big farm anymore so he's moving to a smaller one with Uncle Richard."

"I could've helped him; he always liked me helping."

Mary smiled at her son. "He loved you helping, but we need to look after ourselves now. We came here to get some money."

"Can we go back to Grandfather when you've got some?"

If only it were that easy, Mary thought. "We'll see, but come on, we can't sit here talking the time away, it'll be dark soon and I need to unpack." With that she stood up and untied the string that held the top of her bag. Inside sat a cloth purse containing all the money she owned, a change of clothes for each of them, a bar of soap and two tallow candles. The small wooden train William loved so much and Mary-Ann's teddy bear lay hidden within the bundle.

"My train." William took hold of it and held it to his chest. "I couldn't find it this morning; I thought I'd never see it again."

"Grandmother must have packed it for you as a surprise." Mary took a deep breath. *Why hadn't she thought to pack it?*

"I wish she was here," William said.

"And I do," echoed Mary-Ann.

"Perhaps you can think of her every time you see your train, that way you won't forget her. Now come along, we'd better go and get some bread before it gets late. Leave your toys here so they don't get lost."

When they returned to the living room, Aunt Lucy sat by the fire, still wearing her hat, drinking gin from a large mug. Except for the light from the fire, the room was dark and their shadows danced around the walls. When William saw Aunt Lucy he stopped so abruptly that Mary almost fell over him.

"It's all right, Aunt Lucy won't hurt you," Mary said, pushing him into the room.

"Not if you're good I won't." Aunt Lucy gave William one of her stern looks and he ran to the other side of the room, putting the table between them.

"There's bread on the table and some cheese you're welcome to finish," Aunt Lucy said.

"Is there anyone else living here at the moment?" Mary

15

asked as she sliced and buttered a piece of bread for the children.

"No, there's only one room on each floor. There's another widow, Mrs Gaskill, lives next door with her young son. She works until nightfall most days, but she's around on Sundays; the boy sits in the yard waiting for her." Mary's shoulders slumped at the thought of having no company other than Aunt Lucy, but at least William would have a playmate. "You'll be searching for a job soon, I imagine," Aunt Lucy continued.

Mary sat down with her own bread and sighed. "I can't take a job while the children are so small; I had hoped to claim poor relief."

"You can forget that. The way things are heading they'll want to put you in the workhouse, and no Jackson is going in there."

"They're supposed to let widows claim outdoor relief."

"Maybe they do, but it's not there to take advantage of. There are too many claiming relief rather than putting in an honest day's work; it should only be there for those who are desperate. You have a roof over your head and food on the table; you should thank the Lord for his mercy."

The smile slipped from Mary's face. *If it wasn't for the Lord, I wouldn't be here in the first place.* "How do I buy clothes for the children?"

"We'll all help. People around here won't let you go short."

"I can't expect charity until I find a husband."

"Do you want another husband?"

Mary shifted uncomfortably. "I don't have much choice, do I?"

"Rebecca and I manage perfectly well on our own, so there's no reason why you shouldn't."

"I have two children to care for as well as myself. I have to do what's best for them."

"You don't need a husband for that." Aunt Lucy waved her mug at her. "If you want my opinion, it's the worst thing you could do. There are not many fellows that'll bring up another man's children as their own. If you want the best for them I suggest you remember that."

"Of course I will; I'm not going to do anything to risk their futures."

Chapter 3

M R WETHERBY PLACED HIS PLIERS on the table and rubbed his eyes. The room was dark except for the light of the candle in front of him and the dying embers of the fire. His worktable was placed in front of the window to allow him to work with maximum light, but recently he'd been doing more and more work after dark, which explained his current tiredness. Behind him stood another table, which should have been reserved for food, but was instead covered with reels of wire and packets of hooks and eyes. His bread and butter had been relegated to one of the chairs that surrounded the table.

He stretched his arms behind his head and then rested them back on the table. He had lost track of how long he'd sat there shaping the wire into hooks, but still there weren't enough. The order was due tomorrow and, come what may, he had to have it ready.

This was his biggest order since he'd started out, twelve months earlier, and there would be more to follow if he did a good job. But he couldn't do it tonight. He pushed his chair back from the table and rose to his feet. If he went to bed now, he'd be able to work better in the morning. He reached for his glass of ale and after a moment's thought drained it, picked up the candle and made his way upstairs.

His bedroom was on the first floor. To support his fledgling business he let out a bed in his own room as well as the room on the top floor. His roommate was a labourer he'd met in the local alehouse. He'd been looking for digs and was happy to take the second bed in Mr Wetherby's bedroom. They had little in common but occasionally they would sit in the living room, drinking beer and putting the world to rights. As he approached his room, Mr Wetherby could tell he was already asleep so he undressed quickly, slipped into bed and blew out the candle in silence.

The following morning, Mr Wetherby woke with a start. He usually rose before six o'clock, but this morning the sun blazed into the room. He cursed under his breath and glanced at the empty bed opposite; his roommate had obviously got up as usual and left without disturbing him. He leapt out of bed and pulled on his trousers and shirt before making his way downstairs. He made up the fire, then went outside and walked through the entry into the yard at the back of the house. He usually managed to get to the privy and water pump ahead of everyone else, but this morning there were people everywhere and he had to queue to use the facilities. He finally returned to the house over fifteen minutes later with a large jug of water. He poured some into a pan, which he placed over the fire, before he took the rest upstairs to the washstand.

Once back downstairs, he thanked the Lord that the girls from the room upstairs had left some bread on the table. He buttered himself a thick slice and made some tea before he sat down at his worktable. At least Mrs Barker would be here soon. He had barely started when a knock on the door disturbed him.

"Who is it?" he shouted. When he got no answer he peered out of the window but couldn't see anybody there. At the second knock he pushed himself up and went to answer it.

A young boy stood in front of him, with whom he had no acquaintance. "Can I help you?"

"Mother says she won't be in today because she has a fever." With no further explanation the boy disappeared.

"Who's your mother?" Mr Wetherby shouted after him, but the boy didn't stop. "That's all I need." He'd now have to carry on and hope it wasn't Mrs Barker with the fever. Mrs Gower wasn't due until midday and he hoped to be finished by then.

By ten o'clock he realised he wasn't going to get any help and carried on alone until Mrs Gower let herself in.

"What a day it is out there," she said without so much as a greeting. "There are people everywhere." It was the same statement every morning, but today she changed her routine. "Now, Mr Wetherby, what are you doing still sitting there? Mrs Barker should be there."

"Apparently she has a fever and someone has to do her work. I have to get this order finished and out to Grimshaws today. I want to get another order from them and being late with this one isn't an option."

"A fever is it today? Wasn't it that last week as well, or was that the week before? I tell you, she doesn't deserve someone as considerate as you. You have the patience of a saint."

"That's as maybe, but all this idle gossip won't get this

order out and so if you could kindly take over from me I'll start packaging it up."

"Right you are, Mr Wetherby. You can rely on me."

Three hours later, Mr Wetherby left Shadwell Street with two large parcels under his arm. Grimshaws was an up-and-coming business about a mile from the house. They bought cloth, thread and buttons directly from manufacturers and then sold them to tailors and couturiers. Mr Wetherby had been supplying them with the occasional small order for nearly a year, but last week Mr Grimshaw had surprised him by ordering a thousand hooks and eyes. He had landed a contract with a couturier in London who made women's undergarments and demand for the fasteners was increasing.

He had met Mr Grimshaw on a number of occasions and didn't care for the man; but business was business. He knew what it took to impress men like Mr Grimshaw and if it meant he had to massage his ego in order to get the contract, so be it.

"Good afternoon, Mr Grimshaw," he said as he entered his office. "I trust I've called at a convenient time."

"Is there ever a good time in this day and age?" Mr Grimshaw sat at a desk, mopping his forehead with a large white handkerchief. "It would appear that I have to do everything around here myself. I shouldn't be checking in stock, I pay men to do that for me. Didn't you see anyone outside?"

"No, I didn't, but to be honest I'd hoped to catch you. It's always preferable to talk to the man in charge."

"Of course it is, but I'm busy. What do you want?"

"As you know, you ordered one thousand hooks and

eyes from me only last week and I wanted you to know they're all here."

"I should hope they are. Is that all you wanted? One of the men could have dealt with that."

Mr Wetherby looked at his feet and took a deep breath before he answered. "I wondered how many you'll need for the next order."

"You're a bit forward, aren't you? You've only just delivered these."

"Forgive me, but I know how important you are to your customers and I'd hate you to run out of stock and disappoint them. I expect you'll be getting more business from London now that you have your card down there."

"Fair point. They were impressed by the service I offer. How many can you do in a week?" Mr Grimshaw asked.

"I'm about to move into new premises and take on some more women; if you give me a number I'll recruit accordingly. I don't want to let down such a valued customer."

"You're a man on the up, I see. Do you have any other major customers?"

"I've supplied a number of small tailors, but no one as important as yourself. You'd be my first priority," Mr Wetherby said.

Mr Grimshaw pulled back his shoulders and puffed out his chest.

"Well, yes, of course. There are not many businesses like this around these parts. I think we can continue to do business together, Mr Wetherby. Let's say we'll have double the order next week and repeat that each week for the next three months. We can re-assess the situation after Christmas."

Two thousand! Mr Wetherby struggled to keep the smile from his face as he offered Mr Grimshaw his hand. "It's a pleasure doing business with you. I'll see you next week."

Mr Wetherby had planned to stop at a beerhouse on his way home, but now he had no time. The order was more than he could have hoped for but he had to find a way to produce it. A friend on Summer Lane had told him about some empty workshops in the area and he made his way straight there.

The weather was fine for the time of year and he found his friend sitting outside his front door smoking a pipe.

"Have you finished for the day?" Mr Wetherby asked as he approached.

"Not much call for coal at this time of year; it'll get busy soon enough."

"Can you show me around some of the empty workshops then? I need one pretty quickly."

"What's the hurry? Can't a man smoke his pipe in peace?"

"Not today you can't." Mr Wetherby kicked the man's feet. "Come on, I need to get a move on."

As they walked, Mr Wetherby explained what he wanted.

"We need to find Charlie Harris," his friend said. "He leases out a lot of these workshops. Once we find him, I'll leave you to it."

It took about twenty minutes but eventually they spotted Charlie walking towards them on Hanley Street.

As Mr Wetherby explained what he wanted, the furrows across Charlie's forehead deepened.

"I did have one that would have been ideal, but I let it out yesterday. Another fellow planning on making hooks and eyes."

"Someone else? Where's he from?"

"Didn't say, he just told me he was setting up and needed space for about twenty workers. I've got a smaller unit on Hanley Street, with space for ten."

A look of exasperation crossed Mr Wetherby's face. "That's no good. If I have competition I need somewhere bigger, not smaller. What else do you have?"

"I've a place on Hatchett Street. You'd easily get thirty workers in there, possibly more."

Mr Wetherby frowned; it might be too big. "Can we go and see? I don't suppose I need to fill it immediately."

The workshop on Hatchett Street was bigger than he needed but he couldn't let the chance pass.

"What's the rent?" he asked once they had walked around.

"One pound ten shillings a week."

One pound ten shillings. That'll finish me off if the orders dry up.

"It's a good price for what you get," Charlie continued. "If you were in other parts of Birmingham you'd pay more than that."

Mr Wetherby went over to the nearest workbench and kicked the leg. "What about the benches and trestles? Are they part of the price?"

"I'm moving them to another workshop. Someone's interested in them."

"Leave them in and you've got yourself a deal." Mr Wetherby was conscious of a bead of sweat running down the side of his face.

"They're worth another two shillings a week, they are."

"I don't have another two shillings. Take it or leave it."

Charlie looked around the room and then back at Mr Wetherby, who stood with his hands clasped before him. Charlie's eyes narrowed. "You've got yourself a deal," he said eventually, offering Mr Wetherby his hand. "And a damn good one at that."

"So have you." Mr Wetherby wiped his hand on his trousers before he shook on the deal. "There's not many around here could afford that. I'll arrange to take possession on Monday morning."

When he returned home, Mrs Gower was still working.

"What a marvellous afternoon that's been," he said, causing her to put down her work. "I've secured a large, regular order from Grimshaws and found some new premises. We'll be moving on Monday morning. Do you know anyone who might be able to join us?"

"Well, Mr Wetherby, that's a big step, and so sudden. Are we moving far?"

"Not far; just up Summer Lane to Hatchett Street. The premises are in Hanover Court."

"In that case I know of a few who'd join us; I have friends around there. Shall I tell them to come and see you?"

"Yes, do that. I need five women now, but more later. The sooner they can start the better. We'll have to use the dining table as a makeshift workbench to train them, and they'll need to be quick learners. I only want women who are reliable though, no troublemakers or any who are ill all the time. If they don't turn up for work they won't get paid. If you need to speak to them, go now. We've had a good day and we can start next week's order tomorrow."

Never one to miss an opportunity to finish early, Mrs Gower reached for her cloak. "Right you are, Mr Wetherby. I know those who won't let you down, I'll tell them to come here tomorrow." With that she left Mr Wetherby alone.

He sat down at the table again and smiled; it was all going so well. Despite his concerns for next week he would have the night off and perhaps take his roommate down to the local alehouse. Maybe if he saw them, he might even invite the sisters from upstairs to join them. He hadn't enjoyed any female company for a long time, too long for someone of his age, and suddenly the thought of it was very appealing.

Chapter 4

MARY WASN'T SURE WHETHER IT was because she now lived in the town, but the winter seemed particularly harsh this year. She had started making women's shawls and selling them by the Town Hall, but already she hated her visits into town.

Today she'd been there since mid-morning and had only sold two of her three items. She held them out for everyone to see the detail, and for the most part nobody had looked at her. In some ways she preferred those who ignored her, to the women who looked at her. They were the ones who had the money to buy anything they wanted, but Mary could see the disdain in their eyes as they looked her up and down before turning to their fawning companions with a laugh.

It had been trying to snow for most of the day, and as the light faded she folded up her remaining shawl and put it back in her bag. Her hands and feet were numb and all she wanted to do was go home and have a cup of tea. It wouldn't be so bad if she made enough money to buy some decent food, but she needed the money she'd earned today to buy William a new coat. Why couldn't he stop growing, at least over the winter? She pulled her shawl tightly around her shoulders and bent down to pick up her bag. She was about to walk away when the sound of a familiar voice stopped her in her tracks.

"Aunt Lucy said I'd find you here." Her brother-in-law Richard stood beside her. "You look frozen. Let me buy you a hot drink."

Mary couldn't speak. Hadn't she dreamed of him coming to find her, but she'd never thought he would.

"Have you lost your tongue?" Richard said as she stared at him.

"No … not at all. You just surprised me. What are you doing here?"

"I needed to come to Birmingham and decided to see my favourite sister-in-law. I miss those beautiful blue eyes watching me."

Mary sighed. "I had no choice, you know that."

"You're not still mad with me, are you?"

How could she stay mad with him when he looked at her like that? "It wasn't you I was cross with, well, not only you."

"Come on, let's not dwell on the past. Let me get you some broth and you can tell me what you've been up to."

Once they'd finished their drinks, Richard took her arm and walked her towards Weaman Street.

"What do you do with the children while you're out?" Richard asked.

"They stay in the court. It's warm around the washhouse and they're never alone. I didn't think William would settle when we first arrived, but he seems happy enough now. I'm sure he'll be pleased to see you."

"I've missed having him around the farm, but I'll have a son of my own soon."

Mary stopped. "What do you mean?"

"What do you think? I'm going to be a father … in the summer."

Mary pulled her arm from his. "Is that what you came to tell me? Did you want to dig the knife in deeper?"

"Of course not, I thought you'd be pleased."

"Pleased. Have you no idea?"

"We've moved on, Mary. Why are you surprised?" Richard reached for her hand but she pulled it away.

"You didn't have to come and tell me yourself. It's like you're deliberately trying to upset me."

"Now you're being silly, that's the last thing I'd do. You're obviously cold and tired; let's get you home and we can talk properly."

"While you sit and tell me how wonderful Mrs Richard is? No thank you." Mary snatched her bag from him. "I need to get the children their tea. Don't bother coming with me."

Chapter 5

SINCE HER ENCOUNTER WITH RICHARD, Mary hadn't been to the Town Hall; all she'd wanted to do was curl up by the fire and hide from everyone. Even Aunt Lucy irritated her. If she needed any money she did the laundry for neighbours who needed to work, but it didn't make much. Certainly not enough to buy Mary-Ann the new shoes she now needed; how she'd managed to get her feet into her old ones for so long she didn't know.

With no desire to sell any shawls, and with Aunt Lucy out for the day, she decided it was time to visit the guardians. She was a widow and her young daughter needed new shoes. Wasn't that what they were there for?

Mary arrived outside the workhouse just before ten o'clock. She was horrified to see a queue extending from the central door, across the front window and around the corner of the building. She hesitated when those near the front turned to look at her. *Why were they staring?*

Putting her head down, Mary hurried around the corner, but it didn't ease her discomfort. Eyes were still following her, most encased in gaunt faces that wore the expressions of those with little hope of getting anything for their troubles.

In an effort to make herself invisible, she joined the back of the line and put her head down.

"Freezing again, isn't it?" A woman in front of her stood rubbing her hands. "Not seen you here before."

"I only moved to Birmingham after my husband died."

"Have you got children an' all?"

"I left them at home ... my daughter has no shoes," Mary said, hardly able to meet the woman's eyes.

"You look as if you're doing all right though, with that fancy cloak."

Mary looked down at the cloak her mother-in-law had given her. "It's not mine ... I had to borrow it."

"Lucky for you that you can. I've darned and patched mine so many times they call me Joseph at home ... you know like Joseph and his multi-coloured coat."

"Really?" Mary missed the humour in the woman's voice and stared at her makeshift cloak. "I'm sorry. It must be hard."

"I can't complain; the guardians are good to me. With five children and no husband I get more than most."

"It must be terrible to lose a husband with so many children, it's hard enough with two. When did he pass?"

"He's not dead." The woman let out a bitter laugh. "I wish he was, I'd get more relief then. No, he ran off to Coventry with another woman. I'd have killed him if I'd found him, but then what good would that do? No, the guardians are good. They're after him, trying to get something from him, and I have my friends and neighbours. They won't see me starve or get taken indoors." She nodded to the workhouse.

Mary looked again at the faces around her and at the

children clinging to their mothers for warmth. Several wore no shoes and their feet were almost the colour of the pavement.

"Will you excuse me? I've just remembered something." Mary pushed her way out of the queue. "I hope you get what you need from the guardians."

"They're not likely to give me a husband who earns five pounds a week, but I'll settle for some meat." The woman laughed as she turned to the next woman in line.

Mary couldn't get away from the queue fast enough. What had she been thinking? She shouldn't have been asking for relief when others needed it far more than she did. She had a roof over her head, was kept warm and fed and Aunt Lucy would lend her money if she needed it. She should be grateful she could go to the Town Hall and earn some money.

When she arrived home she was relieved Aunt Lucy was still out. She made a cup of tea and sat by the fire to warm her hands. As she relaxed, the question of whether to go to church or not on Easter Sunday came back to disturb her peace. Until last summer she had gone without hesitation. It used to give her a feeling of calm and security like nowhere else could. Since arriving in Birmingham, however, she had only been once, and that was at Christmas. Yes, she knew she should go, and she took the children to Sunday school, but was it right for her to go when she didn't believe a word the vicar was saying?

Now Easter was upon them, her conscience was pricked again. Her sister-in-law Martha was living in Birmingham now and wanted to go with her. It would make it easier, but it didn't feel right. Why had God put her in this position? It was His fault; He didn't deserve her praise.

As she was slicing some bread for tea Aunt Lucy came home with Aunt Rebecca.

"I don't often see you two together at this time of day," Mary said as they walked in and settled by the fire.

"We've been looking at a couple of properties and we're going to a Friends meeting later. There was no point me going home," Aunt Rebecca said.

"We also wanted a word with you," Aunt Lucy added. The icy tone of her voice sent a shiver down Mary's back. "We have it on good authority that you went to see the guardians earlier."

It was a statement rather than a question and Mary struggled to answer. "I didn't see them. I just walked that way and then came back."

"Don't lie, you were seen in the queue. Do you have no shame? I told you the day you arrived that no Jackson should ever be seen begging for hand-outs."

"Didn't it occur to you it would reflect badly on us?" Aunt Rebecca said. "How do you think we feel when folks say we're not doing our duty by you? You don't want for anything living with Lucy. She gives you everything you need and yet you disgrace her by claiming relief."

"I'm sorry, I didn't think anyone would see me. I only wanted some new shoes for Mary-Ann."

"Why didn't you ask me?" Aunt Lucy said.

"I've already had so much from you." Mary lowered her head to hide the colour rising in her cheeks. "I promise I didn't go in. I stood in the queue but was so ashamed I came away. I won't ever do it again."

"See that you don't," Aunt Rebecca said. "I won't stand by and see Lucy's name disgraced. Do you hear me?"

Mary nodded but as they all sat down for tea, she couldn't eat anything; the atmosphere was tense even with the children at the table. Eventually the two aunts left. Maybe she needed to go to church to pray for forgiveness and thank the Lord for Aunt Lucy's generosity. Yes, she would go to St Philip's on Sunday. At least Martha would be happy.

Chapter 6

ALL THROUGH WINTER AND THE dull, cold spring, Mary had longed for summer, but now it was here she wished it didn't have to be so uncomfortable. It was her first full summer in Birmingham since she arrived at Aunt Lucy's and it seemed so much worse than when she had lived here with Charles. It wasn't the heat that troubled her, so much as the fumes from the factories. They hung heavy in the air and there wasn't any breeze to stir them. There were days when she struggled to breathe. Even having the door open, as she did this afternoon, failed to generate the faintest of drafts and she sat with a fan and a glass of gin to quench her thirst.

She was about to make some tea when she heard her sister-in-law Sarah-Ann shout over to William and Mary-Ann in the court.

"What are you doing here?" Mary popped her head out of the door.

"I've come to see you. I hope you don't mind."

"Of course I don't, but shouldn't you be at work?"

Sarah-Ann stepped into the house. "Mr Rashford let me finish early so I could be the bearer of good news."

"What's happened?"

"Mrs Richard's had her baby. A boy. Joseph William they're going to call him."

"Oh … is that all." Mary placed the pan of water over the fire, trying to keep her face from Sarah-Ann's gaze.

"What do you mean; is that all? It's a healthy baby boy to carry on the family name. Until this, we only had your William."

"I thought you might be here to tell me you're getting married or something."

"Do you think I'd come in so quietly if that was my news?"

Mary turned around and smiled. "You're right. Knowing you I'd have heard your voice carry all the way from Bath Street. No sign of anything from Mr Gilbert then?"

"Nothing. He's been leading me on for too long now. It's about time I told him he should either make an honest woman of me, or let me find someone who will."

"What if he leaves you?"

"If he goes, he goes. I'm twenty-three already, and if I don't get a husband and baby soon, I'll never have one."

Mary took the teapot off the shelf and poured some of the nearly boiling water into it. "You could live like Aunts Lucy and Rebecca."

"No thank you, can you imagine it?"

"If I had the money that's what I'd do," Mary said as she swirled the water around the pot.

"It's all right for you, you already have your children. Besides, you look like you have some money. You're looking as well as I've seen you since you moved here."

Mary walked to the door and tipped the water out of

the teapot, before she went back to the table and spooned in some tea leaves.

"I went to St Philip's on Easter Sunday and they gave me a box of food. Now, whenever I go they have something for me. I don't like to take it really, but it's difficult to say no when it's given with such good intentions."

"You shouldn't sound so surprised, the church always helps those in need. Why didn't they give you anything sooner?"

Mary shrugged and turned to get the water from the fire. "I've no idea. It probably won't last though. There are plenty in greater need than me. Now that William's six I suppose I'll have to look for some work."

"What will you do?"

"I've no idea, but whatever it is, it needs to be better than selling shawls by the Town Hall."

Chapter 7

MARY WALKED OVER TO THE costermongers and bought a couple of potatoes and a small piece of bacon. The food parcels from the church had dried up long before Christmas and, unable to get a job, she had returned to selling shawls. After a day like today, the very least she needed was something warm when she got home.

With the shopping in her bag, she set off up Colmore Row. It had barely turned three o'clock, but the night was already drawing in and the icy wind brought tears to her eyes as she made her way up the hill. As she entered the court she saw the children huddled outside the laundry with their friends.

She let herself into the house and found Sarah-Ann, sitting opposite Aunt Lucy, wearing her Sunday best blue dress with matching bonnet. With her fair hair framing her face, and dusky eyes shining in the firelight, she looked striking.

"What are you doing here looking so smart?" Mary said. "Have you finally had that marriage proposal?"

"Sadly not. I've just come from Mr Gilbert's, hence the clothes, but it's over. He has no intention of marrying me, but that's not why I'm here. I've got something to tell you and I wanted to do it sooner rather than later."

Mary looked at Aunt Lucy and then Sarah-Ann. "There's nothing wrong, is there?"

"It's Mother. Her eyes are worse than ever and Pa says she's struggling to do even the most basic chores around the house. Mother says Adelaide's too young do everything by herself, so they've asked me to go back and help."

"I didn't realise she was so bad. Will she be all right?"

"The doctor thinks she'll go completely blind, but fortunately not yet."

"I must save up so we can go and see her." Mary poured herself and Sarah-Ann a cup of gin.

"I'll give you the money," Aunt Lucy said. "It'll do Ann the world of good to see those children while she can. I might even come with you."

"I've tried to tell them they'd be better off here," Sarah-Ann said. "But Pa has his properties up there and someone has to collect the rent."

Mary sensed the sadness in her sister-in-law's voice and sat beside her. "What about you and your job?"

"I finished work yesterday. Mr Rashford obviously knows about Mother's problems but business is slow at the moment. He's been planning on letting some of us go and I gave him an easy option."

"How can business be slow? Surely men haven't stopped drinking ale."

"A number of new breweries have opened recently and competition is tough. Inns are either not taking our ale or else they're ordering less. We've already brewed enough to last until summer."

"I'll miss you." Mary took hold of Sarah-Ann's hand. "I'll visit when I can."

"You'll be fine here; you're making a living for yourself now."

"It's hardly going to make me rich," Mary said. "I had been wondering if Mr Rashford would give me a job at the brewery, but I suppose I'll have to forget that."

"He might make an exception for family." Aunt Lucy reached for the gin and refilled her own cup.

"I'm not really family, not as far as Mr Rashford's concerned," Mary said.

"Of course you are. Mr Rashford married Eliza and you married her brother Charles, that means you're family."

"I still don't think it would make a difference," Sarah-Ann said. "He'd have let me go, even if I'd wanted to stay. It's no place for you anyway."

"We're managing well enough," Aunt Lucy said. "The rents pay all the bills and we've enough for food and coal."

"I still have to buy clothes though. Today's been bitter again. Why is it always winter when I need to do this? I wish I could get a job indoors. I hate standing outside the Town Hall when the weather's so bad."

"It's February soon," Sarah-Ann said, as she stood up to leave. "It won't be long before it starts getting better."

Once Sarah-Ann had gone, Mary prepared the evening meal and called the children in. They ate in silence but as Mary tidied up, Aunt Lucy found her voice.

"I've been thinking," she said. "There's someone on Hatchett Street with a small workshop. He's been hiring workers recently; would you like me to see if he has a position for you?"

"What sort of work does he do?"

"Makes fastenings for clothes. It's not a strenuous job … and it's indoors."

"If you wouldn't mind; I suppose it's worth a try."

Chapter 8

M R WETHERBY WALKED AROUND THE benches inspecting the workmanship of the women he now employed. This latest batch of recruits seemed to have settled in well and today he had little to complain about. As he returned to his desk, the door to his left opened and an elderly woman walked in. She had a commanding stride and was dressed in a heavy brown cloak and hat.

"Miss Jackson. This is unexpected," he said.

"Good afternoon, Mr Wetherby." She looked around the workshop. "You look as if fortune's been with you since I saw you last."

"Indeed it has, but what brings you here today? I'm sure it's more than a social visit."

"I won't beat about the bush. I've heard you've been hiring women and I've come to ask a favour of you."

"Surely you're not searching for work?" A puzzled expression crossed his face. He didn't know this woman well, but he'd heard she lived by independent means and was proud of the fact.

"Indeed not, Mr Wetherby, I'm perfectly well provided for, thank you. No, I have a young niece by marriage. She was widowed several years ago and wants some work. I wondered if you'd be able to take her into your employment."

Mr Wetherby gave Miss Jackson a long hard stare. When he could take her gaze no longer he walked back around his desk.

"If I'm being honest, Miss Jackson, I already have twenty women and I'm not hiring at present." When her eyes remained fixed on him, he continued. "If you're vouching for her then maybe I can make an exception. Can you send her here on Monday morning?"

"I most certainly can. Her name is Mrs Charles Jackson, and I'm sure she'll be an asset to you."

"As with all of the women," Mr Wetherby continued, "I'll take her on a week's trial. If she fails to grasp the job, I'll let her go."

"I wouldn't expect anything else. Thank you, Mr Wetherby, you've been most helpful. I'll see myself out."

Once Miss Jackson left, Mr Wetherby sat back in his chair. He didn't need any more workers at the moment and he hated being told what to do, especially by a woman, but she was unusually influential around these parts and he didn't want to upset her. He'd expanded his workforce a little too quickly if he was being honest, and already had more fasteners than he had orders for. His margins were tight enough as it was. Perhaps he could pay her less than the others, she wouldn't know, and he could get rid of her at the end of the week.

ॐ∂∞

Mary arrived for work at seven o'clock as Mr Wetherby counted the women in. He was younger than she expected, probably only about her age, and was tall and slim with dark blond hair that he wore swept back and cut into a neat shape around his neck and ears. It matched his neatly trimmed moustache. She supposed he might be described as desirable in his matching trousers and knee-length frock coat, if you liked that sort of look.

"Mrs Jackson, I believe … Mr Wetherby." He bowed his head slightly as he introduced himself. "Please come in. I've a place for you over by the wall."

Mary surveyed the room. There were four rows of benches with five places set at each of the first three and then six places on the back row. Each woman had a pair of pliers and a pile of wire in front of them, as well as a candle to light their working area. The light from the window barely reached the front bench.

"If you'd take your place at the bench I'll be with you shortly." Mr Wetherby indicated to the empty space on the back row.

Mary sensed Mr Wetherby and the women were looking at her, so she walked quickly to the place indicated, sat down and rubbed her hands up and down her arms. Mr Wetherby would have to put more coal on the fire if the heat was going to reach her side of the room. She listened while he gave his instructions to the other women, and then watched him make his way towards her.

"Right, Mrs Jackson, let's get started shall we?" He sat beside her at the bench and over the next hour showed her how to make the eyes for the hooks. It wasn't difficult work and Mary wondered why he needed to spend so much time with her. She particularly didn't like it when he held her hands to show her how to shape the metal. She breathed a sigh of relief as he stood up to leave her and determined to keep her head down. She worked slowly but steadily for the rest of the morning and at midday, Mr Wetherby clapped his hands and brought the work to a halt.

"Twenty minute break," he announced.

He sent a couple of women to get some water from the yard and allowed them all one slice of bread. Mary noticed that most of the women didn't bother with the water. It had a nasty taste at the best of times, and instead they brought in their own bottles of gin. She would remember that tomorrow. This break was the only time throughout the day the women were allowed to talk. As Mary moved to the front of the room, the woman who had sat beside her all morning turned and waited for her.

"Thank the Lord for that," she said. "These mornings seem to get longer."

"It's not that bad, is it?" Mary said.

"I suppose it could be worse, but it could be a lot better. It's so tedious; if only he'd let us talk while we worked; it wouldn't slow us down."

"Have you been here long?"

"Nearly a year now and I could make these damn hooks in my sleep. Mrs Lewis is the name, by the way. What brings a young woman like you here? Mrs Jackson, isn't it?"

Mary looked at her feet, not wanting to go into detail. "I guess I'm here for the same reason as everyone else."

"He wasn't for taking anyone else, you were lucky you had that old aunt looking out for you. He wouldn't have taken you on otherwise. If you want my opinion, he's bitten off more than he can chew. He doesn't see himself as a worker; he wants to be a *gentleman*. A fat chance of that if you want my opinion. He should simply accept his place and be happy with it."

"Isn't business going well?"

"Not as well as he'd have us believe, if you ask me." Mrs Lewis stopped and glanced around them. "I've a friend who says he's always asking around for orders. He'd get rid of us easy enough though if he wanted to. Don't trust him, that's all I can say."

"Now, Mrs Lewis, I hope you're setting a good example to our newcomer." Mrs Gower waited at the table to make sure they only took one slice of bread. "Are you telling her about the business and how lucky she is to be working for someone like Mr Wetherby? A proper gentleman he is."

"Something like that." Mrs Lewis touched Mary's arm before moving on to talk to someone else.

As she'd been working with Mr Wetherby since the beginning, Mrs Gower assumed herself to be his deputy and took no time filling Mary in on her history with the business. Before long, however, Mr Wetherby clapped his hands and the women were back at their benches.

At the end of the day Mary had a small pile of eyes that she left on the table for inspection. Mr Wetherby walked around the benches, checking the quality of the work. Most of the women had gone before he got to her.

"You seem to have picked up the work well." He smiled as he counted out her pieces. "Tomorrow you can have a go at the hooks. I'd prefer it if you could concentrate on them once you know what you're doing; they take longer to make, so I need more of you working on them. Here's your money for today. I pay everyone for a full ten-hour day.

Money is deducted if you need to take time off or if the quality or quantity of the goods is unsatisfactory."

Mary looked down at the money and bit her lip; she could earn more selling shawls. At least this was regular money, and didn't involve standing outside the Town Hall, but it would barely cover the cost of a meal let alone buy clothes for the children. She clearly needed to work quicker.

"Thank you, Mr Wetherby," she said. "I'll see you tomorrow. Good evening."

At the end of the first week Mary waited to be dismissed, knowing she would be left on her own with Mr Wetherby again.

"You've picked up the work well this week." Mr Wetherby stood so close to her that Mary instinctively took a step back. "Have you done this sort of thing before?"

"No, sir," Mary replied.

"What did you do previously?"

"I worked on the family farm." Mary looked around the room, willing him to hurry up.

"I hear you've also been in town selling goods of your own. Is that right?"

Where had he heard that from and what did it matter to him? "Only a few shawls, sir. I took to making them over the summer when I had no other work."

"Have you enjoyed your time here this week?"

"Yes, sir," Mary lied. In truth, Mrs Lewis had been right. The work was tedious, the room was cold and she worried about leaving the children ... not to mention the money, but it was a job and Aunt Lucy had personally arranged it for her.

"In that case, I'll make the position permanent."

"Thank you, sir. May I take my leave now, please? I need to get back to the children."

"Children?" Mr Wetherby said.

"Yes, sir. May I go?" Mary spoke more abruptly than she intended.

"Yes … of course."

Mary didn't wait for him to say anything else. She hurried to the door, pulling her cloak tightly around her as she sensed his eyes crawling over her. By the time she reached the door, her heart was pounding. She pushed through and into the darkness without a backward glance.

Chapter 9

M R WETHERBY STOOD AT THE front of the workshop and surveyed the women before him. Twenty-one of them with their heads down and hands working quickly. Twenty-one women who all relied on him and who were going to raise his status in society. He had already come a long way since he'd moved to Birmingham five years earlier. It had been a gamble but he'd always known he wanted more out of life than his father had achieved. Working just to put food on the table wasn't the life he wanted to live. Since he'd moved to Birmingham he'd seen men make something of their lives, become respectable members of the community and earn themselves some decent money into the bargain. If they could do it, so could he. Never again would he be poor.

That was why he stood no nonsense. These women needed to respect him. His gaze rested on Mary at the back of the room. There was something about her that made her stand out from everyone else. He hadn't known what to expect when old Miss Jackson had asked him to employ her, but not this. She was young for a start and, if he dared to admit it, rather attractive. She had the most beautiful eyes that shone when she smiled at him. She had also surprised him with her speed and ability to learn. As he watched her now, concentrating absolutely on the job in hand, his admiration grew. Some of her hair had broken free from its hold on her neck and hung loosely around her face, creating an elegant frame. She wasn't abrupt and loud like many of the women, and she never complained. Although she'd tried to hide it, he'd seen her disappointment when he'd paid her for her first day's work and the sense of guilt hadn't left him. Already she was one of his best workers and she hadn't missed a day since she started. Perhaps he was being unduly harsh on her. He decided to rectify the situation that evening.

Mary wasn't sure if it was the extra money that had done it but she'd been happier at work since she'd had a pay rise. She even smiled at Mr Wetherby now when she arrived for work. The only downside was that as soon as she walked past him she could sense his eyes following her, and often if she looked up from her work she found him staring at her. She shuddered at the thought and quickly put it from her mind, he probably looked at all women like that. She liked the independence the money gave her and she wasn't going to let something silly like that jeopardise it.

With the end of the day approaching, Mr Wetherby made his way around the room, and eventually stopped in front of her.

"You look like you've had another good day, Mrs Jackson," he said with a smile.

"Yes, sir. I always try to do at least one more hook than the day before."

"That's what I like to hear; I wish everyone worked as hard as you. Tell me, do you go straight home when you leave here of an evening?"

"Yes, of course."

"In that case, I wonder if you'd allow me to walk you home this evening?"

Mary's cheeks turned crimson. "Walk me home … whatever for? I only go to Weaman Street."

"I'll be walking that way myself and I'd enjoy the company."

"I suppose … if you're already going that way …"

"Excellent. Let me get my hat and coat and then we can go."

Within minutes, Mr Wetherby held the door open for her before he followed her and locked up behind them. "How long have you been in Birmingham?"

"I've lived here on and off over the years, but most recently, almost a year and a half."

"And you've lived with your aunt all that time?"

"Yes, she's good to me."

"How long have you been widowed?"

Mary glanced at Mr Wetherby and moved away from him before she answered. "It'll be five years this summer." The sadness in her voice was obvious.

"You mentioned you had children; they must have been young at the time."

"They were two and one, but please, I'd rather not talk about it." Tears glistened in her eyes.

"I'm sorry." He reached down to take hold of her hand.

"What are you doing?" Mary's heart skipped a beat and she moved away.

"Don't go." Mr Wetherby reached out, caught her around the waist and pulled her towards him. Mary gripped his fingers, trying to prise them from her, but he turned her around to face him and held her tightly.

"What are you doing, get off me." Mary thrashed at his arms and torso, determined to break free, and a moment later found enough energy to drag herself from his grasp.

"Please don't go, I didn't mean to hurt you. I only want to know you better," Mr Wetherby called as she ran from him. She dashed down one of the alleyways and stood still in the darkness, praying he wouldn't hear the sound of her breathing. Once she knew he wasn't following her, she crouched down on the floor and let her tears flow. She didn't know why he was taking an interest in her or what his intentions were, but she was still Mrs Charles Jackson and as God was her witness that was how she would behave.

The next morning Mr Wetherby arrived at the workshop early. He hadn't slept that night as the image of Mrs Jackson, frightened and running from him, refused to leave his mind. He wasn't sure how to approach her this morning, but felt he should apologise. Gradually the women started to arrive but seven o'clock came and went with no sign of Mrs Jackson. *Where was she?*

As the women started work he walked to the door to look for her. Nothing.

"I've told you before, we work in silence," he shouted at several women whispering on the third row. "Any more of that and you'll be sacked."

He spent the rest of the morning walking between his

desk and the door. As noon approached, and he was about to end the morning session, the door opened and Aunt Lucy walked in, followed by Mary. There was no preamble.

"Mr Wetherby, I understand there's been an incident between you and my niece which is quite unacceptable. We're here to inform you that Mrs Jackson will not be returning to work. She's a decent hard-working woman and we don't expect a man in your position to take advantage of her."

"Madam, I was merely trying to be friendly, I didn't do anything wrong."

"If you see nothing wrong in what you did, then you clearly don't respect women as you should."

The women in the room no longer pretended to work and looked between Mr Wetherby and Miss Jackson.

"Ladies." Aunt Lucy turned to address them. "Can I remind you that in the eyes of the Lord all people are equal and that means women should be regarded in the same way as men. For men to expect women to do things they don't want to is not acceptable and I'd advise each of you to remember that."

"I'll have no more of that, Miss Jackson. I'm a perfectly respectable man and I'd never harm any of these women."

"You may not harm them, Mr Wetherby, but you don't treat them as equals. There is a difference."

Stung by the attack, instinct told him to fight back. "That's enough, Miss Jackson. If that's the way you feel, then I can't say I'm sorry your niece is leaving us. I'd like to point out she was only here at your request, I had no need of the extra labour and she's done nothing but cost me greatly in wages. If these are the ideas you're indoctrinating her with then you'll be doing me a favour by taking her away from here."

Mary stood behind Aunt Lucy, her face flushed with indignation. "How dare you say that?" She pushed in front of Aunt Lucy. "You told me I was one of the best workers you had."

"I imagine he had an ulterior motive for flattering you," Aunt Lucy said. "If that's the case you're better off away from here."

"Is that true?" Mary's eyes welled up as she glared at him. Mr Wetherby ignored her and turned away.

"Who told you to stop working?" he shouted at the women. "The show's over now, our visitors are leaving." He made a point of looking back at Miss Jackson. "I said you were leaving. Good day to you both."

"It will be a good day once we rid ourselves of men like you," Aunt Lucy said. "Come on, Mary."

Mr Wetherby watched them leave before he went over and slammed the door behind them. He walked back to his desk and sat with his eyes fixed firmly on the wall ahead of him. His mind was racing, but all he saw was the anger in those beautiful blue eyes. How could he have been so stupid?

Chapter 10

MARY SAT BY THE FIRE, her knitting needles clicking frantically. Following the incident with Mr Wetherby, she had taken to knitting baby clothes, and needed to make as many as she could. Last week she had made and sold six dresses, six bonnets and ten pairs of bootees. It wasn't much but it was enough to buy the children some long overdue shoes. She also did laundry several days a week, so she could buy them clothes as well.

She much preferred being at home compared to that dreadful workshop. It was warm and comfortable, and close to the children should they need her. With summer approaching, even going to the Town Hall wasn't as bad as she remembered. As she worked, there was a knock at the door. Although she wasn't expecting anyone, she shouted for the visitor to come in while she carried on with her knitting. She heard the door open but there was a pause before anyone spoke.

"Good afternoon, Mrs Jackson."

"Mr Wetherby!" Mary jumped to her feet, sending the chair spinning. "What are you doing here?"

"I'm sorry, I didn't mean to startle you; I just want to talk."

"You can't come in." She moved to the far side of the table. "Aunt Lucy will be back soon and you can't be here when she arrives."

"I want to apologise for what I said when you left the workshop. I didn't mean to upset you."

"You don't understand. If Aunt Lucy finds you here we'll both be in trouble. You must leave, now … please." The tone of Mary's voice grew higher with each sentence.

"I need to talk to you, we shouldn't have parted as we did. If we can't talk here, is there a place we can meet?"

"No, I'd rather not. I want you to go."

"Please, give me another chance." Mr Wetherby stepped further into the room.

"No. Don't come any further."

"I'm not going to hurt you, I promise. Please tell me where we can meet and I'll leave you in peace."

Mary hesitated. She didn't want to see him again but suddenly there was something in his eyes that made her pause.

"Please," he said again.

Could it do any harm to meet him in public? It would only be for a few minutes. "If you must know, I'm outside the Town Hall on a Wednesday afternoon. Now please … go."

Mr Wetherby nodded and said farewell before he moved and closed the door behind him.

Mary walked to the fireplace and flopped into Aunt Lucy's chair, grabbing the arms to stop her hands shaking. She genuinely didn't want Aunt Lucy to come back and find him at the house, but she knew Aunt Lucy wouldn't be back for hours yet. The truth was he frightened her and

she didn't want to spend any time alone with him. Aunt
Lucy had convinced her she could take care of herself, even
suggesting she could work with her and maybe one day have
her own house to let out. Mary didn't need Mr Wetherby,
but there was something about the way he had looked at
her; something unsettling.

She sat for several minutes taking deep breaths, but
when the fluttering in her chest refused to stop she reached
for the gin and poured herself a full cup. She certainly
didn't want to be in this state when Aunt Lucy got home.

Mr Wetherby walked out of the court, wondering what
had just happened. His visit hadn't gone at all the way
he'd planned. Although he hadn't acknowledged it, he'd
been building up to that afternoon since the day Mary
had walked out of the workshop. At first he'd pretended he
didn't care, even that he was glad to see the back of her, but
he knew it was a lie and over the weeks he hadn't been able
to get her from his mind.

Knowing she lived with Miss Jackson made him angry.
The old woman was so dominant and independent he
worried she would influence her niece for the worse. Over
the weeks, he imagined that her aunt treated her badly
and he became concerned for her well-being. The more he
thought about it, the more he resolved to take her away
from the terrible life she was living.

Only it hadn't been like that. In the seconds before she
had seen him, she'd sat with a contented air about her. It
was only when she had seen him that she'd changed. As
he replayed the scene in his mind, the only positive he

could think of was that he now knew where to find her. She clearly wouldn't have told him if she hadn't wanted to see him again. It wouldn't be easy to leave the workshop on a Wednesday but Mr Carrick, a neighbour who usually worked nights, was always willing to help out. He would ask him to keep an eye on the workers next week.

Chapter 11

MARY ROLLED OVER AND SAT on the side of the bed, careful not to disturb the children. It was still dark but she could see the shape of the chamber pot in the glow from the night-light. She needed to have it close by. A feeling of sickness had been building since last night and was getting worse. Sensing movement from her stomach she threw herself to the floor and grabbed for the handle, certain she was going to vomit. She wasn't wrong. When the retching stopped she reached up for her face cloth and, with trembling hands, wiped the perspiration from her face.

Once the sickness passed, she stood up and took a mouthful of water before moving to the window for some air. The sun would be rising soon and with few clouds in the sky it looked as if it would be a pleasant day. Not that she would enjoy it. What had she been thinking when she'd told Mr Wetherby where she would be? The plain and simple truth was she didn't want to see him, not today, not ever.

The only way she could avoid him involved cancelling her trip into Birmingham. If she wasn't by the Town Hall surely he would take the hint and leave her alone? It had to be worth a try. The problem was she wouldn't earn any money if she didn't go. She didn't normally do laundry on a Wednesday, but maybe today she could make an exception.

She stayed by the window enjoying the cool air on her face as she watched the sunrise. Shortly afterwards, she pulled on a dark grey pinafore dress and made her way downstairs. She hadn't been there long before Aunt Lucy joined her.

"You're up early this morning," Aunt Lucy said. "Couldn't you sleep?"

"I'm going to do some laundry and I want to get to the big houses before anyone beats me to it. I've got my own to do when I get back so I don't want to be late."

"It's Wednesday, why aren't you going to the Town Hall?"

Mary shrugged. "I haven't done much knitting this week so I'll earn more money with the laundry."

"Are you that desperate? What do you need?"

"Nothing in particular, but I don't like having nothing saved for when I need it."

Aunt Lucy wasn't convinced. "You haven't been yourself this week, is something wrong?"

"No, I'm fine. Let me get the bread this morning, seeing as I'm ready."

Mary hadn't been gone five minutes, but by the time she got back Aunt Lucy had brewed a pot of tea and set two cups on the table.

"Sit down with me for a moment," Aunt Lucy said. "I don't like the idea of you walking the streets looking for laundry. It's beneath you."

"It's not much different to selling baby clothes."

"It is. At least your knitting shows you have a degree of skill. Anyone can do laundry."

"Does it matter if it earns me some money?"

"It matters because you're a capable woman and you shouldn't be wasting your talents." Aunt Lucy passed Mary her cup of tea. "By the time I was your age I ran my own business, I had premises and everything."

Mary stopped buttering the bread in front of her. "What did you do?"

"To start with I wasn't on my own, I went into partnership with five of my sisters and we bought and sold bed-linen and other ready-made items."

"How did you have enough money to start buying things in the first place?"

"We didn't have much in the beginning, but we'd seen our mother and brothers, shall we say 'struggle' with money over the years and we were determined it wasn't going to happen to us. If we earned anything we kept it safe. Once Mother died and we had to look after ourselves, we put all our money together and started slowly. My sister Eve was the eldest and she took charge of us all.

"Eventually four of them left. Eve and I carried on until she got married; that's when I went on my own. I had a warehouse on New Street for a few years, don't you remember? It was when you lived on Bath Street."

"Yes, I do, now you mention it. I remember calling with Charles just after William was born. Why are you telling me this now?"

"Because I think you could do something similar rather than messing with all this laundry. Rebecca and I could set you up and help you out while you get started."

Mary didn't know what to say; she'd never imagined

running her own business before. She looked at the grandfather clock and then back at Aunt Lucy.

"Can we talk about this tonight?" she said. "If I'm going to do any laundry today I need to go, but I like your idea. That's a good thing about laundry, you can do a lot of thinking while you're scrubbing those collars."

It was turned three o'clock when Mary returned to the court. The children were waiting for her and when she saw that the washhouse was empty she got them to fetch her some water while she went indoors to get her washing. Once there was enough water in the copper tub, she added some twigs to the fire and stoked it up. As she waited for the water to boil she waved to her neighbour, who was arriving home from work.

"You look busy; did you manage to pick up some work today?" Mrs Gaskill said.

"I was out early and got into one of the big houses. What about you, you're back early? Have you lost your job?"

"No, I've found something better, making buttons. It's much easier work and more regular money. You should try it."

"I don't know that I'll need to. Aunt Lucy said something this morning about helping me set up my own business. I've been thinking about it all day. It sounds quite exciting."

"I wish someone would give me the chance to do that," Mrs Gaskill said. "Maybe I could come and work for you."

"I don't imagine I'll be needing any staff, but if I do, you'll be the first I come to."

Chapter 12

THE FOLLOWING DAY IT HAD turned noon by the time Mary arrived at the Town Hall. The weather was so beautiful she had the children with her and, once she'd laid out the baby clothes, she sat and watched them play. In between customers, she thought about running her own business and realised for the first time in months, she couldn't keep the smile off her face.

By two o'clock all the jackets had been sold, each with a matching bonnet, and only a handful of items remained. She was discussing the price of a dress with a customer when she saw Mr Wetherby walking towards her. For an instant she froze, but was brought back to the sale when the woman handed her a half crown coin. Knowing he now stood next to her, Mary could do nothing to stop her cheeks colouring. *Why wouldn't he leave her alone?* She rummaged in her pocket for some change but dropped several coins that scattered across the pavement. Mr Wetherby watched as she picked them up and counted the correct change into the customer's hand. Finally, once they were alone, she had to acknowledge he was there.

"Good afternoon, Mrs Jackson," he said. "You're a

difficult woman to track down. I expected you yesterday. I must have been mistaken."

"No, you weren't mistaken." Mary struggled for the right words. "I had an upset stomach and didn't come."

"I'm sorry to hear that. I hope you're feeling better."

Mary placed a hand on her stomach as a wave of nausea passed over her. "I'm not fully over it."

"Would you like me to walk you home?"

"No, thank you. I'll be fine."

Mr Wetherby looked at her. "I want to apologise for the way I behaved the day you left the workshop. I shouldn't have spoken as I did. Your aunt annoyed me but I had no right to take it out on you. You were a fine worker; I didn't want to lose you. Will you accept my apology?"

Mary said nothing but looked at him; her expression showing not a jot of warmth.

"I hoped we could move on and make a fresh start," Mr Wetherby continued. "Can we be friends?"

"I don't think so," Mary said. "It wouldn't be right for a master to befriend one of his workers even if she is an ex-worker. I don't know why a man in your position would be interested in a widow like me, but I'll tell you now, I'm a respectable woman and I won't have my reputation ruined."

"The thought hadn't entered my mind; I promise that was never my intention."

Mary maintained her gaze; sure she hadn't misjudged him. "I'm sorry, Mr Wetherby, but you'll have to excuse me. I need to sell these clothes this afternoon and I can't do that if you stand talking to me."

Mr Wetherby spoke without pausing for breath. "I'll buy them."

"I'm sorry?"

"I said, I'll buy them."

"I didn't know you had children."

"I don't, but I know the orphanage always needs clothing and so if it helps you out I'll buy them and donate them to the orphans."

Mary looked down at the clothes on the step. "But ..."

"No buts. Here, let me take them." He reached into his pocket and handed her some money. "This should cover it."

Mary opened her mouth, but it was a few seconds before any words came out. "This is more than the asking price."

"It's what I want to pay for them. Now please, no more arguing."

Mary reluctantly handed him the bag of clothes and was about to call the children, when William ran up to her.

"Can we go now?" he said, when he was close enough to be heard.

"Yes, we're going soon."

"Good afternoon, young man." Mr Wetherby smiled down at him as he came to a halt by Mary's side. "Who might you be?"

William glanced towards his mother, unsure whether he should answer or not.

"Mr Wetherby, this is my son, William."

"What a fine name you have," Mr Wetherby said. "Can you believe my name's William too?" William shook his head. "How old are you, William?"

"Nearly six and three-quarters."

"Nearly six and three-quarters, that is a good age. So

your birthday must be coming up soon. Let me think, is it in July?"

"How did you know that?"

"A lucky guess I suppose. Am I right?"

"Yes it's the twelfth of July," William said. "Then I'll be seven."

"Will you indeed? I tell you what, William, as it's nearly your birthday I've a little present for you." Mr Wetherby fished into his pocket and dropped a penny into William's hand.

"Mother, look, a penny," William exclaimed. "The man's given me a penny."

"What do you say?" Mary said.

"Thank you, sir. I've never had a penny of my own before. I'm going to show Mary-Ann." He raced off to find his sister.

"What do you want from me, Mr Wetherby?" Mary said when they were alone again. "You've come here today, paid me too much money for the clothes and now you've given William a penny. I can't repay you and if I'm being honest it makes me uncomfortable."

"I don't want anything from you other than your company. I want to see you happy."

"I am happy, such as I can be without my husband."

"Why's William got a penny?" Mary-Ann said as she arrived in front of them. "I want one."

"I'll give you one when we get home," Mary said. "Now run and get William, we're going."

Mary picked up her bag. "Goodbye, Mr Wetherby. Please don't come looking for me, I don't know when I'll be here again, but it won't be on a Wednesday." Without another word, Mary left Mr Wetherby alone and followed her daughter into the crowd.

Once they arrived home, Mary buttered some bread and put it on the table with some ham and cheese before she poured herself a large mug of gin. She'd developed a taste for it since arriving in Birmingham, and loved to feel the tension leaving her as the liquid coursed its way through her body. After seeing Mr Wetherby again, she needed it.

She was tidying up after tea when Aunt Lucy arrived home with Aunt Rebecca.

"Do you have a Friends meeting tonight?" Mary asked.

"No, we want to talk to you about a business idea," Aunt Lucy said.

Mary stopped what she was doing. "What are you thinking?"

The sisters took their seats by the fire while Mary sat at the table.

"Rather than setting you up completely on your own," Aunt Lucy said, "there's something we've been considering for a while and we wondered if you'd like to manage it for us."

"Manage it? What sort of venture?"

"Dressmaking and alterations mainly, but also repairs. We'll start by taking on a couple of women, although we may need more once people realise they're happy to pay for such work."

"I don't sew nearly well enough for that." Mary's shoulders slumped.

"You don't need to. We want you to talk to the

customers, take down their requirements, order items of stock and collect the money, keep the books in order, that sort of thing. We'll help if you're unsure of yourself."

"Would I have a say in who we take on?" Mary thought of her neighbour Mrs Gaskill.

"Of course. We'll arrange it so it'll be your business to run, but doing it this way means you don't need to borrow any money to get started. Rebecca and I will pay for everything and take half the profits to pay back our investment."

Mary had been excited about having her own business and somehow this was a disappointment, but maybe it was better. At least she wouldn't be the one taking the risk.

"We still need to find some premises and seamstresses, so it won't be starting for a month or two," Aunt Rebecca said. "What do you say?"

"I think I'd like that." A smile spread across Mary's face. "Thank you so much."

Chapter 13

ALTHOUGH IT WAS WEDNESDAY, MARY sat by the Town Hall confident she wouldn't see Mr Wetherby. She had made herself clear about not wanting to see him again, and he couldn't go there every day looking for her. It was pleasant sitting in the sun and as she still had several jackets left to sell she wondered whether she should stay for another half an hour. Deciding against it, she collected her things together and was putting them in her bag when she heard a voice behind her.

"The weather's been nice again. It must make it more pleasant for you."

Mary hadn't seen Mr Wetherby arrive. She jumped at the sound of his voice and inched away from him as he sat on the step beside her. "What are you doing here?"

"The clothes I bought last week were so popular at the orphanage, I came to get some more. I also wanted to see you again … do you mind?"

Mary looked at him and wondered if the butterflies in her stomach might be an overreaction. "Should I mind?"

"I hope not. I mean you no harm."

Mary stood up to put some distance between them but said nothing.

"They're fine looking children you have."

Mary smiled. "William's just like his father, he's going to be very handsome one day."

"You do well to care for them yourself," Mr Wetherby said.

"Aunt Lucy's a big help."

"Does she treat you well?"

A frown appeared on Mary's face. "Of course she does, why wouldn't she?"

"No reason, but she's a little … different to most women."

"Because she looks after herself rather than taking a husband?"

"That's part of it, I mean it's not normal. Women should be looked after, not working."

"And does the fact that women work offend you?" Mary was surprised at the tremble in her voice.

"It depends. If she has no husband or she marries a scoundrel then she has no choice. My workshop would suffer if such women didn't work; but it can't be natural for women to choose to look after themselves if they don't have to."

Mary let out a long breath. She could easily imagine Aunts Lucy and Rebecca, if they were listening to the conversation.

"Aunt Lucy says women are just as capable as men at earning a living. Both her and Aunt Rebecca are doing well enough, you have to admire them."

Mary noticed Mr Wetherby glance at the sky before he changed the subject. "You seem to have sold most of your clothes already this afternoon. Can I take what's left? I'd hoped to take more than that; perhaps I should call earlier next week. If you don't mind, that is."

Did she mind? The fact that her heart raced and her head pounded told her that she probably did, but if he was going to take her stock, and save her from sitting on these steps all afternoon, would it be that bad?

"If the orphanage needs clothes, then who am I to object? I'll be here at midday."

Chapter 14

THE SUN WAS HIGH IN the cloudless sky and Mary sat in the shade of the Town Hall, a smile on her face. The new workshop was about to open and this was the last time she would need to sit here. As usual William and Mary-Ann played in the square in front of her.

"I'm hot," she heard William say to Mary-Ann. "Let's go to the water pump and cool down."

"I bet I can get there quicker than you," Mary-Ann said.

"No, you can't." William raced away leaving Mary-Ann trailing behind him. As Mary watched him run his hands under the pump, Mr Wetherby sat on the steps next to her.

"They look as if they're having fun." He nodded in the direction of the children.

"They do. What is it with children and water? If I ever try to wash them there isn't the same enthusiasm."

Mr Wetherby smiled and looked at the clothes she had laid out. "You look as if you've been busy this week. It's a good job I bought some extra money with me."

"Please don't think you have to have them all. I should be able to sell at least half of them."

"Don't be silly. I enjoy helping you out, and the orphanage is grateful. Let's get them back in the bag."

As she stood up, Mary heard the sound of footsteps running towards her. "What have you two been doing? You're soaking wet."

"We went to the water pump to cool down." William looked at his shorts and shirt as if it was the first time he'd noticed how wet they were.

"Good afternoon, William, and you too, Mary-Ann," Mr Wetherby said.

"Good afternoon, Mr Wetherby." They spoke as one, standing up straight with their hands by their sides.

"Wait a minute," Mr Wetherby said. "I've just remembered; doesn't someone around here have a birthday soon?"

"Yes, it's me, Mr Wetherby." William put his hand in the air and bounced on the spot. "I'll be seven next week."

"It's my birthday soon too," Mary-Ann said. "I'll be six."

"Will you indeed? I've been thinking, as you both have birthdays soon, I wonder if you'd like to come to the Handsworth Fair with me in September. With your mother, of course." He looked at Mary with a smile.

"Yes, please," they said together.

"Please say we can go, Mother, please," William added. "We've never been to a fair before."

Mary hesitated. Despite the fact Mr Wetherby now came to the Town Hall most weeks, it was only because of the orphans. She wasn't comfortable with him forcing his way into her life.

"It would be a good day out for you too, Mrs Jackson,"

Mr Wetherby said. "When did you last spend a day not working?"

Mary couldn't answer him, simply because she couldn't remember. She didn't particularly want to go, but with the children pleading and Mr Wetherby looking at her expectantly, she believed she had little choice.

"Let me think about it," she said.

"Please, Mother," William said. "We promise to be good."

"I said I'll think about it, now I don't want to hear any more."

"I really, really want to go," Mary-Ann said.

"If I hear another word, we won't be going, now be off with you." Mary turned away and studied the steps of Christ Church opposite her.

"Before you go," Mr Wetherby said to the children, "let's see what I have in my pocket. Look, two pennies, one each, here you go."

"Thank you, Mr Wetherby," they said together. "Mother, can we go and buy some sweets from the stall?" Before she could answer, they'd gone.

"I didn't realise you were so interested in children," Mary said.

"I'm not without practice. I have a number of younger sisters who, for the most part, were born when I was in my teenage years. I hope you decide we can go to the fair. I promise you won't regret it."

Chapter 15

MARY STOOD IN THE LIVING room, her cheeks burning red, as Aunt Lucy looked at her with disgust.

"You've agreed to go with him … after the way he behaved with you?" Aunt Lucy picked up her cup and had a mouthful of gin.

"I haven't said I'll go, but would it be so wrong? I'm sure the incident was a misunderstanding."

"Misunderstanding! You came in here in floods of tears, accusing him of trying to take advantage of you. It didn't look like a misunderstanding to me."

"I overreacted. He said he was sorry and that he didn't mean anything by it."

"And you believe him?" Aunt Lucy took another mouthful of gin. "He tried to take advantage of you in the street and you think it was a misunderstanding?"

"I don't know what to believe." Mary moved to the nearest chair and sat down. "I thought he was going to force himself on me, but now he seems different. He comes to the Town Hall when I'm there and often buys the clothes I knit, for more than I'm asking, and donates them to the orphanage. He's good to the children too and you can't say that about many men. They haven't had much of a life and a trip to the fair would be a treat for them."

"Since when did children get treats? They should be grateful for a roof over their heads and food on the table, never mind going to the fair. But why, may I ask, is he so keen on taking you out for the day? He must have an ulterior motive, because you've nothing to offer him. A man in his position would be able to attract many an eligible woman if he was looking for marriage, not resort to a widow with no money and no personal property." Aunt Lucy turned away, and then spun back around. "Not to mention the children. He won't bring them up as if they were his own. You mark my words. Men only look for less eligible women when they have other things on their minds."

Mary's cheeks flushed brighter as her eyes filled with tears. "Do you think I haven't thought of that? Of course I have, but when he asked me I believed his intentions were honourable."

"If you ask me, you're looking for trouble. If you must go, I suggest at the very least you take Sarah-Ann or Martha with you, and don't come crying to me if it all goes wrong."

Mary kept out of Aunt Lucy's way over the next few days. She couldn't stand another dressing down; she was a grown woman, if she wanted to go, she didn't need to ask permission. Within a week, however, Aunt Lucy was back to her usual self and invited Mary to see the new workshop. It was only small, but they discussed how Mary wanted it arranged and what equipment they needed. She also suggested she find a couple of seamstresses.

Mrs Gaskill was the first person she employed. Mary enjoyed working with someone she knew and together they employed one other seamstress and someone who could darn. After the first couple of weeks, Aunt Lucy let her take charge and she became absorbed in her work. She had never worked so hard in her life, but it seemed to be paying off. Every new customer brought someone else with them and soon she had a regular list of clients. She barely noticed the weeks passing by until one morning she turned over the page in her workbook to see it was the first of September. A week to go before the Handsworth Fair and she hadn't told Mr Wetherby she wasn't going. The only ways she knew how to find him were to go to his workshop, which she didn't want to do, or go to the Town Hall and hope he was there. Still needing to advertise the new business she decided to kill two birds with one stone and take some of her hand written leaflets into town the following Wednesday.

When Wednesday arrived, she was busy as usual and didn't arrive at the Town Hall until two o'clock. Once there she kept herself occupied for most of the afternoon, talking to potential customers, and by four o'clock she decided to leave. Mr Wetherby would have to assume she wasn't going to the fair. She walked over to the costermongers to buy some pies and was turning to leave when she saw him round the corner of Christ Church. He was heading straight towards her.

"Where've you been?" he asked as soon as she was in earshot. "I've been worried about you."

"Aunt Lucy's given me the chance to run my own workshop so I don't need to come into town anymore. I only came today on the off chance you'd be here, so I could tell you."

"How will I see you?" The concern on his face was obvious.

"There won't be any need. I'm not knitting any more so there won't be any clothes for you to buy."

"Do you think that's the only reason I meet you here?" He put his hand to his head, unable to hide his exasperation. "I come to see you; I only buy the clothes to make you think better of me."

"So you don't take them to the orphanage?"

"Yes, I do, and they're grateful, but that's not why I do it. I had hoped we were going to the fair together."

Mary hesitated. Why was it so hard to tell him she wasn't going? "I'm very busy at the moment … and I wasn't sure if you still wanted to go."

"Of course I want to go, I've been looking forward to it. Please say you'll join me."

Just tell him you're not going. Aunt Lucy's words swirled through her head. "Perhaps it would be better if I don't."

"How can it be better? Don't the children want to go anymore?"

Mary thought of William and Mary-Ann, they'd probably forgotten about it. "They haven't mentioned it."

"You haven't asked them, have you? When will they get another chance to go to the fair?"

Mary shrugged.

"I only want to spend some time with you," Mr Wetherby said. "You've had some difficult years and I want to make you happy. Please say you'll come and bring the children with you."

"I don't know … would we be there all day?"

"I've arranged a carriage to pick me up at eight o'clock in the morning."

"Eight o'clock." Mary looked at her feet as she kicked a small stone around. "I suppose we could be ready by then. I need to check with my sister-in-law, I'd like her to escort me."

Chapter 16

M R WETHERBY LEANED OUT OF the carriage to see Mary on the corner of Weaman Street, with William, Mary-Ann and an elegant woman he hadn't seen before, presumably her sister-in-law. It was a bright day and he hoped they'd be spared any rain.

William was peering down the road, clearly unable to hide his excitement.

The two horses pulling the carriage came to a halt and Mr Wetherby stepped out, tipping his hat to the waiting party.

"Good morning, ladies, and good morning, William and Mary-Ann."

"Good morning, Mr Wetherby," Mary said. "May I introduce my sister-in-law Miss Martha Jackson?"

"Delighted to make your acquaintance, Miss Jackson." He raised his hat to her before turning to William.

"Now then, who'd like to ride in the carriage?"

"Me," both children shouted together.

"Come on in then. William, gentlemen sit facing backwards so why don't you sit over there by the window and then the ladies can all face forwards."

He smiled at Mary, a twinkle in his eye, before holding out his hand to help her into the carriage.

"Thank you for coming," he whispered as she stepped past him.

The journey took less than an hour and for much of the time Mr Wetherby entertained William by pointing out things of interest. As they approached the fair the number of carriages increased.

"Look, Mr Wetherby, that carriage has a picture on its side."

"So it does, it's a coat of arms. It means somebody important is inside. I wonder who it belongs to?" he added to himself.

William had his nose pressed up against the window. "Will that man own the carriage?"

"He would indeed. The coat of arms can only be used by that family."

"Do you own this carriage?" William turned to Mr Wetherby.

"Not this one, but one day I will."

"And can I go in it with you?"

"I hope so." Mr Wetherby glanced at Mary, but she was staring out of the opposite window.

"Do you expect your business to take long this morning?" Martha asked, breaking the silence that had descended in the carriage.

"I can't say at the moment. I've a number of people I want to see and I'll be done when I've seen them. I've arranged a stall to display my fastenings and wondered if William would be able to help me out. If he does a good job there might be a shilling in it for him."

"A shilling! Please, Mother, can I help?" William begged.

Mary turned back to face William. "Only if you promise to be good and keep out of mischief."

"Yes I will, I promise. Are we nearly there yet?"

"Any minute now," Mr Wetherby said.

The horses slowed to a walk as the carriages gathered outside the entrance to the park. William was straining his neck to see what lay ahead.

"We should be able to get out soon," he said. "There are men opening the doors of the carriages and we're next. Can I get out first?"

"You wait your turn, young man, the ladies get out first." Mr Wetherby pushed him back into his seat. "We've got plenty of time."

"Will we get to see any lions today?" William asked as his mother, aunt and sister climbed from the carriage. "I'd really like to see some lions … or camels."

"This is only a small fair so I can't promise. Come on, you can get out now."

Mr Wetherby escorted Mary and Martha through the gates. The children followed them along a rough path towards the trade stalls. Trees shielded the view but they hadn't walked far before William pointed ahead of them.

"Look Mr Wetherby, those tents over there. Is that where we're going?"

"You'll have to be patient. We have to sell all these hooks and eyes first." He held up a large bag. "A penny for ten pairs. Can you do that for me?"

"I can count to ten and I know what a penny looks like."

"Good lad. Let's go and get you started and then I can make sure your mother is settled."

∽⌣∾

The ladies and Mary-Ann left Mr Wetherby and William and strolled through the stalls that surrounded them.

"Look over there." Mary pointed to a stall covered with sewing threads. "All those colours. There isn't a great choice in Birmingham but it looks like you can buy anything here."

"This is supposed to be a day out for you, not a day for business," Martha said.

"I can't give up a chance like this; can we go and see?"

They spent several minutes looking and were ready to leave when Mr Wetherby found them. "What have you found here?"

"Look at all these threads." The smile lit up Mary's face. "The only problem is, there are a lot I'd like to buy, but I haven't brought any money with me." She glanced at the threads again.

"Let me get them for you."

"Are you sure you don't mind? I'll pay you back."

"You'll do no such thing, which ones do you want?"

After a little deliberation on Mary's part, Mr Wetherby paid for the thread with a half crown coin and handed Mary the change.

"What's this for?" Mary asked.

"In case you see anything else you like; there are plenty of other stalls. Now, is there anything else I can do for you?"

"First you must agree to let me repay you, for the thread at least, seeing as it's for the business. Also," Mary hesitated, "would you mind if Mary-Ann stays with William? She's bored with us already and she's no trouble."

"I'm not sure it'll be any more fun with us, but she can if she wants to. I want you to enjoy yourself."

Mary-Ann broke free from Mary's grasp.

"Thank you, I'm sure we will. Shall we meet you near the carousel when you're ready?"

"If you can get anywhere near it by then. I'll be as quick as I can." Mr Wetherby looked Mary up and down. "It's such a waste having you here and not being with you."

"Be gone with you." Mary smiled. "Just bring my children back to me when you've finished with them."

Mr Wetherby returned her smile and raised his hat before he took Mary-Ann's hand and went back to William.

"He's certainly got a soft spot for you," Martha said.

"I wish he didn't. I'm perfectly happy as I am, and the new business is taking all my time. I only came because I didn't want to disappoint the children."

"Are you sure?" Martha raised her eyebrow.

"Look over there." Mary turned, ignoring Martha. "A toy stall."

"Don't change the subject."

"I'm not, but look at those little trains; William would love them."

"Why don't you buy one with the money Mr Wetherby gave you?"

"Don't even suggest it; I want to give him the money back, not encourage him. Coming here was enough," Mary said.

"So why did you come, especially after everything that's gone on before?"

"I told you."

"No you didn't; you made an excuse."

Mary said nothing as they walked past the stalls. How could she give Martha an explanation when she couldn't explain it to herself? Why indeed had she come today? She looked at the people surrounding them; if they had children with them, she couldn't see them. She couldn't use them as an excuse. It was just so hard to say no to Mr Wetherby. She looked around at the stalls and rides that surrounded them. "There's a lot more happening than I imagined," she said eventually. "It's a lot busier too. It looks like most of Handsworth and half of Birmingham are here."

"We don't get many fairs so people have to make the most of it. It's such a lovely day too."

"Folk won't be able to get on those fairground rides this afternoon when the stalls close. I'm glad we'll be walking over to see the animals." With the swell of people, Mary found it difficult to look at the stalls and after several minutes she saw a clearing surrounded by trees. "Shall we go and sit over there in the shade?"

Martha followed her to a spot beneath a large oak tree. Once they were settled, Martha tried again. "Are you going to tell me the truth?"

"I wish I could, but I don't know what the truth is." Mary stared over the grass to the livestock enclosure in the distance. "I can't help thinking he wants to take advantage of me. Why else would he be interested? I've nothing to offer him."

"I think you're wrong. He's fond of you and it wouldn't surprise me if he has longer-term plans judging by some of the things he's said. Do you have any feelings for him?"

"Not in the way you mean; he could never take Charles's place. He's been kind to me since that first night, and he seems to like the children, but I still don't trust him. I'm hoping that once we get today out of the way, I won't see much more of him."

"I wouldn't be so sure," Martha said. "Besides, you'll have to see him again if you want to give him the money for the thread."

"I'd forgotten that. Why didn't I think to bring some money with me?"

A moment later Mary jumped as a thunderous roar echoed around the field. She stood up and peered at the pens of cattle but she couldn't see anything. "What was that? It was like nothing I've heard before. Do you think there really are wild animals here?"

"I hope they're well tied up if there are. I wouldn't like to come face to face with whatever made that noise."

"Maybe it's a lion," Mary said. "William will be so excited if it is."

Shortly after midday, Mary and Martha were interrupted when William spotted them and ran towards them.

"Look, Mother, a shilling all for me. Mr Wetherby said I was a good help."

"And indeed he was," a voice said from behind him. "I have a good student on my hands here."

William beamed with pride. A moment later, Mary-Ann joined him looking less happy.

"What's the matter with you?" Mary asked.

"I want a shilling."

Mary pulled her daughter towards her to wipe a dirty

mark off her white pinafore. "William was helping Mr Wetherby. You don't get paid if you don't do any work."

"I helped him join the hooks and eyes together before he counted them."

"She didn't, I did them all," William said. "She was playing handstands on the grass."

Mr Wetherby looked at the two of them. "I think I did see her help you a couple of times. I'll tell you what, you can't have a shilling, but you can have a penny for being a good help. Will that do?"

Mary-Ann smiled and nodded. "Thank you Mr Wetherby."

"Now, I see you're not too far from the drinks stall," Mr Wetherby said. "Can I get you something? The children deserve one too."

"That would be lovely," Mary said. "We'll walk with you if we may. We've sat here for long enough."

"Mother, did you hear that noise before?" William said. "Mr Wetherby says it's a lion and we can go and see it."

"Did he indeed. Well, I wouldn't get too close if I were you."

"I was talking to a customer who said they have a camel and a bear as well," Mr Wetherby said. "They're in the field at the top end of the park, well out of the way. Let me get some drinks and then we'll go and see what all the fuss is about."

As they sat with their drinks the atmosphere of the fair changed. The business was coming to an end and the entertainers were arriving. Time for some fun.

"William," Mr Wetherby said. "Do you want to go and see the magic show?"

"Aren't we going to see the animals?"

"We are, but the magic is on first. You won't believe some of the things they can do. We can see the animals later."

William didn't appear to be convinced and glanced at the tent at the far end of the park before they all followed Mr Wetherby to a row of chairs. Half an hour later as they left, however, all William could talk about was the magician and the way he had made a lot of balls disappear from three cups.

"I told you he'd be good, didn't I?" Mr Wetherby said. "Now, do you want to see the animals?"

"Yes, please! Can we go now?" As soon as he got permission, William ran to the furthest tent. By the time the others arrived, he stood no more than ten feet away from a huge lion, its mouth wide open.

"Oh my word." Mary put her arm out to stop Mary-Ann going any closer. "Is it safe?"

"He's behind bars," William said.

"He might be, but look at those teeth."

"It's perfectly safe as long as you don't put your hand through the bars," Mr Wetherby said. "Do you want me to protect you?"

"I'll be fine, thank you." Mary edged closer to Martha. "It's the children I'm thinking of. Let's move on."

Once they'd seen the camel and the bear, they made their way to the acrobats and jugglers. Soon it was time for their last show.

"Thank you for today," Mary said as they waited for the show to begin. "I've enjoyed myself, but we'll have to leave soon."

"I have the carriage on standby so we can go whenever you're ready." Mr Wetherby smiled and looked deep into her eyes. "I've enjoyed myself too, I just regret that I've spent so little time alone with you. Once we get back to Birmingham, will you let me to call on you and perhaps we could walk out together?"

A shudder coursed through Mary's body. "See me again?"

"Don't sound so surprised."

"You can't come to the house."

"I don't need to come to the house, please, let me see you again."

Mary looked away, fighting to catch her breath.

"Perhaps we could meet at the Town Hall after work and go to one of the gardens," Mr Wetherby said when she remained silent.

"I don't know; it all feels too soon."

"I promise I won't lay a finger on you and, if it makes you more comfortable, you can bring the children."

Chapter 17

THE THICK GREY CLOUDS BLANKETING the town made it feel later than quarter past five. In many ways Mary wished she could go home and sit by the fire, but she had arranged to meet Mr Wetherby outside the Town Hall, and she couldn't let him down. It was over a month ago that they had been to the fair and she had only seen him once since. Calling William and Mary-Ann from the court, she pulled her shawl tightly around her and headed towards Colmore Row.

She was a couple of minutes late arriving and expected Mr Wetherby to be waiting for her. When he wasn't there she walked around the building to check she hadn't missed him. Eventually, when she saw no sign of him, she let the children have a run around while she stood beneath one of the arches, studying everyone who passed. *Where was he?* It wasn't like him to be late. Perhaps he had changed his mind and found a more suitable companion? She couldn't blame him; she'd always said he should have someone young and beautiful … with no children. Definitely a spinster, likely to have a wealthy father too. He might even find someone who loved him. She wanted to think she was pleased for him; it was no less than he deserved, but if she was, why did she still hope he'd walk around the corner and give her that special smile? The clock on the front of Christ Church showed quarter to six; it didn't look like he was coming. She supposed she'd brought it upon herself; now she'd have to make do with Aunt Lucy and the business.

She shouted to the children and pulled her cloak tightly around her as she left the shelter of the Town Hall to head back up Colmore Row. As she passed St Philip's church she heard her name being called and turned to see Mr Wetherby running after her.

"Mrs Jackson, please forgive me." He gasped for breath. "We had an incident at the workshop and I couldn't get away. I was afraid I'd miss you."

"I thought you'd changed your mind," she said.

"Of course I've not changed my mind. It was that irresponsible woman, Mrs Gower. Do you remember her? She's been with me for years but as she was leaving tonight she collapsed right in front of me. I thought she was dead. Turns out she'd drunk too much gin. She'll be for it tomorrow."

"Don't be too hard on her; she may have her reasons."

"I don't care what her reasons are; I nearly missed you. Can we still walk to the gardens?"

"I'd like that." Mary let a smile remove the tension from her face. "There's still time."

They turned and walked back past the Town Hall and headed towards the park. As they approached Christ Church they had to fight their way through the crowds. Mary held onto the children tightly, only releasing them once they were out of the town centre. It was another ten minutes before they reached the park and the children ran on ahead of them.

"I didn't get the chance to tell you," Mr Wetherby said when they were alone. "I secured several large orders while we were at the fair. It means I'm going to have to take on more workers."

Mary stopped and looked at him.

"Don't look so worried," he said with a laugh. "I know you wouldn't want to come back, but I need some errand boys and I wondered if you'd let William work for me? He showed some real talent last week and it would be good to teach him something about business."

"William?" Mary said. "He's only seven."

"I was working at his age. It'll do him good."

"Aunt Lucy says he needs to go to school ..."

"Of course he needs to go to school. He's a bright boy but he doesn't need to go yet. He can come and work for me for a year or so and then he'll be ready to go. Do you know where you'll send him?"

"Not really. Aunt Lucy wants him to go to one of the Friends Society schools."

"A Quaker school? What on earth for?"

Mary's face reddened. "They're good schools."

"They'll indoctrinate him with all sorts of strange ideas."

"Their ideas aren't strange; they make a lot of sense."

"Are you a dissenter?" Mr Wetherby stopped abruptly and looked at her.

"No, Church of England."

"Well, you've clearly been living with her for too long."

He started walking again. "Does she make you go to the meetings with her?"

"I went when I lived in Aldridge, and I go to the Friends Burial Ground every week to visit Charles's grave."

"What possessed you to marry a Quaker?"

"I fell in love." Mary could feel the venom in her eyes, but she wasn't sorry. She might like Mr Wetherby but he was never going to replace Charles.

"I'm sorry, forgive me." Mr Wetherby stepped in front of her. "I didn't mean to be rude, it's just unusual for someone to be allowed into the Quaker *community*."

"They were kinder to me than you'll ever know and I won't hear a word against them. Now if you'll excuse me, I need to get home."

"I'm sorry, please, let me walk with you. You shouldn't be out on your own at this time and we need to talk about William."

Mary's glare softened. Had she jumped to the wrong conclusion again? Her heart pounded as she prayed, once again, that she had.

Early on Monday morning, Mary took William to Mr Wetherby's workshop. By the time they arrived the room was full and Mary noticed there were a lot more places set out than there used to be; it looked positively overcrowded. Several of the women saw her and stopped what they were doing to watch her encounter with Mr Wetherby.

"Good morning, William, Mrs Jackson." Mr Wetherby nodded his head to them.

"Good morning, Mr Wetherby," William said. "Mother

says you have a job for me and you'll pay me some real money. Is that right?"

"It is indeed. I hope you have your best running legs with you, I need you to run some errands."

"I can run really fast, shall I show you?"

"No, not yet; save your energy. Go and sit with those boys by the wall; their names are Albert and Frank." Mr Wetherby waited for William to leave before he continued. "I'll need him until mid-afternoon and then I'll let him go. Will you pick him up?"

"I'm sure there's no need for that, he can find his own way home. Good day, Mr Wetherby." Mary waved to William and turned to leave, but before she had reached the door Mr Wetherby called after her.

"Mrs Jackson, may I have a word with you?"

"What is it; is there a problem already?"

"No, not at all, but can we go outside?" Mr Wetherby escorted her into the court and then stopped. He appeared to be studying the detail of her face.

"Is everything all right, Mr Wetherby?" Mary asked when he failed to say anything.

"Yes, I'm sorry, actually I wondered if we could walk out again?"

Mary flushed as he spoke; she'd been expecting something like this.

"Weekdays are out of the question with the dark nights, but perhaps we could make it on Sunday after church," he continued.

Why was it so hard to say yes? She liked him, didn't she?

"Aunt Lucy always gets meat in for Sunday dinner and then I take the children to Sunday school at St Philip's."

Mr Wetherby's shoulders dropped.

"Maybe we could go after that?" she said. "As long as I'm back in time for evensong?"

A broad smile spread across Mr Wetherby's face and he straightened up again. "Sunday it is then. I'll pick you up from St Philip's when you drop the children off."

Chapter 18

MARY WASN'T SURE HOW IT happened, but as she and Mr Wetherby fell into a routine of seeing each other every Sunday, she finally relaxed and found she enjoyed his company. They usually spent time in the park and if there was a band playing they would sit and listen, but today it was too cold. Mary wore the new cape she had been able to buy with her wages and carried a matching hand muff. Despite that, the cold still managed to find its way in and she hoped they wouldn't be outside for long. Mr Wetherby had been quiet since they had left the church and she wondered if there was a problem.

"Not a problem as such," he said when she asked.

"Do you want to talk about it?"

Mr Wetherby coughed to clear his throat. "Please don't take this the wrong way, but do you remember when I asked about your late husband? I didn't go about it very well but I'd still like to know more about him. Is it still too painful to talk about?"

Mary said nothing, searching her mind for the right words.

"I'm sorry. I shouldn't have brought it up again." Mr

Wetherby thrust his hands into his pockets and looked at the ground.

"No, it's me who should be sorry." Mary spoke in a whisper. "I don't want to spoil our friendship, but it is painful; I can't pretend otherwise."

"Can you tell me about him?"

"There's not much to tell. He was only twenty-three when he died. Consumption. William was only two-years-old, Mary-Ann was one. They never even knew him." She pulled out a handkerchief and wiped her eyes.

"Why did you come back to Birmingham? Didn't you have a family to go to?"

Mary stopped walking and looked away. *Why did he always want to know more?* "I don't have any family and I couldn't keep relying on his."

"You don't have any family of your own?" She felt Mr Wetherby's eyes studying her.

"If you must know, Charles was born in Birmingham, so I came here to claim poor relief."

"Why did you need relief if his family were looking after you?" he asked.

Mary could feel the heat colouring her cheeks and checked herself before she spoke. "I couldn't stay with them. I'm entitled to claim relief from the union of my husband's birth and so I came here."

"I'm sorry, I didn't mean …"

"You don't know what you mean because I imagine you've never been desperate. For your information I haven't made any claims. Aunt Lucy's taken care of me since the day I arrived and I'm very grateful to her. Now, if you'll excuse me."

"No, please don't go. I didn't mean to criticise. I do know how hard it is to have nothing."

"Well, you have a funny way of showing it. Good evening Mr Wetherby, I'll see myself home."

"No, please." Mr Wetherby moved to stand in front of her. "I'm sorry, I always manage to say the wrong thing when I really don't mean to. I wanted this afternoon to be special and I've gone and ruined it."

"What's so special about this afternoon?"

Mr Wetherby searched Mary's eyes with his before he spoke. "It's the afternoon I was going to tell you that I love you and I want you to be my wife."

Mary's gasp was audible. "How can you say that, we hardly know each other?"

"I know all I need to." Mr Wetherby held her gaze.

"I don't know what to say." Mary shivered as she took in his words.

"You could say yes and make me extremely happy."

"But why would you be interested in a widow with two young children? I've no personal property and you could have your pick of any number of eligible women."

"I don't want anyone else. I love you and if I'm honest, I think I've loved you since the day we met."

Mary looked around for a bench and went to sit down before her legs crumpled beneath her.

"I'm not the man you think I am," Mr Wetherby continued. "I wasn't born with money, everything I have I've earned myself. I spent my early years making cloth with my father and the only education I had was at Sunday school. I came to Birmingham with nothing. Literally. By the time I got here the only thing I knew for certain was that I never want to be poor again. That's what's driven everything I've done since I arrived here.

"I don't need anything from you, except yourself. I want to take care of you. I've enough room for the children to have their own bedroom and I can pay for William to go to school, Mary-Ann too, for that matter. You won't have to work again. Someday I'm going to buy my own house, but it will all be meaningless if I'm alone, and so I'll ask you again, will you be my wife?"

Mary didn't know what to say. She'd known he liked her and she was fond of him, but marriage. It had never occurred to her. And then there was the family to think of. Aunt Lucy wouldn't be happy, nor Aunt Rebecca. She needed to speak to Martha and Sarah-Ann; they'd be honest with her.

"I can't give you an answer right away." Mary ran all the possibilities through her mind. "There are too many things to consider, I need time to think and speak to the family. You need time to reconsider as well ... in case you change your mind."

"I won't change my mind, I've known this day's been coming for a while now."

"It's time we were heading back." Mary shivered again, this time due to the cold. "It's nearly time for evensong."

☙❧

As they left the gardens, Mr Wetherby struggled to act normally. *What was it about her that made him act like this? Why did he always manage to upset her?* Yes, she was a fine looking woman, and she had the most beautiful eyes when she smiled, but he had got to the point where he thought about her constantly. He'd actually grown fond of the children too, although that hadn't been part of the original plan. He was used to getting what he wanted and this wasn't the reaction he had expected. When he had asked her to marry him, all he had seen was confusion swimming behind the tranquil blue façade of her eyes. It was clear she didn't feel the same way for him as he did for her, and as they walked he vowed that one day he would make her love him.

Chapter 19

MARY SAT MENDING WILLIAM'S JACKET again. It was the second time in as many weeks he had put the elbow through but she wasn't buying him a new one. The children were in the yard and, with Aunt Lucy at the Friends Society, the only sound came from the fire as it roared in the grate. She was deep in thought when a knock on the door made her jump in her seat.

"I wasn't expecting to see you today," she said as Martha walked in.

"I bumped into Aunt Lucy in the market yesterday and she said you're not your usual self. She asked me to call to see if everything's all right."

"That was good of her, but why didn't she ask me herself?"

"She suspected it was to do with Mr Wetherby and she didn't think she was the best person to offer advice."

"She's right there."

"So, will you tell me?" Martha hung her cloak on the stand and sat down.

"I will, but let me pour a couple of gins first, it calms me down."

"That doesn't sound good."

"I don't know whether it's good or not, to be honest." Mary handed Martha a cup. "I've been having arguments with myself since last Sunday when it happened."

"When what happened?"

Mary took a mouthful of gin. "When Mr Wetherby proposed marriage to me. I don't know what to make of it. Why would he want to marry me when he could have anyone he wanted?"

"I've told you before; he's in love with you. I could tell by the way he looked at you at the fair. I'm sure he doesn't care that you have nothing. Besides, why is it such a difficult decision? I thought the whole reason for coming back to Birmingham was to find another husband."

"That was your mother's idea, I was never keen. Nobody can replace Charles."

"What about the children? You have to consider them," Martha said.

"I consider them all the time, that's part of the problem. I've seen what men can do to children that aren't their own. Money isn't everything." Mary warmed her hands in front of the fire.

"Mr Wetherby dotes on William; I don't think for one minute he'd mistreat him. You seem to be making excuses rather than seeing the positives in this."

"Would I still be part of the family if I accepted? I don't even know if Mr Wetherby would let me visit Mother and Pa again. You're the only family I've got now and I won't accept the proposal if he stops me seeing you."

"You could talk to him about it, but surely there's only one question that's important. Do you love him?"

"Love?" In all her thoughts it was the one thing Mary

hadn't considered and she looked at Martha blankly. "I don't suppose so, it hasn't crossed my mind."

"Do you think you could ever love him?"

"I don't know, I've grown fond of him, so perhaps I could, given time."

"And would it matter if you didn't love him? Could you still be his wife? Satisfy his needs, if you know what I mean?"

Mary shuddered; she didn't even want to think of that. "I don't know. What do you think I should do?"

Martha reached over to the table and topped up their drinks. "I think you should accept. He's got a lot going for him and he clearly adores you. He thinks the world of William too and that's something you shouldn't take lightly."

"Would it mean I don't care for Charles anymore?"

"Of course it doesn't. I'll tell you what, why don't you come to Great Barr with me for Christmas and you can talk to Mother and Sarah-Ann; see what they say."

Mary hesitated. She wasn't sure she was ready to see Richard again. "I don't know. Mr Wetherby might not let me go."

"He doesn't own you yet. Now, I'm not going to take no for an answer. I'll book you some seats on the stagecoach so you can give the poor man an answer before the New Year."

Chapter 20

Great Barr, Staffordshire. England.

THE SNOW WAS EARLY THAT year, making the carriage ride slow and uncomfortable, but at least they had inside seats. Mary sat alongside Mary-Ann, with William and Martha sitting opposite.

Mr Wetherby was so patient with her. It had been almost a month since he'd asked her to marry him and she still didn't know what her answer would be. When she told him she wanted to go to Great Barr he accepted her decision without question and even offered to pay for the stagecoach. For the bulk of the journey the two women travelled in silence. Mary didn't want to discuss the situation in front of the children and, given that she could think of nothing else, she made no attempt at conversation.

They arrived in Great Barr around mid-afternoon and the sky was already darkening. It would take time to walk to Hardwick, especially with the snow on the ground, but they set their heads into the wind and set off as best as they could.

Twenty minutes later they approached the farmhouse.

Mary's father-in-law opened the door, his wife closely behind him.

"Is that you, Martha?" she asked. "I'm so glad you're here, you too, Mary, I was worried the weather would delay you. Come in quickly, all of you."

Sarah-Ann ran down the stairs. "Come and sit by the fire and I'll put some water on to boil."

Mary watched Sarah-Ann prepare the tea and offer everyone some cake.

"You look tired," she said. "Is there anything we can do to help?"

"There most certainly is." Sarah-Ann took a large slice of cake and sank into the nearest chair. "Richard's cut some holly and ivy to decorate the room and I want the children to help me make some paper decorations I've started but I don't have nearly enough. Next year I'm going to lock myself in for a few days to get everything ready; there's too much to do. I'd like you and Martha to make some more mince pies too."

"Do we have the goose hanging already?" Martha asked.

"We've got two. It might have been easier getting a turkey, but it's not the same. They've been in the outhouse since Monday; Richard has sent some potatoes and parsnips as well, so they need peeling."

"It sounds delicious already," William said. "I wish it could be Christmas every day."

When she woke the following morning, Mary struggled to get herself out of bed. She'd had a restless night and she wondered what had possessed her to want to discuss the proposal when the whole family would be here. She should have waited and come to see Sarah-Ann when she was alone.

As it was Sunday, the family made their way to church but the snow made the walk difficult and she stayed with William and Mary-Ann to avoid any awkward questions. Once they arrived home, she helped her mother-in-law place the decorations in the front room, before she went into the back room to make a batch of mince pies.

"I think it's time I took these little ones carol singing," Mother said wiping her hands on her apron. "Will you come with me, Pa? I can't go on my own and William doesn't know the place well enough to act as a guide."

"Do I have to?" Mr Jackson rolled his eyes at her. "You know I find all this fuss quite unnecessary. Tomorrow's just another day to me."

"I know, but everyone else is busy and I don't want to leave you out. Please."

"My mother will be turning in her grave at all this commotion."

Once they were alone, Mary, Sarah-Ann and Martha went into the back room to make a last batch of mince pies.

"At least your father's making an effort to join in," Mary said. "Aunts Lucy and Rebecca refuse to even have a special meal tomorrow."

"I admire them," Sarah-Ann said. "If they don't celebrate Christmas, there's no need to do anything special. Pa only joins in because of Mother. He lets her do what she wants; the only thing he won't do is come to church with us."

"Mother really changed this family, didn't she?" Mary reached for the rolling pin before covering it with flour.

"I don't think she had an easy time when she first married my father," Sarah-Ann said. "From what I hear, she didn't get on with our grandmother, but she died before we were born and so we never knew her."

"I get the impression our grandmother was like Aunt Lucy," Martha said, mixing the mincemeat.

"Your mother must have been strong to stand up for herself. You wouldn't think it now, would you, she's so gentle with everyone."

"She's tougher than you think," Sarah-Ann said.

Martha looked at the clock. "She said they were going to Richard's when they'd finished singing; if we hurry up we can join them."

"Aren't we seeing them tomorrow?" Mary stopped what she was doing.

"Only in the evening. Can you believe they want to have some time to themselves?" Sarah-Ann shook her head in disbelief. "They have the rest of the year to themselves for goodness' sake, but Mother persuaded them to have us all for tea when Louisa and Adelaide's gentlemen join us. I can't believe they're both getting married; Louisa especially."

"I know. She was heartbroken when Ann died, but at least it's given her a second chance to be happy. I don't suppose Mr Robson knows anything about it?"

"I doubt it," Sarah-Ann said. "Why would she admit to having an illegitimate daughter when there's no need. No, best to keep quiet and say nothing. What about you Martha, is Mr Chalmers any closer to proposing marriage to you?"

A scowl crossed Martha's face. "No, and I'm beginning to wonder if he ever will. There could still be a third wedding in the family next year though."

Martha looked at Mary, and Sarah-Ann followed her gaze.

"Mary? Have you had a proposal of marriage?"

Mary's face turned bright red. "Don't sound so surprised."

"Why didn't you tell me?" Sarah-Ann's shriek pierced the air.

Mary put her hands to her cheeks as they looked at her. "It was too important to put in a letter, I wanted to tell you in person."

"So what is there to tell, is it Mr Wetherby?"

"Well, I haven't been seeing anyone else." Mary giggled.

"I bet Aunt Lucy had something to say about it."

"I haven't told her yet, in fact I haven't told anyone because I don't know if I'm going to accept."

"Of course you must," Sarah-Ann said. "You've said in your letters that he's not as bad as you first thought and you've been on your own for long enough."

"You and Martha are on your own and doing perfectly well," Mary pointed out. "Why shouldn't I?"

"We're not on our own out of choice." Sarah-Ann banged the cake tins onto the table. "I'm on my own because I'm stuck here, and Martha would love Mr Chalmers to propose marriage to her. Anyway, it's a chance for you to start again."

"How can you say that when you don't know him?" Mary suddenly felt uncomfortable with the whole idea.

"Well, let's be honest, you're not going to get any better offers."

"Yes, but …"

"And I've known you long enough to know you need a new start. You have William and Mary-Ann to think of. How many good reasons do you have for not marrying him?"

"A few." Mary focussed on the mince pies.

"And if they all revolve around Charles then you're being ridiculous. He's dead, you have to move on."

Mary stood with her mouth open and looked to Martha for support.

"She's right," Martha said. "You have to think of the future."

"How can you say that? Neither of you know what it's like to love someone so much it hurts. I gave up everything for Charles and even now, five years later, I can still see and hear him as if he'd only just left the room. Mr Wetherby doesn't even come close." Mary threw her apron onto the table, tears streaming down her cheeks. "Why is it so wrong for me to want to look after myself?"

৵৵

Birmingham, Warwickshire.

Mr Wetherby slumped in his chair with only the light of the fire and a glass of ale for company. It was his third of the evening but it hadn't made him feel any better. He didn't enjoy Christmas at the best of times but this year was going to be the worst yet. With Christmas Day falling on a Monday he'd had to close the workshop for two days and he would be alone for both of them. The sisters who lodged with him were visiting an elderly aunt, and the labourer, who'd once shared his room, was long gone. He hadn't bought anything special for his Christmas meal and he certainly hadn't decorated the room. He didn't know what this young Queen and her husband had started, but he was sure they would rue the day they made Christmas into the occasion it had become.

As he looked around the room, his thoughts inevitably turned to Mary. *What was she doing now?* How different the house would be if she were here. An involuntary smile flickered across his face when he thought of the children and how they would cheer the place up. Such a notion wouldn't have crossed his mind a year ago, but there was one thing for sure, if they were here now he wouldn't be sitting in the dark, drinking himself into a stupor. Nor would he be planning to spend a miserable Christmas alone like that character Ebenezer Scrooge.

He shifted in his seat when he realised he could hardly tell Mary what a lonely Christmas he'd had. He needed to tell her he'd had a pleasant day. He would go out in the morning and buy a piece of beef with all the trimmings. In fact, if anyone at church was going to be on their own he would invite them for dinner. He had a few bottles of liquor they could share. Feeling sufficiently cheered he finished his drink and took himself off to bed.

Chapter 21

Great Barr, Staffordshire.

THE CHILDREN WOKE EARLY ON Christmas morning and begged Mary to take them to see the finished decorations. Convinced she had only just gone to bed, she waited until the clock struck six before she agreed to get up. They hadn't been downstairs long before the rest of the family joined them and set about their morning tasks. Sarah-Ann wrapped the pudding and put it in the copper, while Martha stuffed the geese with some sage and onion before taking them to her brother's oven. Mr Jackson and William went to fetch the Yule log for the fire and Mary helped Mother lift out the best china and lay it out on the table. All too soon it was time to leave for church.

The children raced ahead, making snowballs from the untouched snow, while Mary walked behind with Sarah-Ann. They had forgotten their harsh words of the night before, and were talking about the marriage proposal, when footsteps crunched in the snow behind them.

"Good morning, ladies, and a Merry Christmas to you both."

The voice instantly sent a shiver down Mary's spine

and she turned to face her brother-in-law, forcing herself to smile. "Merry Christmas Richard. You're looking ... well."

"As well as can be expected at this time of year." His smile caused her to tremble.

"Merry Christmas," Sarah-Ann said to her brother. "Is Mrs Richard not with you?"

"She's under the weather this morning. She's been like this all week, although she gets better as the day goes on. You'll see her later." Richard looked directly at Mary. "You'll join us tonight I presume? I missed you yesterday."

"I wasn't feeling well." Mary averted her gaze, willing her cheeks not to go red.

"What a terrible day to feel ill," Richard said. "Are you all right now?"

"I'll have to see." She wasn't sure she would get through a whole evening in Richard's presence, not with Mrs Richard there anyway.

When they arrived at church the pews were filling up and people sat closely together to fit everyone in. William and Mary-Ann were already seated near the front with their grandmother and Martha.

"May I join you?" Richard asked, holding Mary's gaze.

Mary couldn't speak but nodded and moved along the pew to give him room to sit down. They sat so close she feared he would feel her whole body trembling. She looked at him and studied his profile, his firm jawline, dark eyes and olive skin, edged with the familiar dark brown hair falling around his face. How she longed to run her fingers through it once again.

Richard was two years older than Charles but the resemblance was striking. She remembered the times they had spent together after Charles's death. On the first occasion Mary had gone to collect eggs from the barn and Richard had walked in on her unexpectedly. Initially things had been awkward but when Richard had seen her crying he'd moved to comfort her and held her tightly for several minutes. As he'd pulled away he'd looked down at her and the attraction between them had been stronger than either of them had imagined; after a moment's hesitation they had succumbed to their first kiss. They used to meet in the barn most afternoons after that, always making sure they were alone. To Mary it was as if she had Charles back. They'd kept their secret for over twelve months but had realised they were heading for trouble when they'd wanted more from the relationship. In the eyes of the church they could never be married and, although many disregarded the law, Richard had made the decision to stop seeing her. He'd got over the relationship more easily than she had, and within months he'd met Maria Coates, the girl who had become his wife just over a year later. It had broken Mary's heart for a second time and at that point she had known she had to move away.

Richard turned to her and their eyes locked. Mary couldn't breathe and wondered how he could appear so calm after what they had meant to each other. Eventually he smiled and looked away, but for Mary the church service passed in a blur. Usually she loved to sing, especially the new hymn, *O Come All Ye Faithful*, but today she had no voice. Instead she stood as still as stone, praying for forgiveness for the thoughts passing through her head.

With the service over, Richard walked Mary and Sarah-

Ann back to the end of their driveway, before he turned down the track to the right and made his way home.

"He's happily married you know," Sarah-Ann said when he had gone. "Mrs Richard's lovely and they have young Joseph; another one on the way too by the looks of it. How long have you carried a torch for him?"

Mary stopped and looked at her. "What do you mean?"

"You know what I mean, don't pretend you don't. You couldn't keep your eyes off him."

"Was it obvious?" Mary sighed and looked around them. "If you want the truth, ever since Charles died. He reminds me of him so much."

"But he isn't Charles, and he has his own life to lead," Sarah-Ann said.

"I know. It was when he married Mrs Richard I knew I had to move back to Birmingham. I couldn't bear seeing them together, knowing it could never be me. I know they're happy and that's how it should be, but I can't help myself."

"You're going to have to face her later today."

"Don't think I don't know. It's been bothering me ever since Martha talked me into coming. Perhaps she won't miss me if I don't go."

"Of course she'll miss you, she's been asking after you."

Only so she can gloat, Mary thought. "I don't know why, we were never close, even when I lived with you."

"She probably wants you to see Joseph; he's so like your William."

"If he's like William, I've no need to see him, have I? Come on, we're going to be late."

By the time they arrived home, the celebrations were about to begin.

"Where have you two been?" Mrs Jackson asked. "There's work to do and you're busy talking. Martha and Pa have gone to fetch the birds, and the potatoes are ready for mashing. If you can do that I'll finish the gravy and fetch the cranberry pie. Pa will pour out the gin punch as soon as he's back."

Mary and Sarah-Ann did as they were told and soon the dinner was ready for serving. Everything was put on the table and Mother said grace before Pa picked up the carving knife and served out the geese.

"I haven't tasted anything as nice as that in my life," William said as he finished off his last piece of meat. "My belly feels so full."

"I hope there's still room for the plum pudding, young man," his grandmother said. "It wouldn't be Christmas dinner without that."

Chapter 22

Birmingham, Warwickshire.

Mr Wetherby walked into the front parlour of the Grimshaw family home and sat at the table while Mrs Grimshaw set some cutlery before him. He'd gone to the butcher's that morning as planned, but he'd bumped into Mr Grimshaw who insisted he join them and so here he was, sitting opposite Mr Grimshaw waiting for the meal to be served.

"Molly, you come and sit next to Mr Wetherby, I'll help your mother," Mr Grimshaw said when his daughter brought in some napkins.

"No, Papa, you sit down and I'll help." Molly disappeared into the other room before he could argue.

"These women eh, Mr Wetherby, they can't help themselves, can they? She's going to make someone a fine wife one of these days. Now, can I pour you some mulled wine?"

As Mr Grimshaw poured the wine, Mr Wetherby looked around the room. It had clearly been opened up and decorated especially for the day and, in contrast to his small living room, it was filled to overflowing. The large wooden table, at which he now sat, was positioned in the centre of the room surrounded by six ornate chairs of mahogany. Ornaments of every shape and size covered the sideboard and mantelpiece and under the window sat a couch of deep red that barely fitted into the recess it had been allocated. It was covered with cushions and shawls and surrounded by heavy red velvet curtains that looked as if they'd struggle to close should that ever be necessary.

Mrs Grimshaw brought in a large piece of beef and placed it in front of her husband before handing him the carving knife. Once Molly arrived with the rest of the meal, they said grace and Mr Grimshaw served the meat.

"How's business going?" Mr Grimshaw said as he sat down.

"Very well," Mr Wetherby said. "I've recently recruited another twenty women."

"So I heard. The way things are going we'll need to increase our order with you too in the next few months. We work well together, you and me. We have a lot in common, if you know what I mean."

A puzzled expression settled on Mr Wetherby's face. "I'm not sure that I do."

"We're both self-made men for a start, no silver spoons for us when we were born, and we have big ambitions. We need to look out for each other." Mr Grimshaw winked at Mr Wetherby, who still wasn't sure what he meant, but nodded in agreement.

"I imagine you know as well as I do what it's like to face a struggle. Where we differ is that you're closer to Molly's age than mine. I'd guess you're not much older than her. She's never worked of course, but she knows how to keep a tidy house and she's an excellent cook. Played a big part in preparing this meal today, in fact, didn't you, my dear?" Molly smiled but said nothing. "And she's had an education you know. She went to school for a couple of years to learn her letters and numbers. All she needs now is a good husband to look after."

Molly, who sat next to Mr Wetherby, flushed and looked to her mother for help.

"Come now, dear," Mrs Grimshaw said. "Let Mr Wetherby eat his dinner in peace."

"It's very good, Mrs Grimshaw, and you too, Miss. I haven't eaten as much as this for a long while."

"That'll be because you're on your own," Mr Grimshaw continued. "Men aren't meant to do the cooking; you need a wife to look after you. Isn't that right, dear?"

"I said, leave Mr Wetherby be. He didn't come here for a lecture from you."

"It's all right, Mrs Grimshaw, actually he's right. As it happens I'm hoping to be married next year …"

"There you go, dear, us men know what's good for us." Mr Grimshaw gave Mr Wetherby no opportunity to complete his sentence and spent the rest of the meal giving his assessment of what made a good wife. He spoke until he noticed the empty plates on the table. "Has everyone finished? That didn't take long. Come on, dear, we'll tidy up and leave these two youngsters to get to know each other. No, Molly, I insist." He raised his hand before his daughter had a chance to object. "I'm sure Mr Wetherby would prefer more attractive company than me to keep him entertained." With that he picked up the dishes and ushered his wife into the back room.

In the front room, Mr Wetherby straightened the tablecloth in front of him, paying particular attention to the creases the plate had made. After a moment, Molly spoke.

"I'm sorry about Papa, Mr Wetherby. He seems to think I'm too old to be single, but I'm happy to wait until I meet the right man. He doesn't understand that."

"It's not your fault, Miss Grimshaw, I'm sure you'll meet someone soon."

"I hope so." Molly smiled and twisted a ringlet of hair around her finger; her pale complexion accentuated by the redness of her dress.

"You'll know when they're right for you. Your father cut me off earlier when I said I hope to be married next year. I didn't get the chance to add that I've already proposed to the lady in question."

"Oh." Molly dropped her hand to her lap and looked to the door, as if willing her parents back.

Seeing her reaction Mr Wetherby decided it was time to leave. "I'm sorry, I shouldn't have come today. It was never my intention to upset you."

He was about to stand up when Mr Grimshaw came back into the room. "Here we are now, the plum pudding's ready. I hope we're not interrupting anything?" He grinned at Mr Wetherby.

"Not at all, in fact it's time I left." Mr Wetherby stood up. "I hope you don't mind if I excuse myself."

"You can't go before the pudding. Molly what have you been saying? Has she been discourteous?"

"Not at all, she's charming but I have things to attend to."

"What sort of things need attention on Christmas Day?" Mr Grimshaw couldn't get his words out quickly enough. "Even I have time off on Christmas Day."

"Now, George, calm down. Let Mr Wetherby leave if he needs to."

"Thank you for your hospitality, Mrs Grimshaw, and season's greetings to you all," Mr Wetherby said. "I'll let myself out." Without waiting for a reply he retrieved his hat and coat and left them in silence.

Chapter 23

Great Barr, Staffordshire.

MARY COULD SEE WILLIAM EYEING the Christmas pudding greedily as his grandmother served it into seven bowls. She knew it was his favourite part of the meal, and he was holding his spoon in his hand waiting for permission to start. Sensing his impatience, Mary added custard to his portion before she passed it to him and watched him put a large spoonful into his mouth.

"Don't forget to look out for the sixpence," Mary said, picking up her own spoon. "It'll bring you luck if you find it."

As she spoke, William bit down and pulled a piece of silver from his mouth.

"Look, I've got it," he shouted. "I'm going to be lucky." There was a round of applause at the table. "Will it mean I'll get to see more of Mr Wetherby? That would be good luck, wouldn't it?"

"Maybe." Mary glanced first to Sarah-Ann and then to Martha. "There are other things besides that."

"Who's Mr Wetherby then?" Mother asked.

After all the gin punch they had drunk, Mary felt

relaxed enough to share her news. "A local businessman in Birmingham. I worked for him for a few weeks earlier this year; William runs errands for him."

"Isn't he the one you had problems with?" Pa asked.

"It was a misunderstanding." Mary didn't realise the whole family knew about it. "We've sorted out our differences ... and I've started walking out with him."

"Do you have anything else to tell us?" Mother looked at Mary as if she suspected she was holding something back. Mary glanced again at her sisters-in-law, and then at William, before she replied.

"He's proposed marriage to me ... but I haven't accepted."

"Are you going to marry him, Mother? Is that the good luck? Please say it is?"

Mary hesitated.

"Well?" prompted her mother-in-law again.

"I haven't made my mind up."

"But why not?" William was on his feet now. "I like him and he likes me, and Mary-Ann too."

"And I like him," Mary-Ann said.

"I know, but I have to like him as well."

"And don't you?" Pa asked.

"He's nice enough, but he's never going to replace Charles. Perhaps now wasn't the best time to tell you, we'll talk about it tomorrow."

There was an awkward pause before Mary-Ann relieved the tension. "Let's play some games. Can we play blind man's bluff?"

"That's for later when we go to Uncle Richard's," her

grandmother said. "We need to finish the pudding first and tidy up."

"You leave it," Mary said. "I'll do it when you've gone."

"You'll do no such thing. You haven't seen Mrs Richard and Joseph yet and she asked about you yesterday."

Mrs Richard Jackson, the woman who had everything she wanted. How on earth could she be civil to her after everything that had gone through her mind recently?

༄

Birmingham, Warwickshire.

He didn't often drink spirits, but it was Christmas and the burn of the whisky as it ran down his throat felt good. One more wouldn't hurt. How had he been so stupid as to allow the Christmas meal to end so abruptly? Molly Grimshaw might be a spoilt child and her father an overbearing bully, but he shouldn't have walked out like that. Right now all he could think about was the damage he might have done to his business. Mr Grimshaw was his biggest customer and he would surely stop any future orders, especially now there were new suppliers in the area. He took another gulp of whisky and closed his eyes. *Where are you, Mrs Jackson, when I need you? Come and save me from all this.*

༄

Great Barr, Staffordshire.

As soon as Mary arrived at her brother-in-law's house, Mrs Richard made a point of greeting her with her son Joseph.

"He's a little version of your William, don't you think?" she said. "They could be brothers."

123

"Richard and Charles were alike and so it shouldn't come as a surprise."

Mrs Richard ignored Mary's patronising tone. "I'm expecting another baby next year too; around Easter time."

"So I heard. I suppose it's about time, Joseph is nearly eighteen months already; there are only thirteen months between William and Mary-Ann."

"Nobody chooses the hand God deals …"

"Can we play blind man's bluff now?" Mary-Ann interrupted.

Mrs Richard looked down at Mary-Ann and smiled. "Of course we can, but it's a bit of a squeeze in here. Who's going to be blindfolded first?"

"Me," William and Mary-Ann shouted together.

"Shall we let Mary-Ann go first?" Mrs Richard said. "It was her idea."

Mrs Richard called everyone to order and tied the blindfold securely before turning Mary-Ann around several times. Once released, she stumbled around the room, but it didn't take long before she caught hold of somebody.

"It's a lady," Mary-Ann shouted as she grabbed the folds of a skirt. "You'll have to bend down so I can feel your face." She ran her hands over the head and shoulders of her captive. The hair was fastened onto the top of her head, which didn't help, and so she moved down her face until her fingers touched some earrings. "I know who it is. No one has earrings that dangle except Aunt Sarah-Ann." She whipped off her blindfold and bounced up and down when she saw she had guessed correctly. Sarah-Ann took the blindfold from her and they played for the next half an hour before Adelaide was given the blindfold.

"Richard, I think that's you," she said to her brother a short time later.

"And I thought I'd escaped being on," he joked. "Isn't it time for another drink?"

"You don't escape that easily," Adelaide said. "This can be the last round."

"If you insist." He rolled his eyes and smiled before he held the blindfold to his eyes.

Once ready, he was turned on the spot before he moved forward slowly. Mary stood to his right, no more than an arm's length away, and with her heart pounding, took a step forward, hoping he would take hold of her. Instead he moved to his left and swung out his arms, catching hold of a handful of material. Mary's heart sank.

"Who have I here then?" he said pulling the material towards him. He ran his hands up the arms of his subject before he reached her face, which he stroked gently. He seemed to take an age and Mary watched every movement.

"I do believe I've found my beautiful wife," he said as his face lit up with a smile.

"It's a good job it wasn't anyone else, behaving like that," Sarah-Ann said.

"Don't get all righteous on me." Richard took off the blindfold. "I knew it was her by the feel of her dress." He placed both hands on his wife's face and studied her. "I couldn't mistake you." Mrs Richard giggled, but everyone else turned away to find a chair. Everyone except Mary. She continued to watch as they stood together in a world of their own. After a couple of seconds, Richard kissed his wife's nose before they moved to the other side of the room where baby Joseph lay sleeping.

As Mary watched Richard standing with his arm around his wife's waist, something changed within her. She knew she should never have come. Richard was forbidden fruit; they could never be together. She looked at Mrs Richard with renewed dislike, but realised she too could command the love of a man like that. He was back in Birmingham waiting for an answer from her. Suddenly her weeks of doubt disappeared. She didn't need Richard Jackson to make her happy; Mr Wetherby would do that, if only she'd let him.

Chapter 24

Birmingham, Warwickshire.

M R WETHERBY STOOD BY THE door of the workshop counting in his workers; the two-day break had been too long and he welcomed them back with good cheer. He was about to shut the door when he was almost knocked over by William rushing in, apologising for being late.

"You're not late yet, young man." Mr Wetherby looked out into the yard. "Are you on your own?"

"Yes, Mother's busy."

"Busy doing what?"

"Arguing with Aunt Lucy."

A frown formed on Mr Wetherby's face. "About what?"

William shrugged. "She said I'm not allowed to tell you."

"Tell me what?"

"That she's going to … oh no, you nearly made me tell you. Please don't make me tell you, Mr Wetherby. She said she'd see you later. She said you're to meet her on the corner of Bath Street after work."

Mr Wetherby lost count of the number of times he paced across the workshop that morning and by midday he wondered if his pocket watch had stopped. He guessed she was going to give him an answer and tried to remember William's exact words; he said she was going to do something. Going to say yes, perhaps? What if she said no? What would he do then?

He dismissed the women earlier than usual and walked briskly around to Bath Street. It had already been dark for several hours but the moon was full, giving him good sight of the road ahead. There was no sign of Mary. It didn't occur to him that she wouldn't be expecting him so early, but despite that he didn't have to wait long before she rounded the corner. He hurried towards her and it was all he could do to stop himself from embracing her.

"Good evening, Mr Wetherby." Mary gave him a warm smile.

"Good evening, Mrs Jackson, you look well. The country air must suit you."

"It's where I'm most at home. I'm sorry I couldn't see you earlier, there was something I had to deal with."

"So I understand. Shall we walk?" He gestured towards the road ahead.

"Did you have a nice Christmas?" Mary asked.

"I spent it with Mr Grimshaw and his family; we had a nice piece of beef for dinner."

"We had goose. It was good to see everyone again."

"Forgive me for being impatient, but did you discuss my proposal with the family?"

"I did."

"And do you have an answer for me?"

"I do."

Mr Wetherby struggled to control himself. *Why wouldn't she tell him?* "And what will it be?"

Mary took a deep breath. "I'd like to accept your proposal … if it's still offered."

"Of course it's still offered." He reached for her hands and kissed her on the cheek. "You've no idea how much this means to me. This calls for a celebration. I want to tell the world."

Mary laughed. "Maybe an announcement in *The Times* would be appropriate."

"What an excellent idea, I'll see to it tomorrow." He thought he saw amusement in her eyes. "We must make the arrangements. There's no point waiting is there? Three months maybe?" She had once told him she had married her first husband after only three months' engagement. "We can be married in the spring."

"Slow down," Mary said. "There are things that need doing first."

"What sort of things?"

"Things like finding somewhere to live."

"You can move into my house. It's plenty big enough, even for the children."

"It wouldn't be right for us to move in before the wedding."

Mr Wetherby stopped and looked at her. "I didn't mean … why would you … what do you mean?"

"This morning when Aunt Lucy ate breakfast William accidentally mentioned I was going to accept your proposal. It wasn't his fault, he was excited, but to say Aunt Lucy took it badly is an understatement."

"He said you'd argued. I suppose she still doesn't like me?"

"It's not you, it's the business she's worried about. She wants me to carry on managing it. She says women don't need men to be happy and that I have to make a choice between you and the business."

"That's ridiculous. If things are doing so well, why doesn't she run it?"

"She's planning on moving away next year and she was going to leave me in charge of the business and the house. If I marry you I'll have to move out so she can sell the house and close down the business. I told her if that was the case I'd be looking for somewhere else to live because I don't want to spend the rest of my life alone."

"You did the right thing." Mr Wetherby took hold of her hands. "No wife of mine, or my betrothed for that matter, is going to work. I don't want you living with her for a second longer than you have to. We can find somewhere else for you easily enough."

"Could I carry on with the business until we're married ... or at least until they find someone else?"

"Absolutely not, I'm going to look after you from now on."

Chapter 25

Handsworth, Staffordshire.

THE SOUND OF BIRDS WOKE Mary from her sleep and she lay in bed listening to them. She hadn't got used to being back in the countryside, but she loved it. The move out of Weaman Street had been swift once she had made the decision to get married. Initially Mr Wetherby had been keen for her to move closer to Hatchett Street, but when she had told him she wanted to continue working, he made the decision to move her out of Birmingham. It had been their first argument since the betrothal and within days he had found a small cottage in Handsworth. A week later he helped her and the children with the move.

Once she moved into the house, Mary was thrilled. She had always loved the country and the house gave her more room than she had known with Aunt Lucy. The small hallway housed the stairs and off this were two rooms. The front room was only used for Sundays and special occasions; but the one at the back was a cosy room where the fire was permanently lit and where they spent their days. Two armchairs draped with covers sat on the stone flagged floor, while a square wooden table, surrounded by four chairs, was pushed close to the back wall. A picture of cattle hung above the fireplace between two large cupboards that filled either side of the chimneybreast. Upstairs, there were two bedrooms, which meant that for the first time she did not have to share her bed with the children. There was a privy in the back yard and the best part was, they didn't have to share it with anyone else.

She thought about Mr Wetherby and wondered what she'd been afraid of. He was attentive and generous and made no demands of her. He was not harsh with William and she often found them talking about business. She realised she had grown fond of him, and for the first time in years she looked forward to the future.

There was only one problem, for today at least. Mr Wetherby was accompanying her and the children to the wedding of her sister-in-law Adelaide. Normally she would look forward to seeing the family, but today was different. She would see Richard again, and with Mr Wetherby at her side she didn't know how she would face him. She didn't miss him if she didn't see him, but there was something about him that always brought a flutter to her chest. What if Mr Wetherby noticed? She was roused from her thoughts by a noise coming from the room next door. The children were getting out of bed ... she needed to get a move on.

An hour later, the three of them were downstairs ready for the day. There was a knock on the door and a moment later Mr Wetherby popped his head inside.

"May I come in?"

"Yes, of course." Mary walked down the hall to meet him.

"You're looking especially lovely today." He studied the fitted bodice and wide skirt of her new dress.

"Thanks to you," she said, allowing him to kiss her on the cheek. "I love this shade of blue. Can I get you some tea?"

"We haven't got time; it's going to take at least a couple of hours to get there. Why did she decide to get married so far away?"

"Mr Ogden's been offered a farm up there and they wanted to stay local."

"I suppose that's a good enough reason. Are you ready to go, William?"

"Ready, Mr Wetherby."

The journey was uneventful, coloured by nothing but the occasional field of early crops and rare glimpses of the sun as it peeped from between the clouds. William and Mary-Ann were subdued. Mary presumed it was because they had nothing to look at, and soon Mary-Ann fell asleep resting on her arm.

"Are you nervous?" Mary said to Mr Wetherby as they neared the end of their journey.

"Why should I be nervous?"

"It'll be the first time you meet the family."

"That's no reason to be nervous."

"I'm nervous."

"What on earth for?"

Not wanting to wake Mary-Ann, Mary shifted carefully in her seat and peered out of the window. "In case they don't like you."

"Why shouldn't they like me?" Mr Wetherby neatened

the collar of his jacket and sat up straight. "Anyway, does it matter if they don't? It won't change anything, will it?"

"I suppose not, but I hope we can still see them."

"If it means that much, I won't stop you." His smile broadened as she looked back at him. "Whatever makes you happy."

"I didn't tell you, Aunt Lucy and Aunt Rebecca will be here."

"That surprises me, I didn't think they'd go in for weddings."

"They don't like the idea of marriage, but they're part of the family. They wouldn't miss a wedding. It might be for the best if we keep out of their way."

"You'll have no argument with me on that score."

The carriage pulled up outside the church half an hour early, and Mary alighted with the children while Mr Wetherby arranged their pickup with the driver before he left.

"It looks like we're first to arrive," Mary said when he joined them. "Shall we go in?"

"Let's wait outside until other guests arrive, the weather's mild enough."

William and Mary-Ann ran to the end of the lane to keep watch, leaving Mary and Mr Wetherby to stroll around the churchyard.

"Have you chosen a date for our wedding yet?" Mr Wetherby asked as they picked out the path between the gravestones.

"I haven't had time, to be honest with you, what with the move, Adelaide's wedding today and Louisa's next month."

"I'm feeling left out," Mr Wetherby said. "It'd be nice if we could be married in the summer, don't you think?"

"Summer … this year?"

"Yes, why not?"

The colour drained from Mary's face. "Summer will be with us in no time. Don't you think we should wait a bit longer?"

"You're not changing your mind, are you?"

"Not at all, but there's a lot to think about. Will I have to move back to Birmingham after the wedding?"

"I rather hoped we would live together once we were married. Is that what's troubling you?"

"Not the fact that we'd live together, just moving back to Birmingham. I much prefer it in Handsworth."

"The house on Shadwell Street is plenty big enough for the four of us; that would be my preferred option. You've never been inside before; you should come and visit to set your mind at rest."

Mary didn't have time to respond before a carriage drew up outside the church.

"Who's that arriving with Miss Jackson?" Mr Wetherby asked as Martha stepped from the carriage.

"It's Mother and Pa with Sarah-Ann." She reached for his arm. "Come on, let me introduce you."

Once they reached the carriage, Mr Wetherby raised his hat to Martha.

"Can I introduce you all to my intended, Mr William Wetherby?" Mary said. "Mr Wetherby, this is Mr and Mrs Charles Jackson."

"Pleased to meet you." Mr Wetherby lifted his hat again.

"And this is Miss Sarah-Ann Jackson."

"Charmed I'm sure, Miss Jackson. I've heard so much about you."

Mary raised an eyebrow at Sarah-Ann as she stared at Mr Wetherby. "Shall we go in?" she said. "I expect the bride and groom will be here shortly."

Adelaide walked down the aisle on the arm of her father. *She's only nineteen*, Mary thought. *So young and yet the same age I was when I married Charles. May God be kinder to Mr Ogden than He was to Charles.* As the congregation sat down, Mary settled in her seat but paid little attention to the service. Richard sat immediately in front of her and she couldn't help compare him to Mr Wetherby. When Richard and Martha left to witness the signing of the marriage register, Mary turned to look at Mr Wetherby. With his blond hair and pale skin he couldn't compete with Richard, and the flecks of green in his eyes seemed to emphasise their differences. Still, unlike Richard, Mr Wetherby was prepared to take care of her and the children, and that had to take priority. Accepting she would be spending her life with him, she smiled and took his hand.

Once the formalities were over, Mary took her daughter's hand and walked with Mr Wetherby and the rest of the family to the local tavern.

"Slow down," Mary said to Mr Wetherby as they left the church grounds. "Aunts Lucy and Rebecca are ahead of us, we don't want to catch them up."

"You don't have to talk to them."

"I can't ignore them if they see me. They were good

to me, both of them, despite what's happened since. I still feel bad about leaving them with no one managing the business."

"She was the one who forced you out of your home, you had no choice. If they cause you any trouble they'll have me to deal with."

୬୭

Mr Wetherby and Mary waited for most of the family to sit down before they chose their own seats, and once the meal ended Mr Wetherby found himself alone while Mary went to see Louisa.

"Mary shouldn't leave you on your own," Sarah-Ann said as she sat down next to him. "Where's she gone?"

"I don't mind. She wanted to talk to Louisa and I was happy to be given a few minutes on my own."

"They'll be talking about the wedding. Have you set a date for yours?"

Mr Wetherby looked across the room at Mary. "Not yet. Hopefully it'll be this year. Are you walking out with anyone?"

"Not at the moment." Sarah-Ann shifted in her seat before changing the subject. "Have you met Richard?" She pointed to a tall, dark-haired man who was talking to Mary and Louisa. "He's the only son now; everyone adores him. Louisa was always closer to Charles, but he looked so like Richard I think she sometimes forgets."

Mr Wetherby watched Mary's eyes sparkle as Richard spoke to her.

"Does Mary know Richard well?" Mr Wetherby couldn't take his eyes off them.

"Oh yes, they were as thick as thieves before he got married. If the church had allowed it they may well have settled down together."

"Does she still see him?" Mr Wetherby asked lightly, trying to hide his concern.

"Only at family occasions," Sarah-Ann said as she twirled a ringlet around her finger. "As far as I know ..."

Mr Wetherby continued watching. Mary looked as happy as he'd seen her and was certainly relaxed in this man's company. Sarah-Ann changed the subject again.

"I guess we'll be seeing more of each other over the next few months. We've got Louisa's wedding coming up soon and I imagine you'll be spending time in Handsworth. It's not far from us ... I could easily come over." She paused once more. "You're so fortunate to live in Birmingham though, I do miss it. There's so much going on. I understand you're your own master."

"I have a workshop and employ seventy women to make fastenings." Mr Wetherby still didn't take his eyes off Mary.

"I lived in Birmingham before I moved back to Great Barr to help Mother. I like to think I manage a tidy house and keep us well fed. Between you and me, I want them to give up the farm but they won't hear of it. If they do, I'll be straight back to Birmingham."

Mr Wetherby tensed when he saw Mary making her way back to him. "I'm sorry I've been gone so long," she said to him before she turned to Sarah-Ann. "And thank you for keeping Mr Wetherby company."

"You're welcome, we're getting along fine. We've been talking about Birmingham and how we both miss it when we're not there."

"It's not that good," Mary said. "You haven't lived there for a couple of years."

"It's not changed very much, and Mr Wetherby seems happy there."

"Will you ladies excuse me?" Mr Wetherby rose to his feet and reached for his hat.

"Where are you going?" Mary asked.

"I need some air; it's too warm in here."

❦

As soon as Mr Wetherby left the table, Mary took the seat beside Sarah-Ann.

"How are things with you two?" Sarah-Ann asked. "He tells me you haven't set a date for the wedding."

"There's no rush. I've only recently moved to Handsworth."

Sarah-Ann hesitated before she spoke again. "I know I encouraged you to marry him, but now I've met him, I wonder if he's right for you."

"Don't you like him?" Mary asked.

"He's nice enough, but you don't seem to have much in common. Maybe Aunt Lucy was right."

"What was I right about?" A voice boomed from behind them.

Sarah-Ann jumped up. "Aunt Lucy, I didn't see you there. I was saying to Mary that I'm not sure Mr Wetherby is right for her. Isn't that what you said?"

"I'm sure there's some good in Mr Wetherby," Aunt Lucy said. "But after the way he treated her I don't know why she encourages him. Having said that, the way she's behaved recently I would say they were made for each other."

Mary looked between the two of them as they discussed her relationship with Mr Wetherby as if she wasn't there.

"I don't understand." Sarah-Ann looked to Aunt Rebecca who stood behind her sister.

"They're both only out for themselves. He's a single-minded man who'll do whatever it takes to get his own way and she's out for an easy life."

"That's not true, how can you say that?" Mary finally jumped up, her face scarlet.

"Take a look at yourself. You have no need to marry him except it's the easy option. Rebecca and I set you up in the business and it was going well before you left us. There was no gratitude for what we'd done, no acknowledgement of it even, and where do you go running? To the man who tried to take advantage of you, just because he has his own business and some promises."

"You don't know anything about our relationship; you don't even know him," Mary said. "I kept it hidden from you while I lived with you. If you must know, I decided he was the best hope for the children, especially William. He's going to teach him about business and train him properly once he's old enough. One day William might be a successful businessman because of him. I could never offer him that, especially not with sewing."

"As you wish, but I think you're deluding yourself," Aunt Lucy said. "He'll never treat those children as if they were his own. I'm not the only one who has a bad feeling about him either. A friend of mine, Mr Grimshaw, didn't have a good word to say about him earlier this year. The man abused their hospitality and it didn't go unnoticed."

Mary didn't respond to her aunt's barbed comment. Mr Wetherby had told her he'd spent Christmas Day with the Grimshaws but he hadn't mentioned a dispute.

"I'm sorry to say you're of no concern to me now," Aunt Lucy continued. "We rented out the business to a capable young woman who's thankful for the opportunity. I don't wish you any harm, Mary, but don't come running back to me when things go wrong."

❦

Mr Wetherby found the carriage ride back to Handsworth uncomfortable, but it wasn't due to the conditions of the road. They travelled in silence for some time before Mary spoke.

"Did you enjoy yourself today? You seemed to get on well with Sarah-Ann."

"She seems nice enough," he replied, keeping his voice low so as not to wake the children.

"I think she likes you, which is a good sign. You got on well with everyone, didn't you?"

"I suppose I did, except your brother-in-law Richard. You didn't introduce us."

"Didn't I? I thought I did."

Mr Wetherby looked out of the window. "No, you spoke to him for a long time when you were on your own, not when you were with me."

There was a long pause before Mary continued. "You don't seem yourself tonight, is something wrong?"

"I don't know, you tell me."

"What do you mean?"

He turned to face her. "Do you love me, Mary?"

He saw the flash of alarm in her beautiful eyes before she composed herself.

"We wouldn't be getting married otherwise," she said after an unnecessary length of time.

"Are you sure? You don't seem to want to set a date and you seem happier with *the family* than with me. Why would that be if you loved me?"

He waited for Mary's reply.

"We'll get married this year, I promise," she said.

Mr Wetherby studied her. Did she want Richard Jackson more than him? Was he the reason she wanted to be in Handsworth, so he could make the occasional visit while she was on her own? He'd seen the way she looked at him and couldn't fail to notice the close resemblance between this man and William. He looked at the children asleep by her side and decided this wasn't the time to press for an answer.

Once they arrived in Handsworth, Mr Wetherby helped get the children into the house and lit some candles. He then turned to leave.

"I'll let myself out," he said with no affection. "I won't be here on Sunday, something's come up. I'll write and let you know when I plan to call again."

"You shouldn't work on a Sunday," Mary said.

"It appears many people do things they shouldn't. Goodbye, Mary."

Back in the carriage Mr Wetherby put his head in his hands. He didn't have any problems with his orders; he'd managed to placate Mr Grimshaw after the incident at Christmas and they were on good terms again, but he needed time to think. After some distance, he sat back with a wry smile. Tonight was the night he'd planned on staying in Handsworth rather than travelling back to Birmingham. Now he was travelling back alone not sure when, or even if, he would return.

Chapter 26

Great Barr, Staffordshire.

SARAH-ANN SAT AT THE LIVING room table staring at the candle in front of her. It had turned one o'clock in the morning. She should be in bed, but sleep was out of the question. She had gone to her room three hours earlier when her parents had gone to bed, but after a couple of hours of tossing and turning she'd gone downstairs and poured herself a gin.

What was she doing with her life? All she wanted was to find a husband and have a family, but being stuck in Great Barr there was no chance of that. The village was so small that she knew everyone, and there were no suitors she would be happy with. Birmingham had so many possibilities, but her parents needed her and she couldn't support herself without them.

She hadn't been strictly honest with everyone when she moved back from Birmingham. She said she did it for her parents, and that she didn't mind giving up her old life, but nothing could have been further from the truth. She'd left because her brother-in-law had started taking too much interest in her. At first it was a stray hand if ever they were alone, but before long he found ways to make her stay late after work. She'd threatened to tell her sister, Eliza, but she knew it would be her word against his and her sister was always going to defend her husband.

Things had come to a head one evening when he'd asked her into his office. Why she had gone up there alone she had no idea. It was after seven o'clock and everyone had left for the day, yet there she'd been, like a fool. As soon as he'd locked the door behind her and she'd seen the crooked smile on his face she had known what was coming. Even now, over a year later, a shiver ran through her whole body at the thought of it. Mr Rashford had pinned her against the wall and the smell of ale on his breath had forced her to turn her head. He'd pulled it back with more force than was necessary before his wet lips had tried to find hers. Sarah-Ann had squirmed under his touch, trying in vain to escape his clutches. With his body pressed tight against hers he'd reached for the front of her dress, causing Sarah-Ann to let out a sob. He'd put his hand across her mouth to keep her quiet, but suddenly stopped when someone had come up the stairs and rattled the door handle.

"Joseph, are you in there?" Eliza had called.

They'd both stood paralysed before Mr Rashford had looked at Sarah-Ann with disgust and gone to the door to let his wife in. It had taken a second for Eliza to realise Sarah-Ann was in the office, but when she had, Sarah-Ann had known her days in Birmingham were over.

She had left the brewery that night and gone to stay with a friend. She had been too embarrassed to tell anyone what had happened, but the following day she had written to her father asking if she could go home.

She had told Mary there were no jobs at the brewery

because she'd wanted to spare her from Mr Rashford's advances. She'd thought she was doing the right thing but now she wished she had let her go. At least then Mary would never have met Mr Wetherby and she wouldn't be dreaming about coming between them.

As much as she liked Mary, Sarah-Ann wondered why Mr Wetherby was prepared to marry her and take on the children. Mary wasn't remotely interested in him. It was so unfair. She hadn't intended to cause trouble but a thrill had run through her as soon as she'd seen him and once she saw Mr Wetherby's reaction to Mary being with Richard, she'd been unable to stop herself.

The forthcoming wedding of Louisa would be the next time she would see them. Needing to know if she'd done any harm, she stood up, walked to the bureau and took out her writing set. She would offer to pick Mary up on the way to the wedding and ask if Mr Wetherby would be with her. She picked up her pen, dipped it in the ink and wrote her letter. Once she was satisfied, she blotted it and put it in an envelope before heading back upstairs. As she climbed into bed she wondered how she could make Mr Wetherby happy. She could love him, of that she was sure, but there was so much more. She pushed everything else from her mind and as she blew out the candle she saw his face, beckoning her towards him.

Handsworth, Staffordshire.

When she moved to Handsworth, Mary discovered the joy of baking. Eggs were in good supply, flour and fat were easy enough to come by and Mr Wetherby was happy to buy her sugar. Most importantly, however, she now had a fire with side compartments. She wasn't sure whether her favourite time of the day was late morning when she would take the cakes from the oven or later in the day when she and the children would sit down to eat them.

As she stood at the table beating some butter and sugar together, William came in with a letter.

"From the postman," he said, handing it to her. She wiped her hands on her apron before opening it.

"Have you been reading my letters?" she asked before he disappeared. "This is the second one this week that hasn't been sealed properly."

"I can't read such fancy writing."

Mary looked unconvinced. "I'd better have a word with the postman then. I'm expecting a letter from Mr Wetherby any day soon and I don't want him to lose it."

"We have a different postman at the moment, one I've not seen before. He doesn't have a bag as big as the old postman, maybe he keeps losing the letters."

William ran to the door before Mary shouted after him. "Let me know when he's here tomorrow."

Once she was alone, Mary read the letter several times. Sarah-Ann had offered to pick her up on the way to Louisa's wedding. That didn't make sense, she didn't need to come anywhere near Handsworth on her way to Birmingham. Maybe she was being generous so she wouldn't have to arrive alone. She had hoped to meet up with Mr Wetherby beforehand but the thought of him unexpectedly troubled her. He had never stayed away for so long and she wondered if he was having trouble with the business. In truth she hadn't missed him and wondered if Sarah-Ann was right about them not being compatible. She shook the idea from her head, of course they were and they were going to be married. She would probably hear from him tomorrow.

She returned to making her cake and once it was in the oven, she wrote back to Sarah-Ann before she wrote to Mr Wetherby to let him know the arrangements.

A week later, two days before the wedding, Mary still hadn't heard from him. Since Sarah-Ann's letter, she had been worried and she looked out for the postman each day. He didn't call for several days but eventually she saw him when he delivered another letter from Sarah-Ann.

"You're new around here aren't you?" she asked.

"The other chap's ill, so I'm helping out."

"I've been expecting a letter for a couple of weeks now but it hasn't arrived, are you sure you've delivered everything."

"Yes, ma'am, this is all I've been given." The postman showed her his bag.

"Why do all my letters look like they've been opened?"

"Couldn't say, ma'am, must be one of the errand boys up to no good. I'll let them know there's a problem. Good day."

Mary went back inside, a sinking feeling in her stomach. She would have to call for Mr Wetherby on the way to the wedding and hope he was expecting her.

Chapter 27

MARY STOOD AT THE WINDOW waiting for the carriage to pick her up. As soon as she saw it, she shouted to the children and reached for her cloak. A moment later, Sarah-Ann knocked on the door and let herself in.

"Are you ready?"

"Yes we are." Mary stared at Sarah-Ann. "You look lovely, is that a new dress?"

"I've worn it a couple of times, but I wanted to make an effort; it's not every day I go to Birmingham. You never know who you'll meet. Is Mr Wetherby with you?"

"Of course not; he never stays overnight."

The smile fell from Sarah-Ann's face. "I was only checking. How've you both been these last few weeks?"

Mary looked at her hands. She didn't want to tell Sarah-Ann she hadn't seen him. "He's been busy. He works long hours."

"So you haven't seen much of him?"

"Not much."

"We haven't seen him at all, Mother, not since Aunt Adelaide's wedding," William said as he walked into the hall. "Why not?"

"I've just said he's been busy."

"He's never been too busy before. I thought he liked me." William's shoulders slumped.

"He does like you," Mary said. "We'll see him shortly and everything'll be fine."

"I suppose we're picking him up?" Sarah-Ann said, adjusting the neckline of her dress.

"Of course." Mary checked her own reflection as she ushered them out, wishing she hadn't baked so many cakes lately.

Mother and Pa were waiting for them in the carriage, and three quarters of an hour later they drew up outside Mr Wetherby's house. Mary had never visited before, but she knew the address.

"You wait here, and I'll go and get him." She climbed down from the carriage and knocked on the front door. When she received no answer she checked the adjoining properties before getting back into the carriage.

"He must be at the workshop. Pa, can we ask the driver to go to Hatchett Street?"

Several minutes later they pulled up outside Hanover Court.

"Can I go and get him?" William asked.

"No, I'll go, you wait here." Mary took a deep breath and walked down the entry and over to the workshop on the right of the court. When she went in, Mr Wetherby sat at his desk with about sixty to seventy women crowded around the benches in front of him. Mary didn't know how they managed to work, but it was of little concern to her today. Mr Wetherby had his head in his hands and didn't see her come in.

"Mr Wetherby." She spoke gently so as not to be

overheard. He lifted his head from his hands and looked at her. His eyes were red and a beard had grown into his usually well-trimmed moustache.

"Whatever's the matter, you look terrible," she said.

"Thank you," he said, his laugh piercing the air. "You look lovely as always."

"Didn't you get my letter? It's Louisa's wedding today. Aren't you going to join us?"

"There's only one wedding I want to accompany you to, but you don't seem to want to attend."

Mary turned to check that the women were working. "I don't know what this is all about, but if you won't come to the wedding today, will you come to Handsworth tomorrow so we can talk properly?"

"Talk! I don't want to talk." His voice echoed around the workshop as he jumped from his chair, startling everyone. He took Mary by the arm and led her into the court. "You know what I want, but I really don't know if it's what you want. I don't even know if I'm the only man in your life."

"Of course you are, why would you think otherwise?"

At that moment, Sarah-Ann appeared from the entry. "Good morning, Mr Wetherby."

"Miss Jackson," he said, straightening up.

Mary noticed that Sarah-Ann's eyes didn't leave his as they spoke.

"I didn't mean to disturb you. Mary said you were joining us today?"

"No, I can't. Something's come up."

"That's a shame, I was looking forward to seeing you again. Perhaps another time?" There was a sparkle in her eyes that Mary hadn't seen before.

"Perhaps …" he said.

Mary glanced between the two of them unsure of what she was seeing. "We need to go. Sarah-Ann, can you give us a minute?"

"Of course, but don't be long; I told Richard we'd meet him outside church."

Mr Wetherby turned to Mary. "You didn't say you were meeting him ahead of time."

"I didn't know."

"I'm sure I told you," Sarah-Ann said. "Good day, Mr Wetherby."

Mary paused as Sarah-Ann left the court. "I have to go, but please will you call tomorrow? I've missed you."

He looked at her with a sadness she hadn't seen before. "I wish I could believe that, Mary, really I do."

Once the service started, Mary couldn't concentrate. Mr Wetherby was clearly upset and his comments confused her. It didn't help having Sarah-Ann next to her looking so beautiful. After the wedding, Sarah-Ann had a barrage of questions about Mr Wetherby but Mary didn't want to talk about him. Fortunately the interrogation was interrupted when Martha joined them, a smile lighting up her face.

"You'll never guess what," she said, clapping her hands together. "Mr Chalmers has just proposed marriage to me."

"That's wonderful," Mary said. "I trust you've accepted."

"I most certainly have. I'm not giving him any chance to change his mind. He wants to be married this year too. I'm so excited. It must have been all the other weddings that made his mind up for him. When are you getting married, Mary, have you set a date yet?"

"Not yet, we haven't had time to talk about it. What date are you planning?"

"I didn't want to choose the same date as you but if you haven't decided yet, it's likely to be in November. Mr Chalmers wants it to be before advent."

Chapter 28

O N MORNINGS SUCH AS THIS, Mary usually enjoyed the walk to church. The sun was high in the sky, untroubled by the thin clouds floating past it, and the wind was light. This morning, however, she didn't want to leave the house. Prior to his recent absence, Mr Wetherby would normally get to the house in good time for them to walk together, but he hadn't arrived again.

She left the house as late as she dared and returned home as soon as the service finished. She'd prayed he'd be waiting for her, but when she arrived home and he wasn't there she slumped into one of the chairs.

William followed her in. "I'm hungry. Are we waiting for Mr Wetherby or can we eat now?"

"It's not quite ready but we won't wait. Mr Wetherby must have got caught up with work again."

"Do you miss him, Mother? I do." William said.

Mary smiled, but there was sadness in her eyes. "Yes, I do."

Half an hour later, as she prepared to serve the meat, she heard the sound of a carriage outside. She jumped up and ran to the door, her heart pounding.

"You made it." She smiled at Mr Wetherby as he paid the driver.

He turned to look at her but said nothing before he walked into the house.

"Where've you been?" Mary-Ann said. "We've missed you, and Mother's been sad."

"We thought you weren't coming back," William said.

"I'm here now and it looks like I'm just in time." Mr Wetherby took off his hat and coat.

"Come and sit next to me." William pulled out a chair as Mary-Ann went to get some extra cutlery. "I've got lots to tell you."

"Not yet," Mary said. "Let Mr Wetherby get settled and then it's time for grace."

Silence descended over the table as Mary served out the food and gave thanks for it. "Did you manage to get your business sorted out?" she asked once she sat down. Mr Wetherby looked at her blankly. "You said you were having trouble with a client; did you sort it out?"

"Oh that, yes. Have you been all right here?"

"Yes, we're fine."

"We've got a lot of new friends, Mr Wetherby," William said.

"That's good to hear, but I hope you're not leaving your mother to do all the work herself?"

"No, sir," William said. "I helped plant some potatoes the other week and we did carrots and turnips the week after. It's not the same as working for you, but it's still good."

Mr Wetherby said nothing as they ate, preferring to let

the children do the talking, but as soon as their plates were empty he was keen for them to leave.

"Are you ready for Sunday school?" he asked.

"Do we have to go today?" William said. "We've not seen you for such a long time."

"Of course you must go. You don't go to proper school yet, so how else are you going to learn. Off you go; you can take yourselves."

Mary didn't like them going alone, but today she didn't argue. She needed to talk to Mr Wetherby and it couldn't wait. She watched them walk down the lane before she went back inside. Mr Wetherby stood by the fire waiting for her.

"Thank you for coming," she said. "I was beginning to think you wouldn't."

"I wasn't in the best frame of mind for church this morning."

"What's the matter? I've never seen you like this before."

"You tell me." Mr Wetherby walked to the window. "Why are you so reluctant to set a date for the wedding?"

"I need time to adjust, that's all."

"That's a feeble excuse. What about Richard Jackson?"

"Richard?" A frown settled on Mary's face. "What about him?"

"Is he happy you're getting married?"

"Yes … why shouldn't he be?"

"So you've seen him?"

"He was at Louisa's wedding. What's this about?"

Mr Wetherby stood with his hands on his hips. "Is it true he comes here while I'm away?"

"Where did you get that idea from?"

"Maybe it's the way you looked at him at the wedding …

or maybe it was the revelation that you'd have married him if you could. Is that why you're so keen to live here?"

Mary's stomach lurched and she took hold of the nearest chair. "Who told you that?"

"Sarah-Ann said you wanted to marry him."

Mary sat down and clasped her hands together to stop them shaking. "Why would she say that?"

"That's what I'd like to know. From what I saw at the wedding, everything she said looked perfectly plausible. Why would she lie?"

"I don't know," Mary whispered.

"Is it true?"

"Of course it isn't true." Mary summoned up the courage to defend herself. "He's never been to this house; I don't think he even knows where I live. If he does, it wasn't me who told him."

"And I'm supposed to believe that?"

"You have to believe me. It's Sarah-Ann's word against mine."

"But it wasn't just her word. I saw the way you were with him at the wedding; it went on all afternoon." Mr Wetherby paused but Mary stayed silent. "Fortunately, I don't believe he's been here in the last month."

"He hasn't … but, what do you mean? How do you know?"

"Don't think I've been in Birmingham without keeping an eye on you. You're going to be my wife and I won't have you making a fool of me."

"So you've been here all along and said nothing?" Mary felt the blood rising to her face.

"I haven't been here myself, but that doesn't mean I don't know what you've been up to."

Mary stood up. "You've been reading my letters, haven't you?"

"Why would Sarah-Ann tell me about Mr Jackson if there wasn't any truth in it?"

"I don't know ... but she's lying." Mary spat her words out.

"I don't believe you." Mr Wetherby walked towards her. "I think everything Sarah-Ann said is true and that you'd have happily married him if he hadn't been your dead husband's brother."

"He's been married for nearly three years and they have two children ... Why are you saying this?"

"I want the truth." Mr Wetherby turned from her and paced the room. "If you can't tell me the truth now how will I ever be able to trust you?"

"You can trust me." Mary bowed her head as a tear ran down her cheek. "I want to marry you, what's past is past."

"So there was something?" He turned and walked back to her, his tall frame towering over her. "Tell me the truth, Mary, or I'll walk out of that door and this time I won't come back."

Mary sat down as her sobs became uncontrollable. *Why was he doing this to her?* "He was there, he helped me ... we knew there couldn't be any future."

"Is he William's father?"

"Of course not." Mary's indignation temporarily stopped her tears. "I can't believe you even asked that. William was two years old when his father died."

"What about since ... after your husband died?"

"No." Mary's voice returned to a whisper.

"I can't hear you, what did you say?"

"Stop this," Mary shouted. "There's nothing to tell. I left Aldridge of my own accord to get away from the past, not to have it follow me. If you don't believe me then perhaps you'd better leave."

Mr Wetherby stood in the middle of the room, looking down at her, before he walked to the window and stared out.

Mary's tears continued. Sarah-Ann was her friend as well as sister-in-law. *Why would she do this to her?* If Mr Wetherby left her now, she would be in the workhouse within a week. *Is that what Sarah-Ann wanted? What would happen to the children then? She may never see them again.*

Eventually Mr Wetherby turned to face her. "I'll believe you … for now, but I'll have my eye on you. You're going to be my wife and I won't have you seeing or thinking about anyone else." When Mary didn't speak, Mr Wetherby pulled her to her feet and wrapped his arms around her, resting his head on hers.

"I'm going for a walk," he said when he eventually loosened his grip. "By the time I come back I want all this forgotten."

It was almost four o'clock before Mr Wetherby returned, acting as if nothing had happened. "I've been to see the rector. We'll be married on the twenty-fifth of August, at ten o'clock. It's a Saturday; I trust you've nothing planned."

"No." Mary stood at the table buttering some bread, unable to look at him. *How could she marry a man she no longer recognised?*

"I've been thinking about my father recently," Mr

Wetherby continued. "I'm going to write again and invite him to the wedding. Who will you ask to give you away?"

Mary shrugged. She had no idea.

"Don't you have any brothers or sisters?"

Not anymore, none that would want to see me anyway. "No."

"What about your in-laws?"

Mary sighed. *It would have to be.* "I'll ask Pa."

"As long as it's not the brother, I don't even want him at the wedding."

As the evening set in, and the children went to bed, Mary sat with Mr Wetherby. She was tired and wanted him to go, but instead he stood up and came over to her.

"I'm not going back to Birmingham tonight."

"Where will you stay?"

"Here."

Mary's heart skipped a beat. "In this house … what will the neighbours say?"

"The neighbours needn't know and even if they do, it doesn't matter. We're going to be married. I'll use the spare bed in William's room; Mary-Ann can come in with you."

Mary bit down hard on her lip. It was against all her principles, but after the last few weeks, she had little choice.

Chapter 29

THE LANE THAT BROUGHT THE carriages to Handsworth was little more than a single track. It was lined with several blocks of terraced cottages, made of grey stone and slate roofs, each with a small garden to the front. Fields surrounded the whole area and it was unusual to see more than two carriages a day. Mary's cottage nestled in the middle of the lane and, as it was a warm afternoon, she sat outside her front door under the shade of a sycamore tree.

Her work for the day was done and the tea was waiting for the arrival of Mr Wetherby. Against her better judgement he had become a regular visitor every Saturday and Sunday night. He would close up the workshop around mid-afternoon on Saturday and take a carriage straight to Handsworth to arrive in time for tea. He would then leave at six o'clock on a Monday morning to open up at seven.

She heard the sound of the late afternoon carriage and sat upright to straighten her hair. As usual the carriage went past the house towards the New Inns, but Mary was astonished when it didn't stop. Mr Wetherby should be getting off. She stood up and looked up and down the street but saw no sign of him, all she saw were the children as they ran towards her.

"Has Mr Wetherby gone indoors already?" William shouted as he reached his mother.

"He wasn't on the carriage." Her voice sounded distant as she spoke.

"I thought he was coming today."

"So did I."

"Why isn't he here, Mother?" Mary-Ann asked as she arrived. "Have you fallen out again?"

"I don't think so." Mary sat back down, remembering their last meeting. She didn't think she'd upset him; in fact they'd been getting on well under the circumstances.

The children sat on the ground by her feet and remained silent for a long time. Eventually Mary stood up.

"We'd better go in for tea. It's all ready."

The children followed her into the house, but with one last look down the street William saw Mr Wetherby walking towards them.

"Mother, he's here, look." William ran down the track to greet him before Mary could say anything. "We thought you weren't coming."

"Of course I'm coming; I always come on a Saturday." Mr Wetherby continued striding down the road.

"I was worried about you," Mary said when he reached her.

"I had some business to attend to and so I stopped off on the way to see to it."

"I'm glad that's all it was." She wanted to ask what it was about and why he hadn't told her he'd be late, but she knew better. It wasn't her business.

After they had eaten, the evening was warm enough for them to take a walk. They headed towards the woods and once the children disappeared, Mr Wetherby reached for Mary's hand.

"I need to take on more women at the workshop this week," he announced.

"Business must be going well."

"It is. I've had some orders from Stafford, Coventry and even the Black Country and I need to expand the workshop."

"It must be overcrowded, why don't you move? If you came to Handsworth it would save you the trouble of travelling," Mary suggested.

"I am going to move but it won't be to Handsworth. All the women live around Summer Lane, so I'll stay there. The way things are going, I'll be one of the biggest manufacturers of hooks and eyes in Birmingham by the end of the year."

"I'd no idea there was such a market for them." Mary smiled.

"It's growing too, but that's not all I've been doing this week."

"What have you been up to?" she said, catching his enthusiasm.

"I've been giving some thought to where we'll live once we're married."

"Oh." The sparkle disappeared from Mary's eyes.

"I decided to look for a bigger house in Birmingham and as chance would have it, there's one on Hatchett Street near the workshop."

Mary's heart sank.

"It's on the front so we won't have to face the court," Mr Wetherby continued. "It's bigger than the one I'm in now. The upper rooms extend out over the entry and the whole of the top floor belongs to the property, both the front and back rooms."

"It still only has one room downstairs though?"

"It does, but there's a scullery and it has a fireplace much the same as you have here for your baking. I've spoken to the landlord and I can have it for little more than I am paying for Shadwell Street. You can move in next week."

"Next week?" Mary stopped dead in her tracks.

"I want you with me in Birmingham."

Mary blinked to hold back her tears. "What about the wedding? We won't be able to be married here if I don't live in the Parish."

"I'll speak to the rector and tell him what's happened."

"He won't marry us if neither of us live here."

"He will if I offer an extra donation to the church; he'll do what we want."

"What you want, you mean." Mary turned and walked away.

"I beg your pardon." Mr Wetherby ran after her.

"I'm sorry." Mary couldn't stop her tears. "I'm not going to Birmingham next week, it would be wrong."

"You'll do as you're told. You're going to be my wife and you won't speak to me like that."

Mary looked at him before she walked away again. *Was this what life was going to be like?*

"Come back," he said. "I thought you'd be pleased. It means we can be together and William can come back to work for me."

"Don't bring William into this; it's got nothing to do with him. You don't understand, do you?"

"I want you in Birmingham and the end of August is too long to wait."

"Would I see that much more of you? We already see each other on a Saturday, Sunday and Monday morning and I won't see much of you when you're at work. August isn't very long to wait. Why can't I stay here until we're married?"

"I don't understand why you dislike Birmingham so much. Everyone else in the county wants to move there, why not you?"

"Please, let me stay here a little longer." She took hold of his hands and looked up at him, her body pressed against his.

He looked down at her. "If it makes you happy." Mary's smile brightened her whole face and he stroked her cheek before kissing her gently. "Although why I've just agreed to live without you for longer than I need to, I don't know."

The following day, Mary cleared away the dinner dishes and went outside to find Mr Wetherby. He smiled as he saw her and beckoned her to sit beside him.

"I've been thinking," he said.

"Again?" The uncertainty in Mary's voice was obvious.

"The house on Hatchett Street I told you about, it's too good a house to let go. I'm going to sub-let Shadwell Street and move in there myself."

"That makes sense."

"I won't need all the rooms straight away, and so I'll let out the top floor. That way it will actually cost me less each week as the rent will pay the extra expense." He paused before he continued, "I've also been thinking about William."

Mary's heart froze. "What about him?"

"He'll be eight in a couple of weeks, he should be working by now. Once I move into Hatchett Street I want him to come back to work for me."

"He can't travel all that way."

"He can stay with me. If we leave Handsworth on a Monday morning we can stay in Hatchett Street and come back here on Saturday."

"You can't do that ... he needs me."

"You'll still see him on a Saturday, Sunday and Monday morning and you barely see him during the week because he's always out. Besides you'll be joining us by the end of August, which isn't that far away, is it?"

"No," Mary whispered.

"I suggest we start the arrangement two weeks from tomorrow, once I've settled myself in."

Chapter 30

MARY SAT AT THE TABLE, staring at the bottle of gin. She often had a cup before she went to bed, but tonight she had drunk more than usual. Mr Wetherby had actually taken William to Birmingham and she wouldn't see her son again until Saturday. *How could he?*

Often, if she was upset, gin made her feel better, but it wasn't working tonight. All she wanted to do was cry. She thought about the man she was marrying and realised she didn't know him at all; she wasn't even sure she liked him. Maybe her first impression had been right after all. She knew he had taken William out of spite and could still hear his voice using her words against her. How could she tell him she would miss her son a lot more than she would ever miss him? *She didn't miss him at all.*

Initially William had been pleased to be going back to work; he liked Mr Wetherby and earning money, but when he realised it meant he would be separated from his mother for five days at a time, his enthusiasm had waned.

"Who'll look after Mother if I'm not here?" he had said.

"I'm looking after her now," Mr Wetherby had answered. "She'll be fine."

"Why don't you come with us, Mother?"

Mary hadn't been able to answer. Mr Wetherby had watched her closely, and his silence had troubled her. It was worse than anything he could have said.

"He's too young to be away all week," she had said eventually.

"He's eight years old and it's high time he was working. He won't get a better chance to learn how to run a business. You're too soft with him; you should both be grateful to me."

All the time he'd spoken he'd worn a smile, but it hadn't fooled her and the tone of his voice had sent a shiver down her spine. Once again she'd seen a side of him she didn't like and for the first time in months she had questioned whether she should marry him. Not that she could have done anything about it. If she called the wedding off, she would be homeless and the only place she could claim poor relief was Birmingham, the one place she didn't want to go.

She thought about William. Mr Wetherby would give him the opportunity to learn about the business. *I have to do it for him,* she thought. It might be the best opportunity he has to improve his lot in life. Maybe she should move to Birmingham after all. She stared at the gin bottle for a moment longer and poured herself another cup. If she gave in to his bullying now, where would it end? It was likely to set a precedent for the rest of her life. She wouldn't do that but, thinking about it, perhaps there was one other option.

There was a chill in the air and rain threatened, but nothing could dampen Mary's spirits. William was coming home today. She had missed him so much she had completed her chores in record time, prepared the bread and cakes for tea and rushed to sit by the front window to wait for him. She couldn't keep the smile from her face. Mary-Ann sat beside her with the same anticipation. Every minute that passed seemed to drag, but eventually they heard the sound of horses' hooves approaching. They both ran to the front door and as soon as they saw the carriage, William waved to them. It drove past and stopped in front of the New Inns allowing William to clamber down and run back up the street. Mary waited for him, her arms outstretched, and gathered him to her. Mr Wetherby's arrival went unnoticed.

"Don't I get any attention?" he growled after a few seconds.

Mary straightened herself up and wiped her eyes on her sleeve before she moved forward and gave him a peck on the cheek.

"Did you have a good trip?" She moved back to put her arm around William.

"Yes, we made good time. Are we going to go in? We're going to get wet if we stay out here."

Mary led the way and once they were seated she gave all her attention to William. "How was your week?"

"I missed you," William said, eyeing the pies on the table.

"And we missed you," Mary-Ann said. "I don't like it here without you."

Mary noticed the smirk on Mr Wetherby's lips but chose to ignore him.

"But were you good for Mr Wetherby?" Mary persisted.

"I tried to be."

"He has the makings of a good student," Mr Wetherby said.

"That's good."

The conversation was difficult until Mr Wetherby excused himself from the table and went outside. As soon as the door closed, Mary asked what she really wanted to know.

"What was this week really like? Was Mr Wetherby kind to you?"

"Yes, he was kind. He showed me lots of things and gave me some bread. He even let me use the other bed in his room, but he wasn't you. He didn't hug me or make me nice cakes."

"What was the house like?"

"Like Aunt Lucy's but with an extra bedroom. He has some other people living there so I'm not allowed to go to the top floor. I saw the boy we lived next door to in Hanley Street one night. I played with him for a while but when I saw Aunt Lucy walking down the road, I ran off."

"Will you be happy for a little while longer without me?"

"I suppose so." William's shoulders slumped as his bottom lip jutted out.

Mary heard the back door open and changed the subject as Mr Wetherby returned. "Right, have you both finished? I'd better tidy up."

"Isn't it about time they were going to bed?" Mr Wetherby asked.

Mary didn't pause for breath. "I said they could stay up a little later tonight, we haven't seen William all week,"

The following day as they finished dinner, Mr Wetherby asked about their plans for the afternoon.

"Are the children going to Sunday school today?"

"It's closed. The lady who runs it has gone to see her sick mother and there's nobody to take her place. It doesn't matter though; the four of us can go for a walk together."

"The children don't usually come with us," he said.

"I want to spend as much time with William as I can. You want to come with us don't you, William?"

William, who was finishing some jam pudding, nodded. Mr Wetherby pursed his lips but said nothing. The children would disappear once they were out.

As usual they headed for the woods, but unlike all previous occasions William held his mother's hand throughout the outing. Even once they were home, he didn't leave his mother's side, helping her to lay the table and put out the bread, jam and cakes for tea. He then helped to tidy up. All the while Mr Wetherby watched but said nothing.

When they returned from evensong, Mr Wetherby expected the children to take themselves to bed but Mary fussed around William, making sure he had everything ready for the following week. She then took them up to bed, leaving Mr Wetherby alone downstairs. It was over half an hour later before she returned to tell Mr Wetherby she was having an early night so she could spend some time with William in the morning before he left.

"Do you realise you've hardly spoken to me since I arrived? We've had no time to ourselves and you acted as if I wasn't here last night."

"It was so much easier when William was here all week. It meant I could give you all my attention when you were here. Now I don't see either of you I have to give him as much attention as I give you."

"You seem to be giving him more than his fair share." Mr Wetherby stood up and walked towards her.

"He's never been without me before. It's going to take some getting used to for both of us."

"So is this how it's going to be for the next couple of months?"

Mary shrugged. "It depends on how well he settles in. The happier he is with you I suppose the less he'll miss me."

"In that case I may as well join you upstairs; I hope you've put the children in their own beds."

"You can't sleep in my room," Mary said, her eyes widening at the thought.

"I can do as I damn well want. In case you've forgotten, I pay the bills around here."

Mary recoiled when she saw the smug expression on his face. "In case you've forgotten, we're not yet married. William wanted to sleep in my bed and I'm not going to wake him."

Mr Wetherby picked up a candle and went out into the hall. "Things are going to change around here. I'm not happy about this one bit."

By the time Mary helped William into the carriage the following morning, Mr Wetherby was already seated.

"Have a good week, William." For the first time in months Mary noticed him clutching his wooden train to his chest.

"He'll be fine," Mr Wetherby barked. "Just stop fussing over him."

Mary looked directly at Mr Wetherby, her eyes full of loathing, before she took a deep breath and stepped back. At least he had confirmed she was about to make the right decision. *You're going to regret you ever took my son from me.*

Chapter 31

A S THE CARRIAGE PULLED AWAY, Mr Wetherby leaned forward to look out of the window. All he'd wanted to do was encourage Mary to move to Birmingham, to give her a bit of coaxing, but his plan had backfired spectacularly. He never imagined she would turn against him so vehemently. Initially he'd hoped her anger would be short lived, but he knew he was fooling himself. The look she had given him as he and William left had cut him to the core and she had not had a kind word to say to him.

When he asked her to marry him, he knew she didn't feel the same about him as he did for her. At the time he had vowed to make her love him, but he clearly wasn't doing a very good job. He had started a battle of wills because his ego couldn't deal with the fact she didn't want to move to Birmingham. He knew she had few options and that she would have to accept whatever situation he imposed on her, but he also realised that if he wasn't careful he'd have a wife who hated him. He looked at William sitting beside him, fighting to control his tears. He was a good lad and didn't deserve to be a pawn between the two of them. He patted him on the shoulder, causing him to turn to him, but Mr

Wetherby fixed his eyes on the view from the window and remained silent.

They arrived in Hatchett Street just before seven o'clock and opened up the workshop. Mr Wetherby waited for everyone to arrive before he issued orders for the day. He then sat down at his desk and stared at the back wall. It didn't take him long to realise what he needed to do.

At five o'clock that evening, he distributed the wages and dismissed the women. William waited for him with a sullen expression and, as the last woman disappeared, Mr Wetherby turned to him.

"Do you want to go home?"

William shrugged and got down from his chair, ready to walk to the door.

"I don't mean to the house around the corner, I mean back to your mother."

"When?"

"Tonight."

"Really, do you mean it?" The smile lit up William's face. "Yes please, Mr Wetherby. I miss her so much, and Mary-Ann too."

ৎ৯৽৻

Mary sat at the table in the back room once again looking at the bottle of gin. It was the second of the week and she'd already had a cup, but Mary-Ann was in bed and she had the rest of the evening to face alone. She picked up the bottle and poured another glass before she heard the sound of horses hooves on the road. When they stopped outside the house she went to the front room and peered through the window. Moments later her heart leapt and she ran to the front door and threw it open.

"What are you doing here?"

William ran towards her open arms. "Mr Wetherby said I could come home."

"Aren't you pleased to see me as well?" Mr Wetherby's face appeared from inside the carriage.

Mary stood up and glared at him, the change in her voice obvious. "What are you doing here? Is everything all right?"

"No, not really." He got out of the carriage and let the driver go. "Can you bear to leave your son alone for long enough to talk to me?"

"William, go inside," she said, stroking his cheek. "I won't be long."

She waited until they were alone and took a deep breath. "Before you say anything, I've got something to tell you." Mary felt her stomach clench. "I went to see the rector this morning and I've cancelled the wedding."

Mr Wetherby's jaw dropped. "You can't do that."

"I can and I have. I don't want to marry you."

All colour disappeared from Mr Wetherby's face. "You'll be back on the streets by tomorrow morning."

"I had hoped I'd be here until Saturday, but if you want to make me homeless tomorrow, then so be it." Mary turned to leave.

"Are you mad? You'll be in the workhouse before the end of the week."

Mary stopped by the front door. "No, I won't. I'm going to Great Barr. I should have done it months ago but

I'd forgotten how generous my father-in-law is. He says we can stay with them for as long as we want."

Mr Wetherby stared at her.

"I'm sorry it had to end like this," Mary continued. "I won't marry someone who treats me or the children the way you do. The children mean more to me than anything in this world and you're not going to change that. Now, if you'll excuse me, it looks like I have some packing to do."

"No, don't go, not yet." Mr Wetherby moved towards her. "I've paid the rent until the end of the month, you can stay until then."

"We'll be gone before then, but perhaps we'll stay until the end of the week. I'll leave the key in the back of the door before I go. Goodbye, Mr Wetherby."

Chapter 32

THE FOLLOWING SATURDAY, AT MR Jackson's request, a carriage arrived in Handsworth with a driver to help Mary load her personal property. She didn't have much, but it was more than she'd had three years earlier when she left Aldridge. She helped the children into the carriage before she went back to the house to give it a final check. Satisfied it was as it should be, she turned to leave and collided with Mr Wetherby.

As soon as she saw him she took a step back and stood up straight. "I didn't expect to see you. I've left everything in good condition and cleaned the place from top to bottom. It shouldn't cause you any problems."

"Stop, please, I haven't come to check the house. I've come to see you."

Mary felt a shiver run through her body. "We've said everything there is to say."

"Maybe we have, but I don't want to talk." He looked down at her before he took hold of her face and kissed her. Mary immediately pulled away and walked to the other side of the room.

"Don't be like that," Mr Wetherby said. "I don't want you to go."

Mary didn't move but faced him with determination in her eyes. "I won't be treated with contempt any longer. I lived with a family of Quakers for long enough to accept that everyone is equal in the eyes of God. If I ever re-marry, I'll choose someone who believes that as well. It took me too long to realise it, Mr Wetherby, but you're a bully and I won't put up with it."

"Please, give me another chance, I can change."

"Why should I do that? I'm all packed and ready to go; Pa's expecting me."

"I can send word to him; let him know what's happened. Please don't leave, not like this."

Mary hesitated and walked to the window to check on the children. "The driver has to get back. You've got five minutes and then we're going." She leaned back against the windowsill, her arms crossed against her chest, not sure how she was managing to stay so calm.

"I'm sorry for the way I've been over the last few months," Mr Wetherby said. "I promise I won't take William from you again."

"You're going to need to promise more than that. Aunt Lucy once told me that most men rarely treat other men's children kindly. Now I know what she means. Let me be clear, if you want me, you get the children. If that happens, I expect you to take care of them as if they were your own."

Mr Wetherby looked at the floor. "I will. I already treat William like a son."

"Using him to get back at me is hardly fatherly behaviour and you barely acknowledge Mary-Ann."

"I know and I'm sorry. Please believe me when I say I won't do it again."

Mary continued to look at him with indifference. "How do I know you mean it? You could say anything you want but it could all change if we get married."

"It won't, I promise. I want you to love me, not hate me."

"Well you're going a funny way about it." *How could she ever have thought of marrying him?* Mary turned away from him and saw William and Mary-Ann climbing down from the carriage. "The children are getting restless, I need to go and see them."

Mary walked out and left him while she persuaded the children back into the carriage. It was almost five minutes later when she returned and stood in the doorway.

"There won't be a wedding in August," she said as if she had only just finished her previous sentence.

"I know that, but I want you to stay here. I'll pay the rent and bills for as long as you want, on condition that you let me visit occasionally."

"I need to think about it. I have to know you've changed before I commit to anything. I told you before, the children mean more to me than anything else; if anything or anyone threatens their happiness, I'll walk away. I can go to my in-laws at any time."

"Whatever you want, I love you too much to lose you."

Mary paused and looked at him again. *Could she really change him?* She leaned on the doorframe, not wanting to rush into anything. Eventually she spoke. "Very well, I'll stay … for now." Her heart was pounding now. *What was she saying?*

"Thank you." Mr Wetherby heaved a sigh of relief as

he walked towards her and reached for her hand. As soon as she felt his fingers touch hers she pulled her arm away.

"I'll let you know if and when I'm ready to see you again."

Chapter 33

MARY TOOK THE LETTER FROM the postman and looked at the familiar handwriting. Mr Wetherby had written to her every day since she'd agreed to stay in Handsworth, and the letters revealed a side of him she hadn't seen before. The harshness had disappeared and been replaced by tenderness and kindness. He loved her and wanted to take care of her and the children. He wanted to spend the rest of his life with her. She'd lost count of the number of times he'd apologised for upsetting her. He said he wanted a new start, but only if she wanted it too.

She'd needed time to clear her thoughts, but once he started calling again she found he was good to his word. Gradually she found herself looking forward to his visits. Where there had been an element of fear, she now found him to be good company, knowledgeable too; it was a side of him she had rarely seen. She smiled when she thought of his impending visit and wondered what little present he would bring for her this week. She was shaken from her thoughts by footsteps in the hall, before William burst into the room.

"We've got a letter." He eyed the cakes that were fresh from the oven. "It doesn't look like a normal letter though, it's got all fancy writing on the front and it's stiff." He put the envelope on the table, grabbed a cake and ran back outside before she could say a word. Mary wiped her hands and picked up the letter. The writing was ornate and her stomach flipped as she realised what it was. She hadn't expected such a formal invitation and she opened the envelope carefully before taking out the card.

Mr and Mrs Charles Jackson
Request the pleasure of the company of
Mrs Charles Jackson, Master William
Jackson and Miss Mary-Ann Jackson
To the wedding of
Miss Martha Jackson
To
Mr Benjamin Chalmers
On Monday 19th November at 10am
At
St Martin's Church, Birmingham
RSVP

Mary hadn't seen the family since Louisa's wedding and at this moment the last person she wanted to see was Sarah-Ann. Ever since she cancelled her move back to Great Barr, Sarah-Ann had been sending a stream of letters wanting to know all the details about Mr Wetherby and whether they were still seeing each other. Mary had no intention of telling her, and stopped replying. She had told Martha that Mr Wetherby still paid for her to live in Handsworth, but she hadn't let her know he had started to call again. For now, she preferred to keep it that way.

Mary stood the invitation on the mantelpiece and returned to her baking. She didn't want to let Martha down but she knew she couldn't go.

It was the following Sunday before she showed Mr Wetherby the invitation. She waited until the children had gone to Sunday school and he settled down to read the paper.

"I got this earlier in the week," she said.

He took it from her and read it slowly. "Have you replied yet?"

"I told them you were visiting Handsworth that day and didn't want me to go."

He said nothing for a long time, before he looked at her. "D'you know, Mary, a lot of our problems revolve around a family you're no longer a part of; perhaps it's time you let them go, I don't want them to come between us."

"I won't ignore them, certainly not Mother and Pa, they're the only family I've got."

"You know I love you more than I've ever loved anyone in my life, but after everything that's happened I still don't know how you feel about me. You seem to think more of them," he said.

Mary twisted her fingers together. "I've grown fond of you these last few months."

"And maybe one day you'll be able to say you love me."

৽৽৵

With the dark nights drawing in, Mary pulled the curtains across the window in the back room. The wind rattled the windows and already she could feel the draft as it worked its way to the centre of the room. She was about to make a cup of tea when she heard the front door open.

"Who's there?" A chill ran down her back. It wasn't William, he'd have made more noise, and she wasn't expecting anyone for at least another hour. When she received no reply, she walked to the door, her hand trembling as she reached for the door handle. Before she could get to it, the handle moved of its own accord and Mr Wetherby walked in.

"Are you all right?" he asked.

Mary put her hand to her chest as relief hit her. "You had me worried."

"I'm sorry. I wanted to see you and so I closed the workshop early."

"It's not often you do that. Is there a problem?"

"I hope not. I've got something to ask you." Mr Wetherby stood before her and took a deep breath. "I know we've been through this before and I hope I'm not rushing things this time, but I want to ask you again; will you be my wife?"

Mary looked at Mr Wetherby, who had gone down on one knee, and smiled. He really had changed since the summer and she wondered if maybe one day she could love him.

"Yes, I will." She spoke without hesitation and knelt down before him, kissing him gently.

"Thank you for giving me a second chance," Mr Wetherby said as tears welled up in his eyes.

"I'm glad I did, and thank you for coming back for me. Did you have a date in mind?"

Mr Wetherby laughed. "After last time, I'm going to leave that to you."

"Why don't we talk to the rector tomorrow? It might be difficult now it's almost advent, but it would be nice if we were married before the end of the year."

Mr Wetherby held her face and smiled. "You never cease to amaze me; I expected you to say next summer at the earliest."

"There's no point waiting, is there?"

"I'd get married tomorrow if we had a licence, but let's see what the rector says."

Mr Wetherby helped Mary to her feet and went to sit by the fire while she prepared the tea. Once they were finished, the two of them sat on either side of the fireplace while the children stayed at the table doing a puzzle.

"You're quiet this evening," Mr Wetherby said, picking up his cup and saucer.

Mary could feel her cheeks turning red and thanked the Lord for the dim light. "I've got something I need to tell you."

Mr Wetherby put his cup and saucer back down. "Go on."

"I've not been strictly honest with you … about my family."

"Your in-laws?"

Mary hesitated when she saw the concern on Mr Wetherby's face. "No. I mean my real family. I lied when I said I had no one."

A puzzled look crossed Mr Wetherby's face. "Why would you do that?"

Mary stood up and walked to the table. "I think it's time

you two were upstairs. You can finish this tomorrow when it's lighter. I'll come and tuck you in bed in a minute." She waited for the children to disappear before she continued. "Because, for all intents and purposes, I've been dead to them for the last ten years."

Mr Wetherby walked behind her and put his arms around her waist. "Tell me about it."

"I don't want to go into details." Tears formed as she pictured her father throwing her from the kitchen door, her bag of clothes landing on top of her seconds later. "Let's just say they didn't want me to marry Charles."

She hadn't shed a tear for her lost family since Charles had died, but now she couldn't hold back the years of pain. Mr Wetherby turned her to face him and held her close.

"Do you have any brothers or sisters?"

Mary nodded but said nothing. Eventually, once her tears subsided, she took a deep breath. "I have an older brother and an older and younger sister, as well as one who's the same age."

"The same age?"

"We're twins."

"You have a twin sister!" Mr Wetherby held her at arm's length and looked her square in the face. "Will I ever know the real you, Mary? We've known each other for nearly three years and I'm only finding this out for the first time. Do they live locally?"

"Shenstone I think; that's where they were when I left. I read in the paper that John and Susannah, the older ones, had married but I don't know where they are now. Katharine's four years younger than me; she's probably married too by now."

"What about your twin?"

"Alice?" Mary shrugged. "I tried to contact her once I got to Birmingham but she didn't reply. I even wrote to tell them Charles had died but I didn't hear back. I thought about visiting when I was expecting William, but I lost my nerve. My father had said he never wanted to see me again." Her tears returned and Mr Wetherby stroked the back of her head as he held her tight.

"It's probably not a lot different to me with my father, except I walked out on him rather than him kicking me out. I've written and told him my address in Birmingham every time I've moved, but I've never had a response. I'm going to write again when we have a new date; why don't you write to your family? Ten years is a long time, they may be ready to see you again."

Chapter 34

Birmingham, Warwickshire.

Mr Wetherby stared down at the letter he held in his hands. He recognised the spidery writing even if he hadn't seen it for over six years. It was only a week since he had written to his father and now, unexpectedly, he had a reply. He took his penknife and opened it carefully, unsure what news to expect.

Dear son

I got your letter. I hope to join you. Will bring Amelia and Betsy.

Pa

Mr Wetherby smiled at the brevity of the letter and imagined how long it had taken his father to write it. He read it again and a whole list of questions came into his head, most notably whether his stepmother was still alive. The fact that his father had answered a letter after all these years was a good sign, as was the fact he'd made no mention of bringing her to the wedding, although that could be because she wasn't invited. He also wondered why his father hadn't mentioned his other sisters and brother.

He went to get his writing set and sat down at the table to send a reply. He would invite his father and sisters to come to Birmingham a couple of days before the wedding so they could catch up after all these years. His letter would make no reference to his stepmother.

Handsworth, Staffordshire.

Mary looked at the clock in the corner of the room, half past four; Mr Wetherby would be here soon. She lifted a selection of cakes from the pantry and placed a pot of water over the fire as William ran in.

"Another letter for you." He threw it on to the table and ran out again. Mary wiped her hands and frowned when she picked it up. The handwriting appeared familiar, but quite unexpected. She took it out of the envelope and turned it over to confirm the name of her sister on the bottom.

> *Dear Mary*
>
> *It was good to hear from you, and especially that you are to be married again. We were surprised to hear you are in Handsworth, we thought you were in Birmingham.*

Mary paused, why did they think she still lived in Birmingham? She'd written to them from Aldridge when

Charles died. She thought for a moment before she continued.

> *I've wanted to contact you for a long time but haven't known where to find you. We've missed you and hope we can forget the past, especially since Charles is no longer with us.*

So they did get her letter. Why didn't they know where to find her?

> *We'd be thrilled if we could see you again. Father's been ill and can't travel but we wondered if you could visit us. We are still in Shenstone but not on the farm.*
>
> *Let me know if you can come.*
>
> *Alice*

Mary sat down at the table and put her face in her hands. How many times since Charles's death had she wanted to go home and now, she had a letter asking if she would. Not to the farm of course, but that didn't matter, they wanted to see her again. *They wanted to see her again.* Tears streamed down her face and before long she feared her sobs would stop her breathing.

It was a full fifteen minutes later before Mr Wetherby walked into the back room, and found her crumpled over the table.

"Whatever's the matter?" He grabbed a chair and put it next to her, placing his arm around her shoulders.

"They … want to … see me … again," she said between sobs. "They haven't … forgotten me."

Mr Wetherby read the letter lying on the table.

"Of course they wouldn't forget you, you're their daughter. Here, use my handkerchief, you'll have the shine off the wood in a minute."

Mary laughed as she accepted his offer and wiped her face. "I can't believe it … after all these years. You will let me go, won't you?"

"Of course I will; do you know where they are?"

"Not in the farmhouse but they won't have moved far."

"I'll come with you."

Mary hesitated. "No, I need to go on my own. We've a lot to catch up on and taking you with me might be difficult."

"I need to ask your father for your hand in marriage."

"I'm not his to give away. Please let me go on my own; you'll meet him soon enough."

Chapter 35

Shenstone, Staffordshire.

MR WETHERBY'S ASSISTANT, MR CARRICK, accompanied Mary on her journey to Shenstone. As the carriage left the houses of Handsworth, Mary took Alice's letters out of her bag and re-read them. Although she'd read them all a dozen times, one phrase kept swirling through her mind.

> *We've missed you and hope we can forget the past.*

Forget the past. How could she ever do that? She had loved her mother and father so much it had broken her heart when they told her they never wanted to see her again. She'd pleaded with them to accept Charles, but her father had been adamant, it was either Charles or them. She could understand his anger, but not her mother's. How could her mother have turned her back on her? As she'd picked up the bag of clothes her father had thrown after her she'd wondered if she had made the right decision. Then Charles had put his arms around her and suddenly she hadn't been able to imagine life without him. She had loved him too much and believed he would be with her long after her parents had gone. How wrong she'd been.

She didn't know how she would react to them now, and as the carriage approached the outskirts of Shenstone, the knot that had sat in her stomach for days tightened, making her feel sick.

It had turned noon when they arrived and Mr Carrick helped her down from the carriage.

"Do your family live far from here?" he asked as the carriage pulled away.

Mary hadn't been to her parents' new home but she knew exactly where it was. Her sister had described it in her most recent letter and Shenstone was too small for any of the houses to go unnoticed.

"No not far, just down here on the left-hand side."

The November air was cold and damp and they walked quickly, not taking the time to look around them. As they arrived at the gate, Mr Carrick spoke.

"Mr Wetherby has booked us onto the three o'clock carriage so I'll be back here at quarter to the hour. If you need me any sooner I'll be in the tavern."

Mary thanked him and then looked at the house. It was as she remembered it, a small cottage the third in a row of four, made of grey stone with a stained wooden front door. As she walked through the gate, the front door opened.

"Mary, is that you?" Alice rushed forward, her arms outstretched.

Mary stopped in her tracks. Was this the same Alice who had stood in the kitchen and watched, without shedding a tear, as she was thrown out?

"Look at you in your fancy clothes," Alice continued. "You must have so much to tell us, let's get you in."

Alice led the way into a small vestibule, took Mary's cape and hung it on the wall. Straight in front of them was a steep flight of stairs and to the left, a door led to the only room on the ground floor. Mary took a deep breath and followed her sister inside. The room was tiny with most of the space taken up with a wooden table that was set with knives and forks for their midday meal. Four chairs were pushed tight under the table while two rocking chairs, padded with cushions, were placed on either side of the hearth. Her father sat in the chair furthest from her and when she saw him she fought to hold back a sob.

"Come here and let me look at you." Her father stood up to walk towards her but the exertion triggered his cough and he collapsed back into the chair.

Mary rushed towards him and patted his back. "Father, are you all right?"

"No need to panic, he'll be fine in a minute," Alice said. "Just pass him that glass of ale. It always gets him when he's excited. Sit down and I'll make a cup of tea."

Mary pulled up a chair and placed it close to her father so she could help him take a drink.

"How can you stay so calm?" she said to Alice. "He could choke to death."

"When you've seen it as many times as I have, you know when it's bad. He'll be fine."

Mary took hold of her father's hand and stroked it as he rested his head back on the chair, the coughing over.

"Thank you for coming today," he said as he opened his eyes.

"Have you forgiven me?"

"I forgave you the day you got married. I heard he made an honest woman of you by having the ceremony in St Peter and St Paul's church."

"That was only a couple of months after I left. Why didn't you tell me then?"

"I should have done. Pride I suppose and we feared he'd only married you to preserve your honour. We weren't going to have you back only to have you produce a child before you should."

"I told you at the time you had no need to worry. We were married ten months before I had William. I wrote and told you."

"I know, that upset your mother too."

"Where is Mother?" Mary turned and looked at the three places set at the table. "She is here, isn't she?"

Alice looked to her father before she spoke. "I went to Bath Street to find you."

A frown appeared on Mary's face. "I'd written to tell you we were in Aldridge. We were there for over a year before Charles died. Why did you want to see me?"

"When we got your letter Mother was ill and wanted to see you. I wrote to Bath Street several times but got no reply, that's when I made the trip to Birmingham."

Mary said nothing; she could guess what was coming.

"When I couldn't find you, I asked around but nobody knew where you were."

"Charles's father owns the brassfoundry; any one of the men would have known we were in Aldridge."

"Well, they didn't say anything so I came home. Mother died the following week."

"So I'll never see her again." Mary twisted her handkerchief with her fingers. "She didn't deserve that, despite what she said to me." A tear rolled down her cheek. "What happened to the letter I sent with the Aldridge address?"

Alice shifted uncomfortably and looked again to her father for help.

"'Tell us what's been happening to you," he said. "What are you doing in Handsworth?"

Mary released her handkerchief and wiped her tears before she looked at her father. "It's a long story. I suppose I'd better start at the beginning."

As Mary came to the end of her account, the room fell silent and Alice stood up to carry the pan from the fire to the table.

"I made some dinner for us," she said as she served out a stew of potatoes, carrots and small pieces of bacon. Mary helped her father to the table and the three of them sat down and ate their meal in silence.

"When did you leave the farm?" Mary asked once they finished eating.

"Shortly after Mother died. It was too big for the two of us and Father had started with his breathing problems."

"What happened to everyone else?" Mary asked.

Alice answered. "Susannah got married a few years ago; she lives in Atherstone now. She had a daughter last year; Clara they called her. We see them from time to time. John and Katharine moved away after Mother died. They write occasionally but we haven't seen them for a while."

"I'd like to see them again. Why did they move away?"

"No reason." Alice answered a little too quickly and Mary knew she wasn't being told the truth.

"When are we going to meet this Mr Wetherby?" her father asked when the silence became uncomfortable.

"If you can come to the wedding, you can meet him then."

"Not before?"

"Can you make the journey twice in a few weeks?"

"Probably not, but you will tell him I wanted to meet him, won't you?"

"He sent you a letter." Mary reached inside her bag and handed it to her father. "He seems to think he needs your permission to marry me."

"Do you want to marry him?"

"I do, and before you ask, he's Church of England."

"Even if it crossed my mind, I wouldn't ask. It cost me too much. As long as you want to marry him and he looks after you, then you have my blessing."

At quarter to three there was a knock on the door.

"That will be Mr Carrick to escort me back to Handsworth." Mary stood up and tucked her chair under the table.

"I can't tell you how happy I am that I've seen you again," her father said. "I'm just sorry I took so long coming to terms with Charles. You won't disappear again, will you?"

"You'll see me at the wedding and you have my address in Handsworth. Please look after yourself." She leaned over and kissed his forehead.

Alice escorted her to the front door and once they were in the vestibule she closed the living room door.

"Have you forgiven me?" Alice asked.

"What for? Ignoring my letters when I wanted to see you or for not telling me about Mother?"

"I never meant to hurt you."

"You had a funny way of showing it. You were my best friend as well as my sister and yet you stood and watched Father throw me out. Why didn't you at least show me some support?"

Alice looked at the floor but said nothing.

"The only reason I wrote to tell you of the wedding was to see Mother and Father again, but I was too late for Mother."

"I'm sorry, if I could change things I would. Can't you see I've paid for my mistakes?"

Mary looked at her sister. Was she really the person she had once known?

"I'll be in touch," Mary said before she turned and walked towards the waiting Mr Carrick.

Chapter 36

Handsworth, Staffordshire.

IT WAS ONLY TEN O'CLOCK in the morning, but Mr Wetherby had been busy for hours. After opening up the workshop he left Mr Carrick in charge before he returned home and set about tidying the house. He left the door open to freshen up the room and peered around. There were bundles of wire, and hooks and eyes, covering most of the surfaces as well as unwashed cups and plates that had found a place on the floor. He should have got one of the women from the workshop to come and do this for him, but his pride wouldn't let them see the mess he'd been living in. He started by collecting up his work materials and separating them into two piles; the raw materials were to be taken to the workshop, while the finished fasteners he parcelled up for storing under the bed. Back downstairs he swept the floor before he took the mat outside and gave it a good beating. With all the surfaces clear he then went to get a couple of pitchers of water and washed everything he could see.

Once finished, a smile spread across his face as he surveyed the room. It looked completely different to the one he had stepped into that morning, and one he could bring his new bride back to with pride. At least she would keep it tidy for him from now on. He drew out his pocket watch and noted the time. His father and sisters would be here in little over an hour and he still needed to clean the bedrooms. He shut the front door and hurried upstairs where he turned all the mattresses, swept the floors and put everything away. With minutes to spare he wiped the dust from his hands and went back downstairs.

His father arrived shortly after midday with his sister Amelia, who was fourteen years old, and Betsy who was twelve. Although he hadn't seen them since they were small, they remembered him and he hugged them both before he turned to his father. Surely it was only six years ago since he had last seen him and yet he looked considerably older. He supposed he was about fifty years old but he had lost most of his hair and that which he had kept was grey, not the light brown it had once been. His skin was pale and his eyes red, as if he wasn't used to getting much sleep. He also had a noticeable stoop, which made him appear much shorter than Mr Wetherby remembered.

"William, how wonderful to see you again." He took his son by the hand and shook it vigorously. "I was beginning to think I'd never see this day. You look as if you've done well for yourself with this fancy house."

"I don't do too badly. There's more to come though, you mark my words."

"Let me sit down and you can tell me what you've been doing these last few years. My legs aren't what they used to be and they've already done too much this morning."

Mr Wetherby helped his father to a seat by the fire

before he told him how he had arrived in Birmingham and started his own business.

"I'll take you to the workshop this afternoon so you can see for yourself. I have over eighty women and girls working for me."

"You know, I was angry with you for a long time after you left. I couldn't understand why you'd gone, but looking around here, I have to admit it looks like it was for the best."

Mr Wetherby's thoughts turned to his younger brother. "Is Thomas learning the trade with you?"

"No, he didn't stay around for much longer than you. Your stepmother turned her attention to him once you'd gone, so he soon joined the Merchant Navy. He could be anywhere. He turns up from time to time when he's in the country."

"What happened to the girls? Do you still hear from them?"

"Anne's still at home, but she looks after the younger children so couldn't come with me. Margaret got married earlier this year to a man called Chapman. Amelia and Betsy visit her occasionally and bring me news. Ellen went into service at one of the big houses and we see her on her afternoon off. She passes a bit of money to us."

"I can't believe Anne managed to stick it out. I still feel guilty about leaving her as I did." Mr Wetherby paused, thinking back to the morning he'd left. "Once I'm married I'll take Mary to meet her."

"There's something else you should know. Young James, who was a baby when you were with us, died shortly after you left, but you have another brother called James and a sister, Emily."

"Emily was born before I left. In many ways she was the reason I went. Not that it was her fault, but that woman became even more intolerable after she arrived."

His father continued as if he hadn't heard him. "There's another one on the way as well, by the looks of it."

"So she's still with us then?" Mr Wetherby couldn't keep the disdain from his voice.

"She is. She wasn't happy when I told her I was going away for a few days, but I was coming here whether she liked it or not. It's about time I stood up to her."

"I hoped you may be a widower again when you didn't mention her in your letter."

"No, she's still with me; she has her uses."

While their brother and father talked, Amelia and Betsy prepared some food and brought it to the table. Over dinner Mr Wetherby senior wanted to know more about Mary.

"Did you say you're marrying someone called Mary?"

"Yes, her name's Mary Jackson, for another two days at least." Mr Wetherby smiled at the thought of her finally being his wife.

"Is she coming with a good dowry?"

"Not exactly."

"What does that mean? What does her father do?"

"He's a retired farmer but I haven't met him. I met Mary when she came to work for me."

"She used to work for you, what are you thinking?" Mr Wetherby senior put his hand to his head. "Are you marrying below yourself?"

"She's not beneath me. I hardly had a privileged background, did I?"

"Maybe not, but look at you now. You need to behave properly."

"Mary's not like the other women who work here. She'd fallen on hard times and needed a helping hand."

"What sort of hard times?"

"She'd been widowed."

Mr Wetherby senior rolled his eyes in horror. "A widow. She got more than a helping hand, didn't she? I bet she had her sights set on you as soon as she saw you."

"It wasn't like that; Mary's not like that. They were living with family when we met and they were looked after well enough."

"They?"

"She has two children by her late husband."

"What are you doing?" The wheezing in Mr Wetherby senior's voice grew more pronounced. You should be marrying someone from a respectable family, not an old widow with someone else's children."

"She's not old, in fact, for your information she's the same age as me. She was widowed when she was twenty-three. Before I met her she'd been on her own for over four years and had survived because of the help she got from her late husband's family."

"They've tired of her now have they?"

Mr Wetherby stood up and towered over his father. "You are unbelievable and you wonder why I left. You haven't even met her and you're judging her. Besides, you can hardly talk about my choice of wife after that woman you married ..."

"All right, all right, I'm sorry, I didn't mean to upset you; I'm surprised, that's all."

"Maybe you are but I won't have you talking about Mary like that. You can't judge somebody you've not even met. Now, I don't want to fall out with you after all this time and so can we please change the subject. You'll see Mary on Sunday, then you'll understand why I'm marrying her."

His father nodded. "Are you going to show me this workshop then?"

Chapter 37

MARY AND THE CHILDREN SAT at the table finishing their tea. The soup had gone but there was still bread to go with the cheese, so Mary spread it thickly with butter for the children. The night had long since turned dark but the fire behind them roared brightly, casting shadows on the walls. She thought about the day ahead and the fact that by this time tomorrow she would once again be a married woman. She was ready now. The events of the summer had done them a favour, although she was sorry it had been necessary.

"Tell me again why we have a new grandfather," William asked before biting into his bread.

"You haven't got a new grandfather, he's always been there. You just haven't seen him before."

"Why not?" Mary-Ann asked.

"Because he didn't have our address and didn't know where to find us."

"But you had his address so why didn't we go there?" Mary looked at William and sighed.

"I did go there and that's why he and your new Aunt Alice are coming to the wedding."

"Will Aunt Sarah-Ann be here as well, along with Old

Grandfather and Grandmother?" William asked once he finished his mouthful.

"No." Mary stood up to clear the table. "It's too close to Christmas for Aunt Sarah-Ann to come to a wedding and Grandfather and Grandmother can't come alone."

"Why couldn't you get married on a different day? I wanted to see them again," William said.

"It couldn't be helped." Mary wiped the table with a cloth.

"Who else will we see?"

"Mr Wetherby will wait for us at the church and he'll be with his father and sisters, your new Aunt Amelia and Aunt Betsy."

"I didn't know he had any sisters," Mary-Ann said.

"He has lots, but we'll only meet two of them tomorrow. Why do you always ask so many questions?"

"You said it's good to ask questions. That's how we learn." William put the crust from his bread on his plate.

"But do you have to ask so many?"

"I have to ask questions if I'm going to be clever like Mr Wetherby. You know Alfie Butcher? He said he's going to school next year. A proper school; not just on Sunday. That will make him clever, won't it?"

"I'm sure it will."

"Will I go to school soon?"

Mary paused and looked at her son. How she wanted him to be able to go to school. "Do you want to?"

"Oh yes. Then I'll be as clever as Mr Wetherby. He's the cleverest man I know."

"It will be up to Mr Wetherby to decide, and so you'll

have to wait and see. Now we have a busy day tomorrow and so it's time you two were in bed."

Mary was up early the following morning. She went to the baker's and then to the shop to buy some cooked ham, cheese and pies for later in the day. Once she returned home she put some water on to boil and helped the children with their breakfast before she went back upstairs to get herself ready.

Mr Wetherby had had a dress made especially for the occasion, and she took it from the cupboard and smoothed the material with her hands before she stepped into it. She looked down at the billowing layers of pale blue silk and cotton that flowed from her waist before she ran her hands over the bodice and adjusted the neckline. She had never worn such a beautiful dress and she wished she could see herself properly. She reached down for the hairbrush lying next to the water basin and pulled it through her hair. How different life would have been if Charles were still with her. Would she still have been happy, would she have ever worn a dress like this? She liked to think so. As far as she knew, the family had always done well for themselves, but then Mr Wetherby was in a different league. As far as money was concerned she wouldn't have any worries from now on. The sound of a carriage interrupted her thoughts and she glanced out of the window to see her father and sister stepping down by the front gate. She finished tying back her hair before she picked up her hat from the bed and went downstairs.

"Father, come in. Did you have a good journey?"

"We did, but can I sit down? I need to catch my breath. It was good of your Mr Wetherby to arrange the carriage for us. Now, let me see these two little ones." He turned to see his grandchildren for the first time.

"They're not little anymore. This is William; he's eight and Mary-Ann's seven. You two, this is Grandfather Chadwick and Aunt Alice."

"Pleased to meet you both." Mr Chadwick offered William his hand.

The children both said good morning but couldn't help looking from this new aunt to their mother and back again. They were so alike.

"You look lovely, Mary," Alice said. "That colour suits you."

"Mr Wetherby had it made for me." Mary swivelled her hips to show off the skirt.

"You've done well for yourself. I just pray that one day I'll find someone who wants me."

It was thirty minutes later before they arrived outside the Parish Church. The Sunday morning service had finished and Alice took the children inside while Mary waited outside with her father.

"He's a lucky man to have found you, Mary. I've missed you over the years. You were always special."

"I hope you like him. I think he'll treat me well."

"As long as you're happy, that's enough for me. Although don't you go disappearing again."

Mary squeezed his arm. "Come on, we'd better go in."

Standing at the back of the church, waiting for the organ to announce her arrival, Mary struggled to hold back her tears. Hadn't she always wanted her father to give her away on her wedding day, but it wasn't meant to be like this. She wasn't even his to give away anymore. He should have been there when she married Charles rather than leaving her to face it with no one but the churchwarden standing in his place. What wouldn't she give to see Charles turn around now and smile at her?

The music started without warning and her father pulled her from her thoughts as he took his first step towards the altar. Mary's smile was faint as Mr Wetherby turned to greet her, but her nerves evaporated when she saw the look he gave her. Surely no one could pretend to love someone that much? As the vicar started the service she finally knew she had made the right decision and smiled at Mr Wetherby before repeating her vows.

Once the service was over, they walked to the back of the church and waited for the guests to join them.

"May I introduce my father, Mr John Chadwick," Mary said, as her father and sister joined them. "Father, this is Mr Wetherby."

"Mr Chadwick, a pleasure to meet you, sir. Thank you for giving me your daughter's hand in marriage."

"No objections from me, although it wasn't really mine to give as I'm sure you know. You're a lucky man, Mr Wetherby."

"I won't disagree with you, sir." He turned to smile at Mary.

Alice had been standing a little behind her father, and Mary was amused by the expression of astonishment on Mr Wetherby's face when her sister stepped forward to greet him.

"Pleased to meet you, Mr Wetherby," Alice said. "Didn't my sister tell you we're identical twins?"

"She told me you were twins, but not that you were so alike. If you weren't wearing different clothes I doubt I'd know the difference between you. You even sound the same."

"We're not that similar; you just need to know what to look for," Mary said. "You'll be able to tell us apart by the end of the day."

As she spoke, Mr Wetherby senior joined the group.

"There you are," Mr Wetherby said to his father. "May I introduce you to my new wife Mrs Wetherby, her father Mr Chadwick and sister Miss Chadwick."

"Pleased to meet you, I'm sure," Mr Wetherby senior said, not bothering to introduce his own daughters. "I've heard a lot about you, young lady, and I hope my son's right about you. You certainly look the part."

"Thank you, Father," Mr Wetherby said as Mary's cheeks turned pink. "It's time we went for something to eat so we can get to know each other properly. After all, we are family now."

Once at the New Inns, William and Mary-Ann joined their new Aunts Amelia and Betsy in the corner of the room while the adults took seats by the fireplace. The new Mr and Mrs Wetherby sat on one side of the table, with Alice and the two fathers opposite them. A decanter of sherry had been placed in the middle of the table.

"I haven't had time to tell you how beautiful you look today," Mr Wetherby said as he held a chair out for Mary. "The dress turned out well; I'll have to compliment Mrs Gower. I didn't realise she was so talented."

"You had it made, did you?" Mr Wetherby senior asked.

"A real gentleman you are, sir," Mr Chadwick said. "It's so nice to see Mary looking so elegant. I need to find someone for Alice next to make an honest woman of her."

Mary noticed Alice shifting in her seat.

"I'm sure that won't be difficult, an attractive woman like her," Mr Wetherby said. "I still can't believe they're so alike."

"They're not that alike," Mr Chadwick said. "Once you get to know them they're quite different. Mary has more delicate features, don't you think? And her eyes are a more vivid blue. Besides, Mary has a different way with her."

Mr Wetherby turned to Alice, and held her gaze as he inspected her eyes.

"Why don't you tell Father about the workshop?" Mary said as she took hold of Mr Wetherby's hand, causing him to look back at her. "I'm sure he'll be interested."

As Mr Wetherby started his monologue, Mary watched her sister staring at the plate of food in front of her. Despite everything that had gone before them, she still pitied her and wanted to draw a line under what had happened.

"Do you have anyone to walk out with, Alice?" she asked.

"I don't have time. If I'm not working then I'm at home looking after Father."

"It must be hard."

"I've learned to live with it; at least I get some company working at the tavern."

"What about moving to Birmingham? There'd be more for you here and I could sit with Father during the day."

"I don't know. Mother always said it was a terrible place."

"It's not that bad and we've got a lot of catching up to do."

"I don't think so, but I'll speak to Father about it when we get home."

"What will you speak to me about?" Mr Chadwick joined their conversation when he heard his name.

"Nothing that won't keep," Alice said.

"No, I insist. What is it with you two?"

Mary turned to her father. "I asked Alice if you'd consider moving to Birmingham."

"To live? I don't know about that."

"Why not? It would mean you'd be closer to us and Alice could meet more people."

"It'd be a big move. I've never lived in the town before and it wouldn't help my breathing."

"I'd like to move to Birmingham," Mr Wetherby senior interrupted.

"There's nothing stopping you, is there?" his son asked.

"It's her isn't it. She won't move and it's always down to her; I tell you I've had it with her. I should tell her we're moving whether she likes it or not."

"I don't know why you don't do that anyway; you're the breadwinner. She'd be nothing without you and you should tell her that. I can make arrangements if you like."

Mr Wetherby senior didn't answer, and a second later he slumped over the table holding his chest.

"Father, are you all right? What's the matter?"

"He was all right a minute ago." Mr Chadwick took a mouthful of sherry.

"Father, speak to me." Mr Wetherby slapped his father's face. "Someone get him a brandy, and William, run and get Dr Hart as fast as you can."

"He'll be at home at this time of day," Mary said, walking around the table. "It's the white cottage at the end of the lane."

"I know where he lives." William set off at full speed.

"We should lie him down," Mary said. "He's gone white."

Together with Mr Wetherby she helped him to the floor. Mr Wetherby knelt over him. "Father, look at me. Don't you dare die."

Mary watched as he cradled his father's head and poured a little brandy to his lips. The only other time she had seen Mr Wetherby flustered was the night he had nearly missed her outside the Town Hall. He usually controlled everything.

"Come on, drink it," he murmured under his breath.

"Here, let me help." Mary wiped the perspiration from her father-in-law's face. "I'll hold the glass and you rub some brandy on his lips with your finger. I think his breathing is settling already."

Mr Wetherby did as she said and within minutes colour started to return to his father's cheeks.

"Mr Wetherby," Mary said. "Can you hear me?"

Within seconds, Mr Wetherby senior opened his eyes.

"The doctor will be here shortly," Mary said. "You lie still. You gave us all a fright."

"Don't ever do that again." Mr Wetherby's concern was replaced by annoyance. "We've only just made contact again, I'm not ready to lose you yet."

It took Dr Hart over fifteen minutes to arrive, by which time Mr Wetherby senior could sit up.

"What happened here?" the doctor asked.

"I got a burning pain across my chest and I couldn't breathe; it's passed now."

The doctor examined him and then looked at the plates on the table. "Has he had a big meal?"

"Yes, and quite a lot to drink," Mr Wetherby said.

"I suspect he's overeaten and it's reduced the amount of blood in his heart. That will be what caused the pain."

"Will he be all right?"

"He needs bed rest for the next couple of days and no big meals. As long as he remains calm he should make a full recovery."

They arrived home half an hour later and managed to get Mr Wetherby senior up the stairs. Mary made him comfortable in William's bed while the rest of the party gathered in the front parlour.

"Whisky, Mr Chadwick?" Mr Wetherby asked.

"I don't mind if I do; it helps open my airways."

"What a to-do that was." Mr Wetherby handed his guest his drink. "He won't be able to travel for a while and it would be as well if he didn't see my stepmother too soon. It was talking about her that caused the problem."

"Looks like he'll be with you for Christmas then," Mr Chadwick said.

"It does. You're going to have to make some beds on the floor," Mr Wetherby said to Mary as she walked back into the room. "Father and the girls will have to stay with us for a few days. Would you like to stay as well, Mr Chadwick, or do you have other arrangements?"

"We're going over to Susannah's house on Tuesday. Mary's sister, that is. We haven't seen her since the summer."

"We must visit them in the New Year," Mr Wetherby said to Mary. "I'd like to meet her; John and Katharine too. It's a shame you couldn't contact them before the wedding."

"Father, look at the time." Alice stood up and reached for her bag. "We'd better get our coats, the carriage will be here shortly."

"Right you are, give me a minute to get up from here. I'm not as quick as I used to be." He looked at Mr Wetherby. "If I could just clear this chest it would help." As he spoke his cough started again and he was forced to stay where he was.

"I'll get your hat and coat," Alice said.

"Let me show you where they are." Mary followed her out of the room, shutting the door behind them. Once in the hallway, Mary handed Alice their coats.

"What are you trying to hide?" Mary said.

"What do you mean?"

"I mean, every time someone mentions John and Katharine you change the subject rather quickly."

"There's not much to say about them."

"I'd like to know why they left Shenstone, especially Katharine, given she's not married."

"I don't know. I think there may have been some words with Father, but I don't want to raise it again. You've heard that cough, too much excitement could kill him."

Mary eyed her sister suspiciously but when she refused to say any more, Mary went to get her father. Five minutes later she waved them off with a promise to see them again soon. She closed the door and went back into the front room where Mr Wetherby sat with another whisky.

"I'll go and fix some tea for us," she said. "It seems a long time ago since we ate dinner. Will you go and see how your father is?"

"No, don't do that," he said. "Close the door and come here."

Mary did as she was told before he stood up and moved towards her, pulling her close.

"I've waited too long for today, I don't want to let you go." He held her face between his hands and kissed her.

"Not yet, wait until the children are in bed." Mary pulled away, aware of nothing but the smell of whisky on his breath. "Let me get tea ready and we can spend some time on our own later."

"I don't want to wait. I want you now."

"I won't be long."

She kissed his hand before collecting up the glasses, and the remainder of the whisky, in case he decided to have any more.

William and Mary-Ann were in the back room with Amelia and Betsy when she went in.

"Have you looked in on your father?" she asked Amelia.

"He's sleeping. He looks quite peaceful now. I hope he'll be all right."

"Dr Hart will call again in the morning so he's in the best hands."

Mary rallied the children to help her with the food and once it was ready, she went to get Mr Wetherby. When she found him fast asleep in the armchair she smiled and shut the door again; she didn't need to wake him just yet.

Chapter 38

THE FOLLOWING DAY, MARY WAS up early. It was Christmas Eve and as well as going to the baker's, she had to go to the farm to see if there were any geese left. She also needed to pick up some extra potatoes and carrots. She left the children making paper decorations, but unusually Mr Wetherby had stayed in bed. By the time she returned home, he had just arrived downstairs and sat at the table, red rims around his eyes.

"You look like you could do with a cup of tea," she said cheerily. "Are you feeling all right?" When he made no reply she told the children to go outside to give him some peace.

"Is there something wrong?" she said when they were alone.

"I can't believe you left me downstairs last night. Four o'clock in the morning I climbed into bed."

"You were asleep before tea and I didn't want to wake you. The whisky must have made you drowsy."

"That was no excuse to leave me. I wanted you last night and you weren't there."

"We can be together tonight."

"I can't wait until tonight. I want you now."

"Now? The children will be back in a minute ... and your father's upstairs."

Mr Wetherby stood up and went to the back door where he turned the key in the lock. "Father won't disturb us and the children can wait outside. Now come here."

"It's the middle of the morning."

"I don't care; I've waited too long for this." He pulled her towards him. "You're my wife now and I won't take no for an answer."

Mary recoiled as he moved to kiss her, but Mr Wetherby held her tighter. "What's up? Do I repulse you already?"

"No ... of course not ..."

"Well, you've got a funny way of showing it."

Mary couldn't speak. It wasn't meant to be like this. She wanted to love him, to melt into his arms, to caress him as she had with Charles, but she couldn't. His narrow frame and pale skin held no appeal for her; how different he was to Charles's muscular physique.

"We're in the living room," she said eventually. "Perhaps if we went upstairs ..."

Mary could feel his tension relax as he led her to the stairs, and she prayed that with her eyes closed she could imagine being back on the farm.

The midday meal ended up being a sparse affair and Mary fussed around the table, acting as if the morning's events hadn't happened.

"Are you putting the decorations up this afternoon?" Mr Wetherby asked as she tidied up.

"We'd better, we haven't got any other time to do it."

"How different this is from last year." He sat back with a smile. "I never want a Christmas like that again."

Mary frowned. "You said you had a nice enough time with Mr Grimshaw."

"I didn't want to be there though. I was waiting for an answer from you if you remember."

"It seems like such a long time ago."

"Far too long, but we've made it now." He put his arm around her waist as she stood next to him.

Amelia interrupted them. "I hope our stepmother received the letter telling her we wouldn't be home for Christmas. I don't imagine she'll be pleased, given that she didn't want us to come in the first place. She probably thinks we did it on purpose."

"Will she be all right on her own?" Mary asked.

"She has Anne and the younger children to keep her company, and the way she's always shouting at Father you'd think she'd be glad he wasn't there." She smiled. "You know, I'm looking forward to Christmas this year."

With the children in bed, the house decorated and the food prepared as much as it could be, Mary sank into a chair and closed her eyes.

"We're so lucky, you know," Mr Wetherby said as he sat opposite her. "We've got a good future ahead of us. The only thing missing now is some children of our own. I want my own sons to work alongside me in the business."

Mary sat up straight. "You have William; you promised you'd treat him as if he were your own."

"Of course I will, and naturally he'll work for me, but I need my own sons. Boys with my name and my brains who'll be able to take over the business one day."

"William can do that, he's a bright lad."

"We don't know that yet. I need to get him to school next year; see how he gets on. I'll have to send him away from Birmingham though, the schools in Birmingham aren't good enough."

"He's not nine yet."

"Don't start that again. He's my responsibility now and he's going away to school."

Chapter 39

M R WETHERBY SENIOR HAD BEEN well enough to join the family downstairs for Christmas Day and by Boxing Day, although he would have preferred to stay, he decided he had better go home. He was in enough trouble with his wife as it was. Mary had enjoyed having them, not least because both Amelia and Betsy had got on well with her children, but she was glad when they had the house back to themselves. She hoped maybe now she could relax and become the wife Mr Wetherby wanted. She had finished tidying up and was sitting by the fire with Mr Wetherby.

"It's nice to finally be on our own," Mr Wetherby said. "I've hardly seen you."

"At least your father's well again and knows not to eat too much."

"There's no danger of that; I seem to remember that woman he married doesn't believe in giving anyone too much to eat."

"You really don't like her, do you?"

"I'd go so far as to say that if I had the choice between spending time with her or with Aunt Lucy, I'd pick Aunt

Lucy every time. Anyway, I don't want to talk about either of them. We need to discuss the move back to Birmingham ..."

"Was that a knock on the door?" Mary interrupted. "I'll go and check."

The smile on Mary's face disappeared the instant she opened the door.

"What are you doing here?"

Sarah-Ann stood on the front doorstep, draped from head to toe in a dark cloak and hood.

"Can I come in?"

Mary clenched the door handle and refused to move. "What do you want?"

"I haven't seen you for months, I've missed you."

"Perhaps you should have thought of that before you decided to cause so much trouble."

"I didn't mean to upset you, please, can I come in?"

Mary hesitated, but finally stood back, guiding Sarah-Ann into the front room. She didn't want her to get sight of Mr Wetherby. "What do you want?"

"It's the season of goodwill and I wanted to see you before the end of the year."

"Just like that? Do you realise what you did?"

Sarah-Ann looked uncertain. "There was no harm done was there?"

"No harm done? Because of you I almost lost my future husband, my home and my security, not to mention the fact I'd have been forced to take your brother's children to the workhouse."

"It wouldn't have gone that far; Father was happy to have you."

"And so that makes it all right, does it?" Mary stood with

her hands on her hips. "You told Mr Wetherby I wanted to marry Richard. Do you think he took that lightly?"

"I didn't mean to cause trouble. We were only talking and I forgot what I was saying. It didn't seem to bother him."

"And you expect me to believe that? He didn't speak to me for nearly a month afterwards."

"I'm sorry, I wasn't thinking."

"You knew I'd accepted his proposal; I'd left Aunt Lucy's and had moved here. How did that manage to escape your attention?"

"I don't know. Honestly, it was an accident. I don't know what else to say."

There was a long pause before Mary turned away from Sarah-Ann. "Fortunately Mr Wetherby and I are now married."

"You got married without telling anyone?" Sarah-Ann grabbed Mary's arm and turned her around.

"I wasn't going to invite you to the wedding, was I? I had to pretend to the rest of the family that we hadn't set a date. I didn't want you to find out."

"When did this happen?"

"On Sunday just gone. We only invited my father and sister, Mr Wetherby's father and two of his sisters."

"You invited your father? He disowned you."

"When I had no other family to invite I decided to write and let them know. Perhaps I should be grateful to you. If it hadn't been for you, maybe I wouldn't have sent that letter."

Sarah-Ann sat down as tears stung her eyes. "Why did you miss Martha's wedding?"

"Because I couldn't bring myself to be in the same room as you. I certainly wasn't going to leave you alone with Mr Wetherby."

As if on cue, Mr Wetherby walked into the front room. "What's going on in here?" He stopped when he saw their visitor. "Oh, it's you. Do you need any help, Mary?"

"I'll be fine. I'll join you in a few minutes."

Mr Wetherby looked at Sarah-Ann, who was now sobbing, and left the room.

"He hates me, doesn't he?"

"Hate's a strong word, but it's fair to say you're not his favourite person."

"Please forgive me, Mary. I'm sorry I spoiled things for everyone; it was a mistake. I promise nothing like that will happen again."

Mary looked at her sister-in-law and knew it hadn't been easy for her to apologise. "Stay here and wipe your eyes. I'll make you a cup of tea."

Mary went into the back room and put the kettle back over the fire before she told Mr Wetherby of the conversation.

"Do we forgive her?" she asked as she poured the tea.

"As God forgives us, so we should forgive others, isn't that what the Bible says?"

"It is, but I don't know if I can ever trust her again."

Mr Wetherby stood up and put his arms around her. "Do you trust me?"

"Of course I do."

"Well, given that I'm the focus of her attention, and knowing that I have no intention of spending any time with her, you have no need to worry. Why don't you ask her to take her tea in here so she can see us together?"

Mary wasn't convinced it was a good idea but did as she was told.

"What will Mr Wetherby think of me?" Sarah-Ann said. "I expect I look dreadful with all these tears."

"Given that he's the one who thinks we should forgive you, I'd say it would be rude not to accept his invitation."

"Before we do, there's something I need to ask you." Sarah-Ann wiped her eyes again and took a deep breath. "It upset Martha that you didn't go to her wedding and she'll be even more disappointed when she hears you've married without telling her. I'll tell her it was my fault, but will you call on her as well? She's missed you."

"Of course I will; she didn't deserve to be caught in the middle of all this."

Chapter 40

Birmingham, Warwickshire - Eighteen months later

M R WETHERBY SAT BESIDE THE fireplace, his back to the window. He had finished his evening meal and, as the night was still warm, the front door stood open, letting the light stream in. Opposite him, on the other side of the fireplace, sat his father. The two men often spent their evenings this way when Mr Wetherby senior came to stay. He was a regular visitor now that Amelia and Betsy lived and worked with their brother, and he no longer had any hesitation about leaving his wife, often for weeks at a time.

Mr Wetherby held a copy of *The Times* across his lap. "The exhibition seems to be going well," he said to his father.

"Which exhibition's that then?"

"You know which one. The Great Exhibition of the Works of Industry of all Nations. It seems that the English exhibits are by far superior to the exhibits from the other countries. Her Majesty and Prince Albert were there again last week. What a sight it must be."

"Will you go and see it yourself?"

"I'd love to; can you imagine all that technology and machinery on display, not to mention the magnificent Crystal Palace itself?"

"If you go, can I go with you?"

"You know, there are many people who'd like to make the trip, it's annoying we're so far away. Perhaps I could arrange to take a group from Birmingham for the day. I've heard of some church congregations who've made the journey. Leave it with me and I'll see what I can do." He returned his attention to the paper, but as he turned the page he caught sight of Mary out of the corner of his eye. "Mary, are you all right?"

"I'm tired. I think I'll go and lie down."

"Here, let me help you." He jumped up and threw his paper to one side. "I don't want anything happening to you."

Mary reached for his arm and let him lead her upstairs. Once in the bedroom he helped her onto the bed and pulled the cover over her.

"Is the baby coming?"

"I don't think so, not yet." She moved to make herself comfortable. "It won't be long though. Will you stay with me for a while?"

"What do you want me to do?"

"Nothing special; just be here. After what happened last year I'm frightened there may be a problem."

"Nonsense. Last year you didn't carry the baby for long enough, it had only just started moving; now look at you, there's a strong young boy in there, you mark my words."

"I hope so." She reached for his hand and squeezed it. "I don't want to disappoint you again."

"You could never do that. As long as I have you I'll be happy."

"I wish William was here, he'd like a baby brother."

"He'll be home soon enough, schools don't keep them all year round. Another few weeks and he'll be back and much the better for it in my opinion."

"I know, but I've missed him. He's growing into a young man far too quickly."

"He'll have Mary-Ann to go with next term; I've managed to get her a place at the school as well."

"That's wonderful, she'll be so pleased. She misses William more than she lets on. I'll miss them both of course, but at least I'll have someone else to watch over." She moved her hand across her heavily swollen belly. "When will you tell her?"

"You can tell her tomorrow if you want to, but for now it's time you got some sleep. I'll take charge of things downstairs. Goodnight, my darling."

❧

It was dark when a sharp pain roused Mary from an uneasy sleep. She let out a piercing scream, which woke Mr Wetherby who lay beside her.

He sat up immediately. "What's the matter?"

"The baby's coming, but something's not right." Her breath was heavy as she spoke. "You'd better light some candles."

Mr Wetherby jumped out of bed and shouted for Amelia as he fumbled around in the dark. Within a minute she rushed in from the room above.

"Did you shout?" she asked.

"We need to get Mrs Tompkins here," Mr Wetherby answered. "The baby's coming. Can you run and get her?"

"Don't leave me," Mary said to Mr Wetherby once they were alone again. "Something's not right, I can feel it. It's never been like this before."

"Calm down, I'm sure you'll be fine. It's nearly ten years since you had Mary-Ann, you've probably forgotten what it's like."

"I haven't." Mary spoke through gritted teeth. "It wasn't like this. The baby feels like it's coming already."

A contraction pulled the muscles of her belly and she cried out as she squeezed Mr Wetherby's hand.

"What do I do?" Mr Wetherby rushed to the window to look for the midwife. "I can't deliver a baby."

"Promise you'll take care of William and Mary-Ann for me." Tears ran down Mary's face.

"Don't talk like that …"

"Please, tell me you will. They'll need you, please don't abandon them."

"Of course I won't abandon them, but you can't abandon me."

Mary let out another shriek as a new contraction ripped through her body.

"Mary, stop, lie still. I can't bear to see you like this."

"I can't do this," she said. "I'm too old."

"Of course you're not too old," Mrs Tompkins said as she walked straight into the room. "You've done it before; it should be easier this time. Now, Mr Wetherby, I think it's time you were leaving." She turned and ushered him out of the door.

"Tell the children I love them," Mary shouted after him. "Something's not right."

"You're imagining it," Mrs Tompkins said. "Everything will be fine. Only a bit of pain."

"I'm not. Why won't anyone believe me? There's something wrong."

Mrs Tompkins bent to examine her patient and Mary saw her freeze before another contraction seized her.

"Hold on there, Mrs Wetherby," the midwife said after a minute. "It looks like the baby's ready to come out but it wants to come feet first. We're going to have to take this slowly."

ৎৡৣ

Mr Wetherby couldn't settle. He'd watched the sunrise and now he alternated between sitting by the fire and pacing the room. Presently Amelia came down to stoke up the fire and make him a cup of tea. He watched as she busied herself cleaning the room, but she hadn't done much before Mrs Tompkins asked her to help.

"Let me know what's going on," Mr Wetherby said as she left.

Over an hour later Amelia had not returned and, by the time Betsy and Mary-Ann arrived downstairs, Mr Wetherby couldn't think straight. He sent the girls for some bread and realised his workers would be waiting to be let into the workshop. He went into the court to open up before he called to ask Mr Carrick if he'd watch over things for the day. He got back to the house as the girls returned from the baker's and helped himself to some bread and butter. He had just sat down when his father arrived downstairs.

"Is everything all right?" Mr Wetherby senior said as he took his usual seat. "There's a lot of noise in your bedroom."

"Mrs Tompkins is here. The baby will be born today but something's not right. Mrs Tompkins asked Amelia to help over an hour ago."

"What can she do?"

"I don't know. I wish someone would tell me what's going on."

As midday approached, Mr Wetherby was about to go and check on the workshop when he heard a loud shriek from the bedroom. A minute later Amelia ran down the stairs.

"We need more water." She didn't stop as she ran out of the front door.

Mr Wetherby followed her into the entry. "Amelia, stop, what's going on? Why is it taking so long?"

"The baby's stuck and Mrs Wetherby has no strength left."

"We need a doctor," Mr Wetherby said. "I'm going for Dr Andrews; Mrs Tompkins doesn't know what she's doing."

Mr Wetherby wasted no time going back for his hat and arrived at the doctor's as he was leaving to make a call.

"Doctor, you must come with me. It's Mrs Wetherby, there's a problem … I think it's serious, you must come now."

"Calm down," Dr Andrews said. "Whatever's the matter?"

"It's Mrs Wetherby, the baby's stuck. You have to come now." Mr Wetherby pulled the doctor's arm.

"Mr Jacobs on Summer Lane needs me too; I must go to him first."

"No, please, doctor, she can't hang on for much longer. You can't let her die."

Dr Andrews looked down the road in the direction of Summer Lane and then to the frightened young man standing before him. "All right, Mr Jacobs can wait. Lead the way."

ৎ৵৶৶

All Mary wanted to do was sleep. It wasn't much to ask, but every time she lost consciousness a searing pain would cross her belly and force her back into the room. Mrs Tompkins was no help either. Why did she keep shouting at her and slapping her face? Couldn't she leave her alone? She didn't care what they did to her, as long as they got the baby out. *Please stop the pain and let me sleep.* She willed herself towards tranquillity when a pain like no other tore through her, bringing with it a scream she felt incapable of. The baby was coming; it must be, why else could she feel a warm fluid leaking from her? The baby was here; it was finally here. A smile flickered across her lips as she relaxed back into the pillow, she could sleep now. At that moment, Dr Andrews arrived.

"Praise the Lord," Mrs Tompkins said when she saw him.

"What on earth's been going on here? How much blood has she lost?"

"It's only just happened. The baby wants to come feet first but it's well and truly stuck. I tried to pull …"

"You've pulled the cord away."

"It was a mistake."

"Damn right it was a mistake, you may just have killed the two of them. Get me some cloths, now."

Mary heard the words, but they weren't talking to her. Someone was in trouble, but it wasn't her. She was going to sleep now; she could feel it. The light was failing, they'd started whispering too; they were going to let her sleep. She didn't need to worry about the pain anymore. She was going to sleep.

Chapter 41

M R WETHERBY SAT WITH HIS head in his hands and prayed harder than he had ever prayed before.

"What's keeping them?" He stood up once again and paced the room. "Why has nobody told me what's happening? I'm going to find out for myself."

His father went to stop him, when they heard the sound of a baby crying.

"A baby! The baby's born. I have a son." Mr Wetherby stood still and listened.

"How do you know?" his father asked.

"Listen to the noise, a girl wouldn't cry like that. I have a son, but I need to see Mary. I can't look after a baby without her."

"You need to wait for the doctor to come down, you can't just go in."

"I know, I know. What's keeping him?"

It was another hour before Dr Andrews came down the stairs. "You can go up now, Mr Wetherby. You have a healthy baby boy who looks to have come through his ordeal unscathed."

"A boy, I told you." He turned to his father, a smile on

his face before it instantly disappeared. "What about Mary, Mrs Wetherby? Is she all right?"

The doctor looked down at the floor before he spoke. "She's lost a lot of blood but she's alive."

There was an audible sigh of relief from Mary-Ann who had been sitting unseen on the stairs.

"The baby was too big for her. I think I've managed to control the bleeding but she'll need complete bed rest for at least the next two weeks, probably longer. I'll come and see her every day to see how she is and to change the packing."

"Thank you, doctor. Due to Mrs Tompkins's incompetence, I believe you saved her life."

"You need to thank yourself. You were right that if I'd gone to see Mr Jacobs first she probably wouldn't have made it. I need to go and see him now; good day to you, sir." Dr Andrews collected his hat and let himself out.

As soon as the doctor left, Mr Wetherby ran up the stairs and knocked on the bedroom door. A tired-looking Mrs Tompkins let him in and he walked to the side of the bed, pulling the chair with him. There wasn't a trace of colour in Mary's face, as she lay motionless on the bed, her eyes closed. Instinctively Mr Wetherby took her hand to check she was still alive. On the bed next to her, wrapped tightly in a knitted blanket, lay his son; his ruddy complexion a sharp contrast to his mother's. He was fighting to free himself and started to cry. Immediately Mrs Tompkins picked him up.

"Why didn't you call for the doctor earlier rather than asking for Amelia? She should never have been put in a situation like that. You could have killed Mrs Wetherby with your incompetence."

"Would you like to see the baby?" Mrs Tompkins held the baby towards his father. Mr Wetherby softened as he looked down at his son and stroked his cheek.

"Welcome to the world, William Wetherby Junior," he said. "My son and heir."

"Mrs Wetherby needs to rest," Mrs Tompkins said.

"I'd like to sit with her for a while. Will you leave us? You can take William Junior with you; Mrs Wetherby can't look after him."

Mrs Tompkins cast one last look around the room before she left. As soon as the door clicked behind her, Mr Wetherby lay down on the bed next to Mary and put his arm around her.

"Don't leave me," he whispered. "I love you and our son needs you. This should be the happiest day of my life but it can't be if I lose you." He rested his head against hers and allowed his tears to roll onto the pillow. He kissed her forehead and continued to lie with her until he fell into a fitful sleep.

When he awoke, the room was dark save for the moonlight shining through the window. It looked as if Mary hadn't moved. He put his face close to hers to feel for her breath, uncertain whether she was still with him. Once he confirmed she was breathing he sat on the edge of the bed and rubbed his left arm to bring some life back into it. As he did, Mary stirred.

"Mary, my darling, are you all right?" He reached for her hand as she tentatively opened her eyes. "I've been worried about you."

Mary managed a weak smile but when she tried to speak no words came out. She tried again.

"Where's ... baby?" she managed. "Alive?"

"Yes, he's alive and well. Mrs Tompkins took him downstairs to let you rest. He'll be fine."

Mary closed her eyes again and sank back into oblivion. It was over.

৩৯৫৫

Three days later, Mary was propped up against a bank of pillows, trying to eat a small bowl of broth. It was the first thing she'd eaten since before the birth and Mr Wetherby sat on the chair next to the bed, helping her. Her face remained white but she no longer floated in and out of consciousness. Dr Andrews had visited earlier and was satisfied the bleeding was under control. She had hardly laid eyes on her new son but as she finished the broth, she asked Mr Wetherby if she could see him.

"I'll get Amelia to bring him up. I've given her some time off work to take care of him and I've hired a wet nurse. He's a strong lad and has a good set of lungs on him."

"We need to decide what to name him."

"It's already decided, he'll be called William, after me."

"But we already have my William. We can't have two sons with the same name."

"My first born son is going to have my name and so we'll have to have two Williams; everyone's calling him William Junior."

Mary didn't have the energy to argue and put her head back onto the pillow. Maybe if she was stronger, but perhaps it wouldn't matter.

A couple of minutes later Amelia laid William Junior in her arms. Mary looked down at his well-developed features and her immediate instinct was to hand him back. This wasn't her child, how could he be? He wasn't like William, with his mop of dark brown hair. That was how her babies should look, not like … this.

"Isn't he adorable." Amelia stood and watched over them.

"Adorable?" Mary was shocked that such a word could be used on a child that could have taken her from her own children.

"I think you need to rest," Mr Wetherby said. "You're clearly not your usual self. Amelia, take William Junior back downstairs."

"He's like you," Mary said to Mr Wetherby once they were alone … and deep down she knew that was the problem.

Chapter 42

WILLIAM JUNIOR WAS THREE WEEKS old before Mary was allowed out of bed, and even then it was only for a couple of hours each day. The fever she'd developed the previous week had subsided and she now had some strength back.

As she cradled William Junior one afternoon, there was a knock on the door and Martha let herself in.

Mary smiled. "What a lovely surprise and you've brought Benjamin too."

"I daren't make arrangements too far in advance because I never know how he'll be, but he's being good today and so I decided to take the chance."

"I can't believe he's six months old already. Why did you have to move so far away? I never see you nowadays."

"It made sense to move when the farm down the road from Richard became empty. Mr Chalmers wanted it and it means I'm closer to Mother and Pa. At least if you want to visit Great Barr, there won't be a shortage of houses to stay in."

"I don't think Mr Wetherby would be happy if I stayed with Richard, I'm not even sure he'd let me stay with you, given how close you are to him."

"I thought you told him there was nothing between you."

"I did, but he still doesn't like him."

"Well, you'll have to come for the day. Mother and Pa would love to see you, and William Junior too."

"Perhaps." Mary looked down at the child in her arms. *Did she have to take him?* Amelia wouldn't mind having him for the day.

"What's the matter?"

"I'm just thinking. Mr Wetherby's going to the Great Exhibition in a couple of weeks. He's taking a group from church; perhaps I could come then, for the day."

"That sounds perfect. Will you bring William and Mary-Ann?"

"William's going with Mr Wetherby. I knew how excited he'd be about going on a train and so I asked Mr Wetherby to take him. I worry that now we have William Junior, my William will get neglected but Mr Wetherby was happy for him to go."

"You're lucky he's so good to them."

William arrived home from school two days later and went straight to see his mother. "I've missed you." He threw his arms around her neck. "Where's Mary-Ann, I thought she'd be waiting for me?"

"I misjudged the time and sent her on an errand; she'll be back soon. Tell me about school, how's it been?"

"It's hard work. We've been learning to write our letters and we have to spell all the words properly. We practise every morning. I'll show you later what I can write, it's quite a lot." He stood up straight, with a smile on his face.

"And what do you do in the afternoons?"

William's smile faded and he looked at his feet.

"What's the matter? What do you do in the afternoons?"

"We have to do numbers."

"That's good, isn't it? Mr Wetherby wants you to do numbers; you'll need them if you go into business."

"I know and I try, but I can't remember them. Sometimes I have to do extra practice when everyone else has gone back to the dormitories."

"If you practise hard I'm sure it'll come."

"I do practise, but the numbers get jumbled up in my head."

"Maybe Mr Wetherby could help you?"

"Please don't tell him." Panic spread across William's face. "I don't want him to be angry with me. Please, I'll make sure I can do them soon."

"Very well, I won't say anything, not yet anyway, but you must tell me if you're struggling."

William nodded reluctantly, but said nothing.

"I have a surprise for you," Mary said. "Mary-Ann's going to school with you when you go back."

The smile reappeared on William's face. "Will she? There aren't many girls there at the moment."

"She's lucky Mr Wetherby's happy to send her. She's very excited."

At that moment William Junior, who'd been asleep in the corner of the room, started crying.

"Is that a new baby?" William asked when he saw the tiny shape in the crib.

"This is your new brother." Mary picked William Junior up.

"When did he come?"

"Nearly a month ago."

"What's his name?"

Mary hesitated before she answered. "William."

"But that's my name. Why did you give him my name?"

"Mr Wetherby wanted to call him William because he said it was special … like you're special."

William smiled. "When I have a son I'm going to name him after Mr Wetherby because he's special too. I want to be like Mr Wetherby when I grow up."

Chapter 43

London, England.

THE TRAIN PULLED INTO EUSTON Station, London, five minutes before eleven o'clock. With a final screech of the brakes and the release of a large plume of steam, it ground to a halt. The third-class carriages at the back of the train were crowded, and William stood by Mr Wetherby's seat as he had for the entire journey. He didn't mind though, he was happy to be there. As the train stopped he moved to let Mr Wetherby and his father out, before he followed them onto the platform.

Outside the station a variety of carriages waited to take the travellers on the next leg of their journey. Mr Wetherby summoned four to take the twenty men from St George's church to Hyde Park.

As they entered the park, William's eyes grew wide with disbelief. The park was enormous and the paths were lined with fountains sited at regular intervals, some shooting water so high that he had to strain his neck to see the top before it fell back to the troughs below. The fountains kept him amused for several minutes before he noticed the Crystal Palace itself. It stood over three storeys high and towered over everything else on the landscape. It was made almost entirely of a cast iron frame with glass walls that carried an elegant arched roof over the centre.

"Mr Wetherby, look," he said. "Isn't that the most splendid thing you've ever seen? Have you ever seen a building built of so much glass before?"

"I don't believe I have. Did you know that most of the glass was made in Birmingham or Smethwick and transported down here later?"

"Was it really? I'd like to make something special one day. Do you think I could?"

"Anything's possible if you want it enough; you just have to believe in yourself and work hard."

William imagined himself working on the metal to make the frame and he took in every detail of the building as they approached it.

"Look, there are trees inside the building all the way through, and have you seen the size of the statues as well. And look over there, is that a row of railway engines and carriages I can see through the glass. Please can we go and see them close up?"

"All in good time." Mr Wetherby looked around. "We'll have to join the queue first, there must be thousands of people here already. I want you to stay close, no wandering off on your own; I'd never find you again amongst all these people and I don't want to tell your mother I lost you."

The queue moved in slow procession towards the door in the middle of the longest side of the building. Eventually they passed under the iron frame and the noise they'd endured outside became a murmur as the Crystal Palace threw a spell over them. A path was marked out for people to follow and they walked through the building in an orderly manner. Initially they were fascinated by an array of machines, unlike anything they had seen before, many of them performing tasks without any input from men. William wanted to stop and watch more closely but the crowd kept moving and he got little more than a glimpse of each. They continued to the scientific section where they saw new instruments that could send messages across great distances, see things that were too small for the naked eye, or keep time with perfect precision. They were still marvelling at the possibilities these devices could offer when they became aware of guards surrounding them. William took hold of Mr Wetherby's hand as they were directed into a specially partitioned room. Once inside he let out a loud sigh. There were caskets of diamonds and pearls alongside intricate work of goldsmiths and silversmiths, all displayed on velvet-covered stands. The gasps of wonder were audible as they filed past.

Finally they approached the section housing the railway engines. They saw for themselves the inside of the first-class carriages before they climbed into the engines to see the fire box and all the mechanisms that made these marvellous machines run. William lingered long after Mr Wetherby had left and it was almost twenty minutes later before he came back for him.

"William, didn't I tell you to stay close to me? We're all waiting for you." Mr Wetherby's voice could be heard over the noise. "You could've been left behind."

"I'm sorry, Mr Wetherby, I'm coming, but I don't want today to be over, it's been the best day of my life. Thank you for bringing me with you."

William feared that he might get a clip around the ear for being late, and was relieved when Mr Wetherby patted him on the shoulder.

"I'm glad you've enjoyed it," Mr Wetherby said. "I've enjoyed it too although I fear we've missed a lot. Perhaps we can come again, but for now we must hurry up. We've a train to catch."

Two weeks later, Mr Wetherby and William travelled back to the exhibition. They walked for over five hours and at the end of the day they were both exhausted. As they left the Crystal Palace they found a bench beside one of the fountains and sat down.

"I enjoyed today even more than last time," Mr Wetherby said. "I didn't need to worry about where everyone was and I could focus more on the machinery. What do you think; will machines take the place of people one day?"

"I don't know, I hope not. People need to work. What happens to their jobs if the machines take over?"

"There'll always be work, but machines could help increase the amount we produce, make us more profitable."

"Do you need to make more money?" William looked at Mr Wetherby. "I bet you already have quite a lot."

"You can never have too much, and there are always things you want to do with it. Besides, money gives you power. The more you have, the more influence you have on people."

"And is that what you want? To influence people?"

"Isn't that what everyone wants? The problem is you have to be prepared to work hard for it, which many people aren't. You don't get anything for nothing in this world."

William thought for a few moments. "What happens to the money when you die?"

"You can leave it to your friends and family, or you could leave it to the church or charity."

"So some people do get something for nothing?"

"But those people have usually been part of making the money in the first place and so it's only fair."

"Who will you leave your money to?"

"I've no intention of dying any time soon. Now come on, we'd better be going."

ভ⤫

By the time they got home, Mary was waiting for them. William Junior lay in his cot by the fire and she had a pan of water sitting over the flames.

"Did you have a good day?" she said as they walked in. She expected William to be full of stories as he had been after their first visit, but he was subdued.

"Better than last time," Mr Wetherby said without taking his hat off. "It's given me so many ideas. You tell your mother, William, I need to go to the workshop for a couple of minutes."

"What's the matter?" Mary asked when she was alone with William. "You don't seem very happy."

"I am, but Mr Wetherby seems keen on all the machines. I think they'll end up taking everyone's jobs and it doesn't seem right."

"I'm sure he knows what he's doing, he'll do the right thing." Mary wished she believed what she was saying.

"You're right. Mr Wetherby would never do anything to upset anyone. He'll only do things to make them better."

Chapter 44

Aldridge, Staffordshire.

Mr Jackson handed the spade back to the rector and bowed his head. His son Richard stood by his side and together they led the mourners away from the graveside, back to the shelter of the church.

Mary waited inside the building with Martha before they made the short journey back to the house. Sarah-Ann had stayed at home to prepare the food and by the time they arrived everything was ready. It was the first time Mary had been to the new house in Aldridge, but it felt as if they had never been away.

"It's such a shame we hadn't been living here long," Sarah-Ann said. "Mother loved it here. At least she was at peace in the end."

"Your father will need you more than ever now."

"He will. I've asked him to move back to Birmingham but he won't hear of it, he has his houses to manage here."

"He has more houses and premises in Birmingham than he does here, surely he'd be better placed down there?"

"He has someone to collect the rents in Birmingham, otherwise it would be too much for him."

"You'll meet somebody one day, you know." Mary understood her sister-in-law's desire to move.

"Maybe, but I worry that I'll never have a child; time's moving on."

Mary squeezed Sarah-Ann's hand, knowing she couldn't argue without wishing her father-in-law dead. She turned to look for Mr Wetherby, when she heard a voice behind her.

"Good afternoon, Mary, it's been a long time."

Her flesh tingled and she took a deep breath before she turned around. "Good afternoon, Richard, you're looking well."

"So are you … very well."

Mary's cheeks coloured. *What was it about his smile?* "I'm sorry about Mother, it came as such a shock."

"It did, but she lived to a good age. At least Father still has Sarah-Ann. Have you heard I'm moving to Birmingham?"

Mary raised an eyebrow. "You surprise me."

"There's no future in farming now they're using machines. I don't like to leave Father at a time like this, but we've four extra mouths to feed and there's not enough to go around."

Mary nodded. "I'm sure he understands. It'll be nice to see you around Birmingham. What will you do when you're there?"

"I'm going to work in Pa's brassfoundry on Bath Street. He asked the tenant to give me a job. Are you on Summer Lane now?"

"Just off, on Hatchett Street."

"Mrs Richard will be pleased, she hoped you'd be close

by, because she doesn't know many people in Birmingham. Is the brassfoundry on Paradise Street still there, the one Charles worked in? I used to know some of the lads and thought I'd pay them a visit."

"It closed a couple of years ago, though some of the men may have moved to Bath Street."

"Who's moving to Bath Street?" Mr Wetherby put his arm around Mary as he joined them.

"I am," Richard said.

Mr Wetherby glared at him; unsure whether he should even acknowledge him. "May I offer my condolences?"

"Thank you. It was good of you to come, you hardly knew my mother."

"I'd met her several times and she was very good to Mary. She wanted to be here and I didn't want to trust her well-being to anyone else."

Richard looked at Mary with concern. "Have you been ill? Did you come into contact with the cholera when it was in Birmingham?"

Mr Wetherby answered for her. "Thank you for your concern, sir, but no, my wife was not affected by the cholera. Unfortunately it would appear she has other, more *delicate* problems, and I insist she takes bed rest every afternoon. I worry that a day such as this will be too much for her. In fact," he pulled out his new pocket watch, "we must be going soon. She needs to get back to the children."

"How old is William now?" Richard asked. "It's too long since I saw him."

"He'll be fourteen in the summer." Mary let a smile cross her face. "Mary-Ann's twelve. They're both at school at the moment."

"I believe you have another son now too?"

"She has my son, William Junior. He's the apple of her eye."

Richard glared at Mr Wetherby before he looked back at Mary. "Let me find you a seat."

"Really, I'm fine, there's no need," Mary said.

"There's every need. I don't want anything to happen to you." Richard led her to a seat. "You must eat something before you leave, I'll get Mrs Richard to bring something over to you."

"There's no need for that," Mr Wetherby said. "I can assist my wife myself, thank you."

"Well, make sure you do," Richard said. "She's a very special lady."

Richard was barely out of earshot before Mr Wetherby demanded an explanation. "What's he moving to Bath Street for?"

"To work. If you remember his father has a brassfoundry there."

"Why's he leaving farming all of a sudden?"

"He said there's no money in it. There are lots of families moving from the country to the town, it's not unusual."

"I don't like it. Bath Street's too close for comfort, we need to move house."

"Now you're being silly, there's no need for that."

"I happen to think there is."

৵৵

Sarah-Ann watched the exchange, and once Mary and Mr Wetherby were alone she walked over to them with a plate of pork pies and cold meat.

"Is everything all right?" she said. "You don't look happy."

"We're fine," Mr Wetherby said. "Mary's tired, but I'm sure she'll feel better now you're here."

"I think she looks well." Sarah-Ann offered Mary the plate. "You seem to have recovered from your latest misfortune. Let's hope there's a healthy baby next time."

"I hope so, although I don't know if I have the energy to carry another one. Losing two so close to each other takes its toll."

"You'll be fine as long as you take enough bed rest," Mr Wetherby said. "You always want to do too much."

"You're so fortunate to have Mr Wetherby to take care of you," Sarah-Ann said. "Mother worried about you for a long time after you moved back to Birmingham, but she was happy once she knew you were settled. She'd be pleased that you were here today Mr Wetherby. Thank you for joining us."

Mr Wetherby puffed out his chest. "That's kind of you to say. I was rather fond of her as it happens, always a happy lady. It's good to see you too of course."

"Are we going soon?" Mary put her hand on Mr Wetherby's arm. "You said we had to get back to the children."

"We do, but I agree with Miss Jackson that you're looking well today. You have a bit of colour in your cheeks. I'm sure Mrs Carrick can manage William Junior for another hour. It would be a shame to come all this way and not spend any time with Miss Jackson."

Chapter 45

Birmingham, Warwickshire.

MR WETHERBY SAT AT THE desk in front of the window frowning at his ledgers. William stood to his right-hand side trying to make sense of the figures. He had recently finished school for good and although he expected to start his apprenticeship within the next few weeks, he wasn't sure he was ready for it.

"Sales aren't going as well as they should be." The lines on Mr Wetherby's forehead deepened. "There's too much competition. Do you realise, another six hook and eye manufacturers have started trading in the last six months? That's over thirty of us by my reckoning."

William said nothing. It looked to him as if the numbers were increasing, but he knew his sums weren't as good as they should be.

"The profit margins should be growing faster too," Mr Wetherby continued. "With the cost of wire increasing as it is, and the wages I need to pay all those women, I'm barely making any money. I've been thinking about it for a while now and I've decided I need to move into something more lucrative."

"What will you do?" William asked.

"Make buttons."

"Buttons?" It was William's turn to frown.

"People can't get enough of them at the moment. They're using them to fasten their clothes as well as for decoration."

"Are we going to get some of the machinery we saw at the Great Exhibition?"

"Not for these. I've been looking into it over the last few months and it would take too long to pay the money back to the bank. No, we're going to make buttons that don't need machinery, pearl buttons. Craftsmen make them from shells, and the workshop will be perfect. It's not like making black or brass buttons where you need to work the metal or melt glass."

"Won't it be more expensive if you have to employ men?"

"It will, but their wages will be more than made up for by the number of women I can get rid of. They're costing me too much. I'll carry on making hooks and eyes for certain customers, but I reckon we can probably get rid of at least eighty women."

William gasped. "That's nearly all of them. What will they do?"

"They'll find something else, I can't keep paying them for work I don't want." He paused and turned to look at William. "I also believe that we should diversify further if we want to grow the business."

"What are you thinking?"

"Toolmaking."

"Toolmaking? How will you do that?"

"I've met a man called Mr Watkins who's a file manufacturer. He has his own premises and he's looking for an apprentice. I know how excited you were about working with metal when we went to the exhibition and I've decided it will be a good opportunity for you to learn your own trade. I've spoken to him and he's willing to take you on for an acceptable fee. We only need to get the indenture signed."

"So I won't be working with you?" Inexplicably, a wave of relief swept over William.

"Eventually you will. Once you're qualified, you can come back and bring your new skills with you."

William shuffled his feet, unsure whether he should hide his smile. He'd expected to work for Mr Wetherby for the next seven years, but he thought he would be much happier as a toolmaker. He'd never met this man Watkins before, and knew nothing about him, but he was excited to be given the chance to show Mr Wetherby that he could do something on his own.

ভ৵৶

Mary had gone to get some water from the courtyard and she stopped to talk to her neighbour. She said goodbye and took a step towards the alley, when she heard Richard calling her name.

"I thought you lived around here." He gave her a broad smile. "Are you alone?"

"What are you doing here?" Mary shot a glance at the front door. "Mr Wetherby's probably seen you pass the window; don't be surprised if he comes out."

"That's unfortunate. You're looking as lovely as ever."

"Richard!" Mary's face flushed.

"Are you harassing my wife?" Mr Wetherby pushed past Richard to stand next to Mary.

"I was only being courteous. It'd be rude, don't you think, to see someone you know and not speak to them?"

"What brings you to Hatchett Street? I doubt you were just passing."

Richard rolled his eyes. "As it happens I've been to see a friend who lives around here, but even if I hadn't, I have the right to walk down the street."

"I'll have less of your impertinence." Mr Wetherby took the water jug from Mary. "You get back inside, I'll fetch the water; Mr Jackson's leaving."

Mary ducked into the house as the two men stood glaring at each other. Eventually Richard raised his hat to her and walked away. She stood in the doorway for as long as she dared, watching Richard disappear from view. She was about to shut the front door when she saw the postman heading towards her. She took the letter from him and tore open the envelope.

> *Dear Mary*
>
> *I wanted to let you know that Father has been ill this week and the doctor's told him to stay in bed. He might not have long left with us. If you could visit soon it might be for the best.*
>
> *Alice*

Mary closed her eyes and prayed that Alice was being overly cautious. She didn't want her father to die. Not yet. As soon as Mr Wetherby came back with the water, she showed him the letter.

"Can I go and see him tomorrow?" she asked as he read it. "I don't want to wait too long in case he doesn't make it."

"Why don't you stay for a few days?" Mr Wetherby said. "Alice might like the company, and now Mary-Ann's back, she can take care of William Junior."

"Is everything all right?" A frown spread across Mary's face. She'd never known him suggest she stay away before.

"It will be. I'll arrange a carriage now while I remember."

Chapter 46

AT NINE O'CLOCK THE FOLLOWING morning, Mary boarded the carriage to Shenstone. It was a slow journey and it had turned midday before she arrived. Alice opened the door before she had a chance to knock.

"Thank you for coming." Alice took Mary's cape and showed her into the living room. "Father's in bed. He was sleeping last time I looked in on him but perhaps you can go and see if he's woken up?"

Mary went up the stairs and opened the door quietly. Her father stirred as she went in and smiled at her.

"You came."

"Of course I came. Why wouldn't I?" Mary pulled up a chair and sat close to him.

"No reason. I'm just glad Alice told you this time."

"This time? What do you mean?"

"Nothing." Mr Chadwick stopped to gasp for air.

"Please, tell me." Mary took his hand. "What do you mean?"

Her father hesitated before he spoke. "When your

mother was ill, she asked Alice to contact you. She wanted you to visit."

"Mother wanted to see me?" Tears formed in Mary's eyes. "Why didn't Alice write then? It wasn't because you didn't have my address, was it?"

"She thought she was doing it for the best."

"What could be better than asking me to visit my mother on her death bed? Especially under the circumstances."

"It wasn't like that; she didn't do it on purpose." He paused to take another breath. "Your mother became ill shortly after Charles died. We thought she'd get well again and Alice didn't want to upset you when there was no need."

"I knew you had my address. Why all the lies about Bath Street? You could at least have invited me to the funeral."

"Alice didn't want you to be angry with her."

Tears dripped down Mary's face. "What did I do to upset her so much? She was the only one who didn't seem to care when you banished me, and now I find out she chose not to tell me about my own mother's funeral."

"It wasn't like that. She grew close to your mother after you left and I suspect she didn't want you to come back and push her out."

"Did Mother forgive me?" The pain of her mother's words had never left Mary.

"She wouldn't have wanted to see you if she hadn't. Now, no more talk of it. What's past is past. Does the fact you're here mean that Alice thinks I won't get well again?"

"Of course not. It simply means I'm strong enough to deal with it now."

"And are you? You've had a hard time this last year or so."

"I'm fine." Mary looked at the floor; her inability to have any more children wasn't a conversation she wanted to have with her father.

"Is Mr Wetherby taking care of you?"

"He is, and he's good with the children."

"I can rest in peace then. You mean the world to me, Mary, you always did."

"I couldn't help falling in love with a non-conformist, I just wanted you to accept him; he was a good man."

"I know that now." He patted her hand and rested his head back on the pillow.

Mary sat for a while longer, listening to the rattle of her father's chest as it heaved up and down, but before long she tidied the bedclothes around him and went back downstairs.

"He'll sleep now," she said to Alice as she entered the living room. "We had quite a chat."

Alice paled. "What did he say?"

"He told me that Mother asked you to find me, but you chose not to. You also made the decision not to invite me to the funeral."

"I thought it was for the best."

"Who are you to make a decision like that? It might have been best for you, but it wasn't for me or Mother."

"Was that all he said?"

"Was there something he missed?" Mary couldn't disguise the anger in her voice.

"Of course not. I just wondered."

"I'm staying at the tavern for a few days, or at least until I know whether Father will get well again. I'll see you tomorrow."

Mary left Alice sitting by the fire. Once she arrived at the tavern, she lay on the bed, but she couldn't sleep. At least she knew her mother had forgiven her, but it didn't help. She should have been with her. Who was Alice to deprive her of that? She closed her eyes and saw Alice's face the night she was thrown out. Cold and hard, without a hint of affection; not the happy face she had once known. As children they had not only shared a bedroom, they had shared their most intimate thoughts and dreams. She remembered telling Alice about Charles and of her excitement when he had tried to kiss her. Looking back, that was when things had changed.

She was about to doze off when she sat bolt upright. Was Alice the reason her father had caught her in the barn with Charles? It had never occurred to her before, but suddenly it made sense. Alice always knew where she was, to the point where Mary often suspected her of spying on her. Had she been jealous of the friendship she was developing with Charles? Did she want Charles for herself? Surely it wasn't a reason to have her banished. What would she have to gain? She remembered the moment her father threw her from the kitchen door and felt sure there was a smirk on Alice's lips. *Dear God, please let me be wrong.*

Mary spent much of the following day with her father. She wanted to mention her suspicions about Alice, but he was too weak to talk and spent most of the day asleep. When she went downstairs for something to eat, she knew she had Alice to herself.

"I hoped to have another talk with Father today," Mary

said as she accepted her plate of food. "Unfortunately he seems to have taken a turn for the worse since last night."

"You should let him rest," Alice said. "He won't get better if you keep disturbing him."

"I wanted to ask him why he came into the barn the afternoon I was there with Charles."

Alice coughed as she choked on some bread. "What do you want to ask him that for? It was his barn; he often went in there."

"Not at that time of day he didn't. I've been wondering whether someone told him we were in there."

"I know you're upset, but now you're being silly," Alice said.

"I remember you telling me the first night Charles came to the farm how good looking he was. Were you jealous?"

Alice stood up and collected up the dishes, even though they weren't empty. "I haven't got time to sit and listen to this, Father may be awake and I need to go and see him."

"I'll come with you; if he's awake, maybe he'll talk to me."

Mr Chadwick didn't wake all afternoon and by the time Mary arrived the following morning, Alice had drawn the curtains and stopped the clocks at twenty-three minutes to six.

"So that's it then," Mary said once the doctor left them. "We'll need to write to John, Katharine and Susannah and let them know, assuming you don't have any objections."

"Are you going to keep this up?" Alice snapped. "I made a mistake, I'm sorry. Can't we let it rest?"

"Maybe, once I know the truth about that afternoon. I

think you were watching me, like you always did, and when you knew we were together you told Father."

"I did no such thing."

"As you wish, but I know what I believe. I'm going back to Birmingham, there's nothing to keep me here. I'll call at the undertakers and register the death on my way. If you've anything to tell me, I'll be back for the funeral."

Chapter 47

Shenstone, Staffordshire.

THE LEAVES WERE CHANGING TO their autumn colours, and the sun no longer sat high in the sky, but as Mary and Mr Wetherby arrived for her father's funeral the day was bright. It was five days since his death and she hadn't slept properly since.

"Is this it?" Mr Wetherby was dismayed when he saw a solitary horse harnessed to the hearse and only two small carriages behind it.

"It's only a small community and most of his friends are already dead," Mary said. "All the villagers knew him, so they'll walk behind the hearse and join us in church. At least all the family should be here. We haven't been together for nearly fifteen years."

"We should have brought William and Mary-Ann to make up the numbers. At least you've seen Alice recently."

"Hmmm."

"What does that mean? You've not been yourself since you came home and you've been quiet all the way here. Is there a problem?"

"Nothing for you to worry about. I just want to get inside before people start arriving."

Mary knocked on the door and let herself in before Alice could answer.

"Oh, it's you." Alice showed no emotion when she saw Mary.

"Why are you so surprised? Did you think I wouldn't turn up for this funeral as well?"

"What's going on?" Mr Wetherby said.

"I made a mistake and she can't let it drop; I'm surprised she hasn't told you." Alice glared at Mary.

Mr Wetherby was about to speak when a tall man with pale ginger hair and a full beard came into the room. Mary recognised him instantly.

"John." She turned and walked towards him. "It's good to see you; remember me?"

"Mary? My goodness, look at you. Where've you been all these years?"

Mary threw her arms around her brother before she introduced Mr Wetherby. Before she could ask him what he'd been doing, Alice interrupted them.

"John," Alice said.

"Alice," he replied, before he turned back to Mary.

The moment wasn't lost on Mary. John had barely glanced at Alice and now acted as if she wasn't there. After a few moments, Alice moved away.

"What did she do to you?" Mary nodded in Alice's direction.

"Didn't you hear? When I was walking out with Mrs Chadwick here, before we were married, Alice introduced her to someone she'd met at work and tried to ruin our relationship. She did a similar thing with Katharine. She didn't want either of us to get married and leave her on her own."

"She is so selfish," Mary said.

"You're right. She couldn't bear to let other people have what she didn't have. Fortunately, she caused no lasting damage for me, but the fellow ended up leaving Katharine; she was devastated."

"Alice was jealous," Mary said, without explanation.

"Why would she be jealous? All she needed to do was find a husband of her own and we could've all been happy."

"Because she couldn't have the man she wanted."

John looked at her. "How do you know?"

Mary glanced at Mr Wetherby, not sure how he would react to her next sentence. "I don't know for sure, but I suspect she was responsible for Father finding me with Charles. She won't admit it, of course, but I think she wanted Charles for herself."

"What are you talking about?" Mr Wetherby asked.

How did she explain herself without getting into more trouble? "Father saw Charles ... with his arm around me ... and threw him off the farm."

"It was more serious than that," John said.

"It wasn't really." Mary's eyes pleaded with John to say no more.

"I meant it was because he threw Charles out that you ended up leaving us."

"Yes, of course, that was it. If it hadn't been for her, things would have been very different."

Mary sensed Mr Wetherby was studying her.

"What do we do about her?" John asked.

"I don't know. Father asked me to forgive her for not telling me about Mother. You know about that, I presume? He didn't mention the other thing."

John looked across to Alice as she talked to Susannah. "We'll talk about it later. It's time we were on our way."

The funeral was short and as the men walked to the graveside, the ladies went back to the house to lay out the food. Mary walked with Katharine and Susannah while Alice walked alone.

"We can't leave her on her own, look at her," Susannah said.

"I'm on my own because of her," Katharine said.

"You must forgive her." Susannah linked her arm through her sister's. "She made a mistake but she shouldn't have to pay for it for the rest of her life."

"She made more than one mistake; she tried to ruin John and Mary's lives as well and she's never once apologised."

"Maybe not, but for the sake of the family can we put it behind us? Let's not forget the only reason we're together today is because Father died; it could be any one of us next. I don't want everyone to lose touch again because of things that happened years ago."

Once the last of the guests had left, the family sat down together to resolve their differences. It wasn't a conversation Mary expected, but it wasn't long before Alice admitted it was a fear of being left alone that had made her cause so much trouble for John and Katharine. She also admitted she'd destroyed Mary's address because she'd feared she would come back and steal her mother's affection. With

Mr Wetherby sat at her side, Mary didn't press about the incident with Charles.

Despite everything she had done, Mary couldn't help feeling sorry for her sister. Once they were alone she sat down with her to ask about her future.

"What will you do now?" Mary asked.

"I don't know. I've never been on my own before."

"What about moving to Birmingham?"

"I didn't think you'd want me so close."

"I've been without you for over fifteen years; we've got a lot of catching up to do."

Alice smiled. "I don't deserve you. Why did you turn out so nice, while I always manage to be nasty, even if I don't mean to be?"

"That's enough, we're not talking about it anymore." Mary turned to Mr Wetherby who stood looking out of the window. "Can Alice have a room in one of your properties?"

"I don't see why not. There's a costermonger in Shadwell Street who's missed a couple of weeks' rent. I was going to move him on."

Mary turned back to Alice. "That's not far from us. What do you say?"

Alice looked around the small room she had called home for almost ten years. "Where would I work?"

Mary looked to Mr Wetherby who continued to look out of the window. "I might be able to get you a job with an acquaintance of mine. He runs a warehouse and often takes on casual labour. Let me talk to him."

Mary frowned. He had over one hundred women and girls working for him, surely he could find room for one more? Deciding now wasn't the time to argue, she turned back to Alice. "Think about it, and I'll write when we have news of a job."

On their way back to Birmingham, Mary's curiosity got the better of her.

"Thank you for agreeing to find Alice a job, but why didn't you offer her a place in the workshop?"

"I'm making some changes and I'm not taking anyone else on."

"Changes? What will you do?"

"I'm going to make buttons. I can charge more for them and use fewer employees. I need to take on a few craftsmen to do the specialised work, but I'm losing about eighty women from the payroll."

"Eighty women?" Mary turned with a look of concern on her face. "Is that why William isn't doing his apprenticeship with you?"

"One of the reasons."

"But what about the women? They need their jobs. Many are the only breadwinners and several have husbands who've gone to the Russian War. They don't even know if they'll come back, let alone when. You've seen in *The Times* how bad things are out there."

Mr Wetherby looked through the carriage window. "I'm sure they'll find something else, but if it makes you happy I'll keep those that need it most. I'm still making some hooks and eyes."

"When will you tell them?"

"Soon. I've found a supply of good quality shells, so all I need to do now is find some men to work for me; an extra shilling a week on top of what they're earning should do the trick."

Mary spent the rest of the carriage ride in silence. What about the children who would go hungry, or worse still, those who might lose the roof over their heads? She'd always been proud that he helped so many families, but this was the other side of it and she hated the responsibility, even if it wasn't her making the decisions.

Chapter 48

Birmingham, Warwickshire.

MARY FINISHED PUTTING THE FOOD on the table and looked at the grandfather clock. William and Mr Wetherby should be home by now, but there was no sign of them. She went to the front door and looked out, but all she saw was Alice walking towards her.

"I wasn't expecting to see you so soon," Mary said as she approached the door.

"It was a quiet day at work so we were allowed to leave early, I'm not sure why."

"It's about time, you've barely stopped since you arrived here."

"I don't mind, at least when I'm busy I can't sit around brooding."

Mary ushered her inside before she continued. "What have you got to worry about?"

"Nothing much, I'm just on my own a lot and I suppose I'd like a little company."

"You're always welcome here, you know that."

"I know, but I can't come every night. I need to make friends of my own, but it's easier said than done."

A look of concern crossed Mary's face. "Aren't warehouses full of women our age?"

"Not where I am."

"It's early days; you've not been there two months yet, give it time."

"If only it were that simple, I can't connect with people the same way you do."

"I'm sure you'll be fine." As she spoke, William arrived home. "Where've you been? Isn't Mr Wetherby with you?"

"He's still in the workshop with a visitor." William took off his hat and coat and hung them on the coat stand.

"Who is it?"

"I don't know, I haven't seen him before, but it looked serious. They were looking at some books, and when I asked if he wanted me to lock up, he sent me away."

It was another fifteen minutes before Mr Wetherby appeared. He took off his hat and coat, hung them on the stand next to William's, and sat down without a word. Mary made a pot of tea and sat down next to him. It was only once they had finished eating that Mr Wetherby spoke.

"I'm going to London for the day next Thursday; I'll need to leave early."

"London! Are you doing anything special?" Mary asked.

"I've been invited to buy some shares in the Birmingham Banking Company. I need to go to London to sign the paperwork."

"That sounds grand."

"It is, but you don't get anywhere in this world without making an effort. We still need to move house as well; this place is too small."

Mary looked surprised. "I didn't think you wanted to move away from the workshop. Will you move that as well?"

"I haven't decided yet. I need to have a good look around and see what I can find."

The following Thursday, Mr Wetherby was up unusually early so he could catch the six o'clock train to London. As Mary tidied away the breakfast things he kissed her on the cheek and went out into the dark morning. It was laundry day and to make the most of the early start Mary-Ann went to the washhouse to get the fire going under the copper.

Mary stayed in the house to tidy the breakfast dishes, but as she straightened up from the table she saw stars dancing before her eyes. She immediately grabbed the back of a chair to stop herself falling, before she managed to sit down. As a wave of nausea threatened to overwhelm her, she took several deep breaths before pouring a cup of gin. Several minutes later, the feelings subsided enough for her to stand up and make her way outside.

"Mother, whatever's the matter?" Mary-Ann asked when she saw her.

"Nothing, why?"

"You've gone white …"

"I'm fine, just went a bit dizzy. Let's get these clothes into the water."

They worked for the next hour pounding the clothes, rubbing the shirt collars and squeezing them through the mangle. Eventually, they took the washing back to the house and hung it on the rack over the fire.

"I think I'll go and have a lie down," Mary said once

they were finished. "I've gone lightheaded again; I expect I got up too early this morning. I'll be fine if I can have another half an hour in bed."

Half an hour came and went but Mary remained in bed. Waves of nausea continued to pass over her and as the day went on, even lifting her head from the pillow made her dizzy. When Mr Wetherby arrived home she was still in the bedroom. He went straight to see her.

"Mary, whatever's the matter? Have you called the doctor?"

"I don't need the doctor; I'll be fine by tomorrow. I'm probably tired."

"At least you're in the right place, but if you're no better by the morning I'm calling the doctor."

Mary sighed. "There's no need for that."

"You'll do as you're told. Now try and get some sleep and I'll be back later."

The following morning Mary was still unable to lift her head off the pillow and Mr Wetherby went for the doctor. He wasn't with her long before he shared his diagnosis.

"Madam, I'm surprised you don't recognise the signs by now, you'll be having another baby later this year."

"A baby? I've never been ill like this before, I'm usually perfectly well, at least in the early stages."

"All pregnancies are different and after your recent losses your body may well have changed. You're older now as well. You must take plenty of bed rest and no more hard chores. We need to keep the baby safe this time."

Five minutes later Mr Wetherby arrived upstairs, a broad smile across his face.

"Another chance for a brother for William Junior, I hear."

"Yes," Mary said, "but he already has a brother … and a sister."

"I've told you before, that's not the same; William's only a half-brother. After what happened last year, and the year before, I'm not letting you leave this bed without my permission. I don't want you losing another baby."

"I won't, please just let me have some visitors, otherwise I'll go mad."

"Selected visitors only; Alice, Martha, and Sarah-Ann when she's in Birmingham, and that's it."

Chapter 49

MARY THOUGHT HER ILLNESS WOULD never end. She had been sicker than she had ever been in her life and instead of looking well for a bit of extra weight, she looked as if she hadn't eaten for months, which in fact she hadn't. The doctor had been at a loss with what to do for her but fortunately over the last few weeks she had managed to keep some bread down and started to feel like a human being again. She knew she must be getting better when she began resenting being in bed all day. As she sat up in bed embroidering one afternoon, Mary-Ann knocked on the door.

"Mother, Aunt Martha's here."

"Martha, how good to see you." Mary straightened herself up and put her needlework to one side. "You should have told me you were coming, I'd have made an effort."

"There's no need for that, I know how ill you've been. I'm just glad to see you sitting up and smiling again."

"Not as glad as I am."

"What's been the problem? It's not all down to the baby, is it?"

Mary shrugged. "The doctor's not sure, but he thinks it could be."

"Still, you must be pleased you're expecting again."

"Would it be wrong if I said I wasn't?"

A look of surprise crossed Martha's face. "Why wouldn't you be? William Junior's five this year, it's about time he had a brother or sister."

"I'm frightened, Martha." Tears welled up in Mary's eyes.

"Whatever for? You've nothing to be afraid of; you've already had three children."

"I nearly died when I had William Junior and all I could think of was leaving William and Mary-Ann alone. What would happen to them if I wasn't here? They're still children and I don't know that Mr Wetherby would take such good care of them without me."

"I'm sure he would, he thinks the world of William."

"And then there are the babies I lost last year and the year before. To know that you have a life inside you, that you can feel kicking, and then suddenly it stops but you have to go through the birth anyway. As much as I'd love another child, I don't know if I can do it again."

"Well, you're doing the right thing this time and Mr Wetherby will make sure you have the best care. Speaking of Mr Wetherby, I was surprised to hear William was doing his apprenticeship with someone else, they haven't fallen out, have they?"

"It's since their visits to the Great Exhibition. Mr Wetherby thinks machines are the future and he wants William to train as a machinist. He's working for someone called Mr Watkins, but he'll come back to work here when he's trained. I worried for a long time that William was too gentle to stand up to Mr Wetherby, but hopefully this will do him good."

"Mr Wetherby always seems to get his own way."

"What do you mean?"

Martha lowered her voice to a whisper. "I hope I'm not telling tales here, but I take it you heard about Richard?"

"What about him?"

"He's moved back to Sutton Coldfield."

"I know that, he went at the end of last year. Why's that telling tales?"

"I take it you didn't hear why he moved?" Mary shook her head and Martha continued. "It wasn't because he couldn't settle in Birmingham. It was because Mr Wetherby made sure he lost his job and couldn't get another one in the area."

Mary sat up straight in bed. "Mr Wetherby wouldn't do that."

"That's what Richard said. He's convinced it was him."

"But he's no proof."

"Nothing certain, but a lot of people have told him the same thing."

"That was September last year, wasn't it?" Mary felt a knot tightening in her stomach. It all made sense now. It was when she went to Shenstone, just before her father died. Her absence would have given Mr Wetherby the time he needed; it would also explain why he dropped the idea of moving house. "I wish you hadn't told me that. Please don't ever cross him will you?"

Martha stood up to leave when Mr Wetherby came into the bedroom, but he insisted she stay to hear his news.

"You remember I said we needed a bigger house, well

I've found one, off Summer Lane in Wilby Place. It has two rooms downstairs and then two further floors with two bedrooms on each floor."

"I thought you'd gone off the idea of moving," Mary said.

"I had, but I happened to come across this and it's perfect."

"Mr Wetherby, forgive me if I'm speaking out of turn," Martha said. "Is Mary in a position to move house at the moment? She needs rest."

"Indeed she does and that's where I hope you can help out. Now you're back in Birmingham can she come and stay with you while we move? I'll arrange a carriage to take her from door to door. Nobody wants her to stay safe more than I do, but this new house will be worth the move. It also means that her sister can move in with us if she wants to."

"She'd like that," Mary said. "She's finding it more difficult than she expected to make friends. When will we move?"

"I've arranged to take possession at the beginning of next month which gives us a few weeks yet, but I don't want you to worry about it at all."

"I already feel better than I was," Mary said. "I should be able to get out of bed for a few hours each afternoon to help with the packing."

"You'll do no such thing, you can leave it to Mary-Ann. She's fourteen now and perfectly capable of doing it."

Three weeks later, Mr Wetherby helped Mary and William

Junior into a carriage and escorted them to Martha's house. She was waiting for them with a cup of tea and as soon as Mary was settled he left and went to supervise the move to Wilby Place.

"How are you feeling?" Martha asked.

"I wish he'd let me stay to help. Now the sickness has passed I've got more energy than I've had for years. I should be helping Mary-Ann, she doesn't know how I want all the furniture arranged."

"After everything you've been through I'm glad he's got more sense. Alice will be there to help her."

"I suppose you're right. He's got a couple of men to help him move everything. They're just back from the Russian War. Mrs Gower from the workshop was so relieved to see Mr Gower again; she's really struggled over the last two years. I can't help but worry about women like her. I know that if it weren't for the grace of God I'd be struggling like that."

Chapter 50

A S SUMMER REACHED ITS HEIGHT, and Mary went past the stage where she had lost her previous babies, she convinced Mr Wetherby she was well enough to go downstairs. Most afternoons she would sit in the shade by the front door, fanning herself with a newspaper, but even then the temperature was unrelenting. Several times over the last week her vision had dimmed as she stood up but, not wanting to be returned to bed, she had told no one.

Late one afternoon she stood up to go back into the house, when she again saw stars swirling before her eyes. She held onto the doorframe until the spinning stopped, but as she walked down the hall her vision narrowed and she tumbled to the floor. She lost consciousness before she hit the floor and when she opened her eyes, people surrounded her. William and Alice were there, but it was Mr Wetherby who spoke.

"Mary, what happened; are you all right?"

"I don't know … everything went black, that's the last I remember."

"Mary-Ann's gone for Dr Andrews and he should be here soon. Let me get you upstairs."

Mr Wetherby helped her up the stairs and onto the bed.

As she waited for the doctor, tears started to roll down her face.

"It's going to happen again, isn't it?" She took hold of Mr Wetherby's hand. "After everything I've been through, with the sickness and confinement, I'm going to lose this baby too, aren't I?"

"You don't know that." Mr Wetherby wiped her tears with his handkerchief.

"I can't feel any movement, I haven't since I came round. I must have killed the baby when I fell."

"Let's wait and see what the doctor says." Mr Wetherby absently wiped the palms of his hands on his trousers.

"I won't be able to live with myself if I lose it now. Please don't be angry with me."

"Come here." Mr Wetherby put his arms around her. "I promise this will be the last time you go through this. It's difficult for me as well as you; I don't want to lose you. Let's pray that the Lord will deliver you safely." Mr Wetherby was about to say a prayer when the bedroom door opened and the doctor walked in.

"Let's have a look at you," the doctor said as he set his bag down. "I expect you just fainted, this weather's far too hot. Did you hurt yourself?"

"It didn't hurt me, but I don't know about the baby. I haven't felt it moving since I fell."

"Let me listen." The doctor cupped his hands around his ear and put it to her belly before a frown settled on his face.

"Can you hear anything?" Mr Wetherby's eyes darted between Mary and the doctor.

"I can hear something, but the beat sounds irregular."

"Does that mean it's still alive?" Mr Wetherby asked.

The doctor pressed his hands around Mary's abdomen and after a moment there were signs of movement. "It looks like it."

A smile removed the tension from Mary's face. "I don't know what you did, doctor, whatever it was, it feels like it's having a fight in there."

"That's a relief," Mr Wetherby said.

The doctor placed his hands on her stomach again to feel the movement. "Nothing to worry about, but I'd advise you to stay in bed until the baby is born. That heartbeat is still concerning me."

Two days later, when Mr Wetherby was at work, the familiar ache started around Mary's belly. At first she thought she was imagining it, but within an hour the pain had intensified and she knew the baby was coming. She shouted for Mary-Ann to get Mr Wetherby and lay back on the bed as another contraction arrived.

"Why didn't you tell me sooner?" Mr Wetherby said as he swept into the room. "I hope the doctor isn't busy."

"I didn't know things would happen so quickly. You'd better go and get him; I'm not sure I can hold on for much longer. Send Mary-Ann for Mrs Tompkins too."

Once she was alone, the contractions became more frequent and as the searing pain set in, her mind became oblivious to everything except the baby within her. Within minutes the contractions were too strong, the pain too intense and she had an overwhelming urge to push. The baby was coming and she couldn't stop it. *Where was the doctor? He should be here. She shouldn't be on her own. What if the baby gets stuck?*

"Somebody help," she cried as one contraction ended and another threatened to start. "I can't do this."

Her voice went unheard in the empty house and as the next contraction came, she couldn't stop herself pushing down on the baby, letting out a scream of desperation as she did. *She was going to die.* Moments later the bedroom door opened and the doctor went straight to her, followed by Mrs Tompkins.

"The head's out," the doctor said. "We haven't got much time."

Mrs Tompkins raced to the door and shouted for some water before she went back to Mary's side.

"Stay calm, Mrs Wetherby, you can do this."

Mary tensed every muscle in her body, praying the baby would be safe.

"It's nearly here," the doctor said. "Push now."

Mary did as she was told and a minute later she heard the cry of her newborn baby.

"A healthy baby boy," the doctor said as he handed him to Mrs Tompkins.

"Praise the Lord." Mrs Tompkins laid him on a cloth and wrapped him up. She was about to pass him to Mary when Dr Andrews held up his hand.

"There's another baby …"

"Another one … ? No, there can't be … Please, make this stop."

Mrs Tompkins put the first child down and hurried to wipe the tears that were running down the sides of Mary's face. Mary reached for the midwife's hands and clung to her.

"Now, Mrs Wetherby, don't you be worrying. The doctor's here and if the second baby's the same size as the first, you won't have a problem."

"What if I do? What if I'm taken? The children still need me."

"The children will still have you," the doctor said. "The baby's head is out already, one more push and this will all be over."

As soon as her second baby was delivered, Mary sank into the bed, every inch of her body shaking.

"It's over," Dr Andrews said. "Two little boys. That explains why the heartbeat sounded like an echo. They both look well enough but they're very small, the second one especially."

Mary lay on the bed; her whole body numb. Mrs Tompkins fussed with the babies before she turned her attention to Mary, arranging the pillows so she could see them.

"This one's tiny." Mary put her finger into the fist of the second child. "I don't know if I have any clothes that small, I'll have to start knitting again."

"Let's try feeding them up, shall we?" Mrs Tompkins handed Mary the first baby to suckle. "There you are, you know how to do it."

"He seems sleepy and doesn't want to attach to me." Mary looked at the child as he dozed in her arms. "Shall I try the other one?"

Mary held the second baby to her breast but it wasn't long before they realised that neither would suckle.

"Never mind, you can try again later," Mrs Tompkins said. "Let me get some milk sent up and we can feed them by hand for now."

Mr Wetherby raced up the stairs as soon as the doctor shouted for him.

"Congratulations, sir," he said. "You have two new baby boys."

"Two! That's marvellous." His smile grew when he saw Mary sitting up in bed. "Are they both well?"

"They appear to be, but the second one is very small; they'll both need constant care."

"That's no problem, I'll make sure either my stepdaughter or sister-in-law are with Mrs Wetherby constantly. We've waited a long time for these boys, we don't want anything happening to them."

"I'll call each day to check on them. If there are any problems we'll sort them out quickly."

After several minutes, Mr Wetherby showed Dr Andrews out while Mrs Tompkins stayed to help feed the twins. She had two glass droppers that they filled with milk and dripped into each baby's mouth. It was a slow process but gradually the babies settled and took the milk they were offered.

By the second day, it was clear the boys were not going to feed from Mary. *What was wrong with her?* Why hadn't she had a normal pregnancy or delivery since the birth of Mary-Ann? Why was she now incapable of nursing her own children? She shouldn't be giving them milk from a goat; they needed her milk. The births of William and Mary-Ann had been normal, no panic, no drama; she had simply given birth and fed them naturally. William Junior had changed all that; maybe he had done some lasting damage?

Mary-Ann disturbed her as she came into the bedroom and sat in the chair next to the bed to help with the feeding. "You're so lucky. I can't wait to have a son of my own."

"You'd better wait a lot longer yet," Mary said. "You're only just fourteen."

"I know, but they're so sweet, look at their little faces. I wish they could stay like this forever."

"We don't want Edwin to stay as small as he is; we need to build him up. Even Albert isn't as big as he should be."

"I don't mean that, it's just that I love them so much as they are, it's a shame they have to grow up."

"When you've sat here feeding them constantly for several weeks you'll be wishing they were feeding themselves. My prayer is that they grow up strong and healthy."

As promised, Doctor Andrews called every day. Mary remained confined to bed and more often than not she was feeding one of the boys when he arrived.

"How much milk are they taking?" the doctor asked when he arrived one morning.

"Not much. We get a cup full every morning but they don't take it all. Albert probably has most of it."

Dr Andrews looked at Albert as he lay in the cot. "Have you noticed anything unusual about him? Does he seem particularly sleepy or does he cry more than you'd expect?"

"Not really. His nappies have been a bit messy this last couple of days, but it doesn't seem to be troubling him."

"Maybe it isn't, but with the size of him, we can't be too careful. He's only five days old. He looks listless to me compared with yesterday. How's Edwin been?"

The doctor took Edwin off Mary's lap and placed him in the cot.

"He's had a bit of diarrhoea too, but not much."

"We need to keep an eye on him because if he has a problem, he hasn't got the strength to fight it."

"They will be all right, won't they?"

"I hope so, but we need to watch them. They're too young to have laudanum yet, but if they don't settle in the next few days, I may have to use it. You need to let me know if there's any change."

Two days later when the doctor arrived, it was Edwin who lay motionless in his cot. His brother cried as he wriggled at the other end of the mattress, but Edwin remained undisturbed.

The doctor looked concerned as soon as he saw him. "We must get some fluids into him."

"He's been taking the milk," Mary said. "I've even tried to give him extra."

"That could be the problem; they both need water. Do you have any water that's been boiled?"

Mary-Ann raced down the stairs to get it.

"They will be all right won't they, doctor?" Mary felt every nerve in her body tingling.

"I don't know. They clearly have upset stomachs but with them being so small, there's not much I can do. Let's get some water into them and if they're not settled by tomorrow, I'll give them some laudanum."

Mary heard Mr Wetherby arrive home from work and mount the stairs to the bedroom. She had been dozing, but opened her eyes when he came in. Mr Wetherby kissed her forehead.

"How are they today?"

"Not good. Edwin still hasn't picked up and it's only been in the last hour that Albert's stopped crying. The doctor said he'll give them some laudanum tomorrow if they're no better." Mary fought to hold back her tears.

"There, there. We need to pray for them." Mr Wetherby walked to the cot and looked in. He reached out towards the babies, but stopped and withdrew his hand.

"What's the matter?" Mary said when she saw him stiffen.

"Nothing. I'm sure everything's fine. I'm just going to put another blanket on Edwin; he's a bit chilly. Actually, I don't want to wait until tomorrow to give them the laudanum. I'm going to get Dr Andrews now. You stay where you are."

As soon as Mary was alone she swung her legs out of bed and took her first tentative steps over to the crib. If Mr Wetherby wouldn't tell her what was wrong, she'd find out for herself.

As she looked down at the cot the blood drained from her face. She could see Albert's chest rising and falling with every breath, but Edwin was still. So still. Why wasn't his chest moving or his lips twitching as he let out his breath?

Why did his lips look grey and his face deathly white? She fell onto the chair beside her and reached for his hand. The pale skin was icy cold, despite a shaft of evening sun falling on him.

She looked at Albert lying at the other end of the cot. His skin was pale but still had a pink tinge, and rosebud lips; he still breathed ... not that it offered any comfort. Her baby had gone ... the baby she had fed no more than a couple of hours ago. It took a few moments for the truth to sink in but suddenly reality burst around her. *Where was everyone?*

"Mary-Ann," she called with a sound she didn't know she had. "Mary-Ann ... get help ... now." Mary lifted her baby from the cot and sat by the bed cradling him. *Her beautiful boy.* He looked like a porcelain doll, he was so precious. "You can't leave me," she squealed, as tears rolled down her colourless cheeks.

Mary-Ann burst into the room. "What happened?"

Mary said nothing as she hung her head over Edwin.

"Mr Wetherby's gone out," Mary-Ann said as she walked to the side of the bed and sat down. "He didn't say where he was going ..."

Mary wiped a tear that had fallen onto Edwin's cheek; it was so soft, so perfect. *Why had the Lord done this to her?* She closed her eyes, maybe in a moment she would wake up and this would all be a nightmare.

Mary-Ann said nothing but sat and stroked her mother's hand as they waited for Mr Wetherby.

They didn't have to wait long before he hurried into the room only to stop when Mary looked up at him, her face etched with pain. He walked over to her and bent down to place a gentle kiss on her forehead. "Let me take him."

Mary shook her head and held Edwin tighter. She wasn't ready to let go.

Dr Andrews followed Mr Wetherby into the room and went straight to the cot.

"I'm going to give Albert some laudanum," he said. "He's looking listless, but he's bigger than his brother and has a better chance of fighting off the problem. Once I've done that, I'm going to need you to feed him for me. Can you do that, Mrs Wetherby?"

Mary looked at Albert and nodded; she wasn't going to lose him too.

Chapter 51

THREE DAYS LATER, THE FUNERAL procession left Wilby Place. It was a quiet affair but still Mr Wetherby had two black horses pulling the hearse and had a second carriage to take him and William to the church. Several mutes followed on foot but Mary did not join them.

At the church, Mr Wetherby watched as his sons were lifted out of the hearse and put onto the trolley in front of him. Albert had only lasted a day longer than his brother. Mary was inconsolable but through her tears had insisted on a coffin wide enough to take the two of them. She had said that she couldn't bear the thought of them being buried alone.

The service was short, but Mr Wetherby struggled to contain his emotions. He hadn't cried since he'd thought he was losing Mary five years earlier, but the loss of these two boys had affected both of them far more than it should. Their lives may have been short but they would not be forgotten.

ভ৵

Once news of the twins reached family and friends, a stream of visitors called at the house. Mary knew they meant well but every visitor made her relive their short lives and she spent her days in tears. All she wanted was to be left alone. She needed to sleep, but at night she would toss and turn thinking of the babies she'd let down. If only she'd been able to feed them herself, maybe they'd still be with her. Everyone told her it wasn't her fault, but how did they know? They had no idea.

Day after day, she went through the routine of keeping the house clean and putting food on the table, but it wasn't enough to distract her. Albert and Edwin's little faces were never far from her mind and seeing them would bring tears again.

Mary knew Mr Wetherby understood her grief, and had done his best to console her, but as Christmas came and went it seemed to her that his patience was fading.

"You're not thinking about the twins again are you?" he said, one evening when he came home to find her in tears again. "You have to let it go, Mary. It's a New Year now and as much as we wanted those boys, these things happen."

"But it's so unfair. They were so tiny and helpless, how can God be so cruel?"

"Let me get someone to talk to you about it, the vicar maybe?"

"I don't want to talk to the vicar, he'll only tell me God was punishing me. I know that already."

"You don't know that, because it isn't true. I want you to snap out of this. I'm going to get someone else to call on you. Someone who'll talk about something other than the twins."

The following evening Mr Wetherby came home with a triumphant smile across his face.

"I've got a treat for you next week," he said as he took

off his hat and coat. "I've arranged for Mrs Watkins to pay you a visit." Mary gave him a puzzled look. "You know, Mr Watkins's wife, William's master. You said you wanted to meet her."

"Not now. I don't even know her."

"That's the whole point. You can talk to her about something other than the twins. I'm sure you'll have other things in common."

"How do you know; have you met her?"

"No, but Mr Watkins has mentioned her once or twice and I'm sure she's pleasant enough. They have a daughter too if I'm not mistaken. I think she's about Mary-Ann's age."

Mrs Watkins arrived at two o'clock the following Wednesday and Mary went to the door to let her in. She was a plump woman, no more than five foot tall, and Mary guessed in her mid-thirties. She offered Mary a limp hand before she walked in, surveying the small living room as she did.

"I rarely come this far up Summer Lane," Mrs Watkins said. "We prefer it nearer to the town centre."

"Mr Wetherby needs to live up here with having the business."

"Yes, of course." Mrs Watkins brushed the chair with her hand before she sat down.

Mary took a deep breath and put the kettle over the fire. "It's a pleasure to meet you, I'm surprised we haven't met before."

"Is there a reason why we should have?" Mrs Watkins said.

"My son William's been working with Mr Watkins for almost a year now … as his apprentice."

"Has he really? My husband never tells me anything; I wondered why he wanted me to come around."

"He's not mentioned William then?"

"He's had a number of apprentices over the years but I rarely meet them."

"I suppose you've no reason to. I believe you have a daughter though."

"A niece. We adopted her from my husband's brother when she was young and raised her as our own."

"How old is she now?"

"Nearly fourteen."

"I have a daughter who's fourteen," Mary said. "She's been away at school for a few years but she came back earlier this year. She's been a godsend these last few weeks." Mary imagined Mary-Ann feeding Edwin and stared into the fire in an attempt to burn the image from her mind.

"Where is she now?"

"Who?"

"Your daughter, you said you had one."

"Yes, I'm sorry. When I don't need her she works for Mr Wetherby, it keeps her busy."

"I wish we had that option," Mrs Watkins said. "Harriet's with me all the time but there's no chance of her working."

"Don't you enjoy having her around the house?"

"Not particularly."

Mary waited for an explanation, but when none came she stood up to make a pot of tea. "That's a shame; at least I'm blessed that way. Has your niece been to school?"

"Oh, she's been to school; that's the problem. She learned to read and write very quickly, but when we told her she didn't need to go anymore she had an attack of hysteria and hasn't recovered since. She seems to think she has a God-given right to carry on going and wants to be treated the same as the boys. She talks about it all the time. Mr Watkins won't tolerate it, and she spends most of her time in her bedroom."

"I'm sure she'll change as she gets older."

"She'd better change before then if she knows what's good for her."

"I have two elderly aunts who'd admire her spirit. They're both spinsters and very independent. They believe all women should be educated, and tell anyone who'll listen that they can look after themselves and don't need husbands."

"I hope they're never introduced to Harriet, she doesn't need any encouragement."

For the first time in months Mary smiled. "There's no danger of that; they disapproved when I married Mr Wetherby and I've not spoken to them for years. I saw them at a family funeral earlier this year and we kept out of each other's way."

"I don't understand women like that and I certainly don't understand my Harriet. Why are they so unhappy to have a man take care of them?"

"I can understand if they're like my old aunts," Mary said. "To suddenly lose everything to a husband would be hard; but I can't imagine why your niece would object."

"She's said she doesn't even want any children of her

own. Can you imagine that? What woman wouldn't want as many children as the Lord blesses her with?"

"I don't know." Mary reached for her handkerchief to wipe her eyes before the tears started again.

Chapter 52

MARY PUT SOME BOILING WATER into the teapot and left it to stand. She felt Martha's eyes on her as she poured milk into the cups.

"I do enjoy a cup of your tea," Martha said. "It's so much nicer than the tea I buy from the market."

"It's one of Mr Wetherby's luxuries. He has it sent up from London."

"Business must be doing well."

Mary poured out the tea and handed Martha a cup, with its matching saucer, before she pushed the sugar bowl towards her. "Since he moved into buttons it has been, but he's still not happy. He came home in such a temper a few days ago I was scared of what he might do."

"What was the matter?"

"It was all to do with Her Majesty's visit. Do you remember when he first found out she was coming to Birmingham? He could talk of nothing else for days."

"I do. I've never seen him so excited."

"Well, he wants to see the Queen close up, so he went to the Town Hall to ask if he could help with the arrangements, hoping it would give him inside access to Her Majesty, but apparently they were quite abrupt with him. They said that unless he was a dignitary or a councillor he wouldn't be at the main venue.

"I don't suppose that's unreasonable." Martha took a sip of her tea.

"That wasn't what upset him. He told them he was planning to stand as a councillor, but they laughed at him and asked if he even had the vote. That was what incensed him most. He said they looked down on him as if he were a common workman."

"I can imagine he didn't like that. What will he do?"

"I don't know. He's wanted the vote for over a year now but he's done nothing about it. Now he's desperate to see Her Majesty, goodness knows what he'll do. Whatever it is, he won't stop until he's done it. In the meantime he's at the Town Hall again trying to change their minds."

"Do you think he will?"

"I've no idea, but if he doesn't, we're going to be in for a terrible evening. I've already warned William and Mary-Ann."

"Will he take it out on them?"

"No more than the rest of us, but it won't be pleasant."

"Why don't you tell them to come around to our house for tea? It's not long before we move to Kings Norton and I'd like to see them before we go."

Mary stood up and poured them both another cup of tea. "Why do you have to move away again? It seems no time since you came back."

"It's not that far away; I'll still be able to call. Anyway, what about you? How are things between you and Mr Wetherby?"

Mary sighed. "We get along."

"Is that it?"

"What else is there to say? He works all day, sits in on a lot of council meetings and when he's at home he's tired."

Martha raised her eyebrow at Mary. "Is there a reason he spends so many evenings out?"

"He's interested in local politics and wants to know what's going on."

"That's not what I meant, and you know it."

"We'll be fine, don't worry about me."

Several minutes after six o'clock, Mr Wetherby stormed into the living room. He threw his hat onto the sideboard and sat down by the fire with *The Times*. After several minutes of being ignored, Mary broke the silence.

"Are you ready for something to eat?"

"Do I look ready? I've not finished the paper yet."

"No, I'm sorry, I didn't mean to disturb you." She sat down at the table and stared out of the window into the street. Life carried on as normal out there; men and women made their way home looking forward to possibly their only meal of the day. Mr Wetherby glanced up from behind his paper.

"I can read this later," he said. "Let's eat now, you look as if you're ready." Mary smiled and beckoned for William Junior to join her at the table.

"Are William and Mary-Ann not joining us tonight?"

"They've gone to tea with Martha and Mr Chalmers. How did you get on this afternoon?"

"I won't be defeated you know, I'll get the vote one day soon. I should have bought my own house years ago;

I just didn't get around to it because unlike that bunch of buffoons I was too busy building a business. I have connections at the bank now. I'll show them. I'll borrow as much as I can. I'll buy my own house for certain, my own workshop maybe, possibly both or perhaps even more than that. They've done me a favour."

"Will the house be in Birmingham?"

"Of course it will; I can't move the business and I need to live close by. Don't look at me like that; there are still some respectable places around here and I'll start looking tomorrow."

Chapter 53

M ARY FELT THE THICKNESS OF the envelope she held in her hands and looked at the elegant handwriting. It was addressed to Mr Wetherby, but it wasn't his usual sort of correspondence. She was glad it had only arrived in the late post and she hadn't had to sit looking at it all day. She placed the letter between the knife and fork she had set on the table for him, and hoped he wouldn't be late in.

He arrived home a little after six o'clock and immediately picked up his letter opener. Mary stood close by as he made a slit across the top of the envelope.

"It's from the bank," he said as he read it.

"Why are you getting a letter from the bank?" Mary looked up at him, a frown across her face.

"They're going to lend me some money. I've found a property I want to buy."

"A house?" Mary asked.

"A workshop. It's twice the size of the one on Hatchett Street and there are houses nearby that the landlord thinks will be for sale soon."

"Where is it?"

"Frankfort Street, at the top end of Summer Lane.

You don't often go up there, but it's much quieter and less crowded than here. I'm sure you'll like it."

Mary wasn't so sure, but she bit her tongue. "That's wonderful. How long will it take?"

"It won't be quick but I'll go and see my solicitor in the morning to get things moving. What a relief. This is going to change everything. Can you imagine, me being a property owner. Then I'll be back to the Town Hall for some respect."

⚜

As the town prepared for the visit of the Queen; the place swarmed with people. She would only spend a couple of hours in Birmingham but everything had to be perfect. With his newfound sense of importance, Mr Wetherby managed to secure himself the role of supervising the erection of crowd control barriers around the Town Hall. He had been busy all week, and now fussed over an elegant canopy of purple velvet that was being positioned on the spot the Queen would alight from her carriage.

"You're putting that in the wrong place," Mr Wetherby said as he walked over to the foreman. "It should be over there." He pointed at a spot ten feet from where the foreman stood.

"Mr Digby said to put it here," the foreman replied.

"Well, he's wrong. My barriers need to go where you're standing. He wasn't here for the briefing this morning."

Reluctantly the foreman gave the signal for the men to move the canopy, and Mr Wetherby guided it to exactly where it should be. "Good. Now I can put up the barriers."

As he worked, a messenger from inside the Town Hall came to find him.

"Mr Wetherby?"

"What do you want?"

"Mr Digby wants a word with you," the messenger said.

"Can't he see I'm busy? He'll have to come and find me."

"He wants you to go and see him in the Town Hall."

"I'll do no such thing." Mr Wetherby started to walk away before he changed his mind. An invitation into the Town Hall, into the area Her Majesty would be visiting. *What was he thinking?* "Not just yet anyway. Tell him I'll be there in two minutes."

"Now if you don't mind, Mr Wetherby."

Mr Wetherby sighed, but followed the messenger into the Town Hall. Once inside his pace slowed as he took in his surroundings. On either side of the entrance hall he passed two luxurious reception rooms, decorated for the benefit of their guests, but his attention focussed on the vases of flowers. They were everywhere, brightening the place with colour and filling the entire space with their scents. He continued into the main hall and the first thing he saw was a magnificent dais at the far end of the room covered with a canopy of purple velvet. The carpets were new and his feet sank into the pile as he walked. As he approached the dais he studied the three chairs within it. The large chair in the centre was covered with a crimson material embroidered with gold and was clearly intended for Her Majesty. Two smaller chairs were set to either side on a carpet of rich purple and crimson that perfectly complemented the decor above it. Plants and flowers were everywhere. Mr Wetherby was so taken with his surroundings that he failed to notice Mr Digby walking towards him.

"Mr Wetherby," a voice called.

"Mr Digby, what an honour to be here," he said.

"I've no time for pleasantries. I wanted you to come and see the work we've done with this most special room."

"And I thank you for that, it looks magnificent." Mr Wetherby looked around once more.

"The canopy here, covering the dais, I trust it meets your approval."

"Indeed it does. It looks splendid."

"So may I ask why you've contradicted the orders I gave about the dais outside?"

Mr Wetherby gritted his teeth. "I was told this morning the exact position the Queen would alight from the carriage and I want the canopy to be in the right place."

"The canopy was already in the right place, I checked it myself. Now, I brought you here to show you I am perfectly capable of supervising the work myself and I'd remind you not to change anything unless you have my express permission. I've been working on this for months and I won't have the arrangements changed at the last minute by one of the casual workmen. Do I make myself clear?"

The smile disappeared from Mr Wetherby's face.

"Now see to it that you put the canopy back where it was." Mr Digby waved his hand in dismissal and walked away. Mr Wetherby glared after him before he turned and made his way back to the door. The beauty of the place had ceased to exist and he didn't turn his head once to take a final look around.

The following day, Mr Wetherby was up before dawn. Yesterday was forgotten because today was the day he would see his Queen. The whole town had the day off work and he woke Mary and the children early. Alice was already downstairs when they arrived and after eating a slice of bread each, they walked to the Town Hall.

It promised to be a fine day and as they approached the magnificent building the crowds were already gathering. Mr Wetherby knew the best place to stand and he pushed through the people to get to his chosen spot. As soon as he looked over the railings, a huge grin spread across his face; the purple canopy stood exactly where he'd wanted it yesterday. He left the family under the pretence of checking the barriers, but he had unfinished business to attend to. It took him a while to find Mr Digby but when he did, he was spoiling for a fight.

"Perhaps you weren't as clever as you thought yesterday," he shouted as he approached Mr Digby.

Mr Digby turned to see who had spoken and turned away as soon as he saw Mr Wetherby.

"Don't ignore me." Mr Wetherby pulled Mr Digby's shoulder to turn him around. "Perhaps you should know what you're talking about before you start giving orders in the future."

"How dare you talk to me like that?" Mr Digby squared his shoulders and stood to his full height.

"I'll talk to you anyway I like after the way you treated me. You're going to regret your little outburst yesterday unless I get a lot more respect from you. I've got a feeling you've no idea who you're dealing with."

"I'm dealing with a nobody, who is frankly delusional."
Mr Digby cracked his knuckles.

A smirk settled on Mr Wetherby's lips. "You'll regret
that remark, you wait and see."

Without waiting for a reply, Mr Wetherby turned and
walked back to his place behind the barriers. He hadn't
been back long before William Junior became bored.

"What time will they be here?" he asked.

"We still have a long wait ahead of us." Mr Wetherby
looked at his pocket watch. "They'll arrive at the train
station at midday and travel past the Market Hall, down
Bull Street and on to Colmore Row before they reach us.
It'll take about half an hour."

"Can't we go to the Market Hall, to see them sooner?"

"You'll get the best view here, trust me. Now be a good
boy and be patient."

As the hours crept by, the lingering clouds disappeared
so that by midday the sun was fierce. Despite the heat,
the crowd remained patient until at twenty-five past the
hour they heard the sound of cheering in the distance.
Immediately everyone strained for their first glimpse of the
Royal Carriage but they were cheering long before they saw
it. Eventually the glass carriage rolled into view. The Queen
faced forwards holding a bouquet of flowers, while Prince
Albert sat opposite her. Exactly on cue, the carriage stopped
in front of the canopy and the royal couple emerged, less
than ten yards from the Wetherby family. Within two
minutes they passed into the Town Hall.

"Doesn't she look beautiful?" Mary said. "Did you see
her dress? I'm sure it was silk but it looked like silver."

"I'm sure it is," Mary-Ann said. "And yes it was

beautiful, as she was. Much nicer than I imagined her to be and she looked so happy; did you see the way she looked at the prince? She clearly adores him."

"It must be wonderful to still love someone like that when you've been married for nearly twenty years," Alice said.

"It's not unusual though," Mary said. "They were only married a month before I married Charles and I still love him."

Mr Wetherby turned to look at the women and saw Alice nudge Mary with an elbow.

"Not that I'd change anything now," Mary continued. "Things happen for a reason, don't they?"

Mr Wetherby grunted before he turned away again. He had to let it go.

The silence remained awkward until twenty minutes later when the royal couple appeared again outside the Town Hall. They made their way back to the carriage and this time the Queen stopped to wave. The crowd cheered and many waved flags, but all too soon the royal couple were back in the carriage, heading towards Aston Hall.

As the carriage pulled away, many of the children ran after it, but the Wetherby family turned to make their way back to Summer Lane.

"What a day," Mr Wetherby said with a smile on his face. "Who'd have thought we'd get so close to Her Majesty. I have to stay and supervise the removal of the barriers, but I tell you what, I'll remember this day, and this month, for a long time to come. After the way I've been treated by the council, nobody is ever going to treat me like a workman again."

Chapter 54

MR WETHERBY WALKED WITH HIS head high and shoulders back as he escorted Mary down Frankfort Street. He was making his way to the unusually large workshop situated amongst the terraced houses that lined either side of the road. The key to the workshop was in his hand.

"Look at the size of the place." He pushed the door open and stood back for Mary to go in. "It's more than I dared dream of when I first came to Birmingham."

"You'll need to get more than one fire in the winter," Mary said as she looked around the cavernous room. "Hatchett Street was always cold, never mind here."

"Trust you to come up with something like that. What do you think of it?"

"It's an improvement on the old place, but it depends how many women you want to squeeze in."

"There won't be many; I need space for the machines."

"William won't be back for years yet."

"Maybe not, but I want to be prepared. I might hire a couple of other machinists before then; there's no point hanging around."

Mr Wetherby showed Mary into the small office at the

far end and encouraged her to inspect the workbenches that filled the room. They were ready to leave when there was a knock on the door and Mr Tanner, the previous owner, walked in.

"Mr Wetherby, I guessed it was you when I saw the door off the latch. Now the place is yours, I wondered if you'd be interested in buying one of the houses as well?"

Mr Wetherby's eyes lit up. "Most certainly, which one?"

"I've a couple. Why don't you let me show you around?"

Mr Wetherby took Mary by the arm and they followed Mr Tanner back towards Summer Lane. Before they reached the corner, he stopped and pointed to the house in front of him. It was a three-storey back-to-back house.

"Shall we go inside?" Mr Tanner said as he opened the front door. Once he had showed them around he excused himself and left them alone.

"We can't all live here," Mary said. "There are only two bedrooms and there are six of us ... unless you want all the women to sleep in one room and the men in the other."

"But it would be mine ... and it's so close to the workshop."

"Well, maybe you could buy it and rent it out so we can stay where we are."

"Is there a problem?" Mr Tanner said as he re-joined them.

"Not a problem as such, but my wife thinks we need more room."

"How many of you are there?"

"Six."

"Would it matter if you didn't all live together?" Mr Tanner asked.

"Of course it would …" Mary said.

Mr Wetherby interrupted. "What are you thinking?"

"I have a second house, the one at the back of this, as it happens; I could let you have the two. You have the entry running down the side and so you'd be able to get between them easily enough. In fact, if you wanted to, you could knock a hole in the back wall and join them up that way. Let me take you around to the other house so you can see for yourself."

As soon as he saw it, Mr Wetherby knew he had to have both.

"I want my family together," Mary said. "That means the two of us with William, William Junior and Mary-Ann. We have to think of Alice as well; we can't put her in the back house on her own while the rest of us squeeze in here."

"It needn't be like that," Mr Wetherby said. "William Junior's at school most of the time and if William lived in the back house with your sister, it would only be three of us in the front house. It's about time William took more responsibility."

"If we do that, I want a door between the downstairs rooms so it feels like one house."

"There's no need for that, the entry's perfectly good enough. I tell you what, why don't we ask William if he's happy to live in the back house. If he is, I'll buy both."

William needed little persuasion to move into the back house and Mr Wetherby immediately instructed his solicitor to proceed with the purchase. Two weeks before Christmas he got a date for completion of the sale and hired a carriage to transport all their belongings. On the day of the move Mary and Mary-Ann were in Frankfort Street early, ready to position the furniture and unpack their personal property when it arrived.

"We're not going to get everything in here," Mary said after they had re-arranged the living room several times. "I'll have to take some of the chairs and ornaments around to William."

"They already have enough; perhaps you can sell them or maybe store them in the bedrooms?"

"Why we had to move to a smaller house I don't know. One of these days he'll realise we need more room and I'll be looking for things like this again. You carry on here and I'll go to the other house and check how they're getting on."

When Mary got to the back house, William and Alice were both home from work, emptying crates.

"Can you use any more chairs?" Mary asked.

"It doesn't look like it." William surveyed the room. "I didn't realise we had so many things in the other house."

"That's because it was bigger. I don't know what I'm going to do with everything. Will you come around to the front house once you've finished and see if there's anything you want? I've enough tea for you both as well, so you're welcome to stay."

"You're a godsend," Alice said. "As soon as we're settled, I need to start cooking again."

"You don't need to do that. You're at work all day and it's no trouble for me."

"But I do. You're the lady of the house now and I can't have you waiting on me, it should be the other way around."

"Don't be silly, just because I have a husband who pays

the bills doesn't mean I can't cook for you. Besides, I need to cook for William, and so I won't hear any more about it."

After emptying several more crates, Mary and William went ahead of Alice to the front house. The night had long since drawn in and William helped his mother down the pitch-black alleyway.

"You will be all right by yourself, won't you?" Mary asked when they reached the front.

"Of course I will, why shouldn't I be?"

"I don't know, it won't be the same with you in a different house." She stopped and looked at him. "You look so like your father, you know. You've grown so handsome and that hair is exactly like his. When you look at me sometimes I think it's him and I suppose that while you're with me, a piece of him is still alive."

"I won't be far away and besides, you have Mr Wetherby. You have a lot to thank him for, we all do. If he thinks it's better for me to live with Aunt Alice then that's what I'll do. You need to concentrate on keeping him happy not reliving the past."

Mary shuddered at the thought of the relationship she'd had with Mr Wetherby over the last couple of years, and changed the subject. "Come on, let's go indoors, it's cold out here."

Chapter 55

Aldridge, Staffordshire.

Mr WETHERBY HELD OPEN THE door to the carriage while Mary climbed inside. Beside him Sarah-Ann waited to wave them off.

"Thank you for coming," she said to Mr Wetherby. "Father was delighted, it meant a lot."

"When a man decides to turn to the Church of England, it's a day to be celebrated."

"It's a day many of us never thought we'd see. Even now, the sight of Father having Holy Water poured over his head brings a tear to my eye."

"Don't let tears spoil that pretty face." Mr Wetherby smiled and climbed into the carriage before she could answer. "We'll see you soon."

Mary sat in the carriage and waited for it to pull away before she spoke. "What a splendid day that turned out to be. It's just a shame Martha wasn't there."

"She could hardly make the journey from Kings Norton in her condition. Why couldn't the baptism wait until she'd had the baby?"

"Pa's wanted to be baptised ever since he took ill; he

thinks he's about to die. Sarah-Ann said he wants to be laid to rest with Mother, and she's buried at the Parish Church. If he hadn't been baptised he'd end up at the Friends Burial Ground with the rest of the family."

The sound of the horses' hooves on the track filled the silence that followed. Eventually Mr Wetherby spoke.

"It's a good job he has Sarah-Ann. I do admire her."

"I hope you don't admire her too much. I still don't trust her around you."

"A man still has needs, and there are worse options," Mr Wetherby said under his breath as he turned to face the window.

"What did you say?"

"I wondered if I needed anything before I go out tonight. I forgot to tell you, I'm joining the Conservative Association."

"What do you need? We've spent half the afternoon eating."

"You're right, I wasn't thinking. I can go straight out once we get back."

Mary shuffled in her seat and looked out of the window. "What about becoming a councillor, wasn't that your next plan?"

"After what happened over Her Majesty's visit I don't want anything to do with that bunch at the Town Hall. Now I'm a property owner I'm going to concentrate on national politics. Given his age I can't see Lord Palmerston lasting long as Prime Minister and so we're likely to have another election soon. After what happened last time, the Conservatives need all the help they can get to give us another Prime Minister."

Within half an hour of arriving back in Birmingham, Mr Wetherby was out of the house again. He had already arranged for someone to propose and second him as a member of the Conservative Association and within the hour he was accepted with a unanimous vote. As soon as he arrived home he offered Mary a glass of sherry.

"Does this mean you're going to be out even more?" she said.

Mr Wetherby passed her a sherry and sat down opposite her. "They meet once a week, I think I can manage that."

"I hardly see you nowadays. You get up, go to work, come home for tea and then go out again. Half the time I'm in bed before you get home."

Mr Wetherby picked up the newspaper and glanced at it.

"It's not only me either," Mary continued. "William Junior never sees you. He's due back at school next week, but he's eight now and too much for me. He needs his father's discipline."

Mr Wetherby turned his attention back to her. "You're right, I've been neglecting him. I don't have any plans for tomorrow so why don't I shut up the workshop promptly and come straight home."

৩৵৻

Birmingham, Warwickshire.

Mary knew she should be pleased to spend the evening with her husband, but as she put the plates on the table she didn't know if she was ready for it. Since the death of the twins their relationship had changed. It was now as if the only reason Mr Wetherby came home of an evening was because he needed somewhere to sleep. She supposed it should bother her, but in all honesty, she didn't mind. As long as he took care of the children, she had done what she set out to do.

She was about to slice some bread, when there was a knock on the door. She shouted for the visitor to come in and as the door opened she found a strange, yet vaguely familiar, man looking at her.

"Can I help you?" Mary said.

"Would you be Mrs Wetherby, by any chance?" the man enquired.

"I am. Do I know you?"

"Not yet, but I've been looking for you for the last week. Mr Thomas Wetherby's the name; I believe you married my brother."

"What a surprise." Mary opened the door fully and ushered him in. "Mr Wetherby said your last letter was from Australia."

"That was a few months ago, but I'm back now, for a while at least. I wanted to call and see my big brother."

"He's at work at the moment but it won't be long before he's home. Come and take a seat while you wait, then you must join us for something to eat."

"Thank you very much; I don't mind if I do."

Thomas took a seat by the fireplace and unrolled the newspaper he carried under his arm. Half an hour later, Mr Wetherby walked into the living room, followed by William Junior. Without looking up he threw his hat onto the sideboard and took off his coat.

"Aren't you going to ask me how I am?" Thomas said from his seat by the fire.

"Thomas! What are you doing here?" A smile spread across Mr Wetherby's face and he immediately went to shake his brother's hand. "I'd given up hope of seeing you again."

"To tell you the truth I nearly didn't come back. If it hadn't been for the fact that I left a woman behind I wouldn't have bothered."

"Come and sit at the table and tell me all about it. This is my son William Junior by the way."

"I've clearly been gone too long. How old is he?"

"Nearly eight, and yes you have been gone too long." Mr Wetherby pulled out two chairs and sat down with his brother. "You're not married are you?"

"No and I'm not likely to be either. I was seeing someone a few years ago, and we grew quite close, but I got an offer to join the Merchants and so off I went. She wasn't happy about it, but I promised I'd come back and we'd get married. Anyway, I stayed away longer than planned and when I went back to see her she'd gone and married someone else. Said I'd been gone for so long she thought I was dead."

"How long were you gone?"

"A couple of years; give or take."

Mary brought a pot of tea to the table and sat down next to William Junior. "You can't have missed her much," she said.

"I didn't while I was away because there was so much going on, but I was looking forward to seeing her again."

"So will you settle here now you're back?" Mr Wetherby asked.

"For the time being I will; at least until the urge to travel comes over me again."

"So what happened when you went to Australia?" Mr Wetherby sliced himself a piece of cheese and put it on some bread. Mary helped William Junior to some food and the three of them listened as Thomas spoke.

"When we arrived I jumped ship so I could have a look at the place. I'd heard they'd found gold not far from where we docked and I wanted to try my luck. I found myself in a place called Ballarat. They'd already found a lot of gold there so I decided to set up a tent and see what I could find. I got lucky quite quickly and found a few pieces of gold, which I sold. I lived on the proceeds for over a year and even managed to keep hold of a few pieces, but then the trouble came." Thomas accepted the cup of tea Mary offered him before he continued.

"I'd expected it for some time, ever since the government put up the prices for the licences to dig. The men weren't going to stand for it and there was talk of a rebellion. I didn't want to be involved in case it got back to the Merchants, so I left."

"I read in *The Times* that a number of men died in Ballarat. Were you there then?" The lines on Mr Wetherby's forehead were prominent.

"No, I got out in the nick of time. I went to Bendigo to see if it was any better there, but it wasn't the same. The licence fees were still too high and men were angry and so I decided it was time to head home. I went back to the docks and boarded a ship a couple of weeks later. I came back to

England in July. I had hoped to stay with my lady friend, but when I found out she was married I went to see Father."

Mary and William Junior continued eating, but Mr Wetherby put down the pie he was about to bite in to and looked directly at Thomas.

"Yes, that wife of his was still there. Needless to say I didn't stay long. He was the one who told me where to find you."

Mr Wetherby shuddered. "I don't think I could ever go back to that house, not with her there anyway. She is, without doubt, the nastiest woman I have ever met. Where are you staying now?"

"I'm travelling round, catching up with people and staying in taverns. I've got some money and a small stash of gold."

"We can find some room for you here if that helps, in fact there's a spare bed in William's room in the back house; you can stay as long as you want." Mr Wetherby turned to Mary. "You'll make a bed up for him, won't you?"

"I'll need to find some clean sheets and let Alice know." She stood up and went upstairs.

"You can come and work for me as well if you want to save your gold," Mr Wetherby continued. "I need a foreman I can trust."

"Sounds like I've come to the right place," Thomas said. "As soon as we finish eating I'll go and get my bag from the inn; I'll be back within the hour."

Chapter 56

M ARY LIKED TO THINK SHE was a hospitable person. She was always happy to entertain when the need arose; but of late she felt her generosity was being abused. She knew Thomas had been invited around for meals whenever he wanted, but it seemed like he was never away from her table … and he ate so much. If he stayed much longer she would have to ask Mr Wetherby for more housekeeping. William was equally irritated with his new lodger.

"He seems to think he has the bedroom to himself," he said to Mary one evening. "He leaves his clothes all over my bed as well as on the floor. If I'm asleep before he gets home, he makes no attempt to keep the noise down."

"He's been at sea for so long he's probably forgotten his manners."

"That's no excuse; if you're on a ship you need to have consideration for other people. Can you talk to Mr Wetherby and see if he can move him on?"

Mary sighed. "He won't like the idea; he loves having him here."

"He sees him all day at work and they go drinking at night, surely that's enough."

"All right, I'll see what I can do."

Every time she saw Mr Wetherby over the next couple of days he was with Thomas. In some ways she didn't mind, he now walked around with a smile on his face, but it wasn't helping William or her housekeeping. The only time she saw him alone was when they were in bed but more often than not, she was asleep before he arrived. She would have to make an effort to stay awake tonight.

It had turned eleven before Mr Wetherby came upstairs and as he opened the door, she put down the magazine she was reading.

A puzzled look crossed Mr Wetherby's face. "Is everything all right?"

"I want to talk to you about Thomas."

Mr Wetherby walked to the bowl on the dresser and splashed water on his face. "What about him?"

The colour rose in her cheeks. "Will he be with us for long?"

"He doesn't know yet. Why?"

"Wouldn't he be better off in a room of his own?"

Mr Wetherby wiped his face with a cloth before he turned to look at her. "Has William said something to you?"

"It's not that ..."

"I can always tell when you're lying. What's the problem?" Mr Wetherby took off his shirt and trousers and climbed into bed beside her.

"He needs more space than he has and he's eating us out of house and home."

"He always did have a good appetite, drove my stepmother mad." Mr Wetherby smiled. "We were always at our happiest when we upset her."

"Don't you have a room somewhere else you can let him have?"

"Not at the moment. All the houses are full and unusually everyone's up to date with their rent. If William wants him out of his room I'll have to buy another house."

"That's excessive."

"If you want me to move him, what's the alternative? I'm going to buy anything that comes up for sale on Frankfort Street anyway."

"That could take months."

"It'll take as long as it takes." With that he blew out the candle and lay down with his back to her.

It took longer than Mary hoped, but the week before Christmas, Thomas was ready to move out.

"I can't believe you're giving me a place to myself." He fastened his bag and slung it over his shoulder before turning to Mr Wetherby. "I've never lived alone."

"You won't be on your own for long; as soon as I find another tenant I'll move them in. At least you're not going far."

"Don't worry about me, I looked after myself for long enough in Australia. In fact, talking of gold, you know what would be nice in here? A Christmas tree, just there in front of the window."

"What a marvellous idea," Mary said as she cleared away the breakfast dishes.

"What on earth do we want one of those for?" Mr Wetherby asked. "And what's it got to do with gold?"

"I've seen a few while I've been travelling. With the

right decorations they look as if they're glittering like gold. One would look nice in the window."

"And that's what people do nowadays," Mary said. "Haven't you seen the pictures of the Royal Family gathered around the Christmas tree at Windsor Castle? Besides, we should be celebrating the fact it's our own house. A tree would make it more special, don't you think? Please can we get one?"

Mr Wetherby stood up and walked to the window. "I don't know where this is going to end," he said. "If you want to decorate a tree, then I won't object. Just don't expect me to help."

Mary clapped her hands together as her smile made a rare appearance. "I'll get Alice and Mary-Ann to help; it'll be a real treat."

On Christmas Eve, with William Junior in bed, William set the tree on a table in the window. Once it was positioned, Mary, Alice and Mary-Ann decorated it while William sat by the fireplace with Mr Wetherby.

"Everything looks splendid," William said as Mary stepped back to give the tree her final seal of approval.

"Doesn't it. Thank you for getting it for us," she said to Mr Wetherby. "I haven't enjoyed the last couple of Christmas's after what happened, but it's going to be special this year, I can tell."

Mary was out of bed early the next morning and arrived downstairs before anyone else. She shivered as she made her way to the sideboard but the fire would have to wait. She put her candle on the table and lifted out the presents she had hidden the day before. She arranged them on the table beneath the tree before she went to clean the fire.

By the time the fire roared into life, her hands were numb and she rubbed them up and down her arms to bring some life back to them.

"You should have put a shawl around you before you started that." Mr Wetherby stood behind her as she crouched in front of the hearth.

"I suppose so; I didn't expect it to take so long."

"Come here, let me warm you up." He pulled her up and put his arms around her. For an instant Mary froze before she forced herself to relax.

"Can't I even put my arms around you?" Mr Wetherby said as he released his hold.

"You took me by surprise, that's all."

"I'm not going to hurt you, you know."

"No, of course not, I'm sorry." She walked to the table and picked up a pan. "I'd better go and get some water; I've made some sweet buns for breakfast and we need a pot of tea to go with them."

Chapter 57

Aldridge, Staffordshire.

THE BITTERNESS OF WINTER HAD passed but it didn't lighten Sarah-Ann's mood. She sat at the table in the living room and looked around; it was comfortable enough but things had changed.

Before Christmas her elder sister Louisa had written to say that her husband had died of consumption. Her letter was emotional, not because she had been widowed, but because she had no way of looking after her three children. With no one else to turn to she had written to her father for help.

Mr Jackson had no hesitation welcoming them in, but for Sarah-Ann it had made her life a misery. Eight years Louisa's junior, she had always found her sister domineering, and as soon as Louisa moved in she had taken control of the household chores and delegated most of the work to Sarah-Ann. Their relationship had deteriorated noticeably and they were at the stage where they couldn't be in the same room without arguing.

On top of that, her father's health wasn't good. His bad chest had grown progressively worse and over the winter she'd been forced to collect the rents when he couldn't do it himself.

She looked down at her hands where the once finely kept nails were now split and broken. It said everything she needed to know about how much she had changed since she'd left Birmingham. She no longer owned any nice clothes and her hair, once her pride and joy, was mostly hidden from view by her bonnet. What was the point of making an effort when the only people she was likely to see were her father and sister?

The sound of the postman brought her back from her thoughts and she went to the door. There was a letter for her father, which she placed on the table before turning her attention to the letter addressed to her. She knew it was from Mary before she opened it, and her heart sank when she read that Mary wanted to visit. It wasn't that she didn't want to see her; she just felt so inadequate beside her. Since Mary had come out of mourning for the twins, Mr Wetherby seemed to buy her new clothes on a weekly basis and Sarah-Ann couldn't compete. Well, it looked like next Wednesday she would have to make an effort; at least Louisa would be out.

On Wednesday morning Sarah-Ann put on her best dress of navy cotton, borrowed a small silver locket from Louisa's room and stood in front of the mirror to give her hair one hundred strokes of the hairbrush. Satisfied she looked as good as she could, she gave her cheeks a final pinch before she went downstairs to answer the knock on the door.

"Mr Wetherby," she said, ignoring Mary who was by

his side. "What a pleasant surprise; I wasn't expecting to see you. Are you staying for the day as well?"

"Unfortunately not. I'm only here to deliver Mary safely. I have business to attend to, but I'll have some time this afternoon. Perhaps you can have some water boiling at around four o'clock, it will give me something to look forward to."

Sarah-Ann's heart fluttered. "I think I can manage that, I'll look forward to it as well."

"You'd better be going," Mary said.

"Yes, of course. I'll see you later." Mr Wetherby kissed Mary on the cheek and returned to the waiting carriage.

"I know I shouldn't say this, but he is charming," Sarah-Ann said. "I'm glad the two of you are happy together, honestly."

Mary looked at Sarah-Ann and smiled. "Tell me what's been going on here. How are you getting on with Louisa?"

"She's driving me mad, telling me how to run the place but offering no help at all. She's gone over to Richard's today to see Emma, her eldest. She's been staying with them for a couple of weeks to give Louisa a break, if you like. I tell you, she has no idea what hard work is. She should try doing what I do every day. I didn't tell her you were coming in case it gave her an excuse to sit and do nothing ... again."

"She wouldn't want to spend the day with me. She's still not forgiven me for marrying Mr Wetherby."

"That's true. She was angry when you named William Junior too. She said you should have named him Charles-Jackson."

"I could hardly do that, given he's Mr Wetherby's son.

Anyway, let's not dwell on her; I need to see your father and then we can go for a walk. It's a lovely day."

The day passed quickly and before they knew it, the clock struck four o'clock.

"I'd better get that water boiling again," Sarah-Ann said. "I don't want to let Mr Wetherby down. I've got some cake as well, I hope he's not late."

Sarah-Ann took out the best china.

"You don't have to go to any trouble," Mary said. "He doesn't usually have tea and cake at this time of the day."

"Maybe not, but it's a treat."

As the water came to the boil, there was a knock on the door. Subconsciously Sarah-Ann tidied her hair and smoothed down her dress before she opened it; a broad smile on her face.

"You made it," she said. "Exactly on time too. Come and make yourself at home."

"I can't stay long, I have a carriage waiting." Mr Wetherby took a seat next to Sarah-Ann. "Have you had a good day?"

"We have and we were saying we must do it again," Sarah-Ann said. "Next time you must come as well, I hardly ever see you."

"I'm afraid you might be in for a long wait. Every day's a work day at the moment. I have plans for expansion, not only in Birmingham, but in London as well. I'm likely to be travelling a lot for the next few months."

"How exciting." Sarah-Ann clapped her hands to her chest. "I'd love to go to London."

"Maybe one day you will, you never know."

"What's it like down there, is it similar to Birmingham?" Sarah-Ann gave Mr Wetherby her full attention.

"Not at all. It's much bigger and busier, and there are people of all nationalities. There's so much more going on and you'd love the shops."

"I'm sure I'd like the shops as well," Mary said as she leaned forward.

"Of course you would." Mr Wetherby looked at his pocket watch. "Look at the time, we really must be leaving."

"So soon," Sarah-Ann said. "I'd hoped you could stay longer."

"There's a meeting at the Conservative Association tonight that I need to go to. You should come and spend a few days with us instead. That way we'll see each other for longer."

"I'd like that," Sarah-Ann said. "Louisa can take care of Father for a change."

"There you are then. Let Mary know when you want to come." Mr Wetherby stood up. "Now what did I do with my hat and coat?"

Sarah-Ann took them from the vestibule and handed them to him. As she did, Mr Wetherby's fingers caressed the back of her hand, causing her to freeze. A moment later she looked up to see him smiling at her.

"I'll look forward to seeing you in a few weeks." The glint in his eye wasn't lost on Sarah-Ann but all too quickly he took Mary's arm and escorted her to the carriage.

လ☙

Once outside, Mary wondered what had just happened. She had spent a pleasant day with Sarah-Ann and yet once Mr Wetherby arrived it was as if she didn't exist. She wasn't happy that Mr Wetherby hadn't told her about his plans to travel to London, and was equally put out that he had invited Sarah-Ann to visit. She sat in silence until he settled beside her and the carriage started moving.

"I suppose you're wondering about the expansion," he said without looking at her. "I'm sorry I announced it as I did, but I couldn't lie to Sarah-Ann. I'm expanding the business and buying a workshop in London; it makes eyelets for boots and sacking. There's a ready-made workforce and a full order book, all I need to do is move in and make it more efficient."

"Does that mean we're moving to London?" Mary couldn't hide the look of concern on her face.

"Good heavens, no. You wouldn't like it and I'll still have Frankfort Street. I'll travel to London a couple of days a week until I'm happy with it and then I'll get a manager in."

Sarah-Ann waited a few days before she wrote to Mary. She didn't want to appear too eager and suggested a visit in early June, which was about the limit of how long she could wait until she saw Mr Wetherby again. She had liked him from the day they met, but she didn't think he cared for her, not in the same way, but there was something different about him lately. She could still feel where he'd touched her hand, sending a tingle coursing through her body. Then there was the smile. It was only for her, not for Mary or anyone else. She knew he would never leave Mary, but then why had he invited her to stay? What did he want from her and perhaps more to the point, what did she want from him? Her heart quickened every time she thought about it and she counted the days until she would see him again.

Chapter 58

Birmingham, Warwickshire.

TWO DAYS BEFORE SARAH-ANN WAS due, Mary went to see Martha. The living room in Kings Norton was large and airy, much nicer than Frankfort Street. Martha had filled it with chairs and ornaments, and the cushions and curtains were all finished with vibrant red velvet. Mary sat in a particularly well-padded seat and told Martha her concerns.

"Do you think I'm being silly?" she asked.

"She liked him a lot, I do know that," Martha said. "It was over ten years ago, though."

"Surely she can see we're happily married now?"

"I know you've been married for over ten years, but are you sure you're happy? I don't see you smile very often these days."

"I'm happy enough."

"Are you sure? Are things as good as they should be between you and Mr Wetherby?"

Mary rested her head on the back of the chair and closed her eyes. "I'm not unhappy but I hardly see him anymore. He goes out nearly every evening."

"Why does he go out so often? I don't doubt he still cares for you but I've seen you tense if he so much as touches you. Are you neglecting him?"

"It's only if he touches me in front of other people." Mary stood up and studied the painting over the fireplace.

"Are you sure that's all it is? Don't forget, at the end of the day, he's still a man."

"If you must know, he's not interested in me like that anymore." Mary turned to look at Martha. "Neither of us wants to risk another baby and this is the only way."

"I'm sorry, it's none of my business."

"No, it's me who should be sorry. I asked your advice. Will you come over one evening when she's here? I'm sure she'll be pleased to see you."

"I will if I can get someone to look after the baby. I'm telling you though, if you show Mr Wetherby even a little bit of affection, he won't look at anyone else."

The afternoon was pleasant as Mary walked down Summer Lane to meet Sarah-Ann. She enjoyed days like this when the fumes from the factories didn't obscure the sun. With nothing to hurry back for, they strolled around the market before making their way home.

"It's only the two of us tonight," Mary said, holding open the door to the back house. "Mr Wetherby's at a meeting, and William and Mary-Ann are out somewhere."

"Won't they even be home for tea?"

"Not tonight, I'm afraid. I'm often on my own on a Tuesday."

Sarah-Ann's smile faded. "What about tomorrow?"

"William and Mary-Ann will be around, and Alice will join us."

"What about Mr Wetherby?"

Mary ran her finger across the top of the fireplace, assessing the dust, before she spoke. "He's going to London tomorrow. He only decided yesterday; he's not sure when he'll be back."

Mary kept her back to Sarah-Ann, but heard a sharp intake of breath before she heard Sarah-Ann disappear upstairs with her bag.

୨–ୡ

On Sarah-Ann's last afternoon in Birmingham, as she helped prepare the evening meal, Mary left her alone while she went out for some bread. Mary hadn't been gone long when the door opened and Mr Wetherby walked in.

"Good afternoon, Sarah-Ann, I didn't know you were here."

"Mr Wetherby." A smile lit up Sarah-Ann's face. "If you're looking for Mary, she's gone to the bakery."

"I've just come to tell her I'm back from London. How long have you been here?"

"A few days."

"Why didn't you tell me you were coming?"

A puzzled look crossed Sarah-Ann's face. "I told Mary a few weeks ago, didn't she tell you?"

"I don't think she mentioned it, but please forgive me if she did. I've had a lot on my mind." He gave Sarah-Ann the same smile she'd seen in Aldridge. "How long are you staying?"

"I leave tomorrow."

"That's a shame." Mr Wetherby walked towards her as he held her gaze. "Does Mary have anything planned for tonight?"

"No, it'll only be me and her."

"No it won't." Mr Wetherby paused and looked at his pocket watch. "I don't need to go to the Conservative Association; there's nothing happening that's more important than seeing you."

"I'd like that." Sarah-Ann bit her lip to contain her smile.

"So would I," Mr Wetherby said. "I wouldn't have gone to London if I'd known you were coming."

As he was speaking, Mary walked in. "What are you doing here?"

"I live here."

"You don't normally come home during the day, what's the matter?"

"Nothing's the matter, I've just got back and wanted to let you know. What's wrong with that?"

"You didn't need to call."

"All right, I'll go then, but I'm not going out tonight. I believe it's Sarah-Ann's last night and I've not seen her. Why didn't you tell me she was coming?"

Sarah-Ann watched him disappear out the door as Mary sat down and reached for the gin. She looked down at Mary.

"There's nothing going on you know."

"I don't know what you mean."

"Yes, you do. You think there's something going on between me and Mr Wetherby. I'll be honest with you, I like him and I want him to like me, but there's no more to it than that."

Mary took a gulp of her drink. "It doesn't look like nothing to me."

🚧

Mr Wetherby had arrived home from work by five o'clock and insisted that Sarah-Ann sit with him while Mary laid out the table for tea.

"I'm certain she didn't tell me you were coming."

Mary bristled as Mr Wetherby nodded his head towards her as if she was a servant.

"I wouldn't have forgotten; after all, I invited you."

"You're here now so let's say no more about it. Why did you go to London?"

"That's the annoying thing, I didn't have to go; it was a routine visit that could have waited until next week."

"You said it was urgent," Mary snapped.

"I said no such thing." A flash of anger crossed Mr Wetherby's eyes.

Sarah-Ann looked from one to the other. "Will you excuse me? I've just remembered I left my handkerchief in the other house. I'll be back in a minute." Without giving either of them chance to say anything, Sarah-Ann disappeared.

"Now look what you've done," Mr Wetherby said. "You've upset Sarah-Ann and made me look like a fool. What were you thinking?"

Mary walked towards Mr Wetherby, her hands on her hips. "I'm thinking that I don't want you and her spending any time together, that's what I'm thinking. She can't keep her eyes off you."

"And I've told you you're being ridiculous; I have a reputation to maintain and I don't intend to compromise it."

"Is that all you care about, your reputation?"

"I'd care about you if you'd let me, but you've made it perfectly clear you're not interested."

"That's not true, you know why ..."

"Well, you've got a funny way of showing it ..." Mr Wetherby picked up his newspaper and held it open so Mary could no longer see his face.

She sat at the table and put her head in her hands. How had things gone so wrong? All she wanted was a civilised relationship, but it had reached the stage where they couldn't talk to each other without arguing. They sat in silence until Sarah-Ann came back into the house.

"I'm sorry, am I interrupting something?"

"Not at all." Mr Wetherby folded his newspaper and stood up. "Let's sit down and eat."

Mary watched as Mr Wetherby held a chair out for Sarah-Ann before he sat down next to her. She may well not have been there for all the attention he gave her. Immediately after tea Mr Wetherby asked Sarah-Ann to sit with him while Mary tidied up. He pulled Sarah-Ann's seat close to his and relaxed back in his own chair.

Mary clenched her teeth and turned her back on them as she collected up the dishes and wiped the table clean. She could hear him telling Sarah-Ann about London, its people and the shops. Occasionally she stopped to take a deep breath when the sound of giggling interrupted the conversation. Once the table was tidy she threw the plates into the sink with such force that she feared they would break. She was mad with herself that she had no water and would need to go and get some from the court. She turned around to excuse herself, but when she saw Mr Wetherby glaring at her, she picked up her bucket and walked out without a word.

Once the house was tidy, she sat next to the fire with her knitting, determined not to look up. As it happened, neither Mr Wetherby nor Sarah-Ann seemed to notice her silence and all she succeeded in doing was making herself angrier. As the grandfather clock struck ten, Sarah-Ann stood up to leave.

"Let me walk you back." Mr Wetherby jumped from his seat; ignoring the look Mary shot him.

"I'm sure there's no need," Sarah-Ann said. "It's only round the back and I've done it every other night this week."

"That's because I wasn't here. Now, no arguing; let me get your cloak."

❧

Sarah-Ann and Mr Wetherby walked down the alley in silence. Once they reached the door, Sarah-Ann stopped.

"Thank you for having me this week, I probably won't see you tomorrow."

"I don't go to the workshop until just before seven. If you're ready by then we could have a cup of tea together."

"It might be better if I didn't, Mary doesn't seem very happy with me."

"Nonsense, it's not your fault. She's not been the same since the twins died and she's getting worse."

"That was years ago, she should be over it by now."

"She should, but she isn't and I'm losing patience with

339

her. Having such an attractive and attentive companion has been a pleasant change. I wish I'd been here all week."

Sarah-Ann flushed when she saw the look in his eyes.

"Please join me for a cup of tea in the morning," he said. "I'll be waiting for you." Before Sarah-Ann could say anything, he kissed her on the cheek and turned to walk back down the alley.

ೞ❦

The following morning Mary was up early and by the time Sarah-Ann arrived there was a pot of tea waiting.

"Good morning, Mary. Has Mr Wetherby gone already?"

"No, he'll be down shortly. He asked me to brew some tea for us."

"So you know he invited me?" Sarah-Ann seemed unusually subdued.

"He told me last night when he came back from walking you home. Come in and sit down." Mary gestured to the chair opposite her.

"You're not happy with me, I can tell. What can I do to convince you that I don't have designs on him?"

"You don't have to say anything. Mr Wetherby reminded me last night that he's a respectable, God-fearing man and that he wouldn't dream of breaking our marriage vows. He didn't need to remind me, but … I don't know, he's so distant at the moment. I needed the reassurance."

"He said you've not been the same since the twins died. Is that true? It's a long time to be unhappy if it is."

"It's not that I'm unhappy, I'm so frightened of it happening again."

"And so you won't let him touch you?"

"I can't help myself. I want to be able to but … You won't take him from me, will you?"

Mary poured the tea and sat down.

"When the time's right, I want a man I can marry," Sarah-Ann said. "I don't want to be someone's mistress."

Mary reached out and patted Sarah-Ann's hand just as Mr Wetherby came downstairs.

"Are you two all sorted out now?" he asked. "The last thing I want is for Sarah-Ann to go home with a cloud hanging over you."

"Yes, we're fine," Sarah-Ann said.

"Good. Now, where's my cup of tea. I've got a couple of minutes before I need to go."

Once Mr Wetherby left for work, Sarah-Ann said goodbye and went to catch the nine o'clock carriage. No sooner had Mary tidied the table than there was a knock on the door and the now familiar face of Thomas appeared before her.

"What brings you here at this time of day?" Mary said. "I thought you'd be at work."

"I'm going away again. There's not much for me around here and the sea's calling. I've heard some good things about America and I'd like to see it for myself before everyone else arrives."

"How exciting. Does Mr Wetherby know?"

"Not yet. I called to ask if I could join you for tea tonight. I need to tell him."

"Of course you can; it could be years before we see you again."

Chapter 59

THICK GREY CLOUDS CLUNG TO the buildings of Birmingham making the town dull and cold. Although it was only two o'clock in the afternoon, the candles in the workshop struggled to give enough light for the workers. Mr Wetherby took out his pocket watch and looked at the time. He didn't usually finish until three on a Saturday, but had been tired all week and wondered if he was sickening for something. Deciding that he'd had enough, he let the workers go and went home to settle himself in front of the fire.

"I see Mr Jackson's not well again," he said as he replaced the letter Mary had left on the table.

"He's been in bed for the last week and doesn't seem to be getting any better; it's his breathing again."

"He's an old man now, almost eighty I would say, he might not get over it, you know."

"I know, I must try and see him before Christmas. Will you come with me?"

"As long as I don't come down with anything." He sneezed into his handkerchief. "We could go next week, write to Sarah-Ann and see what she says."

The following morning Mr Wetherby woke with a

headache but it was Sunday and he needed to escort the family to church. They arrived to see a group of men at the back of the building whispering amongst themselves. Irritated that a place of worship had been turned into a meeting room, he motioned for Mary and the children to go to their pew while he went to find out what was happening.

"It's Prince Albert," he said several minutes later as he sat down beside Mary. "Word's come up from London that he died last night at Windsor Castle."

Mary's eyes widened as she looked at him. "They said yesterday his condition had improved."

"It clearly deteriorated again, typhoid, they say. We may have to postpone our trip to Aldridge; if the funeral's next week I'd like to go."

"What do you need to go for? You won't see much."

"To pay my respects. The man's done a lot for this country and we should recognise the fact. We need to show support for Her Majesty as well."

"I don't know why it's always you who has to do these things. Haven't you got enough to do?"

Mr Wetherby glared at Mary as a couple seated behind them tutted at the noise. He didn't care what she said; he was going.

For days afterwards he checked *The Times* for news of the funeral, but he didn't find what he was looking for until the end of the week.

"Can you believe it," he said as Mary peeled some chestnuts. "They've finally announced the funeral's on Monday but they're having it at Windsor Castle. I can't get to Windsor from here, not there and back in a day, at any rate."

"That's annoying. We should have gone to Aldridge this week instead of waiting. We're not going to get there next week either with it being Christmas."

Mr Wetherby grunted and turned back to his paper. The silence deepened until the postman knocked on the door and handed Mary an envelope. She opened the letter before moving to a chair to sit down.

"It's from Sarah-Ann. Oh my ... Pa's died." She re-read the letter. "Bronchitis ... and I didn't get to see him." She found her handkerchief and wiped her eyes. "I hope he knew how much we all cared for him."

Mr Wetherby paused until she'd composed herself. "Does she say when the funeral is?"

Mary shook her head. "No, but she's asked if she can join us for Christmas."

Mr Wetherby sat up straight. "With Louisa and the children as well?"

"No, I don't think so; just her. She must have had enough of them. I don't suppose I have much choice, do I?"

"I want you to make her welcome," Mr Wetherby said.

"Of course I'll make her welcome; in fact it would be nice if we could all get along without arguing for a few days."

ॐ∼ॐ

By four o'clock on Christmas Eve, Mary had done as much preparation as she could for the following day and sat down for a cup of tea. As she helped herself to a second cake, there was a knock on the door and Sarah-Ann walked in.

"I've made it to Birmingham," she said, trying to smile despite the tears in her eyes.

"Sarah-Ann, come in." Mary jumped up and put her arms around her. "I'm so sorry. Come and sit by the fire and I'll pour you some tea ... or would you prefer gin?"

"I don't suppose you have any brandy, do you? I'm chilled to the bone."

"Of course we do." Mary bent down by the sideboard and looked into the back of the cupboard. She saw the brandy straight away, but there was a box in the far corner that caught her eye. "How've you been?" she said to Sarah-Ann as she tilted the box to see inside. It was full of letters that had been tidied together with string. The top one was written in Mr Wetherby's handwriting. She let it settle back on the shelf before she picked up the brandy. *They were the letters Mr Wetherby had written to her when she cancelled the wedding.* "I'm managing," Sarah-Ann said, when Mary turned from the cupboard. "At least he's at peace now. He knew I was with him at the end so that's something."

"Yes of course. Didn't you want to spend Christmas with Louisa or Richard?" Mary listened to Sarah-Ann but she wasn't concentrating. *She didn't remember putting the letters there. Maybe Mary-Ann had when they'd moved house and she hadn't noticed. She needed to read them.*

"I wanted to get away, to be honest with you," Sarah-Ann continued. "Louisa invited herself to Richard's and I couldn't face being with them all. Thank you so much for having me here. Where is everyone?"

Mary jumped. *Where was everyone?* "Mary-Ann's in the laundry and William Junior should be in the yard; my William and Mr Wetherby are still at work." She handed

Sarah-Ann her brandy and poured one for herself. "They'll finish early today, I should imagine."

By the time Mr Wetherby came home from work, Mary had removed all traces of brandy from the room and set the table for tea. He was rubbing his hands together as he walked in and Mary watched him take off his coat.

"Sarah-Ann," he said when he saw her. "I'm sorry to hear about your father, but I'm glad you could join us."

Sarah-Ann smiled and held his gaze. "I needed to get away from Louisa and the children."

Mr Wetherby frowned. "I hope it's not frivolity you want to escape, because I've brought a Christmas tree home. Will it upset you if we put it up?"

"Of course I don't mind. It might cheer me up. We haven't had one before; there was little point when there was only the two of us."

"It's out in the yard at the moment." He turned to Mary. "Shall I fetch it in now before I take my coat off?"

"Why not; everyone will be home shortly."

Christmas Day was fine but cold, and the family wrapped up well for their walk to church. The mood in the town remained subdued following the death of Prince Albert, but it didn't stop people talking about it constantly. When they arrived home, William stoked up the fire and added the Yule log while Mr Wetherby warmed up the mulled wine and Mary-Ann lifted out the glasses.

As soon as it was ready they took to their feet to toast the Queen, and then Mary handed out the presents. As usual, William Junior handed them out before he opened his own, a wind-up train with a detachable carriage.

"I used to have a train like that," William said to no one in particular. "Do you remember, Mother?"

"We still have it somewhere; I'm sure I saw it the other day." The train had been in the box with the letters and she stood up and rummaged in the back of the cupboard. "Here it is; you can have it again now. Call it an extra Christmas present."

William smiled as he took it from her, a look of fondness in his eyes.

"You used to love that train," Mary said.

"I did, it was the only thing I owned when we moved to Birmingham. I took it everywhere with me." He slipped it into his pocket for safe-keeping. "It still reminds me of Grandmother, although I barely remember our years at the farm."

Mary paused, allowing herself to remember the happy times in Aldridge, before she thought back to the letters. *When would she get a chance to read them?*

"You've left a present under the tree," Mr Wetherby said as she sat down again. "It's for you. Merry Christmas."

"What's this?" Mary said as she picked it up. She unwrapped the brown paper covering it. "It looks very special ... a book, how lovely. Look at this, pictures of cakes and biscuits and instructions how to make them. This is wonderful, thank you. I don't deserve it." A pang of guilt struck Mary; maybe Mr Wetherby deserved more than the handkerchief she had monogrammed for him.

"It's not only a book about baking you know, look at the title, *Mrs Beeton's Book of Household Management*. It's new and has everything you need to know about running a home; things like children's health and servants' pay."

Mary smiled. "The recipes will be the most useful section, given that we no longer have any young children and we don't have any servants."

"You're right about the children, but don't be too hasty to skip over the section on servants, I have plans, you know." They all laughed and Mary looked fondly at her book before placing it on the sideboard.

"Right, it's time for dinner. If you refill the glasses," she said to Mr Wetherby, "I'll put the food on the table."

Chapter 60

THE FOLLOWING MORNING, MR WETHERBY was up early to open the workshop. The ice on the windows, which had melted with the heat of the fire the previous day, had returned with a vengeance and he scratched it away with his fingernail before peering outside. Seeing a light covering of snow on the ground, he turned to the fire and lit it before anyone else came downstairs. As he reached for his coat, Sarah-Ann joined him, a shawl pulled tightly around her shoulders.

"I guessed it was you," she said. "I didn't think you'd open the workshop today."

Mr Wetherby put his hat back on the table. "We've a lot to do; I can't afford to take two days off. I'll try and come back later."

"I'm sorry, I didn't mean to slow you down. I just wanted to thank you for yesterday, it was lovely."

"I'm glad you could join us. Will you stay today as well?"

"I'll stay for a couple of hours but with the funeral tomorrow I need to get back to Aldridge." Sarah-Ann looked at her fingers before turning her gaze back to Mr Wetherby. "Will I see you there?"

Mr Wetherby pushed a stray piece of hair back behind her ear. "Yes, I'll be there."

"Where will you be?" Mary asked as she appeared at the bottom of the stairs.

"The funeral tomorrow." Mr Wetherby fumbled for his hat and made for the door. "I take it we'll be going."

"Certainly. I'm going with William and Mary-Ann, he was their grandfather and they're old enough now. I wasn't sure if you'd be able to spare the time. You're always too busy for anything other than the workshop or the Conservative Association."

Mr Wetherby looked at Mary and then back to Sarah-Ann. "I can spare the time for this; I'll leave Mr Carrick in charge."

৵৵

The following day, Mary was ready early in order to take William Junior to the Carrick's house for the day. When she returned, Mr Wetherby was sat in the living room waiting for the carriage. As she walked in he checked his pocket watch.

"Where is that carriage?" He stood up to go to the door but then stopped to look at her. "You do realise Richard will be there today, don't you."

"Of course I do, it's his father's funeral."

"I don't want to see you talking to him."

Mary glared at him. "I'm not ignoring him. I've known him a long time; at the very least I intend to pass on my condolences. I hope you'll be civil towards him."

"I don't have any intention of going near him."

Mary felt the sting of tears in her eyes and took a deep

breath. "All I ask is that you don't embarrass me. I still shudder at the way you were with him at his mother's funeral."

"We won't go at all if you carry on like that."

"Don't be ridiculous. You want to go as much as I do, although probably not for the same reasons."

Mr Wetherby opened his mouth to respond, but Mary stopped him.

"Don't start shouting, it's neither the time nor the place. Go and see where the carriage is and I'll call William and Mary-Ann."

Once they were in the carriage, Mary barely said two words. Fortunately, William wanted to talk to Mr Wetherby, which gave her the chance to stare out the window and ignore them. She couldn't remember the last time she had seen Richard, but thinking of him took her back to happier times. Back to the days before she'd met Mr Wetherby. Maybe she should have let Sarah-Ann have him all those years ago; then she wouldn't be stuck with him now.

When they arrived at the house, Richard was by the front door talking to some new arrivals. Mary lingered in the carriage as the others got out and watched him smile to his guests. Even now, despite everything, he could still make her heart flutter.

"Are you getting out?" Mr Wetherby stood by the door to the carriage waiting for her to move.

Mary said nothing but eased herself along the seat and accepted the hand he offered her. Once outside, she released her hold only to feel Mr Wetherby's fingers tighten around hers.

"You'll express your condolences and then come straight inside with me. Do you understand?"

Mary pulled her hand from his but he grabbed her arm. "Do you understand?"

"Perfectly," she said, her eyes full of loathing.

Mr Wetherby grunted and released his grip. "Come on then." He ushered her towards the door and as they approached Richard she could feel Mr Wetherby's hand in the small of her back. He was clearly determined that she wasn't going to stop and talk.

As soon as they were through the front door, they went to the kitchen where Sarah-Ann and Martha were busy putting food onto the table. Mr Chalmers joined them with a tray of sherry glasses.

"I know, it's a sad day," he said as Mary wiped her eyes. "At least he had a good innings."

Mary nodded but said nothing. If only it was her father-in-law's death that was the cause of her pain. She remained silent as they travelled to and from church for the funeral service, only relaxing when Mr Wetherby finally left her side.

৩৵৵

With William talking to Richard and Mary with Mary-Ann and Martha, Mr Wetherby went to the kitchen. Sarah-Ann had fussed over the food all afternoon and when he decided she'd done enough, he walked over to her.

"You deserve a sit down," he said. "You've been busy all afternoon."

"You're right; people can help themselves if they want anything else." She looked around the table, making sure everything was as it should be. "Mrs Richard will be back shortly, she can sort anything else out, if she can stay around for long enough. I don't know where she keeps disappearing to."

"Come and sit down and tell me your plans." Mr Wetherby stood to one side and ushered her towards a couple of chairs in the far corner of the room. "I presume you'll move to Birmingham now."

"I will but I don't know when. I've got a lot to sort out here before I move, then I'll have to find somewhere to live and get a job."

A frown spread across Mr Wetherby's face. "What do you need to do here?"

"Pa told me before he died that he'd made me executor of his will, along with a couple of others. We have to sell all his properties and split the proceeds between everyone. I haven't seen the details yet, but I don't know where to start; he must have had over twenty properties."

"Who are the other executors?"

"His friend Mr Hewitt, and the clerk of his solicitor."

"Mr Hewitt of Upper Tower Street?" Mr Wetherby said.

"Yes, that's him."

Mr Wetherby's face broke into a smile. "It would make sense for you to move to Birmingham then. I have a property you can use on Hatchett Street. It'll be easier if you're near the other executors. I presume his solicitor is in Birmingham?"

"Yes, on Waterloo Street."

"There you are then. It'll also mean I can help you if you need me."

Sarah-Ann returned his smile, before her own frown

returned. "I don't have much money at the moment, I'll need a job."

"Stop worrying," Mr Wetherby took her hand. "I'll find something for you."

"Are you sure you don't mind? I don't want to be a burden."

"Whatever you might be, you're not a burden. It'll be nice to have you in Birmingham."

ೂಜಿ

Mary was glad to see Mr Wetherby disappear into the kitchen; at least he couldn't watch her from there. She knew Sarah-Ann was in there but with the house full of people she wanted to trust him. It was only thirty minutes later, when he hadn't returned, that her instincts became troubled, and she went to look for him. At first she didn't see him but when she turned to leave, her heart stopped. He and Sarah-Ann were alone in the far corner and Mr Wetherby had hold of Sarah-Ann's hand. Mary recalled the words she'd managed to re-read in the letters. *I'll love you until the day I die. I'll do everything I can to make you happy.* As she watched, the words sounded hollow.

She stood for several seconds, subconsciously turning her wedding ring around her finger, wondering if she should confront them and risk making a fool of herself. As the seconds ticked by she got beyond caring. The way they were touching was almost indecent. If Mr Wetherby wouldn't let her speak to Richard ... Wait a moment, where was Richard? If Mr Wetherby could behave like that, then she would speak to Richard whether her husband liked it or not. She looked around, and in that moment it was as if Richard had read her mind.

"Shall we go outside?" Richard didn't wait for an answer and took her hand, not taking his eyes off Mr Wetherby until they were out of the room. "It's been too long since we talked and you don't look happy. I want to know what's going on."

Chapter 61

THE OUTSKIRTS OF ALDRIDGE WERE desolate in the middle of winter. For the most part it was an agricultural village made up of a small number of houses along with the church and the Manor House. Surrounding the houses, fields stood empty waiting for next year's crops. As Sarah-Ann waited for the midday carriage, the rain, which had battered the windows overnight, had eased off. With her father's funeral over, it hadn't taken her long to realise she didn't need to stay in Aldridge. At the reading of the will she had learned that as well as being executor, she would inherit all her father's household effects. She still had to sell the house, but there was no hurry. Louisa would stay in Aldridge for a while longer and so within the week she said goodbye to her sister and left.

The ride to Birmingham was uncomfortable and the wheels hit every hole and rut in the makeshift road, but she didn't mind. She had left the fields and hedgerows and entered a world she loved. Buildings replaced the fields and although many of them had chimneys that churned out fumes, it failed to dampen her spirits. This was what she had wanted for many years, so she wasn't going to change her mind now. The countryside might be pleasant on the eye, but the town was where the excitement was and she intended to make the most of it.

The carriage arrived in Birmingham shortly after two o'clock, and Sarah-Ann smiled when she saw Mr Wetherby waiting for her.

"I hadn't expected anyone to meet me and especially not you." She accepted his hand as she climbed down from the carriage. "I'm surprised Mary let you come."

"She doesn't know I'm here, but I wanted to welcome you. I need to show you your new home anyway. Let me take your bags."

"I can't believe how much the place has changed," Sarah-Ann said as they walked up Colmore Row. "The houses look dilapidated and the number of people must have gone up tenfold."

"Not quite that much, but it feels like it."

"It certainly does, and listen to the noise. The metal banging on the machinery will deafen me."

"You'll get used to it soon enough, you'll even get used to the smell, although that can be difficult in the middle of summer."

"It can't be any worse than being in the country." Sarah-Ann smiled and took a deep breath.

"I hope you settle in," Mr Wetherby said as they approached Summer Lane. "It's a good house and you're not far from us. A woman, who was recently widowed, lives there with one of her daughters. Another daughter lives close by and she's often out."

"I'm sure I'll be fine, thank you."

"I've found you a job too, I hope you don't mind."

Sarah-Ann's face lit up. "Of course I don't mind, where?"

"Do you remember someone called Frederick Flemming? I believe he used to live with Louisa; he was somehow related to her husband."

"Yes, I remember him; he was Mr Robson's godson."

"That's him. He runs a pawnbroker's near the market."

"A pawn shop?" Sarah-Ann turned to look at Mr Wetherby. "What sort of respectable woman works in a place like that?"

"It's not what you think. It's only a small place near High Street and he had an advertisement in the shop window. He remembered you and said he'd be happy to give you a job if you called to see him."

Sarah-Ann looked doubtful, but carried on walking. "I wasn't expecting anything like that."

"It'll suit you. You're too much of a lady to do anything manual."

"Maybe I used to be, I'm not anymore."

"You're more of a beauty than many around here, and more refined. I wouldn't let you work in a place like that if I had any doubts about it."

As they talked they arrived outside the house on Hatchett Street.

"Here we are then." Mr Wetherby unlocked the front door and ushered Sarah-Ann into the small living room. It was furnished with a selection of assorted chairs and a small table. The embers in the fire still glowed red. As she took in her surroundings, Mr Wetherby moved to the foot of the stairs and shouted up. When he received no reply he went back to the front door and closed it.

"It looks like we're on our own." Although they stood on opposite sides of the room, Sarah-Ann knew he was watching her and she lifted her eyes to meet his. After a moment he walked towards her, never taking his eyes from her face. Seconds later they were so close she could feel his breath on her cheek. "Would you like me to show you to your room?"

Sarah-Ann couldn't breathe as years of longing were aroused within her. "Would that be right?" Her voice was hoarse with anticipation.

His eyes searched hers and she feared he would feel the pounding of her heart as she waited for him to make a move. He lifted his hand and stroked her cheek, pausing as he did, before he hesitated and turned away.

"No, you're right, it wouldn't; forgive me. I'll take your bag to your room." With that he went upstairs, and moments later returned and left without looking back.

As she watched him go, Sarah-Ann couldn't stop shaking. A thousand thoughts raced through her head and none of them made sense. She wanted Mr Wetherby more than ever and knowing he felt the same way thrilled and terrified her in equal measure. What she wanted to do and what she needed to do were two entirely different things. Only the image of Mary, as it fixed itself in her mind, made her realise she had to stay away from him.

Chapter 62

Birmingham, Warwickshire.

EVEN FOR JANUARY IT WAS cold. The ice on the inside of the windows had been thick for weeks, making it difficult to see outside. Sarah-Ann had lain awake, listening to the howling wind for most of the night, and she shivered as it came down the chimney. The last thing she wanted was to go outside, but that was the one thing she had to do. Today she started her new job. She had called on Mr Flemming soon after she had arrived in Birmingham and once she saw the shop she had no hesitation accepting his job offer. He was younger than she remembered, in fact he was clearly younger than her, but she didn't mind. He was pleasant and courteous and she decided she could trust him.

As she stepped into the dark morning, the wind took her breath away and she battled to stay on her feet. She kept her cloak pulled tightly around her and headed towards Summer Lane. The road was full of people, but they all had their heads bowed into the wind and she made the journey without speaking to anyone. As she reached the market, the black of the night started to break but the faint glow of candles still struggled to light the shops that lined the road. The pawnbroker's shop looked inviting. Walking to the door she glanced at the window full of neatly arranged personal property, which would stay there until the owners reclaimed it or it was sold. As she entered the shop, Mr Flemming stood by the fire smoking his pipe. He smiled when he saw her.

"Miss Jackson, come and stand by the fire, you look frozen."

Sarah-Ann returned his smile. "It's a harsh winter this year, that's for sure. I don't know that there will be many people venturing out today, it's not fit."

"Surprisingly, we do well when the weather's bad; people need money for coal and they can't wait."

"I suppose you see some desperate cases."

"I'm sorry to say you become hardened to it. You'll find it hard for the first few weeks but don't worry, I'll do the customer interactions, at least for those who need to pawn something."

While she warmed herself, Mr Flemming made her a cup of tea before returning to stand beside her. She hadn't expected such kindness. It made a change from other places she'd worked where she'd barely been acknowledged or where men couldn't keep their hands to themselves. As she drank her tea, a young woman with long dark hair entered the shop. She greeted Mr Flemming and continued through to the back room. Within a minute she returned, her cloak removed, and looked straight at Sarah-Ann.

"Miss Gardener, can I introduce Miss Jackson?" Mr Flemming said. Miss Gardener nodded in Sarah-Ann's direction. "She'll be working with us from now on, I decided we needed some help."

"Pleased to meet you," Sarah-Ann said.

"Whatever you say, Mr Flemming." Miss Gardener ignored Sarah-Ann and went to tidy one of the cabinets.

Sarah-Ann noticed that Mr Flemming didn't offer Miss Gardener any tea, or a warm by the fire. She wondered if she had only received special treatment because it was her first morning, or maybe it was due to the family connection. Had Miss Gardener been given tea on her first morning? Perhaps the attention she was receiving explained the woman's lack of friendliness.

Sarah-Ann had barely finished her tea when their first customer arrived. Mr Flemming showed her how to take the portable property and write the receipts. He always did the valuations himself, but then passed the paperwork to the ladies.

Despite her initial reservations, Sarah-Ann enjoyed her first day. She liked to think they were helping people through difficult times, which must be a good thing. There had only been one occasion where she'd wondered how the man in front of her had come about such an impressive piece of jewellery, but it wasn't her place to ask and she kept her thoughts to herself.

The following day she arrived for work at the same time, and a cup of tea sat waiting for her on the fireplace. Mr Flemming stood next to it and beckoned her over as she walked in.

"How did you find yesterday?" he said, blowing smoke rings into the air.

"I enjoyed it. I love to see all the jewellery that comes in, I've never had much myself."

"I'm glad you like it, I think you'll fit in well. Maybe we can sort some nice jewellery out for you one day; the right necklace would set off your eyes perfectly."

"That's kind of you to say, but I can't go spending money on fancy jewellery, I have to keep a roof over my head. It will be a while before I get my inheritance."

Mr Flemming looked at her and smiled. "Maybe one day."

Chapter 63

THE DARK MORNINGS WERE A thing of the past and now, as Sarah-Ann left the house, the air was warmer too. Mr Flemming still waited for her every day with a cup of tea but their morning rituals had moved from casual conversations about work to more intimate discussions about their lives. It was Sarah-Ann's favourite time of the day and she would get in earlier than she needed to. The only downside was when Miss Gardener arrived and glared at her, something she did every morning. At that point, the talking stopped and work began.

As she put away a number of items one afternoon, Mr Flemming came and stood beside her.

"Thank you for doing that."

"I'm only doing my job." She looked at him and smiled.

"I love your smile you know, it makes me happy."

"Thank you. I've a lot to be happy about. My sister-in-law and Mr Wetherby have been very generous to me, as you have, and now that spring's here, it makes me feel so much better about life."

Mr Flemming looked at her as he took a deep breath. "Miss Jackson, would you mind if I walked you home this evening? It's lovely outside and I'd enjoy the company."

Sarah-Ann flushed but quickly composed herself. "Why not, I'd enjoy the company too."

Once they'd put everything away, Mr Flemming locked up, and they walked away from the market towards Snow Hill.

"It's nice to be able to talk without being interrupted," Mr Flemming said. "Miss Gardener's timing is usually less than perfect."

"It's the glare she gives me I could do without. Did you used to have a cup of tea with her every morning before I arrived?"

"No, nothing like that; but she's going to have to get used to it."

"She is used to it, but she still doesn't like it."

"That's not what I meant." Beads of perspiration broke out on his forehead. "Miss Jackson, do you find me good company?"

"After the times we've talked together I should hope you know the answer to that."

"I enjoy being with you and you've cheered up the shop since you've been with us. Even the customers have noticed."

"That's nice to know."

"You've cheered me up as well." Mr Flemming coughed as if a lump had caught in his throat. "I wonder … will you walk out with me?"

Sarah-Ann looked at him and smiled. "I'd like that."

Mr Flemming continued as if he hadn't heard her. "I could walk you home from work each evening, and perhaps we can visit the park if the weather's nice."

"I said yes," Sarah-Ann said when he paused for breath.

"You did? I'm sorry. I'd practised my lines and needed to say them all."

Sarah-Ann laughed before she realised he was being serious and straightened her face. "Now it's my turn to be sorry. Had you finished?"

"Nearly. I wondered, given that it's Easter Sunday this week, if I could accompany you to church."

"This Sunday?"

"Is there a problem?"

"Only that most of the family will be there. What would I tell them?"

"You can tell them the truth; that we're walking out together."

Sarah-Ann couldn't hide the look of concern on her face. "I haven't told them anything about you, they'll be surprised."

They walked up the hill in silence, Sarah-Ann too dazed to talk. *What did she say to him?* She liked him a lot and she wanted to walk out with him, but taking him to church on Sunday? Mr Wetherby would be there. She hadn't seen him since the day she arrived in Birmingham, but how would he react if she turned up with Mr Flemming? He might not be pleased, but she couldn't remain a spinster for the rest of her life waiting for him. She needed a husband of her own, surely he knew that.

Sarah-Ann didn't notice the distance they walked and was surprised to see Hatchett Street approaching.

"This is as far as I go," she said.

"You didn't give me an answer." Mr Flemming turned to face her. "May I join you in church on Sunday?"

She returned his gaze and saw the sincerity in his eyes. "Yes, you may. You know a lot of the family already, although I don't believe you know Mrs Wetherby, my late brother's wife. My sister Martha will be there with her family as well."

"I hadn't realised it would be such a party, but you're right, I know most of them. I'll look forward to it."

Once Mr Flemming left her, Sarah-Ann turned towards Frankfort Street. She needed to talk to Mary, and knew, with it being Thursday, that Mr Wetherby would be at the Conservative Association. When she arrived it didn't take long to tell Mary about Mr Flemming.

"He's going to escort you to church? How exciting. Didn't we say you wouldn't be on your own for long? Only the other day Mr Wetherby was asking how you've settled in."

Sarah-Ann's stomach lurched. "Was he? That's nice, I haven't seen him since I arrived."

"I hardly see him myself at the moment," Mary said. "Since he's joined the Conservative Association he has something on nearly every night. Anyway, he'll be here on Sunday and I'm sure he'll be thrilled to hear your news."

Sarah-Ann took a gulp of the gin she'd been given. She wasn't so sure. "I'm a bit bothered about Mr Flemming's age. I don't know for sure but I think he's a few years younger than me. Should I worry?"

"How old do you think he is?" Mary asked.

"I would say in his late twenties."

"And what are you, thirty-seven?"

"Thirty-eight at the last birthday," Sarah-Ann said.

"You don't look that old, all that country air must have done you good. He need never know."

"I worry about what people will think; you will let me know if I look more like his mother, won't you?"

Chapter 64

SARAH-ANN SAT ON THE EDGE of the chair, her hat and cloak on, waiting for Mr Flemming. He was due at ten o'clock but the large hand of the clock still only pointed to eleven. Five more minutes. She stood up and walked to the window hoping to ease the knot that had settled in her stomach. She wasn't ready for this. She should have seen Mr Wetherby first, but it was too late now. The next time she saw him, she'd have Mr Flemming by her side.

At precisely ten o'clock Mr Flemming knocked on the door. Sarah-Ann muttered a silent prayer and forced herself to smile as she opened it.

"All ready?" he said, looking her up and down.

"As ready as I'll ever be. Shall we go?"

It was a short walk to St George's and when they arrived they sat in the first free pew they came to. Halfway down the aisle to the right-hand side, Mr Wetherby and Mary sat in their usual seats with Mary-Ann, the two Williams and Alice.

Sarah-Ann hardly heard a word of the service and once the final prayer came to a close she urged Mr Flemming outside.

"You're not your usual self today," he said as they stood by the church door.

"I'm fine, don't worry about me."

The arrival of Mary and Alice saved her from further explanation.

"Here you are … and you must be Mr Flemming." Mary extended her hand towards him. "I've heard a lot about you."

"All good I hope." Mr Flemming gave a nervous laugh.

Mary assured him it was as Martha joined them, closely followed by Mr Wetherby.

"It's not usual to see you in St George's." Mr Wetherby spoke without a trace of a smile or handshake. "Where do you usually worship?"

"I have a seat in St Martin's, but I offered to escort Miss Jackson here this morning."

"And why did you do that?"

"I've grown fond of her over the last few months and we've started walking out together."

"So I've heard, but I wouldn't say that going to church is a place to enjoy someone's company."

"Come now." Mary took Mr Wetherby by the arm. "Let Mr Flemming be, he came here to meet us all, not undergo an interrogation."

Sarah-Ann noted the furious glance Mr Wetherby shot at Mary, followed by the cold stare he turned on both her and Mr Flemming. The next moment he unhooked his arm from Mary and strode off ahead of them.

"I'll see you at home," he shouted back at Mary.

Sarah-Ann watched him walk away and took a deep breath. She'd never seen him like that before.

"Come here," Mary said, linking her arm and waiting for the rest of the group to walk ahead. "He's been in a strange mood for months; don't let him spoil the day. Is Mr Flemming walking you to Frankfort Street?"

"I doubt it, I didn't tell him I'd been invited for dinner. He'll think I'm going back to Hatchett Street. I don't suppose he's happy that I'm not walking with him now."

"He looks happy enough with William. Would you like me to invite him for dinner? I've a piece of ham that's big enough for all of us and I can do some extra potatoes."

"I don't think so. Mr Wetherby didn't look very pleased to see him."

"I've told you not to worry about him," Mary said. "He's always moaning about something at the moment."

"I think Mr Flemming should join us," Martha said as they caught her up. "Easter's a family time and if you're going to be walking out with him, we need to get to know him better."

Sarah-Ann hesitated. "I'm not sure."

They were fast approaching the corner where Mr Flemming and William were waiting for them.

"I'm going to invite him," Mary said.

"As long as you're sure it won't cause any problems with Mr Wetherby."

"I'll get him to open a bottle of sherry. After a couple of glasses he'll be fine."

Mr Flemming hadn't known what to say to the invitation. On the one hand, he'd wanted to be with Sarah-Ann, on the other he realised that Mr Wetherby was less than happy with his presence. In the end, Mary had refused to take no for an answer and five minutes later they'd all walked into the small living room in Frankfort Street.

As soon as he saw Mr Flemming, Mr Wetherby shot him a hateful glare.

"I invited Mr Flemming to dinner," Mary said. "It seemed a shame for him to be the only one not sitting down with us. Now, will you be a dear and pour the sherry?"

"It's very generous of you to invite me." Mr Flemming stood beside Mr Wetherby as he poured the drinks. "I hadn't expected an invitation."

Mr Wetherby grunted and continued to pour the sherry. He passed the glasses around, handing Mr Flemming his last.

"Is business going well?" he asked him.

"Very well." Mr Flemming smiled. "We're never short of customers needing money."

"I don't know how folks get themselves into such a mess," Mr Wetherby said. "If they all did an honest day's work, they wouldn't need the likes of you."

"Well I'm very glad they do."

"I imagine you are, but you must feel like shaking some of them when they come in?"

Mr Flemming took a sharp intake of breath. "There are some deserving cases …"

"Give me some examples." Mr Wetherby said.

Mr Flemming spoke about his customers and the broader financial condition of the inhabitants of Birmingham. He finally relaxed as Mary directed them to their seats at the table.

As dinner came to an end, Mr Flemming scowled when Mr Wetherby turn his attention to Sarah-Ann.

"I understand you're walking out with Mr Flemming," he said. "Are you happy about this?"

"Yes, of course. He wouldn't be here now if I wasn't." Mr Flemming studied Sarah-Ann as she fidgeted with the lace tablecloth.

"If you're sure, I'll give you my blessing."

When Sarah-Ann said nothing, Mr Wetherby turned to Mr Flemming. "I expect you to take good care of her."

"Of course I'll take care of her."

"And another thing, she doesn't have time for a protracted courtship. If you have any further intentions towards her, please make them known, otherwise leave her to find an alternative suitor."

How could this pompous man talk like this in front of everyone? He'd done everything he could to be pleasant to the man, and this was the thanks he got. Despite having her head bowed, Mr Flemming could see Sarah-Ann's cheeks had coloured and decided it was time to leave.

"I need to be going." He stood up and looked at Sarah-Ann. "Will you join me?"

"Yes, of course." Sarah-Ann almost knocked over her chair in her haste to stand up. "Thank you for your hospitality," she said to Mary. "I'll see you in the week."

Mr Flemming took her cloak from the stand and helped her on with it before he opened the door and almost pushed her onto the pavement.

"I don't know who Mr Wetherby thinks he is," he said as they set off towards Hatchett Street. "*I'll give you my blessing*, indeed. He's not your father."

"He's just protective of me because I'm on my own."

"I hope that's all it is. You know I'd like to spend more

time with you but I don't want him interfering. At least he approved of our walking out together. At one point I thought he was going to object."

"He could hardly do that with Mary there," Sarah-Ann said absently.

Mr Flemming gave her a sideways glance. "Of course he could if he'd wanted to. I don't see how someone like Mrs Wetherby could stop him. It seems to me as if she agrees with everything he says."

Chapter 65

Mr Flemming placed the money in the safe and turned the handle to the locked position. It was late and he and Sarah-Ann were the only ones in the shop. He walked over to the door and locked it before he went back behind the counter.

"We've had some nice things in today," he said.

"We have, but I do feel sorry for people who have to pawn things so they can eat."

"Don't feel too sorry for them. Most of them drink the money rather than spend it on food; they've nobody but themselves to blame. They're glad we can help them until they get paid again."

"I know that, but think of the children; it's not their fault there's no food on the table, is it?"

"I suppose not, but it's not our problem either. What do you think of the rings in the first tray here?" Mr Flemming indicated a tray of rings under the glass counter. "If you could have one, which would you chose?"

"I could never afford one of these."

"Maybe not, but imagine if you could. What sort of rings do you like?"

"I like this one." She reached under the glass and

picked up a yellow gold band studded with an assortment of coloured stones. "I love the different colours."

"Who brought it in, do you remember?" Mr Flemming asked.

"Old Mrs Pearson. Since her husband died she's had to sell the few personal possessions she has just to eat. She said she doesn't know what she'll do when she's sold the last one."

"So it doesn't look like she'll be back for it then?" Mr Flemming took the ring from her.

"I'm afraid not, the poor thing."

"Are you nearly finished here?"

"Yes. Let me polish the counter and I'll be on my way."

"I'll get your cloak." Mr Flemming slipped the ring into his pocket and hurried to the other side of the shop. "I'll walk with you; it's a lovely evening. You know, I can't believe you only came into my life at the beginning of this year; I feel as if I've known you much longer."

"We have known each other for longer. Don't you remember me from when you were living with Mr Robson?"

"I do and I remember then thinking how nice you were. Then you moved to Aldridge and I didn't see you again."

"It wasn't all my fault, I seem to remember you moved to Birmingham around the same time."

"I needed to mend my broken heart." He held his hands to his chest.

"Get away with you, you did no such thing." Sarah-Ann laughed. "If you liked me that much you'd have followed me to Aldridge."

"I did think about it."

"Now I know you're teasing. Nobody except my father

would want to live in Aldridge when they could move to Birmingham. Anyway, I'm glad you arrived here before I did; where would I work otherwise?"

Mary placed the casserole of sausages and potatoes on the table and sat down while Mr Wetherby said grace. The table comfortably sat four people and it was a squeeze with seven of them, but it was worth it. It wasn't every day your eldest son reached his coming of age. Earlier in the week William had also become a qualified toolmaker and been released from his apprenticeship with Mr Watkins. Mr Wetherby had already offered everyone a glass of sherry, but as the meal came to an end he re-filled the glasses and proposed a toast.

William stood up to respond. "Thank you, Mr Wetherby, thank you, Mother. Not only have you spoilt me with this lovely meal, but, Mr Wetherby, I owe you a special thank you for everything you've done for me. I wouldn't be where I am today without you and I want you to know how grateful I am. I'd never have thought of being a toolmaker, but I'm so glad you suggested it; I've enjoyed working with Mr Watkins."

"Mr Watkins was impressed with you," Mr Wetherby said. "In fact, he's so pleased, he asked if he could keep you on. I said no, of course. It was always my intention for you to come back here once you were trained and I've no reason to change my mind. We can start our own workshop making tools now you're here."

William sat down again. "Does Mr Watkins know he'll have competition?"

"He does, but I've promised we won't make files so we don't take any of his business. He seemed happy with that."

"He's been good to me over the years and I'd like to carry on seeing him and the family. Would that be possible?"

"I'm sure Mr Watkins will always be pleased to see you, but why would you want to see the rest of the family? I didn't know you knew them."

William flushed. "They're always pleasant when I see them."

"Mrs Watkins is certainly friendly once you get to know her," Mary said. "I've heard the niece is rather strange though. They've had a lot of trouble with her."

"No, she's lovely, I mean friendly; not at all strange. Anyway," he said changing the subject, "I've been looking at that cake on the sideboard for far too long. Are you going to offer me a piece?"

"Yes, of course." Mary glanced at Sarah-Ann and Alice as she stood up.

"Once you've finished that," Mr Wetherby said, "I think it's high time we left the ladies and went for a pint of ale."

Within half an hour the party had broken up.

"What do you know about the Watkins's niece?" Sarah-Ann asked as Mary made a pot of tea.

"Only that they've had a lot of trouble with her over the years."

"It sounds as if William likes her. What will you do?"

"I'm not too worried." Mary put the teapot down on the table. "Mrs Watkins told me the other week she's going away shortly."

"I suspect William doesn't know."

"He'll find out soon enough."

৯৽৵৻

As the suffocating days of summer persisted, Sarah-Ann wished she were back in the countryside. With the sweltering temperatures, the smog generated from the chimneys made it difficult to breathe. Even now, at nearly seven o'clock in the evening the air was oppressive. Not only that, she still had her laundry to do; a job that made her warm even on a cold day. She worked as quickly as she could and an hour later she was ready to hang her clothes out to dry. She left the washhouse and found space on a line, when she heard her name being called.

"Mr Flemming, what are you doing here?" She dropped her basket of washing and immediately reached to tidy the hair that hung limply around her face. "I've only just finished the laundry, I must look dreadful."

"I am looking at you, and very nice you look too." His smile failed to convince her he was being serious.

"Don't tease me. Here, have a seat while I go and straighten myself up." Sarah-Ann pushed a stool towards him.

"There's no need and I wasn't teasing, you look lovely. Now come and sit with me ... or we could go for a walk?"

Knowing she couldn't possibly go for a walk looking as she did, Sarah-Ann found another stool and sat beside him outside the laundry.

"What brings you here? I didn't expect to see you until tomorrow."

"I needed to get out for a walk and found myself here. I hope you don't mind."

"It's always nice to see you, but I'd have liked some notice to make myself presentable."

"I told you, I don't mind. In fact, I like you like that."
He stopped to look at her and gently pushed a loose piece
of hair behind her ear. "There is a reason I found myself
here, you know."

"Is something wrong?"

"Do you remember on Easter Sunday when I joined
you for dinner, and Mr Wetherby told me to make my
intentions known sooner rather than later?" He paused
but Sarah-Ann gave no response. "Well, he was right, you
deserve to know my feelings towards you."

Sarah-Ann's heart skipped a beat. She didn't know what
to expect or what she hoped for.

"Since that first day you came into the shop I've known
you were special. I now know I want to spend my life with
you and so ..." He paused again and got down on one knee.
"Will you marry me?"

Sarah-Ann looked down at the man in front of her,
his dark brown eyes gazing at her, and became aware of
the silence surrounding them. She looked up to see people
staring at her. *What should she say?* A moment later she
looked back to Mr Flemming, but all she could see was Mr
Wetherby. *No, she couldn't let him take this chance from her.*

"Don't keep him waiting," one of her neighbours
shouted. Sarah-Ann smiled when she realised they were
willing her on.

"Yes," she said, a smile breaking out over her face. "Yes
of course I will." *I need a man of my own, not someone else's.*

Her neighbours broke into spontaneous applause and
Mr Flemming took hold of her hands and squeezed them
tightly.

"I have something for you as well." He put his hand

in his pocket and pulled out a small box. He fumbled to open it, before he took out the gold band with coloured stones she had admired weeks earlier. "Will you wear this to seal our betrothal? I've always said you should have some jewellery and you liked this. I hope it's the first of many things I'll get you."

"I don't know what to say; it's lovely."

"You deserve it. I promised Mr Wetherby I had your best interests at heart and I do. I'll make you happy, Miss Jackson."

෴

Mary stood in the living room, mixing a cake under the direction of *Mrs Beeton*. The heat from the fire made the room oppressive, something the open front door did little to relieve. She was deep in thought, when Sarah-Ann burst in.

"What are you doing here?" Mary said. "Why aren't you at work?"

"I don't have to go anymore." The smile on Sarah-Ann's face was as broad as any Mary had seen. "Mr Flemming's asked me to marry him and I've accepted. Look, he gave me this ring."

Mary wiped her hands on her apron and took hold of the hand Sarah-Ann offered her. "That's lovely; congratulations. When did this happen?"

"Last night, he came to the court after work. It was so unexpected."

"Have you set a date?"

"December. In fact we'll get married a year to the day after Father died."

Mary reached for the bottle of gin and two glasses. "That's still five months away, why are you waiting?"

"I want to get all this probate sorted out. Everyone wants their money and it's not the sort of thing I should be doing as a wife."

"William and Mary-Ann are in no hurry, you don't have to rush on their behalf."

"Maybe not, but Richard and Louisa could do with it. One hundred and fifty pounds is a lot of money. I don't know why Pa didn't give all Charles's share to William and Mary-Ann, I feel mean only giving them nineteen guineas each."

"They get everything they need from Mr Wetherby; he probably thought they didn't need so much. What would they do with that sort of money anyway? Have you sold the properties yet?"

Sarah-Ann sighed. "There's a couple to go but I have some interest in them. I'd no idea it would take so long, and unfortunately I haven't had much help. The other executors do their bit, but they don't seem in any hurry, and then Mr Wetherby, well ..."

"Did he offer to help? He shouldn't have raised your hopes; he's far too busy. At least he's selling the business in London; apparently he's made it more efficient and so he hopes to make quite a profit. All the travelling is too much for him; he wastes over ten hours a week getting there and back and he hasn't got ten hours to spare."

"I've hardly seen him since I arrived in Birmingham. I hope he'll be happy for me."

"I'm sure he will. He gave Mr Flemming his blessing so why shouldn't he be?"

Chapter 66

THE DARK GREY SKY SILHOUETTED the church as the rain lashed against it. It stood as a lone figure amongst the gravestones and only the flicker of candles through the stained glass windows gave any sense of life. A carriage pulled up at the bottom of the driveway and the driver dismounted, waiting for the signal to open the door. It didn't come. Inside Sarah-Ann sat with Mr Wetherby, listening to the rain pounding the sides of the carriage.

"Why does the weather have to be so bad, today of all days?" she said. "I'll look washed out by the time I get inside."

"We have the umbrella, and your cloak will keep the worst of the rain off you." He ran the material through his fingers.

She looked at him and smiled. "Thank you for agreeing to give me away, I didn't know if you would."

"Once Richard couldn't do it, I didn't have much choice, did I? I can't pretend I'm happy about it though. Are you sure you want to go through with it?"

"Yes, I'm sure. Mr Flemming's a good man and I need a husband."

Mr Wetherby reached out and took her hand. "How different it might have been."

"Once you married Mary it was never going to be any other way."

"I know, but ..."

"No buts, not today. This is my wedding day, please be happy for me."

"Very well." He raised her hand and kissed it. "I hope you know I'll always be watching out for you. He's a lucky man."

"Not as lucky as Mary." Sarah-Ann failed to hide the trembling in her voice. "What I wouldn't do to swap places with her." She looked down at the bouquet in her lap.

Mr Wetherby raised her chin and looked at her. "You've no idea how much I've longed for you." He leaned forward and kissed her, gently at first, but then with a growing urgency. Sarah-Ann made no attempt to stop him and yielded as his hands moved down her back and pulled her towards him. When he released her, they were both shaking.

"I shouldn't have done that," Mr Wetherby said, regaining his composure. "Forgive me."

"There's nothing to forgive. I've kissed you a thousand times in my dreams; it's only now that it feels unreal. My only regret is that it's taken you so long."

Mr Wetherby looked at her and she thought he would see her soul; such was the intensity of his gaze. She held her breath wondering what he would do next. A moment later he leaned towards her and took her face in his hands. "May God forgive us," he said.

৯৯

Inside the church, the muttering from the congregation was growing louder. It was usual for the bride to be a few minutes late, but so far they had waited over fifteen minutes and there was still no sign of her. After looking at his pocket watch for the umpteenth time, Mr Flemming approached Mary in the opposite pew.

"They should be here by now."

"They were ready to leave when I left," Mary said. "I'm worried myself."

They both looked to the back of the church, but the heavy doors were shut against the weather.

"I'll go and see if they're here," William said as he overheard the conversation.

He went to the church door and saw the carriage outside with the driver ready to open the door. He was about to turn away when he looked again. Despite the rain, the driver stood at an angle to the carriage, and looked like he had been there for some time. William watched for a minute before he went back to his seat.

"They're here," he said as he sat back down. "I think they're waiting for the rain to go off."

"Well, they can't stay there all day," the vicar said. "I've a meeting this afternoon."

ço~e

It was another five minutes before Sarah-Ann and Mr Wetherby appeared at the back of the church.

"How do I look?" she said as he took her cloak from her shoulders.

The look in his eyes said all she needed to know. "Lovely

as ever, although you might want to fix your hair. At least you can blame the weather."

ঙ্গৢৢ

Mr Flemming gave a broad smile as he saw Sarah-Ann walking towards him. She wore an emerald green gown with a tightly fitted bodice, and a skirt that billowed out beneath her waist. Her hat was the same shade of green, decorated with white spray roses to match those in her bouquet. She looked beautiful with her face powdered and her hair swept over her left shoulder.

ঙ্গৢৢ

All the family were there, but she didn't see them. She fixed a smile on her face and stared at Mr Flemming, but her mind wouldn't leave the scene in the carriage. Her body still trembled and she held tightly onto Mr Wetherby as they walked down the aisle. Once they reached the front of the church, she kept hold of him for as long as she could.

The vicar hurried through the service and before long turned to Mr Wetherby. "Who gives this woman to this man?"

Mr Wetherby hesitated and looked to Sarah-Ann for approval. She gave a barely perceptible nod of her head, and reluctantly he offered her hand to Mr Flemming. He stayed beside her while the vicar blessed the union and then retired to the seat next to Mary.

ঙ্গৢৢ

By the time the service ended, the rain had subsided enough for the wedding party to walk to the tavern for the wedding breakfast. Sarah-Ann spent the first fifteen minutes explaining that she had arrived at church on time, but that the rain had been too severe for her to walk up the drive.

While they waited for the food, Mr Wetherby noticed a familiar face in the corner of the back room, Aunt Lucy. He had forgotten she'd be there and presumed the elderly woman sat with her was her sister Rebecca. Aunt Lucy looked directly at him but he turned away. He had no desire to engage with her, today of all days, and he went to find Mary. She stood talking to Martha and Alice. They were also with someone else he vaguely remembered.

"You remember Emma, don't you, Sarah-Ann's sister?" Mary asked once he had acknowledged the group.

"I do, good morning Mrs ..."

"Dainty." Mary helped him.

"Of course, Mrs Dainty."

"I understand you've been very generous to my sister, Mr Wetherby. In fact I hear you were actually responsible for her meeting Mr Flemming."

"So it would appear, although that wasn't my intention."

"I don't suppose you could have foreseen it, but I know she's grateful to you. She's wanted a husband for so many years. They do look happy together, don't they?" They all looked across the room towards the bar area. Mr Flemming had his arm around Sarah-Ann and laughed as he talked to several of their guests. Sarah-Ann looked as if her mind was miles away. After a couple of seconds she saw them looking and gave a weak smile.

"Sarah-Ann doesn't look as happy as she should," Martha said.

Mr Wetherby was about to respond, when he saw

Richard approaching her. "What's he doing here? I thought he was ill."

"He was, but he's feeling better."

"Why didn't he give her away?"

"Because she'd already asked you and didn't want to let you down," Mary said.

Mr Wetherby looked at his pocket watch. "It's time we were leaving. I'll go and find William and Mary-Ann."

"Not yet, please. We've not eaten and Sarah-Ann'll be disappointed if we leave so soon."

Mr Wetherby glanced at Sarah-Ann and then looked at Mary. "We'll stay until we've eaten, but be quick, I need to get back ... and you need to get back for William Junior."

Mr Wetherby was quiet for the rest of the dinner, speaking only when required, and even then keeping his answers brief. Once they'd finished eating, he grew impatient to leave and ordered Mary back to the waiting carriage.

"I don't know what's wrong with you today," she said. "I've never seen you like this. We can't go without saying goodbye."

"You say goodbye, I'll wait outside."

"You'll do no such thing. You've just given Sarah-Ann away and you don't even want to say goodbye to her. What will she think?"

Mr Wetherby glanced over to Sarah-Ann and saw she was looking at him. She released herself from Mr Flemming's hold and walked over to them. "You're not leaving already, are you? I've hardly seen you."

"You saw me in the carriage if you remember," Mr Wetherby said.

"I'm hardly likely to forget."

"You'll have to excuse him, he isn't feeling his usual self," Mary said.

"He was fine in the carriage, but I suppose I haven't been myself since then either."

A frown formed on Mary's face. "You were only travelling for a couple of minutes, surely the ride wasn't that bad? Perhaps it's the excitement of the day."

"Yes, that must be it," Sarah-Ann said.

"You look to me as if you've taken everything in your stride," Mr Wetherby said.

"Appearances don't always reflect how you feel on the inside."

Mr Wetherby looked at her and saw the sadness in her eyes. "I'm sorry. I really need to go."

Chapter 67

Birmingham, Warwickshire.

WITH THE COLD, DULL DAYS of January upon them, Mary struggled to get out of bed in the mornings. It had been dark when she got up that morning and the thought of another couple of months of nothing to look forward to saddened her. She loved the sun and the clear skies, even if they were often hidden by smoke from the factories. Nowadays the fire, with its light and warmth, had come to be her best friend.

It wasn't like her to feel down, but of late she hadn't been her usual self. Mr Wetherby had been more distant than ever, something that hadn't been helped by the news that his sister Amelia would marry later in the year. It wasn't the wedding itself that caused concern, but it raised the prospect of seeing his stepmother at the wedding.

Not having the energy or will to do even the smallest of tasks around the house, she agreed to see the doctor. He found nothing physically wrong, but said her body was changing and that she may feel '*different*' for many months to come. The diagnosis made her even more miserable. Not only could she expect to feel tired for the foreseeable future, she'd spoken to Alice and she wasn't having any of the symptoms she had. *Why was it only her?* On top of everything else, it was unlikely she'd be able to have any more children. She didn't know why this upset her, she hadn't wanted any more children since the twins, but suddenly she could think of nothing else.

That evening, once they finished tea, Mary excused herself and went upstairs. Shortly afterwards, Mr Wetherby went after her.

"Whatever's the matter?" he said. "You've barely said two words since I came home tonight."

Mary looked at him, but her voice faltered.

"Mary, what is it?" He walked towards her and took hold of her hands. "Please talk to me."

She shook her head as tears fell down her cheeks. Mr Wetherby wiped the first with his finger, but within seconds she was sobbing.

"Come here." He took hold of her and wrapped his arms around her. "It can't be that bad surely, we have everything we want, don't we? My goodness, what am I thinking, I didn't ask what the doctor said. You're not ill are you?"

She shook her head before burying it in his shoulder. Taking the opportunity to hold her, he let her cry. Finally the tears subsided and he lifted her chin so he could see her face.

"Please talk to me."

"The doctor told me I'm too old to have any more children."

A frown formed on Mr Wetherby's face. "You said you didn't want any more children after what happened with the twins, that's why we haven't … you know. You should be delighted. Why are you crying?"

"I don't know, there's just something final about it; I feel like my life's over."

"Don't be silly, of course it's not. Was the doctor sure?"

Mary nodded.

"Come here." Mr Wetherby lifted her chin and kissed her with a passion that had been missing from their marriage for years. "I love you and I'm glad you can't have any more children, at least we don't have to worry about it anymore." With that he led her to the bed and the barrier that had been between them for so long was broken.

Chapter 68

MARY KNEW HOW DISTANT SHE'D become from Mr Wetherby, but now it was as if she was living with the man she had originally married. As spring arrived, even though she felt physically sick, she was happier than she had been for years. She sat by the fire with a cup of tea, thanking the Lord for His mercy, when there was a knock. Moments later Sarah-Ann burst into the room.

"I'm going to have a baby," she shrieked before Mary could say anything. "Can you believe it?"

Mary's smile mirrored Sarah-Ann's. "That's wonderful, congratulations. When?"

"I only found out yesterday. The doctor thinks it'll be another five or six months yet, so sometime around early autumn. I don't know if I'll be able to wait until then."

"I bet that smile hasn't left your face since you found out."

"I can't help it, I'm so excited. It's all I've ever wanted."

Sarah-Ann sat down at the table, expecting a cup of tea, but Mary remained where she was, holding onto a chair.

"Are you all right?" Sarah-Ann stood up again. "You look very pale."

"Just a little dizziness. The doctor said my body's

changing. I do wish it would hurry up. I don't want to feel like this for the next few years."

"A friend of Mother's went through that years ago; I did feel sorry for her. I hope it doesn't last long."

"I'm sure I'll be fine. If I'm no better in the next couple of days I'm going to ask the doctor for a tonic; I need to stop the sickness at least."

❧

When he arrived home that evening, Mr Wetherby didn't have a lot of time. He had a guest speaker coming to the Conservative Association and wanted to be in good time to meet him.

"Will you be out late?" Mary asked as he put on his hat and coat.

"I don't think so, no later than usual. Why?"

"No reason, but I haven't told you Sarah-Ann's news. I wondered if you'd be back before I went to bed."

"What news?" He tried to hide the note of concern from his voice.

"She's expecting a baby. She's so excited, you should have seen the smile on her face."

Mr Wetherby clutched the pocket watch in his hand, trying to process what she'd said. "Sarah-Ann's having a baby? Since when?"

"Since shortly after she got married I presume. Does it matter?"

"No … of course not. I'll see you later, I must be going."

All thoughts of the Conservative Association were forgotten as Mr Wetherby made his way down Summer Lane. He prayed Mr Flemming would be in the beerhouse because he needed to see Sarah-Ann alone. He knocked on the door and gave a sigh of relief when she opened it.

"Is he out?" Mr Wetherby stepped into the living room and locked the door.

"He is, but he'll be back any time. What are you doing here so late?"

"Mary told me your news."

"Isn't it wonderful?" Sarah-Ann's eyes shone as her smile returned.

No smile crossed Mr Wetherby's lips. "Whose is it?"

Sarah-Ann's smile faded. "Does it matter? Mr Flemming will bring it up and nobody need suspect anything."

"If you're carrying my son, I want some say in how he's brought up."

"But we'll never know. Can't you assume it's Mr Flemming's and let me be happy?"

"If I see a hint of green in his eyes, I'll know he's mine, and I can't let Mr Flemming think he's the father of my child."

"You can't think like that. Please let me be happy to have a child of my own without adding complications."

"It shouldn't have happened like this." Mr Wetherby put his arms around her. "It should be me looking after you, not him."

∽◆∾

As the days passed, the sickness dragging Mary down failed to subside and she knew she had to see the doctor again. Not wanting to worry Mr Wetherby she waited until one morning when she saw him leave the workshop before she walked to the doctor's.

"Mrs Wetherby, I don't often see you here," the doctor said. "Why didn't you arrange a visit?"

"I wondered if you'd give me a tonic."

"I told you your body's changing …"

"I know, but it's got so much worse. I can't go on like this for much longer."

"All right, let me take a look at you." The doctor gestured to the bed at the far end of the room. He examined her in silence for several minutes before he straightened up, a frown across his face. "I don't know how to tell you this, but you're going to have another baby."

"A baby?" Mary sat bolt upright. "I can't be. You told me I couldn't have any more."

"It looks like you're three or four months into the pregnancy, so the baby will be born in late autumn."

Mary stood up and paced the room. "I can't go through that again, not after what happened last time. You have to do something."

The doctor looked at her over the rim of his spectacles. "I hope you're not suggesting what I think you are."

"Surely at my age it could be dangerous and it's not yet quickened."

"That, my dear lady, is completely irrelevant and has been for years. I suggest you go home and tell Mr Wetherby. I'm sure he'll be delighted."

"He won't be." The trembling in Mary's voice was obvious. "He'll be furious."

Mary saw nothing and acknowledged no one as she walked home. Her head spun and the prospect of telling

Mr Wetherby terrified her. When she arrived home she sat by the fire and pulled her shawl tightly around her.

Shortly before seven o'clock, she heard footsteps outside the front door and sat up straight, waiting for him to come in. When he saw the table empty, and Mary making no effort to prepare the tea, a puzzled expression crossed his face.

"Will we not eat tonight?"

"We will, but I didn't want to get it myself. I have some news … please don't be angry with me."

Mr Wetherby hung his coat on the stand and turned back to her. "Go on."

"I went to see the doctor today. I didn't want to worry you, I only wanted him to give me a tonic."

"And did he?"

"No." She paused and took a deep breath. "I'm going to have another baby."

Mr Wetherby looked as if someone had struck him. "Another baby?"

Mary nodded.

"Good God, Mary, how did that happen? You told me you couldn't have any more."

"That's what the doctor told me."

Mr Wetherby sat in the chair opposite and put his head in his hands. "Did you trick me into this?"

"Of course I didn't. Do you think I want another baby? I don't want to go through childbirth again."

"When will it be born?"

"Late autumn."

"You should be in bed." Mr Wetherby took her hand and led her towards the stairs. "I don't want to see you lift a finger around this house; and you can write to Martha and tell her you're not going to her daughter's baptism next week. May the Lord preserve you, this should never have happened. Mary-Ann and Alice can do all the chores."

"I need to tell Sarah-Ann." Mary said as they reached the top of the stairs.

"Sarah-Ann? What's it got to do with her?"

"She's having a baby too, probably only a couple of weeks ahead of me and so we can keep each other company."

"You'll do no such thing. You need to look after yourselves, not be travelling across Birmingham; in fact, I don't want you going to see her. I'll go and tell her and ask if she's able to visit you."

☙❧

Mr Wetherby knocked on the door and went straight in.

"What are you doing here?" Sarah-Ann jumped up, scattering wool across the floor. "I wasn't expecting you."

"That's a nice welcome. Aren't you pleased to see me?"

"Of course." She put her arms around him. "But I worry he'll come home early."

"He won't today, I walked past the shop and he looked busy."

"Then what can I do for you?" A smile spread across her face.

"I've come to tell you Mary's expecting another baby."

"She can't be." Sarah-Ann pulled away. "You told me you didn't have that sort of relationship."

"We didn't, it just happened … she was upset."

"What's she got to be upset about? She has everything anyone could ever want."

"She thought she couldn't have any more children."

"And so you thought you could do what you wanted with her and I wouldn't find out?" Sarah-Ann turned and went to the other side of the room.

"Sarah-Ann, you're being unreasonable. She's my wife …"

"You've been using me … to get what you couldn't get at home."

"It wasn't like that, besides, I have to put up with you being here with Mr Flemming."

"That's only because I was practically married before I knew how you felt."

"I'm sorry. It should never have happened." Mr Wetherby walked towards her and wrapped his arms around her. "I don't want to say this, but I think we should stop seeing each other, it's getting too complicated."

"You can't end it like that." She threw his arms from her. "Not with the baby and everything, I won't survive without you."

"Of course you will. You have Mr Flemming and I need to spend more time with Mary; I don't want anything happening to her. I told her I was coming here to let you know about the baby. Are you well enough to visit her?"

"How can I visit when you've told me you don't want to see me anymore?" Sarah-Ann couldn't hold back her tears.

"Please don't cry." He wrapped his arms around her again. "It's not that I don't want to; I just don't think we should see each other as often. I'll always look out for you, don't ever forget that."

Chapter 69

THE WATKINS FAMILY LIVED A short walk away from Frankfort Street and William set off as soon as he finished at the workshop. He had been invited for tea, and knocked on their front door exactly ten minutes after he left work. The domestic help answered and took his hat before showing him into the back room.

"Mr Jackson, come in." Mr Watkins stood up and shook his hand. "It's good to see you again."

William hadn't been to the house before and was surprised at its size. A large window overlooked the back yard and an impressive fireplace sat in the middle of the back wall. The table in the centre of the room was set for four people, and for a moment William wondered who would be joining them. Mr Watkins had taken on a new apprentice so perhaps it was set for him.

"Is the new apprentice joining us?" William pointed at the table.

"No, he doesn't eat with us. It's my niece. She's back from school."

"She's back!" William put his hand to his face to smother his grin.

"She is, for the summer at least," Mr Watkins said.

"She'll be here soon enough, but tell me, how are things with Mr Wetherby, what are you doing?"

Soon enough for Mr Watkins wasn't soon enough for William, and he kept his eye on the door while he explained he was now making buttons.

"Is that what you want to do?"

"Not really, but with Mr Wetherby away on business so often, I have to oversee the workshop. I still do some toolmaking but it's buttons that make the money and so that's his priority."

"That's very disappointing. I'm going to speak to Mr Wetherby again about having you back here."

William was about to tell Mr Watkins he would be wasting his time, but the door opened and Mrs Watkins and her niece came into the room. A moment later the domestic help followed and placed some food on the table. William's eyes followed Miss Watkins around the room, watching the sway of her skirt as it moved with her marvellously curvaceous body. She stood tall for a woman, only a couple of inches shorter than him, but with her hair arranged in ringlets around her face, she had an elegant look.

As soon as William sat at the table he was unable to concentrate on Mr Watkins. His niece looked so lovely, his eyes were constantly drawn to her. He had admired her from a distance since the early days of his apprenticeship, but they'd been young then and had never been left alone together. He had been upset when she went away, but he hadn't forgotten her, and this was the closest they'd been to each other.

Mr Watkins brought him back to his senses when he asked a question about his future plans. The truth was he would do whatever Mr Wetherby told him to, but he didn't say that. Instead he talked about expanding the toolmaking part of the business and over tea they had a protracted conversation about the future of manufacturing in Birmingham.

As the evening wore on, William found that whenever he looked at Miss Watkins, she was already watching him, her mischievous blue grey eyes dancing with delight whenever he turned his attention to her. Over the course of the evening he took in every detail of her face. He wanted so much to get to know her, but knowing she would be going back to school soon, he knew he had to bide his time and create an image of her he wouldn't forget.

A week later, when Mr Wetherby got home from work, he slammed the door behind him before he realised Mary had a visitor.

"Sarah-Ann!" He couldn't hide his surprise when he saw her. "What are you doing here? You shouldn't be out in your condition."

"I needed some company and didn't think a walk would do me any harm."

"You can't make these decisions yourself. Does Mr Flemming know you're here?"

"I only decided after he left this morning."

"Well, I'm going to take you home in a carriage right now and I'll have no arguing. You can't just do what you want."

"I'm sorry, but please stay for a cup of tea first, I've not seen you for weeks."

"You look like you could do with one," Mary said to him. "What's the matter?"

"Nothing for you to worry about, only that fellow Watkins. He's been to see me again to ask if William can go back to work for him. He doesn't think he should be making buttons when he's a trained machinist. I don't know what I have to do to make him realise William's not going anywhere."

"It's nice that he values him," Mary said.

"Not when it's at my expense. I've invested a lot of time and energy into that lad; I want my money's worth."

"He seems to be spending a lot of time with the Watkins family at the moment, I wonder if they've been planning something?" Mary said.

"Is the niece home?" Sarah-Ann asked. "He seemed quite keen on her last year and it could be another reason why he's there so often."

"Whatever it is, he's not leaving the business and I want no more talk of it. Now, let me go and get a carriage."

Once they were settled in the carriage, Mr Wetherby instructed the driver to drive slowly and avoid all holes in the road. He knew it would double the journey time and he wanted time to talk. As they set off he took hold of Sarah-Ann's hand.

"How've you been?" he asked.

"I've been better. You used to lighten up my days, now all I have to look forward to is Mr Flemming coming home each evening."

"Is he treating you well?"

"He is and he's delighted about the baby, but he's not you." Mr Wetherby heard the disappointment in her voice.

"God's punishment is severe indeed. Many would say we deserve it."

"Maybe we do, but how can you stop yourself falling in love?"

Mr Wetherby lifted her chin to look at her. "Don't talk like that; you have to focus on the baby now and give it all your love."

"I already am. I'm counting the days until it's born and maybe if he has fair hair I'll pretend he's you."

Once they arrived back at the house, Mr Wetherby helped Sarah-Ann down from the carriage and opened the front door before he locked it behind them. Once in the small living room he took her cloak.

"What time will Mr Flemming be home?"

"Probably not yet, he often calls in the beerhouse for a drink, but you'd better not stay."

Mr Wetherby reached down for her hands and ran his eyes over her. "Pregnancy suits you, you look beautiful."

"I feel well, I just wish I'd been able to start sooner."

"Don't ever regret anything. You can't change things, and everything we do becomes part of us."

He leaned down to kiss her but before he could, the door handle rattled and a second later Mr Flemming shouted through the door.

"Why's the door locked? Sarah-Ann, let me in."

Sarah-Ann's eyes widened with horror. "He's going to find you here."

"Don't worry; I'll tell him I brought you home."

"Sarah-Ann, are you in there?" The door rattled again.

"What about the door being locked? I never lock it."

"I'll tell him I did it, say I forgot where I was. Don't worry."

Sarah-Ann looked unsure but unlocked the door and let her husband in.

"Why was the door locked?" Mr Flemming asked as he walked into the room. "And what's he doing here?"

"I'm sorry, it was my fault." Mr Wetherby held up his hands. "Sarah-Ann called to visit Mary this afternoon and I wanted to make sure she got home safely; I must have locked the door by mistake."

"A likely tale. You don't lock someone else's front door by mistake. Get out of my house; you've no right to be here with my wife."

"She shouldn't have been out in her condition and I didn't want to leave her alone. You need to look after her." Mr Wetherby glanced at Sarah-Ann who kept her eyes on the floor.

"Don't tell me how to look after my own wife. I don't know who you think you are but ever since I met Sarah-Ann you've been interfering where it's not wanted. She's my wife and I don't want you seeing her again unless I'm with her. Is that understood? I'm perfectly capable of looking after her and our child myself."

Mr Wetherby flinched at his words and watched as Mr Flemming looked from him to Sarah-Ann and back again.

"There's something going on here, isn't there?"

"Don't be ridiculous," Mr Wetherby said. "I'm a happily married man."

"So was I until I came home tonight. Now tell me what's been going on before I beat it out of you."

꽁쏙

Two days later, Mary was so engrossed in her knitting she wondered if she had imagined the knock on the door. When nobody came in, she heaved herself out of the chair and went to check. It took her a minute to open it and when she did, Mr Flemming had turned to leave.

"Mr Flemming, what brings you here; won't you come in?"

"No I won't. I've come to tell you Sarah-Ann's lost the baby."

"No … she can't have." Mary put her hand to her chest. "She was only here the other day, she looked marvellous. Mr Wetherby took her home."

"You knew Mr Wetherby was with her?" The colour drained from Mr Flemming's face.

"Yes, he wanted to make sure she got home safely. What happened?"

Mr Flemming shifted uncomfortably. "She fell down the stairs and triggered the birth … it was a boy … he looked exactly like her … she's devastated."

Mary clutched the doorframe, a feeling of dizziness passing over her. "I'm so sorry, I know how much she wanted that baby. What made her fall?"

Mr Flemming shook his head but said nothing.

"I can't take it in." Mary sat in the chair nearest the door. "I must call and see her."

"Please don't. She needs plenty of rest, and seeing you like that might upset her." Mr Flemming pointed at Mary's swollen belly. "I don't want Mr Wetherby calling either."

"Why would Mr Wetherby call?" Mary said, but Mr Flemming raised his hat and left without another word.

Chapter 70

MARY SHIFTED TO ADJUST THE pillows behind her and leaned back. It was half past eleven in the morning but she dared not get out of bed, not until Mr Wetherby came to help her. Since Sarah-Ann's accident he had confined her to her room and, although she desperately wanted to regain some independence, she knew there was little point arguing. It was for her benefit, she knew that, but still each day dragged more than the one before.

He usually came home between twelve and one o'clock and helped her wash and dress. Today she prayed he would be early. The baby was unusually active and she needed to move for the sake of her ribs. Not only that, Martha was coming to see her and she wanted to be ready. Much to her relief, he arrived at quarter past twelve and helped her out of bed.

"I can do this myself, you know."

"I don't want any accidents," Mr Wetherby said as he led her to the washbasin.

"I've told you I won't go near the stairs."

"That's beside the point; what if you have a rush of blood to your head? I don't want to come home and find you on the floor." Mr Wetherby passed her a towel.

"I feel fine, really I do. Please could I at least get out of bed and get ready to go downstairs before you come home?"

"You haven't got long left now, is it worth the risk for such little benefit?"

"You're not the one confined to your room. Please, I'm losing my mind."

Mr Wetherby stood and looked at her as she fastened her skirt. "I'll ask the doctor when he comes tomorrow. If he has no concerns I'll allow it. You're too special to me, I won't risk anything happening."

Once downstairs, she sat with Mr Wetherby and Mary-Ann for dinner before Mr Wetherby went back to work.

"Things are looking up," Mary said to Mary-Ann when they were alone. "I should be able to get myself out of bed and dressed in the morning. At least I'll be able to look out of the window while I wait for him."

"Once everyone's at work, there's not much to see." Mary-Ann began to collect up the dishes. "I often wish I could do more than just clean the house."

"You're twenty-one now, you should be going out more often. William can escort you. Have you seen him lately?"

"No, I never know where he is. He spends a lot of time at the Watkins's house, although not as much as he did over the summer."

Mary stood up to stretch her legs before moving to the fire. "Your aunt Sarah-Ann suggested it could be to do with the niece."

"She could be right," Mary-Ann said. "She came home over the summer but she's back at school now."

"I hope you're wrong; I don't want him having anything

to do with her. Even her aunt thinks she's trouble. Have you met her?"

"No, and I haven't heard much about her either. William seems to want to keep her secret."

Shortly after two o'clock, Martha knocked on the door and let herself in with her young daughter.

"I'm sorry I had to bring Catherine with me," she said, taking her daughter's cape off. "The last thing you must want is a small child disturbing you but I had nobody to leave her with."

"I don't mind, I don't see enough of her."

"If she gets restless, I'll take her out of your way," Mary-Ann said. "I love looking after little ones."

"You wait until you have some of your own and you can't give them back," Martha said with a smile. "You won't be so keen then."

"I'm looking forward to it," Mary-Ann said. "What could be hard about looking after your own children?"

"I'll remind you of that in about ten years' time," Mary said with a laugh.

It only took half an hour for Catherine to tire of the living room, so Mary-Ann took her into the court. Once they were alone, Martha turned the discussion to Sarah-Ann.

"I went to see her yesterday and she looked dreadful. The baby should have been born last week and she's grieving as if he's just died. She's wearing black and everything."

"As if I didn't have enough to worry about with this baby," Mary said. "I don't know how I'll face her again, I feel so guilty."

"It's not your fault."

"I know, but I still feel uneasy. What if she hates me because she lost the baby rather than me?"

"Of course she won't. She didn't say anything of the sort to me."

"I suppose that's something. I'll be glad when this is all behind us and we can go back to how we were."

Despite how much she wanted the ordeal to be over, when she was alone, Mary was often in tears at the thought of the birth. The doctor visited every morning and evening to check on her, but still it did nothing to allay her fears. After all, Albert and Edwin had been born without incident, and look what happened to them. What if she had two babies now? Surely they would go the same way.

As the middle of October approached, the position of the baby changed and Mary knew the time was near. When Mr Wetherby came home from work on Saturday afternoon, she asked him to take her upstairs. She lay on the bed, breathing hard. The pain from the baby hadn't started but every nerve in her body was on edge. She couldn't do this.

"Don't leave me." Tears rolled down her cheeks as Mr Wetherby stood up to go. "I can't go through this again."

"Of course you can." Mr Wetherby put his hands on hers. "I'll get the doctor, so you won't be alone."

Mary watched the door close behind him and felt sick. What if he took too long and the baby was born before he came back; what if she was carrying two babies again? They were bound to die; she couldn't go through that again. Her heart was pounding; she needed to be calm. She needed to stay calm … to take deep breaths … but she couldn't. She couldn't breathe, not properly, only small breaths. Her heart was beating faster and her throat had closed in on her. She needed to breathe, shallow breaths and lots of them. She didn't want to die.

By the time the doctor arrived, sweat covered Mary's face and conversation was out of the question.

"She needs to calm down," the doctor said to Mr Wetherby. "I'll give her some laudanum; it will steady her breathing and help her sleep. The baby won't be born today but I'll be back tomorrow to see how she is."

Once they were alone, Mary let Mr Wetherby wipe her brow with a wet cloth. Her breathing had steadied but if she drifted off to sleep the image of Albert and Edwin invaded her thoughts. *Why was it so hard to have another child?*

By Sunday morning the pains had started and became so severe Mary writhed around the bed, unashamed of the screams that accompanied them. The doctor arrived to witness the terror on her face and immediately gave her a low dose of laudanum before he sent Mr Wetherby downstairs. He warned him to expect a long wait but once they were alone and he examined his patient, he was amazed to see the head of the baby.

Within the hour and without incident, Mary gave birth to a healthy baby girl. There was nothing small about her and, despite feeling drowsy, Mary was able to sit up in bed holding her daughter.

"It's over," Mr Wetherby said with a smile as he walked

to the bed and kissed her head. "I told you everything would be all right, although I believe it's a girl."

"She's beautiful, look at her. How could I ever think I didn't want something as wonderful as this?"

"She might be beautiful, but after all this time, what use is a daughter to me? I can't believe it."

The smile left Mary's face. "Don't be angry, it's not her fault. At least come and look at her."

Mr Wetherby pulled back the blanket protecting his daughter and took his first glimpse of her.

"She's just like you," Mary said, looking down at the fair hair and snub nose. "I can't wait to introduce her to everyone."

"No ... you can't, not yet." Mr Wetherby covered his daughter's face with the blanket.

"What's the matter? Anyone would think you're not proud of her."

"We need to keep her well wrapped up ... away from the cold. That's all."

"It's only October." Mary didn't normally raise her voice, but he wasn't making sense.

"You won't be going out for a couple of weeks and by then, it'll be too cold for her."

"I can still have visitors?" Mary said.

"Yes, no ... not Sarah-Ann ... or Mr Flemming."

Mary stared at Mr Wetherby as he paced the room. "Why not?"

"You told me Sarah-Ann was still upset about losing her baby; I'm sure Mr Flemming is too. It wouldn't be tactful to invite them around, not while she looks like ... a baby."

"Now you're being ridiculous, I can't put off seeing them until she's grown up."

Mr Wetherby wiped his hands on his trousers. "You need to wait."

"I've invited them for Christmas, is that long enough?"

"That's only two months away." The pitch of his voice was noticeably higher and he coughed to clear his throat. "What did you do that for; why didn't you ask me first?"

"Why would I do that? I always arrange Christmas and I thought it would be nice after the year they've had. Now I don't want to hear another word about it. We shouldn't argue on such a special day, we need to decide what to call our daughter."

Mr Wetherby took a deep breath and looked down at the child again. It was a long time before he spoke. "I know what I'd like to call her. Charlotte ... after my mother."

"Yes, I like that," Mary said. "Welcome to the world Miss Charlotte Wetherby."

Chapter 71

WHEN HE ARRIVED DOWNSTAIRS ON Christmas morning, Mr Wetherby was surprised to see Charlotte already asleep by the fire. He assumed Mary had gone for some water, and crouched down at the side of the cot to stroke the delicate cheek that turned towards him. He had never wanted a daughter but now she was here, he knew he would do anything for her, even at the expense of Mary or William Junior. He just wished she didn't remind him so much of Sarah-Ann. He thought of the day that lay ahead and shuddered. It would be the first time he had seen Sarah-Ann since the 'accident' and he still prayed she would send word that they wouldn't be joining them.

The last time he'd seen her, Mr Flemming was standing over her wearing a shameful look of satisfaction. Even now, he could feel his heart rate quicken merely thinking about it, but then, with every fibre of his being he'd wanted to knock the smile off his face. Instead, for Sarah-Ann's sake, he'd turned and walked away. If he had his way he would never see the man again, but thanks to Mary he would be a guest in his house this evening. He needed to make sure he had several glasses of sherry before they arrived. He stood up from the cot as Mary came back with the kettle full of water.

"It's busy out there," she said. "Everyone's up early to get the meat to the baker's."

"Do you want me to take ours?"

"It's gone. Alice came around about ten minutes ago and took it. You sit down and I'll make a cup of tea before everyone comes and disturbs the peace."

By five o'clock, Martha and Mr Chalmers had arrived at Frankfort Street with the children, but there was no sign of Sarah-Ann and Mr Flemming.

"Are you sure they're coming?" Mr Wetherby said. "They haven't had a change of plan?"

"I saw Sarah-Ann on Wednesday and she said she'd see me here," Martha said.

"And I had a letter earlier in the week saying how much she wanted to see Charlotte," Mary added.

Mr Wetherby's face paled. "Maybe it's Mr Flemming then. He's an odd fellow."

"Well, don't you go annoying him, you always seem to upset him one way or another."

"I don't know why I ever agreed to her walking out with him …"

"That's enough," Mary said. "Why don't you open the bottle of port and pour us all a drink while we're waiting?"

Mr Wetherby walked to the sideboard and was still pouring the port when the door opened and Sarah-Ann walked in followed by Mr Flemming.

"Merry Christmas," Mary said with a smile. "We were beginning to wonder where you were."

"We just had a few things to sort out … didn't we?" Mr Flemming turned to Sarah-Ann.

Sarah-Ann said nothing but stayed by the door, looking at the floor.

"Well, you're here now. Will you take their coats?" Mary said to Mr Wetherby.

"I'll take my wife's, thank you." Mr Flemming dragged the cloak from Sarah-Ann's shoulders. "Go and sit in the corner out of everyone's way."

Sarah-Ann gave a compliant nod and moved to the chair beside Charlotte's cot. As soon as she sat down, she pulled back the blanket that obscured the child's face and let out a gasp.

"She's beautiful," she said when everyone turned to look at her. "I'll cover her up again, I don't want to disturb her."

Mr Wetherby saw the fear in Sarah-Ann's eyes and turned to Mary. "Perhaps you'd better take Charlotte upstairs. I'll look after the guests. Mr Flemming, will you have a port?"

Mr Flemming eyed him suspiciously before turning to Sarah-Ann. "Why don't you go upstairs and help Mrs Wetherby, seeing it's your fault she has to go."

"It's no trouble," Mary said. "I was about to take her anyway, this room's too small."

As soon as Mary lifted Charlotte from her cot, Sarah-Ann stood up and put herself between the baby and Mr Flemming.

"I'll bring the cot," Martha said as she jumped up to follow them.

A moment later, Alice was on her feet. "Mary-Ann, you come with me. We'll go next door and get the rest of the food."

"I'll help you." William scurried after them.

"Nothing like breaking up a party before it's started." Mr Wetherby glared at Mr Flemming.

"You look at my wife like that again and it'll be more than the party that's broken up."

"Let's stop this right now." Mr Wetherby put down the bottle of port and stood inches from Mr Flemming. "It's Christmas Day and you're a guest in my house."

"Don't think I'm here out of choice."

"And don't think the invitation had anything to do with me. I don't want you here, but I won't have you spoiling the day for Mary or Sarah-Ann."

"That's enough." Mr Chalmers rose to his feet and stepped between them. "The children are still here."

Mr Wetherby glared at Mr Flemming before turning his back on him. "You're right. This isn't the time or place. Let's sit down like civilised human beings while we wait for the ladies."

"Don't think you'll see much of us after tonight," Mr Flemming snapped as he accepted a glass of port. "We're moving down to Highgate."

"What in God's name are you going all the way down there for?"

"To get away from you."

Chapter 72

DESPITE THE LATENESS OF THE year, the sun was still warm. Mary sat outside her front door, Charlotte in the pram beside her, trying to catch the few breaths of wind that passed down the street. Mr Wetherby had gone to observe a council meeting and she wasn't expecting him home any time soon. Around five o'clock, William walked down the street towards her. What a handsome young man he had become. He was taller than Mr Wetherby and with his dark hair and deep brown eyes was the image of his father. He had an extra spring in his step tonight as well.

"You look happy," Mary said as he approached. "Have you had a good day?"

"It wasn't the day that was good, more the conversation I had last night. It looks like I'm moving to Handsworth."

"That's wonderful." Mary clapped her hands together. "Are we all going? Mr Wetherby hasn't said anything to me."

"Mr Wetherby doesn't know yet. Can you keep it to yourself until I get a chance to talk to him?"

"If you're not going with Mr Wetherby, who are you going with?" Mary stood up, but still had to crane her neck to look him in the eye.

"Mr Watkins. He's moving his workshop up there and wants me to help him set it up."

"You'll come back once you've finished?"

"That's not the plan, he wants me to move permanently."

Mary felt a sinking feeling in the pit of her stomach. "Mr Wetherby will never agree to that, he's told Mr Watkins often enough that he won't release you."

"I'm sure he will when he hears the deal; let me talk to him and see what he says."

❦

As the council session came to an end, and Mr Wetherby stood and picked up his hat, Mr Watkins approached him from the other end of the gallery.

"Good evening, Mr Wetherby."

"Mr Watkins, I didn't know you were in the chamber."

"I was interested in the discussion on the property rates. I'm fed up of them being increased."

"You're not alone. You'd think they were trying to force us out of businesses the way they're going up."

"I'm glad you agree," Mr Watkins said. "I'm ready to leave Birmingham. I've decided to move to Handsworth and set up a workshop there. The rates are cheaper and the air will suit Mrs Watkins's bronchitis."

"It's tempting but it's not for me, not yet anyway."

Mr Watkins paused and looked around before he spoke again. "Has William spoken to you today?"

"No, I've been out of the workshop, why?"

"I've asked him to move to Handsworth with me. I need someone I can trust to set up the new workshop."

"You had no right to approach him without asking me

first." Mr Wetherby spat the words through gritted teeth. "I've already told you I'm not prepared to release him."

"Now he's of age it's only right that he should have some say in the matter."

"He's still my employee. Has he given you an answer?" Mr Wetherby could feel the vein in his neck pulsing.

"I only asked him last night, and I did suggest he talk to you before he makes his decision."

"What makes you think he wants to go?"

"He's developed a fondness for my niece. He doesn't know I know, but I don't think he's happy at the prospect of not seeing her again."

Mr Wetherby's eyes widened. "When did this happen?"

"My guess is that he's liked her for years but they were too young. Now, however, I'm wondering if we can work it to our advantage."

"What do you mean?" The more usual squint returned to Mr Wetherby's face.

"Bringing the two families together would be good business for both of us. I could source plenty of business for you in Handsworth and you could return the favour for me in Birmingham."

Mr Wetherby paused and stroked his chin. "When are you moving?"

"I don't know yet. I've only just decided I'm going and haven't started looking for premises yet. I'm going up there for a few days next week."

"I wasn't aware William had feelings for your niece, but maybe you're right. Bringing the two families together is an attractive proposition. We could do a lot of business between us. Let me think about it."

❦

Mary sat at the living room table, waiting for Mr Wetherby to come home. The food sat in front of her, but she wasn't hungry; she was too preoccupied thinking of William. Surely Mr Wetherby would stop him. She was deep in thought when the door opened.

"Have you had a good day?" She smiled as Mr Wetherby took off his hat.

"Yes, very good. It was an interesting meeting and they arrived at some good decisions." He sat beside her and helped himself to some bread and cheese. "I met Mr Watkins when I was there; he's a decent sort, don't you think? He told me he's moving to Handsworth."

Mary stiffened. "Yes, William told me earlier this evening."

"Did he now, and did he tell you he's been asked to move with them?"

"He wants to speak to you about it. You won't let him go, will you?"

"I need to think about it, it could be a good opportunity for us … for him."

Mary coughed back the mouthful of gin she'd just swallowed. "What do you mean? You've always said you wanted him to stay with you."

"I said I need to think about it. He may be more valuable to me in Handsworth."

Mary's face turned pink. "If Handsworth's so good, why don't we all move there? You know I've wanted to live there ever since we were married."

"Maybe we will one day, but not yet. I've still got work to do here."

"You can't let William go by himself."

"He won't be by himself, he'll be with the Watkins family, and from what I hear he's taken a liking to their niece."

Mary shot her husband a furious glance. William hadn't mentioned that to her.

"That girl's a troublemaker; we can't let him become attached to her."

"Don't be silly, there's nothing wrong with her. Mr Watkins sent her away to school and apparently she came back a changed girl. I believe she's charming; you just don't want him to leave."

"Of course I don't."

"Well, it's about time you considered the possibility. You have William Junior and Charlotte to take care of now and they need you more than he does. He isn't eight years old anymore."

Mary wiped her eyes with the back of her hand. "I'm going upstairs, I'll tidy up later."

◈

Several days later, Mr Wetherby knocked on the door in Shadwell Street and took a step back. It was a smart looking house, clearly well looked after, always a good sign. He didn't have to wait long before a maid opened the door.

"Is Mr Watkins home?" he asked.

"Yes, sir. Please come in, I'll let him know you're here."

Mr Wetherby looked around the hallway and decided that William could do a lot worse for himself. Mr Watkins clearly had money, and judging by the personal property, Mrs Watkins liked to spend it.

A moment later Mr Watkins joined him and showed him into the front room.

"A nice house you have, Mr Watkins. Have you been here long?"

"A few years now; Mrs Watkins wanted help around the house so we needed the extra space to accommodate a domestic help. Have you come to talk about the move to Handsworth?"

"I have, but I still haven't come to a firm decision. I know William's keen to move with you, but if you wouldn't mind, I'd like you to introduce me to your niece. She seems to be the main reason he wants to leave, and I'd like to know what I'm up against."

"Of course, come into the back room. She's with Mrs Watkins at the moment doing a spot of darning."

Mr Watkins led the way into the back room and Mrs and Miss Watkins both looked up and smiled when they entered.

"Mr Wetherby's come about some business," Mr Watkins said.

"I'm sorry to disturb you," Mr Wetherby said when both sets of eyes rested on him. "I didn't want to call and not wish you good evening."

"It's very nice to meet you, Mr Wetherby." Mrs Watkins remained in her chair. "I've heard a lot about you from your wife. I've not seen her for a few months. Is she well?"

"Yes, very well thank you, just busy with the baby. I'm sure she'll be in touch soon."

Miss Watkins said nothing but carried on with her work.

"You look very busy there, Miss," Mr Wetherby said. "I imagine they taught you well at school."

"Yes, sir, they taught me everything I need to know about looking after a home and family ... as well as plenty of things I didn't need to know."

"I believe you know my stepson, Mr Jackson."

"I wouldn't say I know him, sir. We've met obviously, but we don't speak to each other. Uncle is always talking to him about the business, I only sit and listen."

"As it should be, my dear, you don't want to be bothered with all that." Mr Wetherby smiled when she looked up at him. "Well, I think I've taken up enough of your time and so I'll wish you good evening."

Mr Wetherby walked back to the front parlour with Mr Watkins.

"I heard you had trouble with your niece a few years ago, but it looks like the school did the trick."

"Yes, I've been very pleased. We don't get any insolence from her nowadays."

"I'm pleased about that. I like the idea of doing business together, although I can't let William move with you just yet."

"How long do you think you'll need?"

"That, I'm afraid, is a question I can't answer."

Mr Watkins took a deep breath and walked to the window. "How am I supposed to plan? Do you think you'd be able to let him move by spring of next year?"

"Why don't you start looking for premises, and when you can give me more details, I'll re-consider?"

"So you're not ruling it out?"

"I'm not ruling it out ... but I'm not ruling it in either."

ৡৼৢ

William knew that Mr Wetherby had gone to see Mr Watkins, and by eight o'clock he wondered why he hadn't heard anything. He walked around to the front house to see if he had arrived home but, when he saw his mother sitting alone, he immediately regretted his visit.

"Isn't Mr Wetherby home yet?"

"He shouldn't be long now, but I don't know why you're looking so cheerful; he's not going to let you go, you know."

William took a deep breath. "You don't know that."

"I know that he always wanted you to be part of his business and that he's stopped you moving back to Mr Watkins several times already. Why would he let you go now they're moving to Handsworth?"

"Because I want to go and he knows that."

"Well, I don't want you to go and he knows that as well." Mary folded up her knitting and put it on the table.

"Mother, why can't you just be happy for me and let me lead my own life?"

"Because you're making a terrible mistake."

"Why, because I want to work as a machinist with the master who trained me?"

"You know that's not the reason." The colour started to rise in Mary's cheeks.

"Then what is it? Because I'll be leaving Birmingham?"

"In part, yes, you know I don't want you to go, but …"

"But that's not the real reason?"

"It's because she'll be the ruin of you."

William threw his hands in the air and let them slap back on his thighs. "Who'll be the ruin of me? What are you talking about?"

"You know very well what I'm talking about."

"Mother, I know what I'm doing and I'm not ruining anything. I don't want to fall out with you, but please stop this."

"You don't even talk to me anymore, you don't tell me anything. You didn't even tell me about her."

William sat down and put his head in his hands.

"I think she means Miss Watkins," Mr Wetherby said as he walked in and closed the door behind him.

"What about her?" William stood up again and looked at Mary.

"Isn't she the reason you're so keen to go to Handsworth?" Mary asked.

William flushed. "Who told you that?"

"So it's true. Why didn't you tell me? Maybe if you talked to me more, I wouldn't worry so much."

"Is it any wonder I don't when this is the reaction I get? You treat me like a child and I've had enough of it."

"You know nothing about Miss Watkins, who she is or what she's like. Well, let me tell you she's trouble." The venom in Mary's voice was unmistakable.

"That's rich coming from you, you haven't even met her," William shouted. "For your information, she's quite charming and full of fun."

"She's a pretty little thing too," Mr Wetherby said as he moved to a chair by the fire.

"Yes ... she is ... thank you." William looked at Mr Wetherby with a fresh pair of eyes before turning back to his mother. "Is it wrong for me to admire an attractive young lady? I'm twenty-four years old, I should be thinking about getting married, not explaining myself to my mother because I happen to find someone attractive."

"I think you've both said enough for one night," Mr Wetherby said. "Isn't it time you were going home, William?"

"I came to find out how you got on with Mr Watkins. Did you come to a decision?"

"We did, and as much as I think your mother is being unreasonable, I'm afraid to say that you won't be going with them."

William stopped in his tracks and glared at Mr Wetherby. "Not going? Who made that decision? Not me, and I suspect not Mr Watkins either."

"I told you Mr Wetherby wouldn't let you go."

The smile on Mary's face was too much for William. "I wanted Mr Wetherby's blessing to move to Handsworth, not his permission. I'm going to Handsworth whether you like it or not and if I decide to settle down with Miss Watkins you're either going to have to get used to it or our relationship is over. Goodnight."

Thank you for reading
Hooks & Eyes.
I hope you enjoyed it.

If so, please share your thoughts and
leave a review on Amazon.
http://bit.ly/HooksEyesAM

It will be much appreciated.

Further Books in
The *Ambition & Destiny* Series
Part 2: Less than Equals

When you speak, but no one listens...

When strong-willed Harriet upsets her uncle, her punishment is severe. Now, with her freedom denied, Harriet must endure a self-imposed exile to make those who love her understand she will go to any lengths to gain control of her own life.

Part 3:
It started as a dream. It turned into a nightmare.

As tensions within the family build, tragedy strikes and the protection William has enjoyed since he was a child is gone forever.

Part 4:
A new start. A bad business partner.
Two sons who want the truth.

A time of upheaval and heartbreak sees the fate of the family changed forever.

Part 5:

The conclusion to The Ambition & Destiny Series is being planned.

For further details about publication dates and to hear about special offers, sign up to my FREE monthly newsletter at:
www.vlmcbeath.com

Acknowledgements

From start to finish, the process of writing these books has been an experience I am so glad I have undertaken. Not only has it given me a more detailed understanding of the extraordinary lives of my ancestors, it has given me a new perspective on life. It may also have turned a hobby into the next stage of my career.

Naturally, I couldn't have done this on my own and I would like to thank my family and friends for the support they have provided along the way. In particular, I would like to thank my daughters Emma and Sarah; my mum and dad, Marg and Terry; brother-in-law Dave and friends Marie, Carolyn and Rachel for taking the time to read various drafts of the book and either give me words of encouragement or valuable insights into how it could be improved. I must also acknowledge the hundreds of writers who willingly share the knowledge of their craft on the Internet. I've spent many, many hours reading your words and, genuinely, you have been my teachers.

I must also thank Katharine D'Souza and Wendy Janes for their wonderful (if sometimes painful) editorial feedback, and Debra L Hartmann from The Pro Book Editor for proofreading and formatting the document. I learned so much from all of you and I know the book is in a better place than before you saw it.

Last but not least, I must thank my wonderful husband Stuart. Not only has he been my chief reviewer; but he never complains when I spend hour after hour at the computer, even if it means getting left with the chores. At least it gives him time to watch his choice of films most evenings!

The project is not yet over and in many ways, it has only just begun. I have another three books that are ready to be edited and an outline of the final story in my head. Netflix needn't worry that they'll be losing a viewer anytime soon!

About the Author

Val started researching her family tree back in 2008. At that time, she had no idea what she would find or where it would lead. By 2010, she had discovered a story so compelling, she was inspired to turn it into a novel. Initially writing for herself, the story grew beyond anything she ever imagined.

Prior to writing, Val trained as a scientist and has worked for the pharmaceutical industry for many years. In 2012, she set up her own consultancy business, and currently splits her time between business and writing.

Born and raised in Liverpool (UK), Val now lives in Cheshire with her husband, two daughters and a cat. In addition to family history, her interests include rock music and Liverpool Football Club.

For further information about The *Ambition & Destiny* Series, Victorian History or Val's experiences as she wrote the book, visit her website at: vlmcbeath.com

Made in the USA
Las Vegas, NV
14 February 2022

43900837R00256